Beloved Heretic

Eleanor LaBerge

PublishAmerica
Baltimore

First printing

This is a work of fiction. Names, characters, places, and incidents either are the product of the author's imagination or are used fictitiously. Any resemblance to actual persons, living or dead, events, or locales is entirely coincidental.

ISBN: 1-4241-6128-2
PUBLISHED BY PUBLISHAMERICA, LLLP
www.publishamerica.com
Baltimore

Printed in the United States of America

Beloved Heretic is dedicated to by beloved husband Earl, without whose help it could not have been written.

Acknowledgments

There are always more individuals who should be acknowledged than room permits. I would like to know that I am grateful to each in full measure—especially Marc Griesemer and Lim Forgey, computer geniuses, and my friend Celine Nichols, who is always ready with advice and valuable suggestions.

Author's Introduction

Beloved Heretic is the improbable love story of Beryl Charbonneau, a white woman born to wealth and privilege, and Joseph Wolf, an Indian "half-breed" abandoned in infancy.

The "improbability" is multi-faceted. Beryl was born in Maryland to an aristocratic family in the mid 1800s. Joseph is the progeny of a captured white woman and an Indian. Beryl Charbonneau lived as a nun in one of the Catholic Church's strictly cloistered monastic orders, while in the far west Joseph's mother abandoned him to be raised by homesteaders in Washington State's Cascade Mountains.

Beryl, having left the monastic community, comes to the Washington Territory for the purpose of founding a congregation of Catholic Sisters, whose mission is to bring education to the newly settled West. While visiting prospective sites for schools, Beryl meets and rescues Joseph, not yet in his teens, from a situation of abject and hopeless poverty. The boy is hiding from white men who wrongfully accuse him of murder. She becomes his mother, teacher and friend.

Beloved Heretic spans historical events of East and West, beginning in 1855 before the Civil War and continuing through the migration to the far West, the settlement of Seattle, the expulsion of Chinese from Tacoma and Seattle, the development of parochial schools and hospitals in the frontier, the politics of prejudice, the efforts of women to make substantial contributions to life in the northwest, and the Seattle fire of 1889, which almost destroys Seattle.

Against the background of history and politics, the bond between Joseph and Beryl deepens. It is the catalyst which inspires Joseph to develop a talent that elevates him to be a world class sculptor. It is the reality that compels Beryl Charbonneau to examine elements of her faith which would deny the rewards of Heaven to unbaptized Joseph. Beryl, the foundress of an expanding religious order, must come to terms with her personal rejection of certain church laws, knowing that should she publicly confess her conscience, the social structure she has built will collapse. Joseph must resist "conversion," which he sees as contrary to his intellectual and artistic freedom. Ironically, he wishes that Beryl would give him proof of her love by offering to bind him in the chains of her Christian beliefs.

In spite of religious and social restrictions imposed by a church and society that is dominated by men, strong women come to life in *Beloved Heretic*. They form the rich colors and chiaroscuro shades of a panoramic mural of 19th century frontier life. In these characters, we see love and commitment, but we also see hate and interracial conflict; where we see the faith and eagerness of the Christian missionary; we also see betrayal, greed, and jealousy. Throughout the book the pure love of Beryl and Joseph is the vital element that breaks the barriers between Protestant and Catholics; white men and those of color; prejudice and acceptance. There lives the dearest, freshness deep down things.

And though the last lights off the black West went
Oh, morning, at the brown brink eastward, springs—
Because the Holy Ghost over the bent
World broods with warm breast and ah! bright wings.

Gerard Manley Hopkins:
"God's Grandeur"

Part One

I

Maryland
1855

Five carriages had stopped at the entrance to the Charbonneau manor within the hour. Adam, the hostler, was stabling the guests' horses, storing their carriages, and setting aside any tack which seemed to need attention. In the unusual activity, twelve-year-old Beryl Charbonneau saw a chance to take one of the family horses for a gallop. Adam, whose word was law in the stables, would never have let her ride out unsupervised. Wearing britches borrowed from her brother Pierre, which she concealed with a woman's riding skirt, she eased her way past the guest barn undetected. Bareback and astride a spirited bay mare, Beryl rode through a stand of trees that separated the paddocks from the open meadow.

The day was perfect. The rising sap of May had turned the bare branches of maple and beech a deep red. Green buds were beginning to swell on brush growth, and fronds of new grass rose from the damp sod of the meadow. Beryl brought the mare to a halt at the crest of a hill and took a deep breath. The morning was still cool, but in the air there was the hint of warmth to come. From the moist earth wildflowers of blue, purple and yellow would soon carpet the ground. Such a day and such promise filled the girl with joy.

She pushed her thick, dark hair into a cap usually worn by a stable boy, gathered her reins, and pressed the mare to a canter toward one of the brush jumps at the bottom of the rise. Once over this obstacle, she made a sharp turn and cleared the entry gate to another trail. She reined to a stop as she nearly collided with her father and another horseman. Henri Charbonneau's seventeen hand chestnut stallion shied and Charbonneau sprawled over his mount's neck.

Regaining his seat, Charbonneau faced Beryl. "You little fool! Take that mare back to the stables this instant, and tell Adam that..." He did not finish as the stallion needed his full attention to control. Fortunately for both riders, the mare was past her season, and she gave the fretting stallion little regard. A week before and both horses might have bolted in the urgency of nature.

Beryl turned her horse, kicked its flanks and cleared the gate again with a foot to spare. Henri Charbonneau, having calmed the stallion, turned him in tight circles intent on keeping the upper hand. His companion stared after Beryl appreciatively. His horse, a quieter gelding had stood regarding the scene indifferently with the passivity of a horse that had seen it all.

"That stable brat has an enviable seat," he remarked, "and bareback to boot!" As he laughed heartily, he noticed a long strand of dark hair escape from under the rider's cap.

Charbonneau had not observed what his companion had seen. He scowled, thinking it was a good thing that the identity of the rider was unknown to his guest. He was relieved that Beryl had not addressed him as "Father." The child was allowed too much freedom. Perhaps the suggestion of his boys' tutor, Father Louis Bertrand, that she be allowed to attend his sons' lessons was not such an outlandish idea after all.

Henri and Constantia Charbonneau had planned the weekend house party to announce the engagement of Evangeline, their eldest daughter, to Charles Beaufort, heir to industrialist's Claude Beaufort's fortune. Evangeline was the first Charbonneau girl to marry. In time, the others would follow, and Henri planned to bestow generous dowries on each. Clemence, second to eldest, was on the Grand Tour with a maiden aunt, and already there were letters that indicated a match might be made in Europe. Marie Louise was close to marriageable age, and Beryl, twelve, was within a few years of maturity. Yvonne, just two years older than Beryl, was already a graceful beauty. Beryl was the only girl who caused her parents—especially her mother—to worry. She was taller than average, awkward and disinclined to be interested in the future prospects of marriage.

The mare put away and the cap discarded, Beryl entered the house through the kitchen and took the back stairs to the girls' bedrooms. She knew she would be punished, but she was confident that her father would not report the incident to Constantia until after the important engagement party.

When Beryl next saw her father, her tall, lean figure was clothed in a pink

14

full skirted dress, her first floor-length party frock. She hated the color, but at least it was not replete with the ruffles Evangeline preferred. A matching bow held her long hair that hung in natural waves down her back. In the reception line, Henri introduced her to Beaufort senior, who had been riding with him earlier. Beryl's smile was docile and she curtsied as prettily as possible to him and his wife. He took Beryl's white gloved hand and said, "Enchanted," but as he met her clear blue eyes he raised his eyebrows, then winked. Beryl reddened and lowered her lids swiftly, but the gentleman said nothing further. Of all the men to have been with her father—Evangeline's future father-in-law! She was in far deeper trouble than she had realized.

After the weekend festivities ended and the guests had departed, Henri sent for Beryl. When she entered her father's study, she was surprised, and relieved, to find him alone. Beryl had pictured this moment: Constantia tearful and distraught as she conjured the image of her daughter crashing into a future in-law wearing britches on the very day of Evangeline's announcement.

The girl stood, her hands gripped behind her back, waiting for Charbonneau to pronounce the details of her punishment. She had speculated about the possibilities and concluded that she would be sent away to a convent school. She would be doomed to dull days of embroidery and French—which she already spoke perfectly. She would ride, of course, but in a lady's hat and habit, perched sidesaddle on a mount whose fire had long since burned to an ember. Certainly she would not be allowed the unladylike pleasure of grooming a horse, brushing its coat glossy and combing its mane and tail free of tangles. Her mother was most certainly upstairs packing her trunk. She tried to control her feelings, but as she stood in her father's study, she felt her eyes burn with tears.

If she had been older, she might have begged her father to let her enter an order of nuns. At least in this circumstance she could have participated in honest work and avoided the dreaded "finishing" process to which her mother was determined all her daughters must conform. Her sisters prattled on about the social whirl of the "season." These things bored Beryl. She found her greatest pleasure, apart from being with the horses, was in hiding behind the school room door eavesdropping on Father Louis' lessons of history and philosophy. Later she'd slip into the classroom and read the books her brothers had studied. This pleasure would probably end as well. Just a few days ago, Father Louis Bertrand had caught her, and while he did not scold, it was not likely he approved.

Henri Charbonneau took Beryl's misty eyes to mean contrition. This, at least, was to the girl's credit. He cleared his throat. "Daughter, I have concluded that you have too much time on your hands. Your mother will be occupied with the wedding, and I have decided not to burden her with supervising you to the extent that seems to be necessary." As he paused, Beryl could hear the bells of the convent school tolling. "Instead, I shall insist that you join your brothers every day in their studies."

"Father!" Beryl couldn't help but exclaim.

Charbonneau misunderstood, and put up his hand to signal silence. "Now, daughter," he said in an authoritative tone, "I will not entertain any objection. You will study with Pierre and Phillipe, and I shall instruct Father Louis Bertrand that he make no exceptions for you. He will require the same degree of excellence from you as if you were one of my sons."

"Father, I will do the very best I can." Beryl hung her head submissively pressing her lips together as she struggled to suppress a smile.

"Very well." He took a deep breath. "It will be best if your mother does not know the reason for my decision." He turned abruptly from Beryl to affairs on his desk, and she left with as much dignity as she could muster.

She kept to a walk as she went from the study down the long hall where portraits of relatives, mostly dead, were hung. She took the stairs that led to the kitchen one at a time, passed between the long cutting tables and the ovens, out the back door. In the garden, two workmen were tending the rose beds, and she walked by them sedately, still maintaining her dignity. Finally she opened the gate to the back field. Holding up her skirts, she bounded into the meadow with a cry of unrestrained joy.

II

A Remote Valley in the North Cascades

Clutching her infant, the woman slipped under the tent while those who guarded her peered through a narrow slit at the shelter's entrance. They were absorbed by the ritual dance for new chief. It had been but three months since she had seen the same ceremony honoring her mate.

Clear of the tribal compound, she ran to a horse she had tethered earlier outside the corral. Racing against the time when she would be missed, she cantered to the river, guiding her mount to midstream. She pressed the infant close to her breast and rode as swiftly as she dared lest the horse come up lame on the rocky river bed. It was well before first light when she came to a bend where she found a fallen cedar, its roots half exposed on the bank, its submerged branches moving with the current in the water. This was the clue her mate had described.

On the opposite bank there was a shallow crossing. Sliding from the horse's back, she pulled the hemp bridle free, and striking the horse's withers with it, sent it galloping to the opposite bank. She continued to wade at the water's edge, clutching the child and fighting both fatigue and the chill of the stream.

The full moon had risen, which helped her locate the rocky trail that led to a cave concealed in the rock face. Tracking her would be impossible over the loose rocks and boulders if she watched her step. She scrambled up the hill, mindful not to touch any small tree or leave any telltale strand of blanket.

She found the cave, concealed by brush. She had to push the child inside before she could press her body through the narrow opening. How her mate had managed to enter she could not imagine. Once inside, she groped in the dark to find a bed of dry leaves where she gently placed the child. Taking a flint from a fold in the infant's blanket, she made her way cautiously through the blackness to the far end of the cave. A fire was laid, ready to be lit. It provided enough light for her to return quickly to the entry, where she sealed the opening with brush and small rocks.

Satisfied that the cave emitted no telling light, she carried her child to the rear of the shelter. She hoped she was far enough from the entrance that its cries not be heard should she fail to quiet him. The sound of rushing water below would help. Near her fire she found several clay pots of water, and in a hole that was sealed by a heavy flat rock, strips of dried meat. With the aid of a thick branch as a lever she was able to retrieve the store Grey Wolf had left for her.

The woman had begged her mate to run, taking both her and the child far from harm's way. But he had insisted that this would be the act of a coward, not a chief. Grey Wolf had narrowly missed death when his horse tumbled from a narrow trail—a fall miraculously broken when he grabbed a sapling strong enough to hold his weight. The horse had not survived, but an examination of the scene showed a cleverly hidden fault, which was meant to cause a collapse of the trail at the slightest weight. Grey Wolf's brother, Running Bear, had ridden some safe distance behind, supposedly in deference to the sibling who had been named the chief's successor—in spite of his being the younger son.

The woman huddled by the fire and reflected how strange were the twists and turns of life. Grey Wolf had abducted her by force as a prize and proof of his manhood. She had been his prisoner; she would not be his mate. She spat her anger at her captor, and plotted her escape—an effort that had no substance for at that time she had no survival skills. As time passed, she had entered into the daily work of the tribe. Her hands became rough with weaving; she learned to understand the strange language and to appreciate its imagery. Gradually she learned to respect Grey Wolf's strength and to take pride in his arrogance. Ultimately, she came willingly to his tent.

What was more remarkable, she no longer felt oppressed in her captivity. Instead, she realized that other chains had fallen from her. She was not constrained to meet the harsh requirements of her father's domineering philosophy. As a minister and self-proclaimed link to God, he maintained that all mankind, especially women, was intrinsically evil. Humanity stood on a precipice where one misstep would result in a plunge to the fire pit of everlasting Hell. By comparison, the natives she had thought of as godless and barbaric were merely human beings in a day by day, year by year, struggle for survival. And yet, in this battle against nature, adults and children lived free to laugh, dance, and appreciate beauty. She was not blind to another side of the "noble savage." She had seen how greed and ambition for power had set in motion the events that led to her mate's death and placed her and her child in jeopardy.

She had been with Grey Wolf for a little over a year when the old chief, his father, had died—the victim of a cougar attack. How it had happened no one knew, but in the months to come the woman was certain it had been planned. Two weeks ago Grey Wolf had been carried into the compound, an arrow through his heart. An "accident."

The woman remained in the cave until her meager supplies were gone and enough time had passed that she believed she had evaded her pursuers. To cross the mountains safely, she could not wait long. Autumn had already begun to alter the color of the wild huckleberry bushes. The vine maples were blood red against the green of fir, cedar, and hemlock. Any day the chill in the air would bring snow, and it was not unknown to these mountains that the first storm could be a blizzard. She left the cave and began her trek to the valley where her family had long since given her up for dead. There was a homestead in the hills where an immigrant Scotsman and his wife bred and raised horses for settlers and the army. This was her destination.

More than a week of unusually warm weather followed her across the peaks that bordered the cattle runs from Ellensburg to Seattle. One fog-drenched dawn, under the cover of darkness, she approached Douglas McFee's cabin.

The mist lay heavy on the branches of cedar and fir. On the stream's bank, dew laden spider webs, like a hundred strands of pearls carelessly flung over the brambles, quivered as droplets from the trees fell among them. The woman stood motionless in the wood that bordered a stream of clear running water. Amid the ghostly shapes in the fog, she was indistinguishable from any young tree on the near bank. She held her infant, her gaze steadily fixed on the cabin. She shivered in her only garment, the tunic that had clothed her on the night she had crawled from under the women's tent. The child was warm, wrapped in pelts. Next to its skin, the fur of a grey rabbit protected him from the cold. The skin of two beavers sewn together with leather thongs covered the fur. Over these layers, the child was swaddled in a roughly woven blanket of dyed wool in stripes of umber, saffron, and purple.

The woman raised her face to the gold circle of the sun glowing through the mist and realized that the morning fog would not conceal her much longer. The sun would climb higher and burn through the moisture, possibly within an hour. Earlier, under the cover of night, she had taken a horse from the cabin's corral and had stolen a bridle. She tied the animal near another stand of trees at some distance. She would have no need of a saddle, and once she reached the settlement, she would turn the animal loose to find its way home. Riding to the settlement would rest her feet which were swollen and tender.

If the old man did not open the cabin door within the hour, she would be forced to return to her people with the burden of the child she held in her arms. With a half-breed child, she knew that the family who had believed her dead would not welcome her. The child would be shunned. She would be unable to protect him by her love. Still, she knew, though, it was an unkind fate, this circumstance would guarantee that both she and her child would live. If she had failed to reach safety before Running Bear found her, her capture would have meant her death, and certainly the death of the child. Running Bear knew that, like the kitten of a great she-cougar, the young life could grow and in the fullness of time claim its blood right of succession.

The woman's reappearance after four years would have to be explained. She invented a tale of white outlaws who, two years before, had robbed and beaten her, leaving her senseless in the woods with no hope for survival. Friendly Indians—possibly Nez Perce or Cayuse—had found her. She would claim that until recently she had no memory of who she was or where she belonged. When her memory returned, the savages had brought her home, but departed swiftly, fearing their involvement would be misunderstood. The story would insure that there would be no posse riding the trails in search of a renegade tribe that still roamed free. She would not be the cause of more death.

Light had still not appeared in the cabin. The woman considered approaching the dwelling and begging Douglas McFee and his wife to take her child. She could imagine their hesitation, not the least of which was because of their age. She had no time to argue with objections. It would be best to leave him and rely on their compassion. McFee and his wife were not like the settlers her father counted as faithful members of his flock. The Reverend had failed to bring the couple into his fold. He had railed against the sinners who refused the gift of salvation by baptism and acceptance of Jesus Christ the Son of God. He described the pains of hell and eternal fire. Mildly and respectfully, McFee claimed they found their creator in the mountain solitude.

Should she fear that after finding the child at his door and later hearing of her return to the bosom of her family McFee would confront her as its mother? No. Douglas McFee was not a fool. He would realize that by such an action he would condemn an innocent child to society's scorn. As she pondered all that had happened and all that might occur, a light suddenly appeared within the cabin. The door opened and a bright beam from an oil lantern illuminated the porch and the path to the river. The woman did not move. McFee set the lamp on the bottom step and proceeded to the river, a pitcher in his hand. Through the fog she dimly made out McFee's wife adding wood to the stove.

She left her chore to come to the entrance. "Douglas! Are you intending to heat the whole outside?" She closed the door.

McFee passed within twenty feet of the woman, but his mind was on his morning task. Once he had returned to the cabin, the woman in the woods did not hesitate. She had said her farewells, grieved at the separation she knew was best for her child, and now action without delay was imperative. She ran to the cabin, left her burden to one side of the door so that its opening would not touch it, and stepped away. She found several sizable stones which she flung at the porch one after another, making a deafening noise that aroused McFee and his wife. The child began to wail. By the time McFee discovered the child, the woman had disappeared into the mist. It took all her strength of purpose to ride away, tears flowing from her eyes.

III

Six Years Later: Georgetown 1860

Father Louis Bertrand stood as the diminutive nun entered the room, her hand outstretched. "Father! Welcome." She stepped back to look at him. His face was full and had color. His dark hair had thinned in six years and there was a trace of grey around his temples, but the blue eyes were bright and he stood youthfully straight. "You appear well. A remarkable improvement from when we last met. Please sit. Sister Emily is bringing tea."

"I shan't stay long, Mother Eulalie. I have come from the Baltimore Carmelite Monastery and am on my way to the Jesuit house here in Georgetown."

"A change of assignment?" Eulalie asked.

Louis Bertrand laughed. "No, thank God. Tutoring the Charbonneau children was one thing, but a chaplain for cloistered nuns would be too much excitement for my newly regained health."

"It might provide some excitement for the nuns," she teased.

"I had an appointment with Reverend Mother Aimee on behalf of one of my students, Beryl Charbonneau."

Eulalie's raised eyebrows showed her surprise. "I understood you were tutoring the Charbonneau boys."

"True. Beryl attended every lesson hidden behind the old nursery door. Finally, I asked Henri Charbonneau if the girl might study with her brothers, to provide sibling rivalry." Louis Bertrand took a deep breath recalling that situation. "To their credit," he told Mother Eulalie, "Pierre and Phillipe tolerated their sister's presence without complaint, even though she was their intellectual superior. I believe they felt a protective attitude toward her. She was not one of her mother's darlings, nor even a favorite of her father." He smiled at the memory of the twelve-year-old girl eavesdropping as he taught the boys. "The Charbonneau boys were bright, but their sister was brilliant."

"And she wants to be a Carmelite?"

"Yes. I admit I would prefer that she had chosen the Holy Names Sisters or the Madams of the Sacred Heart. But she seems drawn to the contemplative life."

"Somewhat retiring in temperament, is she?"

"Hardly! But you will meet her when she and her mother stop here on their way to her interview in Baltimore."

After refreshment and pleasant conversation with the nun who had founded the new community of the Visitation, they walked in the garden. It distressed Father Louis Bertrand to observe that the nuns still lived in difficult circumstances. He had heard that last winter they had neither sufficient heat nor food. He would ask Constantia Charbonneau to assemble gifts of blankets and provisions to bring when she and Beryl stopped on their way to Baltimore. Father apologized for the brevity of his visit, and after he said Mass for the sisters, he prepared for the last miles of his journey. The Charbonneau coach was as comfortable as the circumstances of carriage travel permitted, and Louis Bertrand was glad for the privacy which he would not have had in public transportation.

The Jesuit eased his back against the leather upholstered seat and attempted to organize his thoughts. His meeting with Reverend Mother Aimee at Carmel completed, he intended to stop at the Georgetown Jesuit House of Studies for the night, and if the Father Provincial were available, he would plead his cause to be sent to the missions in the far West. Louis Bertrand was confident that his appearance would give proof of his restored health.

Six years ago he had been stricken with smallpox, and although he had survived, the disease left him in a weakened condition. Doctors had advised a prolonged period of recuperation where he could rest, eat nourishing food, and have none of the demands of community life and teaching. His superior had been pondering a request from Henri Charbonneau asking him to recommend a tutor for his two sons. The boys needed to prepare for entrance at Harvard University, but at their mother's insistence, Charbonneau had removed them from a private academy in New York because of the smallpox epidemic. The Jesuit Father Superior had decided to send Father Louis Bertrand. For the last six years he had been tutor, friend of the family, and resident chaplain.

Louis Bertrand had been grateful for the assignment. It freed him from involvement in any other teaching post that might compromise his primary ambition: missionary work in the West. His hope was to be part of the creation of a Catholic University in the Northwest. He did not know when he came to the Charbonneau estate that within a few years all his spiritual strength would be necessary to battle the one serious temptation to his vocation: Beryl Charbonneau.

Louis Bertrand was twenty years Beryl's senior, old enough to have fathered her. Older men frequently made good marriages to younger women, and Beryl was mature beyond her years. Such a consideration was pointless. The Charbonneau family would never consent to a daughter's alliance with a defrocked priest. His own family, prominent in Boston social circles in spite of their Roman Catholic affiliation, would be shamed. He could never openly express his feelings for Beryl Charbonneau.

When Father Louis Bertrand arrived in Baltimore to speak with the Carmelite Prioress on Beryl's behalf, he found the nun well informed and intelligent. In this modern day, the Order was not remarkable for its scholarship, and study was not encouraged as it was in the Order of Preachers, the Dominicans' appropriate title. The Carmelite Reverend Mother Aimee was what his confreres would call a "worldly nun." As foundress and superior, she had access to visiting clergy and dignitaries. She managed to keep informed of current events and possessed an adequate classical education. Not equal to the quality of Beryl's, he told himself with a certain amount of pride. He was convinced that Beryl would be understood by this woman. It was more than likely she would be groomed as her successor.

Yet the thought of brilliant Beryl Charbonneau hidden behind cloister walls was almost unbearable to him. She would be separated from her family and all others not only by the thick iron grilles, but by an inflexible rule of seclusion. But he must keep silent. He would beg God to mend his broken heart.

IV

Washington, D.C.
June 1860

Beryl Charbonneau stared at the row of rough bed planks set in a line at the far side of the shed. A thin straw mattress covered each with a muslin sheet, and a neatly folded wool blanket lay across the bottom.

"We've had to push our beds over there." Mother Eulalie told her. "The snow sifted through the cracks on the window side and we would wake up as if we had white feather comforters over us!" She winked at Beryl. "Not that we slept very soundly with our teeth chattering!" The Mother Superior's scrubbed face had a sprinkling of freckles across her nose, and it was not hard to guess that the hair under the coif was bright red. But the face revealed breeding and her speech had the unmistakable inflection of Boston's high society. Beryl marveled that Mother Eulalie could laugh at her community's lack of material goods. The nun didn't complain that only a few sticks of wood each day provided respite from the winter cold, or that their living quarters were little more than shacks. Constantia, Beryl's mother, shivered at the sight, not from the lack of warmth on this fine June day, but from the specter of overwhelming deprivation. Surely Beryl's spiritual advisor, Father Louis Bertrand, could not have hoped that her daughter would give up the idea of entering the Carmelite cloister in favor of this place!

The "Pious Ladies," as they were called, had only recently established the order of the Visitation Nuns with Mother Eulalie as its foundress. Since Georgetown was on the Charbonneau's way to the Carmelites near Baltimore, Father had suggested a visit. He had urged Constantia to take a donation of food and other necessities to the fledgling group. He had not exaggerated when he described the nuns' struggle to survive.

Constantia knew that when this Mother Superior was still in the world, she had been presented to the finest of Boston's society by a family rich in tradition and reputation. It was rumored that she had been disowned when she converted to the Roman Catholic faith.

"Our brougham is ready." Constantia said from the door of the dormitory building. "Mother Eulalie, thank you for your hospitality."

"And thank you for your generosity!" The bright-eyed nun smiled.

Constantia had brought dried fruit, jams, salted meat and had stopped at a local butcher to procure a fresh side of beef. The nuns seldom had such abundance in their larder.

The team of black thoroughbreds was rested and watered. The footman had done his best to wipe the dust from the inside of the carriage. He helped Constantia into her seat as Beryl lingered to say her personal farewell to Mother Eulalie.

Beryl spoke in a low voice, her blue eyes looking down on the Mother Superior, who was a shorter and more delicate figure. "Mother, I wish very sincerely that I did not feel a call to the cloister…"

Mother Eulalie did not let her finish. "There is no need to explain, my dear. Our community home must seem harsh indeed to one who has been brought up with your advantages."

Beryl grasped the superior's hands spontaneously. "Oh, dear Mother! You misunderstand. Truly, I would come to you most enthusiastically! I have no fear of hardship, and I am attracted to your pioneer community. I would be honored to come here!"

"And we would be honored to receive you, Beryl." Mother Eulalie looked up at this young woman, so earnest and honest of expression.

"I believe Father Louis Bertrand wanted me to be impressed," Beryl said, and when she smiled, her plain features had a pleasing quality that was more attractive than prettiness. "He is not pleased with my intention to enter Carmel." She hesitated, but looked unwaveringly into Mother Eulalie's eyes. "If I seem hesitant, it is because I lack the wisdom to know if my feelings are of the Holy Ghost or a temptation put before me to lure me away from the cloister. Carmel is where I feel God wants me. I wish I could tell you otherwise."

Mother Eulalie did not let go of Beryl's hand as they approached the carriage. "I believe you are doing what God asks of you, Beryl Charbonneau, but I also believe I have not seen you for the last time. There are many roads that lead to God. Carmel may be your way. But know this: He will not let you make a mistake."

They embraced before the footman helped Beryl into the carriage where her mother waited. Mother Eulalie watched as the team disappeared down the dusty road. This young woman was forthright and genuine in her efforts to find her calling. Time would tell what that was, even if Beryl were taking the long way around, she wouldn't get lost. Of that much Mother Eulalie was certain.

Sister Francine came from inside the house with a great stiff broom. Keeping the small portico free of road dirt was her chore. She inclined her head to the dust cloud which was all that could be seen of the visitors' carriage."An interesting young lady," she remarked. "And what a time she'll have molding her fine mind to fit the Carmelite cloister! A bad choice," she muttered. She continued to sweep in brisk strokes when her superior had retired without comment to the house.

Dust from the road made conversation inside the coach impossible. Constantia covered her nose and mouth with a lavender scented, embroidered linen handkerchief. Her daughter used her own plainer bit of linen, glad to look out the window in the privacy of her thoughts. Living as one of the heroic Visitation sisters would be a challenge, and she was intrigued by the cultured Mother Superior. Yet, she felt drawn to the contemplative life of prayer. Some months before, Beryl had asked Father Louis Bertrand, the Jesuit tutor to her and her brothers, to investigate the Discalced Carmelites in Baltimore. She sent a message to the Reverend Mother Superior with Father Louis in which she expressed the call she felt clearly and humbly. Reverend Mother invited her to come to the monastery for the visit to which they now traveled.

The journey to the Carmelite Monastery took several hours from the Visitation convent in Georgetown. Toward afternoon, the brougham approached the stone wall of the Carmelite enclosure. It was ten feet high, concealing whatever gardens might be within. The chapel and visitors' entrance stood well back from the road, and there were stables for the carriages of churchmen and guests adjacent to the main buildings. There had been no rain for weeks. The steeds, covered by a patina of dust appeared to be more grey than black. By the time Beryl and her mother departed the coach, road dirt filled the crevices of their traveling gowns and had seeped into their shoes. Their eyes were sore and their nostrils were dry.

They were surprised to see two nuns of the Order approach them from the entry door. The sisters greeted them warmly, took their satchels and guided them inside. The thickness of the stone walls was a barrier to the summer heat, and inside there was not a trace of dust. The wood plank flooring shone with buffed wax. The double oak doors of the public chapel were open, and the altar lamp gave a faint illumination to the sanctuary, which was softly lit by a collection of votive candles arranged at the foot of the Virgin's statue. To one side of the altar, heavy iron bars welded in vertical and horizontal squares with only six inch openings separated the altar from the nuns' cloister. Beryl's keen ears heard a faint cough from the nuns' area. Other than this muffled sound, all was covered in a stillness so profound it seemed palpable. Mother and daughter didn't need to be told to observe silence; the surroundings demanded it.

"Reverend Mother Aimee will welcome you as soon as you are refreshed," one of the nuns whispered. The short, round faced woman had to look up to Beryl and Constantia. Her complexion was ruddy and her manner friendly. Her companion, a woman of slighter build, smiled, but did not speak.

"I didn't realize you were allowed outside the cloister," Beryl whispered to the round woman.

"Ah! Mais non! We are externs, not from inside the walls. Let me show you to your rooms." She turned and said a few words to the other nun before leading Beryl and Constantia down a corridor across from the chapel. "Our accommodations are plain, and no doubt not what you are accustomed to, but if you require anything, please ring this." She placed a wooden handled bell on a small table that stood outside one door. "I will hear it and come." Her voice was still low, but now she spoke rather than whispered.

"Nous parlons Francais," Constantia said courteously. "Perhaps you would be more comfortable speaking your native language?"

"Ah, merci, vous etre tres solicitous! But the Reverend Mother requires us to speak English. If I make the mistakes, perhaps you will be so kind as to correct me!"

The other sister had returned carrying a double-handled copper kettle steaming with hot water. She poured bowls full in each room. There was soap and clean towels.

"There are quarters behind the stables for your driver. Our caretakers, young William and his grandfather, will see to him. Reverend Mother will call for you in a short while." She gave a slight bow and left them to their ablutions.

Constantia noted that the nun was a gentle soul, but not gentile. The little

French she had heard her speak was an indefinable patois, not the Parisian inflection.

When they were summoned by the Reverend Mother Prioress, they were shown into a small room, plain with whitewashed walls, a single crucifix, the same highly polished plank floors, and two straight backed chairs with no cushioning. One wall was an iron grille from table height to ceiling. It had eight inch spikes pointed at the visitors, set uniformly every two of the six inch metal squares. A heavy black curtain on the nuns' side was drawn over the grille. Beryl and her mother stood waiting for the Prioress.

They heard a door open softly and a voice in faintly accented tones said, "Blessed be Our Lord Jesus Christ!" A small figure, hooded under a black veil that concealed her face and upper figure, drew the curtains aside. The nun moved her straight chair closer to the divider and indicated that her two guests should sit. Constantia noted the finely boned hands and delicate long fingers before they were quickly withdrawn under the brown scapular.

"Welcome to the Monastery of the Immaculate Heart of Mary," Reverend Mother Aimee said in a voice that proclaimed her excellent breeding. "And this is Beryl?" she said turning toward the young woman. Both mother and daughter wondered just how much the nun could see through the veil. "After a little chat, we shall have a talk by ourselves if your good mother will excuse us, oui?"

They spoke pleasantly and Reverend Mother told them she had sent some reading material through the turn. "Soeur Felicite tells me you read French, n'est'ce pas?"

"Yes, Reverend Mother," Beryl said as her mother nodded.

Once alone with Beryl, the Prioress wasted no time in frivolous talk. "Your maman does not discourage your vocation?" Mother Aimee asked. She had known more than a few parents who vigorously objected to this austere life for their cherished daughters. "Nor your pere?"

"I am one of eight children, Reverend Mother," Beryl told her. "I have two older brothers and five sisters. All my sisters have made good marriages. My parents are quite willing to give a child to the Church."

"You are eighteen?" The Reverend Mother took the hem of the veil that covered her face and pulled it away.

Beryl looked into the grey eyes of a woman, whose age was impossible to determine. The soft white wimple covered the neck and its headband was set high on the wrinkle free forehead. The brown scapular had been put on over the wimple, and over it the black veil. Mother Aimee's features were perfectly chiseled, as if in classical marble. The nostrils on her patrician nose flared ever so slightly, and the fine bones of her face made her large eyes remarkable. Her eyebrows were superbly arched, but without a hint of arrogance. Her thin mouth did not smile, but neither did it turn down. She was a perfect beauty, one of rare quality. Beryl could imagine that there was aristocracy in ancestors who had somehow escaped the citizens' wrath after the revolution. She had to wrench her mind away from these musings to pay attention to the question she was being asked.

"Have you been to school?" Reverend Mother asked, and Beryl interpreted the question as "finishing school" rather than academic.

"I studied at home, Reverend Mother. Papa permitted this, although he felt it unsuitable that I continue my education outside of our home. He was, I believe, relieved when my brothers' tutor, Father Louis Bertrand of the Society of Jesus, told him of my desire to enter religious life."

The Reverend Mother had already heard of the candidate's academic prowess from Father Louis Bertrand. This young woman was proficient in Latin, French, and German. She had a basic foundation of Greek and had read both Roman and Greek philosophers. She was well versed in ancient and modern history, had knowledge of the arts and wrote with flair and ease. Had she been born a male, she would have been welcomed by the Society of Jesus.

The Reverend Mother studied Beryl's appearance and demeanor. She was a tall girl, not delicate of bone, and though pleasant of expression, not beautiful. Her blue eyes met the Prioress' gaze directly, although her deportment did not indicate boldness. All to the young woman's credit. Furthermore, she came from a family well placed in society. Before Beryl and Constantia left Baltimore, a date was set for Beryl's entrance and a dowry agreed upon.

* * * * *

Yvonne and Marie Louise returned to their childhood home to attend a farewell dinner for their sister. Neither girl was close to Beryl, who had been as absorbed with her studies and horses as her sisters were with fashion and social events.

When she was still at home, Yvonne frequently complained to her mother that Beryl's unseemly preoccupation with books made her too opinionated. "She is insufferably bold!" Yvonne accused. The truth was that she did not want Beryl to impress her suitors. She sensed a heightened interest on the part of some young men who were in their social circle.

When chided by Constantia in this regard, Beryl defended herself. "Mama, I merely crave good conversation."

However, Yvonne took comfort in her favorite suitor's comment referring to Beryl: he felt sorry for any man who would have to justify his politics and ideas to a woman.

The unmarried sisters did not have to worry about competition as far as appearance was concerned. Beryl had a high forehead, straight nose, and cerulean blue eyes. She had a strong chin, even teeth and a generous mouth, but put together, these fine features missed beauty. The imperfections of her sisters were far more striking. Yvonne's slight over-bite and tilted nose was piquant and noticeable. Marie Louise's flawless complexion and ash blonde hair was far more alluring, in spite of her overly plump lips. The willow-like grace of her mother was particularly absent in Beryl, who had to struggle to correct her lumbering gait. Beryl rode gracefully and could sit any recalcitrant or flighty horse in the stable. But her dancing skills were a disaster to which many a young man's sore feet could attest.

Marie Louise was kinder and had been sincerely concerned when Beryl announced her intention to enter the Carmelite Monastery. "Sister dear, are you not making an exceedingly cheerless choice? Do consider changing your mind."

"I'm not at all tempted to change my mind, Marie Louise."

"But surely there is some man who would have you!"

Beryl laughed and pressed her sister's hand. "I am happy with my decision, truly."

What Beryl did not, could not say was that to her the one ideal man was not one who rode to the hounds, or who presented a handsome figure at balls. He was a scholar, a man who passionately explored spiritual and philosophic matters. He was Father Louis Bertrand. This was the measure against which Beryl had compared all suitors who might have sought her hand in marriage. Through Louis Bertrand's fervent dedication to his calling, Beryl had seen the dignity and the merit of religious life. Once she had glimpsed this ideal, she wanted the most perfect expression of it, the most complete devotion to Christ for a Christian woman, and she saw this as the cloistered life of a Carmelite nun.

In one of her last moments with her sisters, Beryl smiled broadly and whispered, "Do you want to know my very deepest regret?"

"Oh, yes, Beryl."

"Confide in us, do!"

"I shall miss our father's magnificent horse."

V

The North Cascades

Douglas McFee led the last of the horses into the corral. Little Joseph stood ready at the gate to enclose the year-old filly whose feet had been trimmed. Douglas leaned against the fence and looked down at the boy. "Twenty horses, shod or trimmed, and if that's not a day's work I'll be eating my cap for supper!"

"Will they go by the end of the week?"

"All but the yearlings, and that young gelding I've had me eye on. That's a fine piece of horse flesh, as fine as any I've seen in my life. I've a mind to train him myself. And you can help, lad."

Joseph, although barely five years of age, had a way with the horses. A stubborn gelding or snippy mare became docile at his touch. Douglas thought perhaps the Indian blood gave the boy an advantage ordinary folk could not put a name to. Joseph didn't "talk" to horses as some charlatan trainers claimed to do. Still, it seemed to be a mind to mind connection.

"Well, lad," Douglas said moving away from the corral, "the stew's in the pot, the frost will be on the pumpkin, and we'll be snug within. Have ye an appetite?"

"I do!" the boy replied, giving the old man the smile that never failed to warm his heart. "Will we have lessons, or…" the boy hesitated.

"Ye'll be thinkin' the old fellow's so long in the tooth he's good for a day's work and then abed!" He ruffled the boy's wavy black hair. "Well, truth to tell, I am fair wearied, but our supper and a wee dram of whiskey will have a restoring effect. Let's have our meal and then our pleasure!"

Douglas never talked down to the boy, and once lessons began, the brogue into which he frequently lapsed was abandoned. Years ago he and his dear Fiona had agreed that life in the raw Pacific Northwest would be easier if they had the mark of the common touch. They were singular enough without arousing the suspicion many settlers felt toward the educated, those who "put on airs." It was no different at home across the ocean. Whenever either was in the village or among the folk, they would, as Douglas said, "Massacre the King's English worse than any Scotsman from the West Highlands could have done."

Douglas had been fortunate in his youth. The Laird's son, Malcolm, was sickly and slow to learn. His tutor suggested that the bright lad who lived with his family in the gatehouse might join the boy, making the learning less lonely. In the schoolroom, Douglas was the shining star the privileged child worshipped. There was no jealousy; no feeling that Douglas should not excel. Instead, there was friendship and admiration. Malcolm absorbed sufficient learning to convince his father that he was receiving a first class education. But he merely spouted facts and would not have been able to form them into a coherent essay. Of the classroom conspirators, no one shared with the Laird the truth that Douglas was the scholar. The tutors, several in succession as it came to be, were intrigued by Douglas' bright mind, and enjoyed challenging him to the fullest extent of their intellectual prowess. The schoolroom kept Malcolm more than content because of Douglas' presence. His father was aware that his son would never excel in the gymkhanas or the games of the public schools and was satisfied to let it be known that Malcolm was preparing privately for university examinations. His suggestion that Douglas, now close to fourteen years, be released from coming to the schoolroom met with Malcolm's panic, tears, and tantrums.

When asked about the boys' relationship, the tutor said, "Douglas gives him competition and keeps him alert, even though," the man lied with a straight face, "Malcolm is the superior scholar." The last tutor employed had determined to depart the manor before the results of Malcolm's university entrance examinations were forwarded to his father. But his resolution was unnecessary. Malcolm became ill of a fever and died before he could sit for exams. The lessons ended abruptly for sixteen-year-old Douglas.

The tutor approached Malcolm's father and begged for his son's friend to be sponsored for a scholarship to the university. "In memory of Malcolm's affection for his schoolmate," the tutor said.

Douglas earned his place at the university and read the classics for three years before he had to return to the Laird's gatehouse to care for his infirm father and, in his place, assume the management of the estate. Douglas did not abandon his studies, although his formal schooling ended. He married Fiona, a local schoolteacher, who shared her husband's love of learning. No children resulted from their union, and when the Laird died and bequeathed all of Malcolm's books to the boy's friend and schoolmate, he also gave Douglas a gift of enough money to purchase passage to the New World and a new life.

The couple homesteaded north of the Washington settlement of Fort Vancouver, and gradually ventured further into the Cascades where Douglas purchased and bred horses to be sold to the United States Army. Douglas made trips to Seattle where emigrants eager to find gold came, as they say, "lock, stock and barrel." As far as their "stock" was concerned, the horses were anything but suitable as pack animals or mounts for the trails. McFee purchased many fine horses from this lot and fitted the emigrants with Appaloosas, Mustangs and grade horses. He earned the reputation of honesty and fairness.

Fiona volunteered as a school mistress in the town, but was forced to admit she was quite unable to meet the needs of these uncultured boisterous youngsters. She had no natural ability to keep discipline, and when her voice rose higher and higher in an effort to gain control, the mimicry of the pupils made the schoolroom sound as if a kennel of yelping dogs were imprisoned and demanding release. She was happy to stay at home. She prayed for a child, but until McFee discovered the infant Joseph on their doorstep, her prayers went unanswered.

It was Fiona who found the carefully crafted note in the child's blankets. The mother had taken a strip of bark from the wild Madrona tree, smoothed its surface, and with a sharpened stone etched her message. Barely discernible when done, she had washed the words she had written with a dye of blackberries, and scraped the surface to reveal the writing. It said:

> *This is Joseph. His father was Grey Wolf. He was a chief, but he was killed. I am a white woman. I have traveled a great distance to save our lives. Please keep my child. You are his only hope.*

Fiona lived until Joseph was in his fourth year. The couple recognized his intelligence and devoted themselves to his education. Before Joseph was two years old, he knew the names of every object in and around the cabin. He would point to anything unfamiliar and then store the name in his remarkable memory. By three Fiona had taught him the alphabet and he could put together simple words. She had kept many of the children's books from her teaching years hoping that a child of her own would one day treasure them. At four years Joseph could read them all, books that spanned the first three grades of regular school.

Douglas and Fiona kept Joseph's presence from being known until he was a strong and curious toddler. Then Fiona fabricated a story for the villagers. She told them that she and Douglas had taken in an Indian worker and his squaw along with their boy—to help with the horses. The settlers were scandalized. They predicted that Fiona and Douglas would soon be dead in their beds, throats cut and scalped to boot. No trader could report having seen the red man or the squaw, but said that the lazy "injins" habitually left their offspring unsupervised to roam the McFee land. When Fiona, a victim of a sudden stroke, died, Douglas told the villagers that his Indians had run off leaving the boy. He said he had decided to keep him on until he was old enough to work.

"Get rid of the vermin! You can't trust an Indian!" the men at the general store repeated.

Douglas seemed to consider their words, but shrugged when men warned him that the boy would ultimately run off with anything of value. McFee said, "Right now he's too small to steal the horses, and the only things of value in my cabin are books! Now what would an Indian do with those?"

A good laugh was had by all, and Joseph was safe.

VI

Maryland: The Charbonneau Estate
1860

Beryl gave the chestnut stallion his head and felt its acceleration to a gallop reverberate through her own body. She rode astride on this, her last morning at home. The sound of hooves against the earth drummed in four four time, and birds twittered an accompaniment from the copse at the edge of the wood. There was that first faint smell of autumn in the air, crisp and invigorating. The hedgerow was in front of her. She gathered the reins, leaned over the great steed's arched neck and lifted to a jumping position, her heels well down in the stirrups. The horse left the earth and they rode the air up and over the stones and bushes. Beryl shifted her weight back as they landed. The two were in perfect balance: the powerful animal and the strong-willed girl who knew just how much freedom to allow her mount and still remain its master.

Beryl slowed the stallion to a trot. He snorted, sending puffs of steam from his nostrils. She patted his muscled neck, and he nickered his response. There was a mist rising from the earth, still warm from yesterday's Indian summer heat. Trees and hills were softened, and Beryl rode through what might have been the background of a Dutch master's landscape. Shafts of early light ribboned through the stand of trees that bordered a rock bed stream. The sound of the water was barely audible over the bird song and the horse's breathing. This morning was a blessing, and she thanked God for it. She guided the stallion in a long turn and cantered back to the stables.

By the time the household was awake, Beryl had cooled her mount, picked the tell-tale dirt and grass from his hooves, and brushed him free and dry of saddle marks. This last ride was their secret. Adam, the hostler, would know and had probably seen her go out, but she could rely on his silence. She took her riding skirt from a hook in the feed room and wrapped it around her waist, concealing the britches she had borrowed from Pierre's closet so she would not need to use a side saddle.

She was to leave for the monastery at an early hour. She bathed quickly and dressed in the simple black postulant's frock. Beryl wore the postulant's dress with surprising elegance. Its simple blouse and skirt with the modest waist-length cape complimented her slender frame. Constantia's efforts to clothe this daughter in feminine pastel fabric and delicate laces to compensate for her angular figure had never achieved the intended effect. This morning Beryl pulled her thick hair back from her face and tied it at the nape of her neck.

Looking at her daughter in this plain garb, Constantia had to admit that in such a style, or the lack of it, Beryl was attractive. *For all the good it will do now,* she thought.

The trunks containing part of Beryl's dowry were already mounted on top of the carriage. Constantia was sending linens, a silver service, and a set of altar candle holders, also in pure silver. Books deemed appropriate were packed in another trunk, with fine British woolen blankets filling the remainder of space.

Pierre and Philippe had left for Harvard University in Boston two weeks before. Their carriage ride had taken three days. Father Louis Bertrand accompanied them as far as the Jesuit Novitiate near the capitol where he was to receive a new assignment from his Master General. His superior had indicated that he might receive permission to go west. Beryl had said her farewell to Father Louis in private, and she promised to write to him. Reverend Mother Aimee understood that he was her spiritual director, so she would be permitted this communication.

"Letters may take some time to arrive if, as I hope I will be in the Pacific Northwest. Don't worry, Beryl, if you do not receive an immediate reply."

There were no tearful farewells. Henri Charbonneau embraced his daughter, patted her back, cleared his throat telling her awkwardly that should she fail, there would always be a place for her at home.

"I am determined to succeed, Father, but it is a comfort to know I will always have a home," she responded formally.

"Then bide you well, child," her father said, and was dismissed.

She remembered the Visitation nuns telling her that their families had disowned some of their number when they had embraced the Church of Rome. When they took the veil, the rejection was total and irrevocable. At least Beryl was within the bounds of family tradition. Also, she was not the favored child, a pampered pet of her parents, and they had made little objection to her choice. Beryl was not easy to pamper. From the time she was old enough to toddle, she had demonstrated an independent spirit.

Unknown to Beryl, her father regretted that she had been born female. Had this bright and determined girl been one of his sons, he would have spared no effort to assure that the Charbonneau name be honored by such an offspring. Now, as she was leaving the family, he felt some regret that he had not taken more interest in this child whom Father Louis Bertrand said was rarely gifted. Undoubtedly, she would make her mark in the Order.

There were tears in Constantia's eyes when she said her goodbye. She was not close to Beryl, but she admired her. She had also worried for her. It was pathetic how this handsome daughter had made every effort to learn the social skills that would make her a good wife. But who would have her? No one had been inclined to court Beryl, although it was well known that all the Charbonneau girls were given generous dowries. Beryl lacked the guile to convince a suitor he was of inestimable worth. She excelled at everything except feminine wiles. Constantia was happy to turn her over to the Carmelites, though for the life of her she couldn't see what the attraction could be. It seemed such a waste. And yet all the tutoring Beryl had received with her brothers was wasted on a female in any case.

The servants stood in the foyer to wish Beryl well—all but Adam, the hostler. He waited outside by the carriage. He was sad at Beryl's leaving. This morning he had been awakened by a movement in the stable and saw the girl riding out on her father's stallion. The elder Charbonneau had purchased the great horse as his own mount and to improve his breeding stock. Yet, Charbonneau, an accomplished equestrian, was wary of this animal. Beryl had no fear of him and the stallion knew it. There was mutual respect between beast and girl.

As Beryl approached the carriage, the hostler came forward with awkward shyness, uncertain that he was behaving appropriately. He thrust a roughly wrapped gift into her hands. Beryl smiled her thanks as she took the lump of wrinkled brown paper. His head bowed, Adam made a respectful retreat.

Beryl embraced her mother one last time and climbed into the carriage. The girl had insisted that the footman and driver and one of the downstairs maids would be all the escort she needed, and that she would prefer to say goodbye to her mother at home.

Father Louis had given her a letter which she was not to read until she was on her way to Carmel. It was difficult to make out the fine copperplate script while the carriage was moving, so she put it aside and opened the hostler's gift. It was a plain cross, shaped and welded from the steel nails used to shoe the horses. Beryl took her rosary from her pocket and worked open the loop that held its cross. She replaced it with Adam's gift. This was the first time she had let tears fall from her eyes.

When Beryl's carriage stopped at the West Shire Inn on the first leg of the journey to Baltimore, she was met by the innkeeper's wife, who had been advised of her coming. Beryl refreshed herself and sat in the dining area for supper. Aware that she was oddly dressed under her cloak, she kept it on. She had looked forward to the stop so that she could read Father Louis Bertrand's letter. Unfolding it, she spread it on the table to read.

1 October 1860

My dear daughter in Christ,

My words to you at your entrance are written after profound reflection and prayer. I am not one to claim prescience, and I admonish you not to make any such interpretation.

Yet, I must advise you that I have a conviction regarding this step which you take so generously in response to God's call. It may be that this calling is a time of preparation for you rather than an end in itself. I risk being imprudent by confiding such an opinion to you, but I trust your abundant gifts of intellect and discrimination.

The life of Carmel is hard, but I do not believe you will find it unbearably harsh. Reverend Mother Aimee is a woman of some education, and certainly no fool. She will find a use for your gifts.

The time of postulancy and novitiate will test you in full measure. Give yourself wholeheartedly to the trial. Promise to bear whatever hardships, mental and physical, for the years of your novitiate until final vows.

Keep me informed of your spiritual progress. If, at the end of your novitiate, you are of firm resolve to take solemn vows, I shall bless and congratulate you, remaining your devoted confessor and friend. But keep your heart open to all possibilities, my child. I am yours in the Heart of Our Lord Jesus Christ and His Blessed Mother.

Louis Bertrand Beauleux, S.J.

Beryl read the letter three times and committed essential phrases to memory. Was Father Louis telling her she didn't belong in Carmel? No, not exactly that. Was he warning her of the hardships of a penitential life? She knew full well that there would be challenges to her resolve and her human nature. "A time of preparation…" She tore the letter in half, put it in the fire that burned in the Inn's hearth and watched it curl into cinders. Father had warned her that privacy was not one's right upon entering Carmel. All correspondence was read, both incoming and outgoing. He had told her that she could seal an inner note clearly marked "matter of conscience," and it would be sent to him untouched. He also advised her to use this means of communication judiciously. As for the letter she had just burned, Beryl judged, and rightly, that Reverend Mother and Mother Mistress Francoise would not wish to read that Beryl's spiritual director and counselor was telling her in effect to put up with almost anything, it was only temporary. That was the message, she was certain of it.

It was late afternoon the following day when the carriage arrived at the monastery. The extern sisters greeted her once again, only this time with effusive affection. They embraced her and murmured, "Welcome, petite Soeur!" Beryl suppressed a hearty guffaw. To have laughed outright would have been unrefined and unladylike, but she was amused at anyone's calling her "petite." The sisters guided her into the chapel. The nuns were reciting the hour of Vespers. She could catch only a few phrases as the chant, plain and without melody, rose and fell with each cadence of the psalms. Two groups of voices alternately chanted the stanzas. *In conspectu Angelorum psallam tibi, prosternam me ad templum sanctum tuum.* She translated it without difficulty: *In the presence of the angels, I shall sing your praise. I will worship at your holy temple.* The voices chanted a hymn, then there was silence. The nuns moved silently, but she thought she could hear them leaving their choir.

The round faced extern who had met her so warmly was at her side, beckoning. She led her to the wide door at the end of the outer hall. A key turned in the inside lock and it swung open. What seemed to be the entire community was on the other side of the door, each holding a lighted candle. All the nuns were hooded with black veils like Reverend Mother Aimee had worn when she and Constantia first met her in the visiting parlor. When the cloister door closed, the nuns lifted these from their faces. A nun on either side of her, Beryl was led into the Choir while the community chanted. Beryl was too overwhelmed to translate accurately at first, but then she recognized The Magnificat. *My soul doth glorify the Lord...*

After the nuns welcomed her. two sisters with white veils led her to a silent supper in the refectory. One nun showed her to her place as the others smiled, still in total silence. They stood until Reverend Mother Aimee took her seat and tapped the table. At this signal, the community sat.

A sister took her place at a small table in the middle of the room and began to read by the light of a candle that Beryl thought must have a double wick. She read from a spiritual treatise of Saint Teresa of Avila. Supper was simple, but ample. There was a thick potato soup flavored with onions and spices; coarse, but good tasting bread with a crisp crust; and strong tea. After the meal, a novice with a white veil brought a tureen of hot soapy water. Each sister in turn washed and dried her own bowl and replaced it on a shelf under the refectory table. At a signal from the Prioress, the community rose, stood in lines on either side of the room and recited thanksgiving prayers. They filed out in order, the eldest leaving first.

Beryl was taken in hand by an older nun who escorted her to another part of the monastery. The white veiled sisters, whom Beryl supposed to be the novitiate, followed.

"Blessed be Jesus Christ in all his Glory!" the older nun said once in the confines of this new wing.

"Amen!" the group responded, followed by a chatter of greetings. They took straight back chairs and placed them in a circle. They sat with their hands circumspectly hidden under their brown scapulars.

The older nun introduced herself. "I am Mother Marie Francoise, your Novice Mistress. She nodded to the white veiled sister on her right who began the introductions of the members of the novitiate.

"I am Sister Jean Albert," the first young woman said.

She was followed by Sisters Marie Claire, Ann Louise, Marguerite, Celine, and Annunciata. Beryl was the only postulant.

"I thought there were other novices?" Beryl said.

"You saw our lay sisters. They do not have the duty of reciting the Divine Office in Choir, and they always wear the white veil. Three of them have entered since we came to America, as have all of our novices here. We are blessed with many vocations."

Mother Francoise spoke perfect English with no accent. Beryl remembered that Reverend Mother Aimee had told her that Mother Marie Francoise had been born and raised in America, as were four other sisters among the professed nuns. They had all begun religious life at the Motherhouse in Belgium and had made their solemn profession there before joining the new cloister in America. It was the dream of the parent community that it would make the first foundation in the Northeast of America. In 1791, when the invitation came from the Archbishop of Baltimore, the community was ready and eager to begin plans for a monastery in America.

As the first weeks of her postulancy passed, Beryl learned the routine of Carmelite monastic life. There were assignments in the garden and kitchen for the sake of training, but manual labor was the task of the lay sisters, not choir nuns. Other work was done in the solitude of each nun's cell. Beryl's cell was a room twelve by twelve furnished sparsely. It contained a hard mattress on a plank, no pillow, but she was given enough blankets for warmth. There was a small table for work and study. A set of shelves contained clothing, which was neatly folded and never more than needed at any given time. The novitiate had its own library, and Beryl's books were shelved there. She was allowed one volume at a time for her private meditation. Anything she needed she was expected to ask for in deference to a spirit of poverty. There was no conversation except at instruction time and at recreation hour when the sisters brought their needlework and conversed in a group. The only contact with the larger community was in Choir, at daily Mass and prayer, and in the refectory.

Beryl slipped into the routine with ease. The daily psalms, responses, and memories of the year of saints and feasts seemed to her to be a magnificent pattern in harmony with the changing cycles of the seasons and the great feasts of the Church. She listened to the Latin lessons in the novitiate with patience and humility, never indicating that she understood the Latin as second nature. She longed to assist the novices who experienced difficulty, but wouldn't put herself forward. When, after some months, the novice mistress asked Beryl to help Sister Jean Albert, whose profession was in jeopardy unless she could master the language of prayer, she took on the responsibility of tutoring gladly.

The exercises of discipline were easy for Beryl to accept, but the spiritual lessons given by Mother Mistress Francoise were trying in the extreme. The nun was reluctant to speak literally, and embellished her lessons with vivid metaphors. Of the need for chastity she said, "We must keep in check the steeds of passion that would hurl us from the edge of the precipice."

Beryl could not hide a smile as she thought of riding her father's powerful chestnut stallion to the edge of the precipice.

"Sister! You find this subject amusing?" The Novice Mistress' voice brought Beryl back to the present.

"Oh, no, Mother Mistress. I was just remembering my father's horse."

Mother Francoise frowned. "We do not discuss our personal histories, Sister." She pointed to the floor, and Beryl rose from her chair and kissed the polished wood twice as a penance for the smile and the inadvertent reference to the past.

During another lesson on the same subject, Mother Francoise said, "Sisters, we must keep intact the original bloom of the pristine flower." This time Beryl covered her mouth and feigned a sneeze. Her Novice Mistress stopped and looked at her class sternly, her eyebrows raised, but Beryl had managed to assume an ingenuous expression, innocently waiting for the next words of wisdom.

For the most part, Mother Mistress Marie Francoise was pleased with the new postulant, but also suspicious. "Sister Beryl is too perfect, Reverend Mother," she confided to Mother Aimee. "She is obedient, cheerful, humble. I find it difficult to fault her, which I try to do for her own good."

"How does she respond to correction?" Reverend Mother asked.

"Very well. Yesterday I scolded her for walking like a peasant field hand. She bowed her head and acknowledged that her mother had told her much the same thing. She promised to correct her fault and asked if little Sister Annunciata could help her learn to walk like a lady, as befitted a nun!"

"Sister Annunciata?"

"Yes! The daughter of a common miller! I don't know, Mother, Sister Beryl is just too good to be true."

"I wouldn't worry, Mother Mistress. What is the American expression? She takes to the life as a 'duck to water?'"

"Very well, Mother. I shall thank God for our little duck!"

Their "little duck" thrived in the monastery. Soon the years of her probation came to an end. Beryl wrote to Father Louis Bertrand.

4 October 1862

My dear Father,

>   *I cannot believe I have been in Carmel for nearly two years! The richness of prayer and the great Office is a delight. In the silence I have learned to still my undisciplined mind, and I have confessed my arrogance before God. He is teaching me that all I have learned is, as Saint Thomas Aquinas discovered, as so much straw. I have been accepted to receive the holy habit on October 15. On that day I will be Beryl Charbonneau no longer, but will receive a name deemed suitable by my superiors. Father, I remember your last written words to me. Be assured that God's grace is pouring over me like sweet, warm rain.*

She continued with a few pages of anecdotes from her first year of religious life, then put the letter, unsealed, on her novice mistress's table. There was no reason to include a "matter of conscience" enclosure. Nothing was troubling Beryl. Her superiors read the letter and were satisfied that Beryl was indeed secure in her calling to Carmel.

The Charbonneau family was well represented when Beryl received the habit of the order. Henri and Constantia came with two of Beryl's sisters, Clemence and Yvonne. Marie Louise was expecting her first child and unable to attend. It was too long a journey for Pierre and Philippe, but they sent messages. Constantia brought pastry delicacies and baskets of dried fruit, and several bottles of fine French wine from their cellars. She also brought the bridal gown Beryl was to wear in the ceremony before she was clothed in the Carmelite habit. At the ceremony Mass, the curtains were removed from the grille and the family and guests watched as Beryl, majestic and more beautiful than she had ever been before her entrance, knelt with a lighted candle to affirm her desire to receive the habit. Out of the sight of guests, Beryl was led away to remove her finery. She returned in the habit of the order.

The climax of the ceremony came when the Bishop said, "In the world you were known as Beryl Charbonneau. In the Order you will be known as Sister Saint John of the Cross."

Later in the day when the guests had left and the hours of visiting in the parlor were over, Beryl knelt in the choir clothed in the habit of Carmel. She loved the brown wool tunic, the soft wimple with the brown scapular covering it so that just a bit of white showed at the shoulders over the tunic. Her white veil covered a head shorn bare of her dark brown hair. It was supposed to be a humiliating ordeal, but Beryl found it practical and comfortable. Before the little bell rang for all candlelight to be extinguished, Beryl began a letter to Father Louis describing the joyous day and telling him of her name in religion. She wondered how long it would take for him to receive it. Her father had said that he was working with Jesuit Father Cataldo in the far west, in Spokane, a city that was being established as an inland empire of the north westernmost United States. He had sent a message, but Reverend Mother had not yet given it to Mother Mistress. Beryl looked forward to receiving it, and she would finish her letter to Father Louis after she read its contents.

VII

The North Cascades
1862

Douglas was glad to be home. Although he had delighted in Joseph's first trip outside the local settlement to the coast, he had been uncomfortable with the charade he and the boy maintained whenever they left their domain. Over the eight years of the boy's life he had prepared Joseph carefully. The child seemed to grasp the fact that ignorant men and women nurtured hatred and ill will to those of their fellow men who were either different or did not believe as they did. Douglas used both literature and history to illustrate his point, all for the sole purpose of building a strong armor of protection for Joseph when in the future the boy would live on his own.

"So I'm Shylock to the people of the settlement?" Joseph once asked.

"As far as he was a victim of hate, yes. But there is a great difference. Can you tell me what it is?" Douglas was astonished by Joseph's answer. Not a day went by but the lad would confound the old man with his intelligence and insight. And all this from an eight year old child.

"The difference is not in the prejudice. You want me to say that I would not ask for a pound of flesh."

"This is true."

Joseph remained silent for a long time. Douglas thought perhaps this was too lofty a subject for a young mind, and was content to let the subject drop. Joseph surprised him yet again.

"I do not mind how we must act in the settlement, not even when I pretend

46

to be stupid and ignorant of speech. But if I had walked on the streets of Toledo when Torquemada burned men alive because they were Jews, or wouldn't believe as he did, I would have hated him." Joseph eyes were bright with anger. "I could have killed him had I the chance."

Douglas met the boy's eyes. "And your act of murder would inspire revenge in return, and on and on until the hatred sent blood flowing in rivers down the streets." He shook his head sadly. "It is happening now. Good men from the North and South murder each other. The army here in the west drives Indians from their rightful land and there is more killing between the tribes and the settlers. So how does it end, or does it ever end?"

"Fiona used to say that God would make everything right. I wouldn't trust Torquemada's God—or the minister's, and He was the same God, wasn't He? I heard the minister tell you that God would send you to Hell unless you came to church every Sunday. And remember when he pointed at me and said I was already doomed to Hell because I was a savage..." He paused. "And then his daughter screamed at him to stop. That seemed very strange."

"Indeed." Douglas remembered that day clearly. "Life is strange, Joseph. I think that is enough philosophy for tonight. Shall we have a game of chess before it is dark?"

Douglas thought about the minister's daughter. After the screaming incident, he overheard two men discussing her.

"She came back a queer one, and that's a fact."

Douglas was standing next to the two and inquired mildly, "Back from where?"

The men told Douglas the story of her disappearance and reappearance. "She came back in Indian clothes. Skin and bones she was, too, but she insisted she hadn't been mistreated. Back when she disappeared, she was attacked by robbers and rescued by the Indians. She said they thought she was nutty in the head since she couldn't remember who she was. The Indians are afraid of crazy people. So, some years later she got her memory back, and the Indians returned her to her father. Nobody ever found out what tribe they were because they just dumped her outside the town and ran off."

Joseph set up the chess board after their supper. Douglas sat heavily. The years were beginning to sap his physical strength, Fortunately, he was not yet infirm and he was far from senile. How could mental inertia overcome him as long as this boy was his companion? He stared at the board, but his thoughts were on the minister's daughter. He was certain she was Joseph's mother, and he understood why she could not have brought a half-breed child home. He

ELEANOR LABERGE

remembered the note etched on Madrona bark. She had risked her life for the child. He would keep her secret.

As Joseph waited for Douglas to choose his moves, his whittling knife chipped away at a piece of dry birch. The boy seemed to have a talent for creating figures from scraps of wood. A rough collection of squirrels, fox, bear, birds and owls occupied a window ledge. Douglas moved his rook.

In response, Joseph moved his queen swiftly across the board. "Check, and checkmate, I think."

"So it is. I must have been wool gathering." Douglas collected the ivory pieces his school friend Malcolm had given him many years before. "Too much pondering on the ways of the world!"

Part Two

I

Carmelite Monastery, Baltimore
1863

In spite of the rule forbidding worldly subjects, the professed nuns were discussing the war at their recreation hour. Reverend Mother Aimee had not yet returned from a visit in the parlor. She was surprised to hear raised voices coming from the community room. She heard the normally soft spoken sister from South Carolina, Marie Jeanine, speaking urgently. "My father and my brothers had to go to war to protect our free trade and our laborers. Our slaves are the lifeblood of our economy."

Sister Agnes, a nun who came from Massachusetts, responded. "But is not yours a way of life that is founded on the sale and ownership of human beings? My father told me that since the invention of the cotton gin, the numbers of slaves have risen to over two and a half million, and seventy-five percent of the number was involved in cotton!"

Sister Anastasia, whose family lived in Boston, spoke up. "Sister Marie Jeanine, is it your contention that slavery is right because the south's economy benefits by it?"

Fragmented comments followed;

"You can't understand,"

"The Bible says to treat slaves well, so slavery is not immoral."

"Would Jesus have kept slaves?"

"George Washington kept slaves!"

"Sisters!" Reverend Mother entered the room clapping her hands,

"Sisters," she repeated, willing her voice to be calm. "We shall not have a war inside the cloister. What happens outside our walls is not our concern. Henceforth, in holy obedience I forbid you to speak of war, either in private conversation, in the parlor, or at recreation."

Mother Aimee blamed herself for the outburst. It was apparent that unmonitored family visits and mail she had forwarded to the sisters without carefully reading the contents had fanned the flames of argument. She herself was aware of the political and moral debate, but she was careful not to appear to take a side in the matter. Whether the North or the South won the war, the monastery could not afford to make enemies. From that day she undertook to censor incoming mail scrupulously, often returning communications to the family requesting that subjects of a more neutral character were desired for the spiritual well being of the sisters. The Southern families could no longer journey safely to Baltimore, and in the novitiate the young women from the confederate states were told just enough to explain their loved ones' absence. Mother Mistress dutifully placed mail that her novices wrote home on Reverend Mother's desk, but most could not reach their families. By April of 1861 bridges from the South to Maryland had been destroyed, and until they could be repaired by a regiment from New York, civilian and military traffic was stopped. Non-military communication between North and South was extraordinarily difficult.

Beryl had not had a family visitor for well over the time she was allowed to receive a guest in the parlor. Unaware of the war, she had assumed there were many reasons, from inclement weather to her sisters' pregnancies. Constantia finally made the journey to Baltimore. Beryl was shocked to hear that the nation was embroiled in mortal combat. Both Phillipe and Pierre had joined the union army, and Phillipe had been sent home after his ankle had been shattered by musket fire at the battle of Antietam forty miles from Washington.

Reverend Mother was present during Constantia's visit, and could not, without being ill mannered, prevent Constantia from discussing her family's involvement in the war.

Not having been among the professed nuns when the Reverend Mother's dictum forbidding war talk was given, Beryl pressed her mother for details, but Constantia knew little more than the fact that the embargoes made life inconvenient. Cotton and muslin were hard to find, and British ships didn't come as before. She complained that her long overdue order of Limoge from France still had not arrived.

"And our picnics to Antietam had to be canceled when that dreadful battle took place. Oh, that dear little stream," she complained tearfully.

"But Pierre!" Beryl was impatient to learn the details of her brother's wounding.

"It was at Antietam that Pierre was wounded, you see," Constantia said. "But hadn't I told you this already in my letters and that your father was wounded in Baltimore after Fort Sumter?"

Beryl sat still in wide-eyed silence. She had not received a single letter. There was no way she could see that behind Reverend Mother's veil her mouth was set in a tight line of disapproval.

Constantia continued, "You must have known that when Mr. Lincoln sent troops right here into Baltimore, he put city officials in jail until the government was sure Maryland was going to side with the North! Henri said it was all illegal, even though he has decided our sympathies must be with the Union." As soon as Constantia had imparted this last bit of information, her voice drifted off. She had been babbling.

The Reverend Mother interrupted the conversation. "I am certain that Sister would not wish to hear more talk of war, Madame Charbonneau."

Although Constantia changed the subject to family matters, she managed to tell Beryl that three of her other daughters' husbands had gone to war. Marie Louise's Stefan was from Georgia, and he fought on the side of the Confederacy.

When the visit ended and farewells were made, Mother Aimee detained Beryl at the parlor door. She lifted her veil and said, "You will not speak of the war to any nun or novice, including Mother Mistress. You will not repeat any information relative to it. You may beg prayers for your brothers and your sisters' husbands, but you will not say why."

Beryl assented calmly. "I realize such talk would be unwise for the peace of the community. I assure you I shall say nothing."

Reverend Mother watched the novice, now bound by her first vows, as she walked down the corridor. She was disturbed by Sister Saint John's words, even though there was nothing of disobedience in their content or in her tone. Why then did she feel uneasy? The simple fact was that Sister had indicated her understanding of the Prioress's policies, and given her assent. The words somehow conveyed their equality. That was it. The exchange, however brief, had not been at the level of subject and superior, but between equals. Sister Saint John had bridged a forbidden gap, and Mother Aimee was not pleased.

Beryl went down the corridor with perfect religious deportment. She looked modestly downward as she passed two professed nuns and entered the door to the novitiate without encountering Mother Mistress or another novice. Her hands were under her scapular, but they were clenched. What her mother described was a war that could destroy the nation. Surely the industrial North would win in the long run, but how many lives would be lost? How long had this gone on? Which states fought? Had President Lincoln made slavery a fundamental moral issue?

It took a great effort of will once she was in her cell with the door closed behind her not to pound her fists on the table. It was study time. Beryl sat with her open breviary in front of her, but she was trembling. The news of the war, of Pierre and of her father had been kept from her! This was the first crisis in her religious life. She had seen two novices and one postulant buckle under public humiliations and unreasonable disciplines.

Beryl knew from the moment of her entrance that she would be tested, and she responded as if in a game of wits. She never showed frustration, nor did she feel any, even when perfectly beautiful stitches were ripped out of her mending and she was scolded for her sloppiness. She knew her stitches were excellent, and she knew her novice mistress knew. And her novice mistress knew she knew. It was a game, and the playing of it amused Beryl.

Father Louis had coached her well. "Always remember that true humility is truth, my child. Do not permit any superior, nor any custom to call into question your God given intelligence. I have seen this happen, even in the Society of Jesus. In subtle ways your mind may be challenged and you may be tempted to believe you should not even think! Resist such efforts to humble you, child, at least interiorly. That kind of discipline is based upon a false premise."

Beryl's analytical mind examined the problem. How, exactly, did knowledge of the war or the lack of it, affect her life as a nun in this house? It should not. She had entered the cloister, not to be a part of the world and its turmoil, but to achieve union with God. The floods of Noah could be rising once again and what would it matter? The waters of change and war could engulf them, and what should their reaction be? Surely not to fight against the trials God sent. Surely not to take musket and guard the convent door! God would, in His Infinite wisdom, send them trouble or leave them in peace. The Carmelite nuns of France had lined up, stripped of their habits, and had marched to the guillotine chanting their affirmation of faith.

At Vespers, Beryl's demeanor was placid and untroubled. She sensed that she was under the keen scrutiny of her Prioress. *With good reason*, she thought. She would give Mother Aimee no reason to suppose she was troubled, and she was not. At least not so deeply as she had been earlier.

Throughout the coming months Beryl suppressed all thoughts that distracted her from the continuity of her prayer life. The solemn profession of the fellow novice, Sister Jean Albert, whom Beryl had tutored in Latin, brought her misgivings to the surface once more. Sister Jean Albert was accepted for her final vows in 1863. Mother Mistress told her group that there was "some trouble" between the states which made travel difficult, and therefore Sister's family would not be present for her ceremony. However, Reverend Mother made certain that the Archbishop of Baltimore would be present to officiate.

Beryl could no longer put her questions to rest. Was Sister Jean Albert making an informed decision? If she knew what conflagration might be raging in her beloved Atlanta, would she make this choice? Beryl tried to put herself in her superior's place. She knew little personal information about the professed nuns, but she could assume they had at least the variety of backgrounds found in the novitiate. How would she, in Reverend Mother Aimee's place, have handled the nuns regarding the war? The good Lord didn't look with disfavor on a daughter of the Confederacy any more than He would spurn a loyal child of the Union. All the considerations of family history and opposing tradition would come together under the monastic roof. Here God's children would embrace each other, Northern woman and Southern woman, bestowing upon each other the balm of healing forgiveness. Given their unity of vocation, that would have been the way Sister Saint John, Carmelite novice, would have led the community were it hers to lead. Which it most definitely was not.

Sister Jean Albert made her vows before the first Passion Sunday and left the novitiate to begin her life as a fully professed nun. In the three days of free time after Resurrection Sunday, Beryl began a letter to Father Louis Bertrand. For the first time since her entrance, she enclosed a brief, sealed "matter of conscience" message with the more general correspondence. The Monday following Easter, she placed it on the novitiate message table for posting.

Several days passed before the sealed portion of her letter was returned to her. With it was a note in Mother Aimee's hand writing which told her that the Carmelite fathers who would be visiting within the month would be able to help in any matter of conscience for a Carmelite novice. Beryl was stunned. Would this have been the response if she had written confidentially before now? The envelope had not been opened. Her privacy of conscience had not been violated. She had given no external indication of her spiritual stress, nor had she been guilty of any behavior unseemly to the contemplative life. Beryl could see no justification for her superior's action. Mother Aimee had severed the lifeline that Beryl had believed would always be there for her.

Beryl destroyed her confidential communication, but in spite of her efforts, she could not silence the questions in her mind. She attempted a confession to one of the Carmelite fathers, but it was clear to her that he did not grasp the magnitude of her problem. She began to admit to herself how much she missed the nourishment of the intellectual life; she yearned for the exchange of ideas and acknowledged this to her confessor. He was gentle in a patronizing way.

He dismissed her concerns and voiced platitudes. "Your little problems will be utterly extinguished by the grace of God when you pronounce your solemn vows, my dear," he told her. "Vows bestow grace." His counsel was meant to console; it plunged her into greater turmoil.

For the first time since she entered Carmel, Beryl made a decision to disobey her superior. She wrote a long letter to Father Louis Bertrand, seven pages in all, and enclosed them in a sealed inner envelope. She marked it "Matter of Conscience." She placed this in an outer envelope addressed to Father in care of the Jesuits in Baltimore. She put no return address on it, and pinned it to her underskirt rather than leaving it in her cell. There were unscheduled searches of nuns' cells by Reverend Mother accompanied by a senior nun. It was part of the Carmelite Rule, but the invasion of privacy that rankled with some novices hadn't offended Beryl. If a nun owns nothing, she cannot be possessive, she reasoned. Everything a nun used was part of shared community property. A sister could be reprimanded by accumulating things for her own use, or admonished if her cell were disorderly or in need of cleaning. Beryl would not risk having this communication found. She kept it with her. As the weeks passed, the envelope became dog-eared and the address faded, but it was still readable.

Constantia had given her yearly visit time to her daughter Yvonne. Beryl was summoned to the parlor. Yvonne had come with a companion who preferred to remain outside. Reverend Mother had mail to read and sort, as well as work of her own. She set up a table outside the open door of the visiting parlor rather than sit idly through the visit. If anything unseemly were to be said, she would be in the room immediately. Beryl encouraged her sister to chat about light things, but shook her head and steered the conversation away from any talk of the war. Yvonne and Beryl recalled happy memories from their childhood, and after one anecdote that sent the sisters into ripples of laughter, Beryl withdrew the letter from her pocket, put her finger to her mouth signaling Yvonne to silence, and rolled it to fit through the grille. Still laughing and saying insignificant things, Yvonne took the letter and swiftly pocketed it. Beryl smiled her thanks and her sister nodded her unspoken promise to post it. Beryl put her hands back under her scapular just as Reverend Mother entered, veil down, to greet the guest personally.

II

The North Cascades
1864

Two men from the town found the old man on the trail. He was barely conscious, bleeding from a head wound and a deep gash in his stomach. "A knife, and a nasty one," the first man said.

"He's trying to say something." The second man put his ear to the victim's mouth.

"F-f-find...Joseph..."

"What's he saying?"

"Something about a 'Joseph.'"

"That's what he calls that Indian."

"We warned him. Nobody can say he wasn't warned."

Douglas struggled to speak again, but consciousness had slipped away and he would not speak again.

"We need to take the body back to town."

"He'll keep. We need to get that Injin if he's still at the cabin."

After they searched the old man's pockets, which they found empty, they pulled his body into the bracken at the side of the trail, "Jesus, he must have had a couple of hundred from the horses he sold on the coast."

"That wasn't the half of it. He was riding that gelding of his—it's worth top dollar."

"Don't we need the law—or help?"

"Hell, no. The day ain't come when two of us can't handle one Indian. He's probably stealing a stash nobody knows nothing about."

They mounted their horses and headed for Douglas' cabin at a canter. Joseph didn't expect Douglas until noon. He might be later if the four horses he was bringing home resisted being roped in a string following Douglas' gelding. The horses the emigrants brought to Seattle by barge were not always docile—at least not in the ways of a western trail horse. He felt uncomfortable letting Douglas make the trek down to Seattle by himself, but one of their best mares was due to foal, and this morning she had been particularly restless. This was not the time to leave her alone.

An hour after Douglas had left, the mare was in labor. The delivery was going smoothly, the front foot presented first, then the other and the head tucked in between. Joseph crouched at the mare's head, calming and encouraging her, but he was alarmed to see that the birth sac covered the foal's head. Swiftly he came to its aid. He tore the sac, enabling the newborn to breathe. Shortly afterward another contraction expelled the foal. It was a colt, healthy and strong. Soon it was standing and nuzzling the mare for food as she nickered to it in wordless pleasure. Joseph wiped it dry with a clean barn towel, gave extra alfalfa for the mare and left them. If he had not been there to remove the sac from the foal's head, it would have suffocated. This was a lesson he must remember, Joseph thought. It would be prudent to keep a minute by minute vigil when a mare was close to delivery.

After his chores, he found the volume written by an American, Nathaniel Hawthorne, *The Scarlet Letter*. In the first pages, Joseph recognized the similarities between the Salem witch trials and the Spanish Inquisition. Here again was evidence that men committed atrocities and persecutions in the name of their many-faced God. Creating God in their own image, as Douglas was fond of saying.

It was Joseph's habit to sit among the branches of the great cedar that rose a hundred feet next to the cabin. He would step carefully to the top of the wood pile from which he could stand on the cabin's roof. From there it was an easy climb up the cedar's branches to a perch some fifty feet above the ground. He would sit on a flat piece of wood which was securely nailed between two limbs. From his lofty perch he could watch the trail from which Douglas would approach, and at the same time see into the paddocks. Today he kept a close watch on the paddock where the mare stood above her foal as it slept.

As mid-day came and passed, Joseph listened for Douglas. When he heard approaching horses, he began to climb down and was almost to the cabin roof when he remembered the book. Douglas trusted him never to leave any volume outside. Scrambling upward, he retrieved and pocketed it. Then he heard angry voices. Two men Joseph had seen several times in the settlement were approaching the cabin. They were shouting his name. One held a rifle, his finger on the trigger.

He heard one yell, "Dirty Injin! Killer! Thief!"

The other voice cried, "Mongrel whelp of a she wolf!" and again that chilling word, "Killer."

Joseph froze.

Both men dismounted and barged into the cabin, then they came out and searched the barn.

"Nobody."

"I'll bet you two day's work the kid's long gone."

"He won't get far. An Injin kid with a wad of cash? Now how believable is that? If he took a string of horses, he'll be easy to track. Let's get help."

Joseph did not move until the men had gone down the hill and he heard no sign of their back tracking. He had to leave and immediately. Douglas would not want him to stay and be hauled to the gallows, or worse. Douglas had met with misadventure, but fear and the urgency to run for his life stilled Joseph's grief.

In the cabin he stuffed some bread and dried meat into a burlap feed sack. He removed every stitch of his clothing and searched for a loin cloth. He found a beaver skin and the many colored blanket Fiona told him he was wrapped in when he was brought to them. It was moth eaten, but certainly not "white man's" clothing. He grabbed a tinder box, some candles, and looked at the books. No. Being found with just one of these could mean instant "justice" administered with a thick rope on the nearest tree. He ran his hand over the precious row, then left them. He remembered his sturdy boots and removed them swiftly. There were beaver pelts in the feed room. He would take some cord and use these on his feet. For a head start he would have to use a horse, but he would let it go as soon as he could. First he piled extra food for the mare who had foaled, then he took a trail seasoned Appaloosa, a breed known for its strong feet and good bone. He'd ride in the stream as long as the water level permitted.

It was almost dark when he encountered the rapids and knew that his horse's way through the water had ended. Joseph dismounted and continued upstream on the calm side. Hopefully, the trackers would pursue the horse, which fortunately did not take off in the direction of the cabin. Soon the stream widened, and on both sides there was a steep granite wall. A million years of water and ice had eroded the sides smooth, but there were hand holds. He climbed in total darkness, and finally tumbled onto a plateau. He was numb with cold and exhaustion, but knew he could not rest. Neither was there time for grief. He listened to the sound of coyotes screaming their night songs. An owl hooted a mating call in the distance. Joseph fought the urge to sleep. Douglas had once shown him the entrance to an abandoned silver mine, but with neither moonlight nor the light of day to guide him, his safety lay in forging ahead into the isolated heights of the mountains.

III
Baltimore
January 1865

Father Louis Bertrand took off his great coat, his suit jacket and removed his stiff clerical collar. He splashed water from the basin on his face and dried with a clean towel. He saw that it bore streaks of road grime. He couldn't decide between a bath and the bed. The luxury of stretching out on a real mattress had the greater appeal. He stepped into the hall to ring for one of the house brothers. He saw that old Brother William was already on his way with a packet of mail set on the edge of a tray of cold cuts, bread, hot tea and honey cakes.

"Welcome home, Father," the ruddy faced brother bowed deferentially. "There's a jigger of whiskey under the napkin to flavor your tea!"

"Ah, William. You always know just what we need. This is a welcome fit for a king. A very, very tired king," he sighed, taking the tray.

"Father General says to rest and he will greet you in the morning. What time will you say your Mass, Father?"

"Wake me at six, Brother, and thank you."

Louis Bertrand removed the remainder of his travel-worn garments, donned a clean flannel nightshirt and put a wool blanket around his shoulders as he sat to eat. He was as hungry as he was tired. The railroads at the end of the trip might be quicker than the old pioneer route by carriage, but it was a noisy, bone jolting ride, especially after a boat journey of over five thousand miles. His trip had been made pleasant by the companionship of Asa Mercer, a learned young man who had been appointed the first president of the Territorial University in Seattle. Mercer had taught for five months and then was returning east to New England where he intended to recruit young ladies of marriageable age to settle in the new West. "I'm seeking a 'calico cargo' for the settlers," he said. "We need the stability of family life in our new community."

Father Louis finished his meat and bread. He poured the generous portion of spirits into his tea and took a grateful swallow. He reached for a sweet cake, but his hand paused as he noticed the worn envelope with the familiar hand in faded ink. His dear Beryl! After these many years! He opened it immediately to find the confidential enclosure.

November 1863

Dear Father,

> *I must tell you that I write to you without the permission of my superiors, and if you are reading my words, I shall have contrived to send the letter without Reverend Mother's knowledge. Having made this confession...*

A deep frown creased the Jesuit's forehead as he read Beryl's description of censorship and her efforts to rise above the misguided policies of her superior. He noted with satisfaction that she didn't sentimentalize her struggle for personal holiness. She wrote not of any blame, but her own acknowledgment that her dilemma regarding her perseverance had its underlying cause in her own selfishness and lack of faith.

> *I flail about in an ocean of doubt, Father, groping for something to hold me above water, but finding nothing. I look to Heaven and see only unsubstantial clouds. I pray for a sign from God and then berate myself for such presumption. Perhaps I am too worldly to understand that I am in a sea of God's love and if I could quiet my soul and sink into its depths, I would find peace. Yet I struggle not to sink and reach for the sky, the empty sky.*

Father finished the letter and sat pondering its contents. He was no longer eager for sleep. From his valise he took papers he had prepared for the Archbishop. He had been prepared for his proposal, but now he thought that his appeal for help would take a different direction. He had intended to ask His Excellency's support in seeking one of several established orders of nuns to come to the western Jesuit province to establish much needed Catholic schools. The hardships of the war and the constraints on travel had delayed the project. Now he was formulating a daring plan: the creation of a new Congregation uniquely American in concept and led by Beryl Charbonneau as foundress. Beryl had prayed for a sign. He would bring it to her.

He put aside the documents and went to the window. Drawing the curtains, he stood looking at the early night Heavens. The sky had not yet turned black, but the single evening star burned brightly just over the horizon. Yes, he would go to Beryl, Sister St. John of the Cross, without delay, but in the first excitement of his new plan he must not act imprudently. He would see the bishop early in the morning.

* * * * *

The monastery had changed little in the five years of his absence from Baltimore. After the initial bloody affair in the city, which killed and wounded more civilians than soldiers, it had been spared. Had the conflict continued to rage in the North, the nuns might have found their structure conscripted for military purposes. The war would not have remained a secret to the community in that event.

He rang the front bell and waited for an extern to answer. When she appeared at the door, Father said, "I wish to speak to the Reverend Mother, Sister. Kindly announce Father Louis Bertrand of the Society of Jesus."

He waited in the visiting parlor. Reverend Mother Aimee entered, without the veil that had covered her face at his last visit.

An interesting courtesy, Louis Bertrand thought.

They exchanged some pleasant conversation, and Mother Aimee inquired about the pioneer life in the Washington Territory. Beryl might not have read all his letters, but this woman clearly had.

After a suitable time he came to the point. "Reverend Mother, I would like to speak to Sister Saint John. As her spiritual father, she may also wish to have me hear her confession." He would not be so bold as to ask for an unmonitored conversation, or to require Beryl to do so. In the confessional there would be privacy.

"How generous of you to come, Father, but it is impossible for you to see Sister at this time. She is deep into her retreat for solemn profession. Of course, on her ceremony day, which I invite you to attend, she will be pleased to see you. She will be delighted that you grace the day with your visit."

Father Louis was not going to argue with this nun, who clearly did not want her retreatant to speak to him. Nuns in retreat for vows often spoke to their confessors. After reflecting upon Beryl's letter, he had anticipated some difficulty and had come prepared. He withdrew an envelope from his breast pocket. "I understand, Reverend Mother. I am also here on another matter."

He rolled an envelope and passed it through the grille. "The Bishop has appointed me extraordinary confessor this year for your community. I will begin to receive the nuns as soon as you notify them of my presence. Will an extern sister direct me to the confessional?"

Reverend Mother Aimee had admirable control. Her expression did not change, although she knew that any effort to prevent his communicating with Sister Saint John had been defeated. Once a year a priest was delegated to hear the confessions of every nun. Canon law decreed that every sister in every house must at least enter the confessional and ask for the extraordinary confessor's blessings. She was not required to make confession, but every nun must report. It was a safeguard against the very kind of control this superior was attempting to exercise. Father Louis would have his conversation with Beryl.

Two days later, Reverend Mother Aimee accompanied Sister Saint John, now simply Beryl Charbonneau. Only minutes ago, the time of her temporary vows had expired. Father Louis Bertrand and two Visitation Nuns from Baltimore were waiting in the corridor. They had sent appropriate clothing for her through the turn, mindful that Beryl's head was shorn bare. Departure was mercifully quick, and Beryl, hearing the cloister door lock behind her, concentrated on the life ahead, which she was certain God ordained. Still, the sound of the key gave her almost unendurable pain.

On the enclosure side, Mother Aimee sank to her knees. During the last year she had waged her own interior battle. Once she admitted to herself that she felt jealous of her novice, she stormed Heaven with prayers for forgiveness. Her desire to make reparation for her own sinful inclinations took a nearly disastrous turn. She protected her subject from any temptation that might stand in the way of perseverance, and intervened lest any distraction in the form of letters or visits disturb her. She had tried to safeguard what she believed was Heaven's plan. Now she was confused.

Should she have contested the young nun's decision to leave more forcefully? She stood, lifted the veil which still covered her face and made her way to the nuns' choir. Sitting alone, examining her conscience, she realized that it must be true, as Father Louis Bertrand had explained to her, that Carmel had been a preparation for Beryl Charbonneau. So be it. This great house, the first foundation of Carmelites in America, would continue to remember its child in their prayers. They would continue to fortify her by their penitential life for the great work Beryl Charbonneau was destined to accomplish.

IV

Obtaining the support and blessing of the Archbishop of Baltimore for Father Louis Bertram's new congregation was not a simple matter. His Excellency did not readily agree that a new congregation was needed, and he doubted that such an innovation could be led successfully by one as young as Beryl Charbonneau.

Father Louis Bertrand pressed his case with an eloquence inspired by desperation. "Your Excellency, the young woman I propose as Mother Foundress is exceptionally qualified. She possesses a brilliant mind and a deep desire to devote her life to the Church. Against my better judgment as her spiritual director, I gave my blessing to her entering Carmel. She was an exemplary candidate, but began to examine the wisdom of a strictly cloistered life for one of her temperament—as was suitable and commendable before taking solemn vows."

The Archbishop sat back in his well upholstered desk chair and folded his hands as he regarded the Jesuit. "You are proposing that I endorse a young woman who has failed to commit herself to a contemplative vocation to found another order?"

"She entered an order which is a veritable desert of solitude and penance. She spent five years, exemplary years, in Carmel which encouraged maturity in her spiritual life. However, when she sought my counsel, I felt compelled to be honest. As I said, I had misgivings from the beginning that she was destined for the hidden life of the cloister. If you are finding fault with her for not making solemn profession, bear in mind that had I not spoken, she would have become a professed Carmelite."

"You took much upon yourself as her spiritual director, Father."

"I am convinced that the years in Carmel have been a unique preparation for Beryl Charbonneau. I also believe that my visit to the monastery, coming at a time when her decision hung in the balance, was the work of the Holy Ghost. I believe most profoundly that Miss Charbonneau is being called by God to fulfill a special role in the Church. You are concerned that she is young, Your Excellency. Youth is in her favor. I have lived in the West. The task I am proposing for her will take a great deal of energy, as well as dedication."

"Where is she now?"

"With the Visitation Nuns in Georgetown. I have witnessed her private vows and Mother Eulalie is pleased to have her with her community for the present."

"What is Mother Eulalie's opinion of this young lady?"

"I hope you will ask her, Your Excellency. In fact, it was her feeling, as well as mine, that Beryl did not belong in Carmel. She believed that in God's mysterious ways it would be a preparation."

"She expressed this opinion?"

"Indeed."

Ultimately, the Archbishop gave a conditional approval for the new community, which was to be called the Congregation of Martha and Mary. He permitted Beryl Charbonneau to recruit women in schools and parishes within his archdiocese. If she inspired followers, the Archbishop reserved the right to examine each to be certain they understood the serious difficulties involved in their undertaking.

Beryl Charbonneau, as Mother Foundress, would remain in Georgetown with her volunteers during their six month period of postulancy. They would then enter into the strict canonical year of novitiate as mandated by the Church. The year was to be spent under the supervision of the Visitation Nuns in their convent while Mother Charbonneau would proceed to the western territory to arrange for a suitable convent building and to prepare for the mission of her Congregation. The Archbishop appointed Father Louis Bertrand to be Advisor and Father Confessor of the Congregation and admonished him sternly to provide a solid theological foundation for applicants. To accomplish this, he was to remain in the East and, if the canonical year were successful, he would escort the candidates to the West.

Father Louis Bertrand's dream was on the way to reality. Rather than separated by cloister walls and three thousand miles of unexplored territory, he and Beryl Charbonneau would be joined in a great venture. It was meant to be.

V

When Joseph found the mine he hoped to use as shelter, he discovered that a group of prospectors had made camp at the site. He observed them from a distance, watched until they lit a fire, ate, and finally prepared for sleep. He counted five men in all. Apart from passing a canteen of spirits and sharing a swallow apiece, these men did not appear to be drunkards.

In the morning, Joseph observed all five men disappear into the shaft leaving no guard. He was in desperate need of clothing, but had to be careful not to alert the men to the presence of a thief. Rummaging through packs and scattering the contents as a bear might do, he took a wool blanket and a pair of boots. The men had hoisted their food stuffs into a bull maple. A bear or raccoon would have found no challenge in reaching the store to claw at it until it tumbled to the ground. Joseph climbed the tree and released the wrapped foodstuffs. After he scattered the contents, he took dried meat and some stale biscuits. When he heard voices in the tunnel he slipped away.

Joseph repeated his marauding visits whenever he encountered a camp. He never stole anything that had value. He left coins, watches, and tack, and no camp suspected more than a visit from a bear, coyote or family of raccoons. By the first snow Joseph had collected blankets, spare boots, a backpack and one sturdy hunting knife. He stole a cooking pan, which he could use to melt snow or stew a rabbit. His hunting skills were sufficient to keep him from starvation, but he never ate his fill. Sated he would not be alert. To fend off boredom, he whittled, but burned each piece when it was finished. He attempted a carving of Douglas which was so like his friend and teacher, Joseph wept as the fire reduced it to ashes.

When an early spring brought cattle herds over the Cascade Trail, Joseph followed them. He learned the locations of trading stops and settlements where men could eat, sleep and drink with good company. Drifting into one of these rest areas, he began to do odd jobs for drivers and traders. The Innkeeper, Harriet Lathrop, thought he had run off from a cattle train and didn't mind his staying to cut wood, haul water, muck out stalls, and feed the stock—all for table scraps and a corner of the barn for the night.

Gradually he became an accepted part of the landscape. He rid himself of the hunting knife and kept only his whittling tool as a personal possession. He was careful not to follow any orders too quickly, but rather to feign a dull-eyed lack of comprehension. Once when he had been in Seattle with Douglas, he had seen an unfortunate young man who walked with a peculiar shuffling gait. "Poor lad," Douglas muttered and gave the boy a coin. It was accepted with a blubber of thanks as if the young man's tongue were too large for clear speech. Joseph mimicked this memory and gave a credible portrayal of an amiable retarded youth, one just bright enough to accomplish the simplest of chores.

He paid a price for his living arrangement, becoming the butt of cruel jokes. Once he was thrown into a pig trough. Joseph sputtered and came dangerously close to fighting back. Before he could vent his anger, another man had picked him up and tossed him into a barrel full of horse water. His drunken tormentors roared with laughter.

"His first bath!" they shouted. "Change the water before the horse's drink!"

Joseph, sobered, crawled out and ran from the premises. He hid outside of the compound until his clothes had dried, then returned stealthily to the blacksmith's place. Without being asked, Joseph would frequently appear at the head of a frightened or unruly horse until it would settle. The smithy was not overly friendly, but kind. He would often talk to Joseph believing the boy did not understand.

"Poor lad. The animals like you sure enough. I wish I could make you understand me. I'd tell you to stay away from those louts with two legs and put all your trust in critters."

Joseph hung his head dumbly but thought to himself that this was good advice.

There was some discussion about giving Joseph a name. The Barkeep said, "How about 'Tom?'

"Yeah," one listener laughed, "as in Tom-Tom the Half Breed!" His cronies guffawed as he pounded out an Indian rhythm on the counter.

"He has two names already," a swaggering cowboy offered, "Moron or Idiot. Which fits him best?"

The blacksmith interrupted this latest contributor. "That moron or idiot saved your crazy horse from breaking a leg when he got himself tangled yesterday. I'd like to have seen you get in the middle of that fray."

It was agreed that the boy had a way with horses. "Oh, hell," someone said, "Let's just call him 'Dumb Ass.' It's as good an Indian name as any."

The blacksmith shook his head. He thought it was better to leave well enough alone and yell 'Hey you!' when he wanted the boy's help.

Joseph lived from day to day. It would not improve his situation to leave this place. At least he had shelter and scraps to eat. He would have to wait a year before he met his future, Beryl Charbonneau.

VI

Georgetown: The Visitation Convent
1866

The brick wall protected the Visitation Sisters' Convent garden from some of the road dust, but it didn't muffle the sound of carriages passing. Beryl was on her knees weeding a patch of beans when she heard her father's voice ordering his footman to attend to the team of horses. Beryl got to her feet, brushed the dirt from her canvas apron and removed her garden gloves. She couldn't make out what Mother Eulalie said to her father, but it was unmistakably her voice coming from the front entryway. She knew her father well enough to be confident of his courtesy, but his voice was raised and Beryl assumed that he had come to demand that she return home. His letters had promised as much.

Beryl had written several times attempting to assure her mother that the conditions at the Visitation convent, which had so appalled Constantia five years before, had greatly improved. She knew that her parents' concern was not about her temporary residence with the Visitation Sisters, but with Beryl's plans to go to the West.

Beryl found her father standing in the visiting parlor of the new wing. To her relief, Constantia was not with him.

Henri Charbonneau wasted no words. "What is this foolishness about going West?" he demanded. "Your letter tells us you shall leave within a week?" His voice was tremulous in anger.

"Please sit down, Father. Sister Francine is bringing refreshment for you."

"The devil with refreshment. I haven't come to sip tea and coat my tongue

72

with honey cake. You must return home, daughter. Your mother is beside herself with worry. I myself cannot imagine what possesses Father Louis Bertrand that he has proposed such an outrageous scheme!"

Beryl remained calm. "Please, Father, sit down," she said as she sat in a straight-backed chair.

Henri had not seen his daughter since she was eighteen. Even under the odd blue and brown nun like attire she wore, the habit that had been adopted by the new Congregation of Martha and Mary, he could see that her slender frame had not taken on flesh. Her face was less girl-like, strong, and authoritative under the wimple and veil. Her clear blue eyes looked at him unwaveringly. This was not the father-daughter encounter he had anticipated.

"Father, if I were going overland on the Oregon Trail, you would have good reason to question my plan. But I will be traveling by steamship with a group of young ladies supervised by Asa Mercer, the president of the Washington Territorial University. It is an excellent season for the voyage, and I assure you it is no more dangerous than your trip between here and home."

"I understand that the manner of your traveling is prudent. But you are inexperienced. Nothing in your background has prepared you to be a missionary to savages and frontier riffraff!"

"I am not called to found Indian schools. This is being done by established orders. The Congregation of Martha and Mary will found parish schools for the white settlers."

"But you will be in harm's way. We've heard about the Whitman tragedy and other killings."

"Here at home we fought against one another, killing hundreds of thousands of our own men and boys. The Cayuse tribe killed the Whitman party because the white settlers brought a deadly epidemic of measles. Marcus Whitman could save his white brothers, but he could not save the Indians. In their grief and confusion, the Cayuse blamed Whitman. But five of their braves came forward and gave their lives as reparation—an act more Christ-like than savage."

Charbonneau had no reply, especially since Beryl chose to allude to the Civil War so newly ended. "There are many areas closer to home where there is great need. Aren't you happy with these sisters with whom you are living?" He had not intended to capitulate by encouraging Beryl to remain with the Visitation community, but clearly Constantia's fears regarding their abject poverty were no longer valid.

"Happiness has nothing to do with my decision or what I know to be God's calling. And, Father," Beryl looked into Henri's eyes, "it is my decision."

Sister Francine knocked softly at the door and brought in a tray of tea and wheat bread. "Look, Father." Beryl smiled. "Plain whole grain bread. No honey coating for your tongue!"

Henri Charbonneau returned home without Beryl.

Part Three

I

December 1866

On board the *Continental*, Beryl had her first look at Asa Mercer, Seattle's Territorial University President, the gentleman who had assembled the "Mercer Girls." She was shocked to see a vigorous young man barely out of his twenties. Why had Father Louis not told her of his youth? Her mental picture had been of a benevolent, bearded old gentleman. Certainly she had not imagined that the man on an errand to bring the stability of family life to the Pacific coast had experienced the use of a razor for less than a decade! As she looked at the group of nervous young women who had entrusted their futures to Mr. Mercer, she prayed that his wisdom was greater than his years. Except for one, the girls huddled together, some giggling, some weeping. A solitary Mercer girl stood apart from the rest, a fragile figure with a dry cough and pale face.

"She's no more than a child," a woman who had joined Beryl said, following her gaze.

"I would say no more than fourteen," Beryl responded, turning to see a woman close to her own age.

"And she's not likely to reach fifteen. I'm Elizabeth Ordway—Lizzie to my friends, and one of that sorry group." She extended her hand, male fashion to Beryl.

Beryl accepted the greeting. "I too, am with Mr. Mercer," she admitted. "I'm Beryl Charbonneau."

"Ah! The nun. You don't look the part," Lizzie said.

Beryl was taken aback. She was not accustomed to this kind of easy familiarity, but surely their circumstances weren't those which would demand that formality be observed. She laughed. "Perhaps it is better to be what one is rather than look the part! And if you would forgive my boldness, you don't appear to have much in common with the rest of our group either!" she rejoined.

"If you mean that I'm not a simpering, dewy-eyed husband seeker, you are absolutely correct. I am a confirmed spinster and intend to remain so. Quite contentedly, I should add." Elizabeth Ordway was an attractive woman with an oval face, dark eyes, and even features. She parted her hair in the center and pulled it back severely in a bun. Beryl reflected that if this were done to appear unfeminine, the style served rather to compliment her strong features. "I intend to make my mark in a man's world on my own terms," she told Beryl. "There are not many of us female pioneers in this new frontier."

Beryl continued to look at the fragile girl who was now with the larger group. "I believe that child should be put off the boat at once," she said to Miss Ordway.

"Mr. Mercer told me that she has lost her parents to smallpox, and that her only surviving family is two brothers in Seattle. She wants to be with them."

"Yes, well—that is different."

The great ship left New York and proceeded south under somewhat rolling seas. Beryl didn't experience seasickness, and neither did the redoubtable Miss Ordway. They joined those passengers inclined to eat at the long dining room table. The food was plentiful and well prepared. The wood strip deck outside was wide enough to accommodate chairs. Some passengers gathered at the railing, and others chose to take some exercise walking around the promenade.

As the journey progressed, Beryl found Elizabeth Ordway, now "Lizzie," excellent company. She was a woman of considerable education and exceptionally well read. The two women soon became friends.

The air was heavy and hot as the ship neared the equator. Lizzie and Beryl spent more time on deck hoping for a breeze. Once they neared Rio de Janiero, the air lightened and the oppressive heat was behind them. The ship docked at Rio, but Beryl remained on board the *Continental*. She welcomed the comparative solitude that gave her time to write to her family. She also wrote to Father Louis and her little band of volunteers who remained in Georgetown for a year of training. She described the ship and the voyage in detail, describing uncomfortable conditions honestly; she intended reality to take the place of romantic fantasies.

In Rio two new passengers came aboard, and were assigned to places at the dining room table next to Lizzie and Beryl. Professor Albert Boucher and his granddaughter Lavinia had departed from New York earlier with the intention of touring Rio, then joining Asa Mercer's party. Professor Boucher was traveling to Seattle where he would assume a post as professor of literature at the Territorial University. Lavinia, recently orphaned, would accompany her grandfather as far as San Francisco where her elder brother had consented to provide room and board in exchange for her services as tutor and mother's helper.

The two were amiable company. Professor Boucher was grey-haired with an enormous walrus style mustache. He was an excellent conversationalist, but, as Lizzie pointed out, he dominated all subjects. It became a challenge for Lizzie to express her opinions fully before the professor had gone on to a new topic.

"Perhaps he is hard of hearing," Beryl offered.

"Which condition would improve mightily if I were a man," Lizzie countered.

Boucher's granddaughter was well educated, but had no income of her own. Professor Boucher was not a wealthy man, not having been born to money. Lavinia would have to manage independently.

"My brother has four school age children," she explained to Beryl and Lizzie. "I shall help tutor them in exchange for my keep."

"An unenviable circumstance," the professor muttered. "They are insufferable and wretchedly undisciplined. I've told Lavinia that she would be far better off living with me, although social life in Seattle is limited."

"I love you, Grandfather, but I would be equally unhappy as a cook and housekeeper. At least with Avery's children I will teach."

Boucher made a sound that conveyed the idea that any teacher would have a difficult time with these grandchildren.

During the voyage, Lavinia, Beryl and Lizzie became friends. Lavinia's parents had been scholarly, and her father was involved with the Transcendentalist movement.

"Is your grandfather a writer? He seems to be intent on a journal," Lizzie commented.

"He is translating works by the Norwegian playwright Henrik Ibsen," Lavinia explained.

Out of Lavinia's hearing, Lizzie commented that it was surprising such a beautiful girl was unmarried. "She's an outstanding beauty. A bit frail, perhaps, but with the ash blonde hair and classic features? I can't imagine that there weren't suitors on the doorstep."

"There was one," Beryl said, repeating the story she had heard from Professor Boucher. "He was killed at Manasses."

As the weeks passed, Professor Boucher read selected passages from his translation to the ladies, and Lizzie was especially fascinated by *The Doll's House*. "I don't think he really gets the point," she told Beryl. When Lavinia and her grandfather learned of Beryl's background, Lavinia pressed Beryl to share more about her community.

"I am a Catholic," Lavinia said, which you probably would not have guessed. My mother was of the opinion that children should be brought up with some religion. My father didn't object—actually, he was indifferent to organized religions. Grandfather doesn't talk about it. I think that be believes that ignoring the fact will make it disappear!"

Before the ship approached San Francisco, Lavinia sought out Beryl while she was alone on deck. "Would you have a place for me in your Congregation of Martha and Mary?"

Spontaneously Beryl gave her a great hug, then apologized. "My bear hug could have compromised your delicate bones!"

"I may have a fragile appearance," replied Lavinia who weighed no more than a hundred and twenty pounds, even though similar in stature to Beryl, "but I'm tenacious as dandelions in a summer field."

"Is your brother depending on you? Will he be disappointed?"

"His plans can change. He can afford proper schooling for the children." She looked at Beryl shyly. "You would be justified in questioning my motives. The boys are a dreadful sort! I had an opportunity to know them well four years ago before Avery accepted a banking post in San Francisco and my own circumstances changed."

"I'm glad that you will escape that life. There are ten applicants studying with the Visitation Nuns in Georgetown. If you take passage on the first boat returning to New York—this time through the Isthmus of Panama, you will be able to join our candidates and return with them and Father Louis Bertrand."

"I don't yet have sufficient funds for the voyage, but I'll earn my passage."

"By no means will you finance the trip on your own. I will arrange to send you back." Beryl was grateful that the generous contribution given by Henri Charbonneau would be put to its first good use.

II

Beryl made arrangements with the Captain for Lavinia to return on the first boat going by way of Panama. Lizzie volunteered to take her trunks so that Lavinia could travel lightly. "It's mostly books and some things from the family home. I can take clothing for the trip in one carpetbag," Lavinia told Lizzie.

The professor was surprised, but didn't offer opposition. He spoke to Beryl privately. "I don't pretend to understand the religious aspect of all this, but I do know that being in Avery's household would have been tantamount to slavery. My son is not a sympathetic person. He would take Lavinia in, but with an eye to his own comfort, not her happiness."

In a way Beryl regretted that she could not ask Lavinia to remain with her so that she would have a companion for the months of work ahead, but contrary to Lavinia's claim of being dandelion tough, Beryl did not want to chance her becoming ill with the deprivations most likely to be encountered.

The ship passed the Straits of Magellan after sailing up the west coast of South America, and the captain informed his passengers that they were now two weeks from San Francisco. When they neared their destination, the passengers crowded at the railing. The ship sailed through the mile wide waters named "the Golden Gate" by San Francisco settlers. It made its way into the harbor anchoring off the Folsom Street wharf. Passengers eager to disembark piled their portmanteaus on the deck, and their great trunks beside the smaller luggage. The port was crowded: clippers, steamers, lumber vessels, and an assortment of foreign trading ships.

Mercer conveyed his group to the Occidental Hotel where the accommodations were remarkably luxurious. The lobby was decorated with deep red carpeting and numerous potted plants which created oases amid clusters of upholstered chairs. The hotel was steam heated, a welcome feature considering the biting cold of the foggy air outside. Plants and trees were perpetually in flower and leaf here in San Francisco, but the dampness was bone chilling.

Beryl was pleased to have a packet of mail waiting for her. She opened the letter from Father Louis first.

My dear Beryl,

There is much to say to you, but I must impart some less agreeable news first. After much prayer, candidate Pru Taite has determined that she is better suited to the Visitation Nuns and their plans for retreat houses for women. I have concurred and have assured her that you would not stand in her way. It would be a kindness to her if you could write a personal letter giving her your blessing. You have nine sisters remaining fast in their determination to make profession as a Sister of Martha and Mary at the conclusion of their canonical novitiate, and two other young ladies who seem interested.

You will be met in Seattle by Father John Baptiste Brouillet. He is a fine priest with an unusual background. When the Cayuse tribe descended upon the Whitman Missions north of Vancouver, Father Brouillet, by himself, went to bury those massacred.

He did so before the Indians burned the remainder of the mission, and well before the area was safely under the control of the army sent from Fort Vancouver. You have no need to worry that such an incident will be repeated.

In Seattle you shall meet Mother Joseph, the foundress of the Providence Sisters from Montreal, Quebec. Since you are fluent in French, you will have no difficulty conversing with her, but she is learning English rapidly. You will appreciate her pioneer spirit. Already she and a few younger sisters have ventured into the mining camps and villages begging for funds. Do not interpret this as a suggestion, my child. I tremble when

I think of you fully astride some western steed in borrowed britches accompanied only by the cattle drivers through the Snoqualmie trail.

Beryl laughed at her good counselor's words. She finished his letter and went on to others. There was one note from her sister Yvonne. She was expecting another child. The family was well, except for some mild lung complaint of her mother's. The letter was written in February when winter still held the East in an icy grip. She prayed the spring would mark an improvement in Constantia's health. She was deeply touched to receive a letter from Reverend Mother Aimee written on the Feast of the Annunciation in February. It was brief, but written with words of warm friendship and the promise of prayers.

Beryl slipped these into the diary, which she had kept faithfully and with great attention to detail ever since her departure from Carmel. If her Congregation thrived, this journal would be the beginning of community archives and a look into the past for future Sisters of Martha and Mary. Before retiring, she wrote of the landing in San Francisco, her surprise at the size of this booming western city, and of the unlikely building sites where homes were under construction on steep hills.

Beryl and the Mercer party began the trip north on a British sloop, *The Kidder*. During the first part of the journey, the passengers were within the sight of land almost all the way. Beryl and Lizzie gaped at the stretches of forests, which were sometimes burnt and standing like giant match sticks down to the very shoreline.

"Most of that burning isn't natural," one of the officers told them. "The Indians sometimes set these fires to stimulate the growth of wild blackberries."

"I've never imagined forests like these," Beryl said to Lizzie. "It's like a jungle. Do you suppose sunlight ever filters through?"

"It wouldn't appear so," Lizzie said.

III

The rain pelted the sloop's decks in a deafening tattoo. The pounding did not lessen as the ship sailed from the Pacific through the Straights of Juan de Fuca, the inland route to Seattle. Canada, to the north, was recognizable as land only because the passengers were told that the vague dark shape they were passing to the north was Vancouver Island. Beryl and Lizzie, huddled under wool hats and blankets, were among the few who stood on deck straining for the first sight of American Northwestern land.

There was a glow of light to the south, and as this turned to a rosy shade, the rain became drizzle. The western coastline emerged through a low fog under a slate sky. To the south, clouds were separating and shafts of sunlight slanted to the land and water.

Beryl was the first to comment. "Either God is blessing the land, or giving us an opportunity to climb to Heaven!" Not hearing a reply, she regarded her friend who was unusually pensive. "What are you thinking?"

"Not proper pioneer thoughts."

"How?"

"The loneliness of this place. The desolation, dark and grey without joy. For a moment I was quite unnerved."

"Nature can lack friendliness," Beryl agreed, "but the joy is something we have to create. It won't be bestowed upon us unearned."

Within the hour the sky had lost its menacing dark solidity and the fog had cleared. High white clouds scudded northward and, gradually, in the south a great mountain emerged first as a pale phantom, then a brilliant snow-covered peak rising above foothills to blue sky. Beryl averted her eyes from

84

the spectacle reluctantly, only to cry, "Oh, look!" To the west a distant line of snow capped peaks appeared.

"We must have passed those mountains yesterday from the other side," Lizzie commented.

"Who could tell?" Beryl laughed

"I take back my dismal words," Lizzie said. "Surely this beauty is a gift of joy."

The two women had removed their hats and blanket shawls. Even the wind had stilled.

"In the words of Macbeth, 'So fair and foul a day I have not seen!'" Lizzie said.

Captain Lipton came from the upper deck toward them. He tipped his hat. "Miss Ordway. Miss Charbonneau. We are anchored and expect a tug boat escort to bring us to the dock. It seems the day will be fine."

Already the waters of the bay surrounding the Port of Seattle were glass smooth, only gentle swells in place of the white capped waves that had rocked the ship for days.

"However," the captain continued, "I have some sad news to impart. President Lincoln was assassinated. It happened just after we left San Francisco."

He recited the details the wireless communications had provided him. The government had not deteriorated, and the political situation was as stable as the circumstances allowed. Lizzie was shocked, but she claimed that it was not a surprising aftermath of the war.

"I have to confess that I am not informed regarding political events," Beryl said. She had not confided the censorship of the monastery to Lizzie. It would have served no purpose except to alienate her Protestant friend further from what she saw as the control of the Church over the minds of its faithful. The momentous historical event did not seem to have affected the passengers of the Kidder. Beryl thought this quite remarkable.

Lizzie was appalled. "It is a wonder we call ourselves a civilized country," she said bitterly.

As the ship was being secured at dock, Beryl sought out Asa Mercer, who was gathering his band of young women. He was dressed in a formal waistcoat and jacket with the polka dot bow tie Lizzie had remarked must be the only one packed in his trunk. The young man wasn't one for a dandy's fastidiousness. His dark beard was not well trimmed, but stood out in shaggy tufts from his jowls. His hair was longer on the sides with a tuft on top, which sat back from his forehead like a little cap. But he was not comical. His dark eyes, under thin, black brows, were piercing. He was slight in build, but not underweight.

He stood at the rail looking at the crowd gathered on the dock. "I've never seen the townsmen so well turned out, and some are even clean shaved!" he commented to a purser.

Another seaman approached Mercer, who left his view spot immediately. Two young men had been permitted on board to escort their frail sister. Beryl and Lizzie looked upon the reunion, grateful that the girl had survived thus far.

The other eight girls in Mercer's group squealed their delight as the men on the dock waved their greetings. "Silly children," Lizzie muttered. "I hope the reality does not overwhelm them."

Beryl approached Asa Mercer. "Thank you once again, Mr. Mercer, for permitting me to travel with your group."

"The pleasure has been mine, Miss Charbonneau. I hope you will arrive at Fort Vancouver safely."

Lizzie indicated a priest and a sour looking woman who had come on board. They were scrutinizing the passengers. "I think your welcoming committee is looking for the nun," she whispered in Beryl's ear. Beryl excused herself from Asa Mercer's company and pressed through the throng on deck, followed closely by Lizzie.

As she approached him, the priest peered at Beryl questioningly. She said, "Father Brouillet?"

"Surely, madam, you are not Mother Charbonneau!"

"I am," Beryl replied. "Mr. Mercer thought that less attention would be directed to me as the eleventh woman in his group of marriageable females if I did not wear the habit. A circumstance," she added, "that will be corrected as soon as possible."

"Yes," the Father said vaguely. He had looked for a nun more in the image of the Sisters of the Holy Names or Providence Nuns. He was unprepared for the tall woman who greeted him, elegant in bearing in spite of her modest attire. He regarded Beryl without friendliness. "I am not Father Brouillet, but a mission priest. I am Father Donnelly."

"Father, may I present Miss Elizabeth Ordway, who has been my companion on the journey?"

"How do you do, Father?" Lizzie put her hand forward. The priest lifted his eyebrows at the masculine gesture, but shook her gloved hand.

"The rectory housekeeper, Mrs. Maloney," Donnelly said, indicating the small woman whose face had the wizened look of a puzzled monkey.

"We didn't expect two sisters!" she remarked, appraising Beryl and her companion with a frown.

Lizzie was quick to respond. "I am not a nun, madam, nor am I ever likely to be!" Although the priest and Mrs. Maloney did not appear amused, Lizzie continued, "However, if my faith and predilections had led me to that circumstance, I would surely have been honored to affiliate myself with the Sisters of Martha and Mary. I congratulate you, Father. Mother Charbonneau is a treasure."

Father Donnelly muttered something unintelligible and picked up Beryl's carpet bag. "We have a carriage waiting for us."

Lizzie and Beryl embraced in farewell as Lizzie whispered to Beryl, "Quite a charmer you're going to work for…"

"Break the news gently to Mr. Mercer that you are not a willing wife," Beryl said in a whisper as she prepared to follow the priest and his housekeeper. "You have my Fort Vancouver address. Write to me, please?"

"I will. Soon," Lizzie replied, regarding the motley group of men on the deck appraising the women who surrounded Asa Mercer.

Father Donnelly delivered Beryl to the Providence Sister's convent where she met Mother Joseph, the legendary superior and Mother foundress. "We have planned a dinner in your honor, Mother Charbonneau—unless you are too tired from your journey?"

"Quite the contrary. But I would like to discard these worldly garments."

"I would hardly call them worldly," Mother Joseph quipped, and in the brief exchange Beryl thought that she would easily learn to call this woman a friend. Just as in Carmel, the habit did not disguise individuality. Yards of black muslin covered Mother Joseph's body, and the pinched wimple and headdress revealed only a small part of her face, but her posture and the way she carried her head spoke clearly of authority. The eyes told Beryl that the woman possessed intelligence, and the comment about her clothes showed humor. *Say what one would about the uniformity of religious garb, personality will win out,* Beryl thought.

Beryl spent an hour's time with Mother Joseph discussing the growth of the Providence Community and the role of the new Sisters of Martha and Mary. Before they discussed their mission, Mother Joseph said, "We have been praying for Mr. Lincoln. Did you know him?"

Beryl realized that this question came from a woman who knew that Beryl had been born to an influential eastern family. She would have had no idea how remote the chances were of an association between the Charbonneau family and the late President. They soon moved to other subjects.

"We have thirty-four of our sisters in Vancouver now," Mother Joseph said.

Beryl wondered if the older nun were questioning the need for another order in a place where her community was so firmly established. She was relieved as Mother Joseph continued, "And there are eight thousand Catholic souls in the Washington Territory. Our main apostolate is health services, and in spite of the blessings of vocations, it strains our community when Bishop Blanchet asks us to take care of the educational needs of the area. I'm certain that your presence here, should your congregation flourish, will be appreciated by the Bishop, and most certainly by us."

The dinner gathering after a short version of Vespers was merry. The sisters, at first startled by Beryl's navy blue habit, brown scapular, and soft headdress, accepted Mother Charbonneau as one of them, notwithstanding the fact that her new order was in its infancy.

It seemed to Beryl that Mother Joseph had treated her in a particularly motherly manner, but she was not offended. The older nun was not patronizing, only concerned. Beryl had no more years than most of the novices in training here at the Seattle convent.

"It would give me great pleasure if you would call our convent in Vancouver home until your sisters arrive." Before Beryl could respond, Mother Joseph continued, "But your school is quite far from our convent, and if I am a judge of character, it will be your choice to be independent."

"Thank you for your kindness, Mother. You are correct. I must be on my own."

"Be assured that we are close enough should you need our help for any reason."

"Thank you."

Mother Joseph led Beryl upstairs to the room that had been prepared for her. As she left her, she sighed. There were so many hardships ahead for this young woman, but clearly she had courage. Mother Joseph found Sister Florence, Superior of the Seattle convent, waiting for her at the bottom of the stairs. When Mother was in residence here it was their custom to check the night locks together.

"Did you have any idea she was so young?" It was the time of night when the community observed silence, and Sister Florence whispered.

Mother Joseph thought it prudent to evade a specific answer. "Father

Louis Bertrand did not refer to her age when he wrote telling us that she was on her way."

"A well-bred young lady barely out of a cloistered monastery?" Sister clucked her disapproval. "And now here in the West all by herself?"

"I believe that Mother Charbonneau may surprise us."

Even as she spoke the optimistic words, Mother Joseph wondered at the title of "Mother" for one so very young. She had other thoughts, which she would also keep to herself. When Father Louis Bertrand had been the Providence Sisters' retreat master shortly after his arrival in the West, she had several private conversations with the Jesuit. An astute judge of character, Mother Joseph had detected more than a fatherly concern when Father Louis described his years of recuperation at the Charbonneau estate. He spoke at length of the girl who at twelve hid behind the classroom door to hear her brothers' lessons. She was nineteen by the time she entered the Baltimore Carmelites, and the priest's disappointment at her choice was apparent even if his words seemed detached.

Mother Joseph stopped at the little chapel by the convent's entry door and knelt to say a good night prayer. Her thoughts were still on Father Louis Bertrand and his protege, Beryl Charbonneau. So now the good priest had snatched Beryl from the cloister just as her vows were about to lock the young nun inside for her lifetime. And he had arranged that this same young woman, still in her twenties, should be a Mother Foundress under his guidance. How on earth was such a proposal given ecclesiastical approbation?

She meant no personal criticism of Beryl Charbonneau, who seemed in every way to be remarkable. It was obvious to Mother Joseph that several of her own young novices would have followed Beryl out the door like goslings after the goose. The "Mother Charbonneau" had a magnetic personality.

Mother Joseph pondered the situation further during a night of uncharacteristic wakefulness. Even if, and she did not know this for certain, Father Louis Bertrand had manipulated all the players in this religious drama, she was not justified in judging the matter. The very unlikelihood of his plan's having come to pass was an indication that it was meant to be. God may and does inspire His children for His own purposes. She would pray for Mother Beryl Charbonneau.

That evening Beryl wrote to Father Louis Bertrand:

> *I don't think Father Donnelly approves of me, but I am determined to be of value to the children of the area he serves.*

The Puget Sound is calm and glassy smooth today, and should continue to be so for the steamship journey tomorrow. I wanted to assure you of our safe arrival in Seattle and post this letter to you before we sail. I don't know what to expect in the south, but I will try not to disappoint your expectations for our future community.

Kindly extend my best wishes to Mother Eulalie and my sisters. I will write again when I am settled.

Your spiritual daughter,
Beryl Charbonneau

IV

"We don't have the comforts you are accustomed to where you come from," Mrs. Maloney said as she yanked open the rain-swollen wooden door to the schoolhouse. Beryl had discovered that she was to use the school as both convent and classroom until the building of her convent was completed.

Work on this project might begin now that she was present to negotiate the purchase of the land. She would develop plans after she had evaluated the congregation's needs. Father Louis had described all too vividly the inadequate housing pastors out West expected sisters to accept. Beryl would not have luxuries, but she was planning for the future, and realized that she must keep her community independent of the whims of pastors. As it was, she was not to expect more than a subsistence wage for opening the school here in Vancouver.

Mrs. Maloney followed Beryl into the dark, musty schoolroom. The single row of windows would have been adequate for light were they washed. They were not well sealed, and drafty. There was a woodstove covered with splotches of rust like lichen on a swamp log. Obviously no fire had been lit for quite some time. Beryl stooped to finger the kindling and small sections of chopped wood beside the stove. They seemed dry enough, but the split cedar was not piled neatly, just dumped.

"Is there a flint?" Beryl asked.

Mrs. Maloney nodded. "On the desk."

If she had been less tired and not chilled to the bone, Beryl might have made an effort to deal with Mrs. Maloney's hostility. If a more friendly relationship would develop, it would only be in time, if at all. For now, she would ignore the woman's antagonistic manner.

91

Pointing to a closet, the woman said, "There's a place off here that you can use as a larder. As you see, there's a copper kettle, some tins, cleaning things, and cupboards. You can have ice delivered for perishables, but you'd best use the pit below where there's sawdust for vegetables. Potatoes and carrots will keep year round." Mrs. Maloney stood in the door throughout this narrative, so Beryl could not see the condition of the space.

"Your sleeping room is in here." Mrs Maloney pushed open the door to a room barely large enough for a plank bed frame and roughly built, ill-shaped wardrobe. Beryl reflected that her father would never have permitted this vulgar structure in his tack room for horse blankets, and certainly not for his stable boys. The straw tick mattress had no bedding on it. Beryl found it odd that as a courtesy it had not been made up. As if to explain, Mrs. Maloney said, "I put bedding out there on the desk chair," the woman said. "I would have made it up, but…" she hesitated, then pursing her lips, "I hate mice." She cast an apprehensive glance in the corner by the wardrobe.

Beryl's eyes widened, but she forced a smile.

"We'll not have Mass tomorrow. Father goes up river to Yakima Crossing every other Sunday. When Father Brouillet returns from Canada, we will have Mass every day. So. I'll bid you good night. Mr. Maloney will bring a supper tray to you in an hour."

Beryl was happy to hear the name of Father Brouillet, of whom Father Louis Bertrand had told her. Not wanting to be rude, she had not expressed her surprise that Father Donnelly had come to meet her in his place. She would look forward to meeting Father Brouillet, the priest made famous when he took it upon himself to bury those killed by the Cayuse in what was called the Whitman Massacre.

Beryl watched the woman hitch up her skirts to cross the muddy vacant lot to the Rectory. She was certain that Father Donnelly's abode in the rectory was warm and his mattress soft. When she had eaten the sparse supper of soup, lukewarm, and brown bread with cheese that Mrs. Maloney's husband brought to her, Beryl wrapped herself in blankets and slept on the unmade bed. To her relief the tick mattress was new. She was exhausted physically and mentally and sank into unconsciousness, not caring that the scratching noises she heard were made by mice. She hoped there weren't rats.

At first light, Beryl built a fire in the stove and put pans of water to heat. She found a bar of brown soap, rags, and a stiff scrub brush and began to scour the floor, windows and schoolroom cabinets. She pulled the wardrobe out of the sleeping area and, without too much, effort broke it apart for firewood.

She found mouse nests behind it and a hole in the wall through which the rodents had entered. She patched this as tightly as she could, and scrubbed her way out of the room.

There were more rodent nests in the filthy schoolroom cupboards, also moldy clumps of what must have been uneaten food and the accumulation of dirt. The textbooks she discovered were chewed and rotted, most beyond repair. She burned all but a half dozen.

When she had scraped and washed all she could, she changed from her work clothes with the intention of purchasing whitewash, wax, and brown paper to line the shelves. Then she remembered that she had labored all through the morning on the Lord's day. "Forgive me, Heavenly Father, but I simply forgot!" Then she admitted to herself that Sabbath or no Sabbath, what she had done was altogether necessary.

Beryl worked into the middle of the week without seeing Mrs. Maloney or Father Donnelly. A few parishioners had shyly approached the schoolhouse with gifts of eggs, bread and assorted supplies for her larder. As she shelved the last of her books that had been carefully packed, she pushed the empty trunks against the windows and placed a plank she had ordered from the lumber yard over them. Yards of calico made a bright coverlet for what she intended to be a nature table. For now, she placed a wild fern which she had planted in a leaky pan she couldn't use for cooking.

She surveyed her domain. In five days she had made shelves for books, with boards the lumberyard cut to her specifications. With a hammer and nails, plus whitewash, Beryl had done the rest. She had laughed all the while at the thought of what her mother and sisters would say if they could have seen her.

She had put a kettle on the stove to treat herself to tea when she heard a knock at the door. Mrs Maloney stood in the entryway with a tin of freshly baked bread. She started to apologize for neglecting Mother Charbonneau with the excuse that her husband had a bronchial ailment, when words failed her. She gaped openmouthed at the interior of the schoolhouse.

"Come in, Mrs. Maloney," Beryl said.

The housekeeper looked at the transformation. The floor planks were waxed and polished to a warm glow. The dingy, brown walls were now white; each student desk was polished with fresh slates on top; the stove was blackened and its copper trim gleamed. Crisp calico curtains framed the windows, which were clean and clear.

"See what I have done in the bedroom" Beryl invited. Just as in the schoolroom, the walls of the small space were whitewashed, and a crucifix was on the wall above the bed, which now had a plain dark blue coverlet and neatly folded blankets at the foot. Instead of the wardrobe, Beryl had built shelves covered by a plain blue curtain for her clothing. There was no decoration aside from an open trunk which contained Beryl's books on shelves she had made to fit inside.

"And I have also changed the larder." Mrs. Maloney peered into this room, which was scrubbed and painted, with tins labeled for rice, flour, sugar and beans. A long shelf was labeled "Pupil lunches," and had ample space for the children's lunch buckets. Along the side wall were hooks and boxes on the floor. "These are for coats and boots," Beryl explained.

"Saints in Heaven!" Mrs. Maloney finally exclaimed. "You did all this yourself?"

"Mostly. I had help from Mr. Larsen cutting the shelf wood to the size I needed."

"Father should see this! I must say, this is hardly what we expected from an…Easterner."

Beryl pressed her advantage as she observed the woman's respectful attitude. "The name of our Order is no accident, Mrs. Maloney. The Sisters of Martha and Mary are not afraid to work, as well as pray. We are not planning to be served, but to be of service."

If the visit were not to be the beginning of a friendship, it was at least the foundation of grudging respect.

Part Four

I

Vancouver, Washington
1867

Beryl's next triumph was the stuff of legends. She hired a man to put the small barn near the schoolhouse to rights. She instructed him to build two horse stalls, and flooring for a feed and tack room. She'd keep grain in a cleaned out oil barrel, alfalfa or timothy hay along one wall, and leather goods on the other. It wouldn't be like the Charbonneau stables, but it would do. At the general store she made it known that she wanted to purchase a horse, one suitable for riding and for the cart. She would not be reluctant to take two animals if one would not fit both needs. Beryl told the storekeeper, Mr. Peabody, that she was able to pay a fair price.

A few days after she had made her needs known, Caleb, the blacksmith's boy, appeared breathlessly at the schoolhouse door. "There's a horse at our place, and you should come see."

Beryl accompanied the boy, and as she approached the farrier's place of business, she heard loud voices.

"I'll not be a party to this," Mr. Peabody the grocer yelled.

"Aw, don't get het up. It's just a joke."

"The hell it is!" This was the blacksmith's voice. "When you sent my boy over there to get the sister I had a hunch you was up to no good. You meant to sell her that beast and the devil take the hindmost. You could have gotten her killed!" he added.

"Excuse me," Beryl said as she approached. "Who is about to murder

97

me?" She smiled at Mr. Peabody and at Willy the blacksmith, and also nodded to the farmer whom she had seen in the feed and general store. He was standing near a horse he had tethered to a yard post.

"Carter here has a wild horse which he was intending..."

Beryl acknowledged that Mr. Peabody was speaking to her, but her attention was fixed in astonishment at the horse Carter had tied to the post. It was not the awkward, heavy boned stock typical of these parts. "About four years old?" she asked.

She circled the animal, patted its flank and withers and pulled the lead rope from the hitch. She took it through a few ground paces, then ran her hand down its front foreleg. Instantly, the horse lifted its foot. Although its feet were not in good shape, it had obviously been trimmed or shod and well trained for the procedure.

"Would you trot him out for me?" Beryl asked Carter. "Or is he too wild as I heard tell?"

Carter took the rope and ran with the horse in a straight line away from the group, then back.

"He may lead," Mr. Peabody said, "but he's unbreakable and that's a fact. He's a no damned good varmint, begging your pardon for my language."

"His ground manners are perfect," Beryl remarked. "Do you still want to sell him?"

"Aw, no ma'am, I got him cheap and I just want rid of him, but I have to warn you..."

"I will take him, Mr. Carter, but in all fairness I must say that this is a very fine animal. You should ask a fair price. How did you come by him, may I ask?"

"I was up in Seattle. One of the cattlemen had this one, but he couldn't break him out. I got him and brought him down here on a Seattle-Vancouver steamer."

"So you bought him for a bargain."

"No. I took him off his hands, but I can't break him out either. I think he's loco. I walked him over here just for a joke, ma'am. You have no use for this animal."

"Nevertheless, if you are willing to give him to me, I'll take him."

"Fine by me, but don't say I forced him on you."

Beryl had to listen to the additional warnings from Peabody and the blacksmith, but she stood firmly by her decision. She asked that the animal's feet be tended, that she would return for him. Later, as she led the horse to her barn, it made no objection to going in the paddock. Beryl changed into her work habit and then spent an hour giving her acquisition a good grooming. The gelding was beginning to lose its winter coat, and Beryl used a curry comb to loosen the hair and then brush him to a healthy gloss. She brought a flake of alfalfa to him and returned to the barn to fork fresh bedding straw in one stall. She took a bucket and dipped it in the rain barrel to leave for the animal. The horse watched her calmly.

"Well, my fine fellow, the problem with you may be a simple one. Or I may get my neck broken. We'll find out tomorrow morning."

The next day Beryl took the gelding into the field, but she was not early enough for secrecy, nor were there trees to shield her from curious eyes. Beryl saddled the horse with her own English hunting gear and a bridle with the mildest of snaffle bits. The grocer's boy saw her crossing the field and ran for his father. Peabody, together with his wife, came to the road where they could observe the spectacle. By this time the blacksmith and a crowd from his place had gathered. "Damn fool nun," Willy muttered, wiping his forehead with the back of his hand.

"Where is this 'damn fool nun?' "

Peabody and the assembled crowd turned to see their pastor, Father Brouillet, who had come from the rectory for the purpose of introducing himself to Mother Charbonneau.

"Father Brouillet! Welcome home." Peabody shook his head and pointed to the field behind the schoolhouse. "Our school nun is about to risk her neck on a wild horse she took 'gainst everything all of us could say."

Coming from the other side of her barn, the gathering saw Beryl astride a lively, but docile mount. They were walking out, the horse in perfect control and Beryl's habit bunched up over the saddle.

"Well, I'll be jiggered," Willy said.

"It ain't ladylike for a nun or any other woman to ride like that," Mrs. Peabody remarked.

"I haven't had the pleasure of meeting the good Mother Charbonneau, but it seems to me she can take care of herself," Father remarked.

The group watched as Beryl walked the horse in large and small circles, then repeated the patterns, first at a trot, then a canter, finally reversing direction and repeating the procedure. All the observers stared in frank admiration.

Later, Beryl wrote to Lizzie:

But the real surprise of the day was Father Brouillet's return to Vancouver. Imagine my shock when, covered with dust from the field and perspiring like any hired hand—I think the phrase the natives would use is "ridden hard and put away wet"—I found Father was at the schoolhouse to meet me. I had the decency to be embarrassed, but honestly, he didn't seem to mind. He came into the schoolhouse for a cup of tea and was well pleased with the improvements. Instead of a picture of a holy nun, kneeling in adoration, he will forever after see me as a bronco buster who is half carpenter and the rest white-washer. I will be coming to Seattle next week, Thursday, I believe. Please be at home, as I have a very important proposal for your consideration.

As ever,
Beryl

II

"What do you mean, 'do I ride?'" Lizzie scoffed. "Being a well brought up Boston Bhramin girl, how could I avoid it?"

"It was a rhetorical question," Beryl admitted.

"Riding lessons!" Lizzie reminisced. "It would have been tolerable if I could gave gotten up on the horse and just learned to sit well. There was all the rest."

"Meaning?"

"Brushing the animal, digging the dirt out of its hooves with the nasty pick, not to mention mucking out a stall."

"I loved all those things. Adam, our hostler, taught me stable management. Father provided equestrians to perfect my riding technique, and Adam sometimes let me sit astride, which was more to my liking."

Lizzie replenished Beryl's cup of tea and offered her a square of sponge cake. "So you came all this way to discuss my skill in the saddle?"

"I came to ask if you're adventuresome enough to ride on the trail with me for the next three weeks, mainly to the settlements along the Columbia, and on toward settlements on the Cascade Trail. With the sisters arriving at the end of next summer, I need to recruit students and settle on the numbers we'll expect."

Lizzie merely raised her dark brows. "You're not going to find many Roman Catholic families out that way. In fact, there are those who would as soon stone a Catholic as speak to one."

"Surely not a nun!"

"Most particularly a nun. And let me remind you that your habit is hardly what the common person expects in a nun. There's a great deal of prejudice out here on the frontier. A Roman Catholic is just a little more acceptable than the Indians. You are tolerated because you're a Charbonneau rather than an O'Brien or O'Reilly."

"I experienced some hostility from the local merchants—until I proved myself on Sir Prize. A few gave me cool courtesy, but now I have respect!" Beryl smiled. The blacksmith had suggested that Beryl name the horse "He Who Laughs Last," but Beryl liked the sound and double entendre of "Sir Prize."

Beryl and Lizzie started their trip with a horse borrowed from Father Brouillet for Lizzie, and a pack mule Beryl procured in Seattle. Beryl rode Sir Prize with English saddle gear, a spectacle that had heads wagging in disapproval. The trip was uneventful, except for the last days when they rode toward Yakima Landing. The rain pelted them with a ferocity equal to the storm that followed the ship from San Francisco to Seattle. As the two women began to descend to the Yakima Landing settlement at the Columbia River's edge, they found an entire section of the trail almost completely washed out. Beryl dismounted and walked ahead.

"If we're careful we can still use this route." Beryl had to shout now that thunder and lightning made deafening crashes. "There's no place to stop. We have to keep going."

"I'm not partial to being struck by lightning!" Lizzie shouted back.

"It's north of us. Just stick close to the hillside!"

Beryl brought the mule to the front of the caravan behind Sir Prize and in front of Lizzie. The little pack train ventured along the remains of the path. With a suddenness that made reaction impossible, a boulder came loose from above and careened down the hillside striking the pack mule. The animal was propelled from the trail, end over pack crashing at the bottom of the ravine with ominous stillness. Almost as suddenly, Sir Prize lost his footing and slipped off the trail. Beryl knew she couldn't control the fall or help the horse with her weight on its back, so she executed an emergency dismount of the kind she had learned when she was a child. She was off her horse's back and prone in the mud on what remained of the path. She watched in horror as Sir Prize slid and rolled to the bottom of the hill. The horse lurched to its feet, trembling, and ready to bolt, which would only have served to endanger him further. Beryl could not tell if he had survived uninjured. The mule was dead.

This was a mercy, as Beryl had not carried with her any means to put an injured animal out of its misery.

As she got to her feet, Beryl saw a boy who seemed to appear from nowhere. He had swiftly secured her horse's reins and stood stroking his neck, calming the frightened animal. Sir Prize was improbably and utterly quiet, flicking his ear at the boy's voice and affectionately butting against his body.

Beryl half slid down the ravine as Lizzie, now dismounted, yelled at her to be careful. Covered with the slime of mud and old leaves, Beryl reached Sir Prize, breathing thanks to the child who held him. She made a quick check of legs, then called to Lizzie, "I think I can walk around from down here. I'll meet you on the other side. There appears to be better footing around the bend."

Beryl looked around, bewildered to discover that the boy had disappeared. "Ho, there!" she called in several directions, but it was as if he had never been there. Her calls were drowned by the noise of the storm. When Beryl and Lizzie rode into the settlement, Innkeeper Harriet Lathrop and a number of her miner boarders went running to them. Once the men were told of their predicament, several left on foot to reclaim the mule's pack.

Harriet was a massive woman who wheezed as she led the two bedraggled women into her barn so they might secure their horses. While Beryl fed, Lizzie accompanied Harriet into the main house to be shown their rooms. Harriet Lathrop puffed her way upstairs, patting her forehead with the end of her apron.

"I'm sorry for the inconvenience, but you and the good sister will have to share my bed. We're full up, what with this storm." Lizzie looked at the bedroom with its wardrobe, chamber pot, and one double bed, all crowded into a space Lizzie thought would be better used as a closet. Lizzie took matters into her own hands.

"Mrs. Lathrop, we will make ourselves comfortable in the barn. Mother Charbonneau prefers to sleep in more private quarters."

"But in a barn?"

"Believe me, on this trip we have had many lodgings not as comfortable. I noticed the stove out there. We'll use it to dry our clothing."

"Well..." Mrs. Lathrop was relieved. She had not been inclined to share her small room with strangers, especially considering one of them was a nun. "Of course I will send out a tray at dinner time," she said magnanimously.

"That would be kind of you."

Beryl was more relieved than Harriet Lathrop. "I must say that I admire the woman's courage. I can't imagine living in such appalling circumstances."

Lizzie sat on a wood apple crate and pulled off her sopping wet stockings while Beryl built a fire in the woodstove. They had improvised a clothesline tied across the feed room's rafters, and their soaked undergarments were hung in the hopes that they would dry overnight. Beryl put on the crumpled habit she had worn when she met the priest who came to the mission station northeast of Yakima Landing. She had safeguarded the garment in a carpetbag well covered by watertight canvas. They had ridden that day with canopies of tenting covering their heads, but it was no protection when the wind blew them like sails.

"What would either of us have done if, like Mrs. Lathrop, we had been widowed in the wilds?" Beryl wondered aloud.

"I would have taken the first sloop back to San Francisco and booked passage home."

"You and I are blessed with that option. We have families that would have welcomed us. From her speech it would seem that Harriet Lathrop is from the British Isles, a long way from home."

Lizzie gave her friend an approving look. Beryl was not encumbered by the excess yardage of other order's garb, nor was she confined by a medieval headdress starched to cutting stiffness. Lizzie had met two Dominican nuns who had come to the West from Newburgh, New York, investigating the possibility of building a hospital south of Seattle. Lizzie later commented to Beryl that it was a good thing the women had maintained calm and unruffled postures. If they had not, the ridiculous configuration on their heads would have sliced their foreheads to bits.

"I must say, I'm getting used to your habit. I have to admit that it's more comfortable than my duds."

"Your duds!" Beryl laughed. "The West is coloring your vocabulary!" The banter was comforting to both women. The ordeal they had been through and the death of the pack mule had left them both unsettled.

A pounding at the door announced that one of the men had brought dinner from the house. He kicked the door, calling for the women to open up. He held a large tray with both hands. Beryl would have preferred that their undergarments were not so obviously displayed on the line, but managed to accept the largess courteously.

The man didn't seem to notice; he was happy to make a quick exit. "Leave yer bits and scraps out in the firewood lean-to when yer done," he said over his shoulder.

"We won't mind bringing the tray back to the kitchen," Lizzie called. "You wouldn't want to attract rats."

"We always leave our scraps out there for Mrs. Lathrop's pet rat," he called back to them.

"What on earth?" Beryl questioned the odd remark. "Surely he's not speaking literally." Before she sat for her meal Beryl pulled a still damp shawl over her head to investigate the outside. Lizzie would have admonished her to eat her soup while it was hot, but she knew there was no distracting Beryl when she had a bee in her bonnet. Or her coiffure, she corrected herself.

And so it was that Mother Charbonneau met Joseph, who had saved her horse. She managed to pantomime that he should come inside the barn, out of the wind and rain, to eat. Joseph did so cautiously. He watched while Beryl spooned out a portion and then, sitting on the bale of straw Beryl indicated, he ate. He was intensely curious, but he dared not look at Beryl for fear of stepping out of his accustomed character.

"You caught my horse on the trail. Thank you." Beryl spoke slowly, but the boy was intent upon his food. However, she noticed that he ate slowly and delicately, the effect of manners regardless of the fact he didn't have a fork. How should she describe this strange boy? He possessed dignity—that was the word she would use to describe Sir Prize's rescuer.

"You know what they say about not feeding stray dogs and cats," Lizzie said from across the barn. "If you make him a pet, he's liable to follow us back to Vancouver."

"If I can make him understand that I'd like him to come with us, that is exactly what I hope will happen."

"Oh, for mercy sakes, Beryl! This is obviously a retarded half breed who is best left in the environment he has become accustomed to."

"Left dirty, lice infested, and half starved? I'll admit he may not be capable of learning the academic basics, but he could be a help in my barn. My immediate concern is that he bathe and put on fresh clothes." She left the barn in search of Harriet Lathrop. Insisting, with as much diplomacy as she could manage, Beryl arranged for a copper tub and some carbolic soap. She also borrowed a pair of sharp scissors. Once again with pantomime, she urged Joseph to shed his clothes, and get in the tub. She put up a blanket for his privacy.

"I don't think he's as dim-witted as Harriet says. I haven't had much trouble getting him to understand about his bath." Beryl remarked as she lifted the boy's filthy clothes with a long stick and removed them to the burning barrel outside. She had purchased undergarments, pants, socks, and a shirt at the general supply store, and a cap for the boy's head. "Mrs. Lathrop wanted me to pay for the boy."

"I beg your pardon?" Lizzie gasped. "Are you out of your mind?"

"I gave her almost all I had."

Lizzie made unintelligible noises of derision.

Joseph permitted Beryl to cut his hair, but there was an accumulation of snarls that only a shave down to the roots would fix. Time enough in weeks to come. Meanwhile, the boy was free of fleas and lice. Out of the bath, dried and dressed in the first clean clothes he had felt on his body in two years, Joseph allowed himself to look into Beryl's eyes. In an instant she understood that there was more to this boy than she had suspected.

"Do you have a name?" she asked, fully expecting an answer.

"I am Joseph. And I understand that you wish me to come with you. I will work hard to repay your kindness."

The reply stunned both Beryl and Lizzie to speechlessness.

They set out early the next morning, Beryl and Lizzie riding, and Joseph leading a borrowed pack mule. At evening camp, Joseph told them his story from the day that Douglas had not returned to the present.

"Your Sir Prize was Douglas' gelding, Mother Charbonneau. No one had been on his back except Douglas and myself. He never had heavy western equipment on his back—only a light hunting saddle. I could ride him with just a halter and lead rope."

"I return him to you, Joseph. He belongs to you."

"No, please. I am happy to know he survived and is well taken care of."

Lizzie was curious. "Have you had any instruction in reading, Joseph?"

Both women were amazed at the extent of the boy's education.

"You never returned to Douglas' cabin? You have no idea of the disposition of the place—what happened to his books?" Beryl asked.

"It would have been too dangerous to return."

"I could make inquiries," Lizzie said.

"Best leave it. Questions might arouse suspicion," Beryl cautioned.

III

Vancouver

From the window of the schoolroom Beryl saw Mrs. Maloney ambling toward the convent carrying a basket. It appeared to be loaves of bread, and if it were, it was welcome. Beryl was grateful for this largess, as she was woefully lacking in kitchen skills. Born to a family who depended entirely upon cooks for culinary arts, cooking was not in the curriculum for young lady's preparing for marriage. Beryl and her sisters were taught home management, and this included supervision of the kitchen. Her inadequate practical involvement came from the Visitation nuns during her short stay in their Maryland convent.

With Joseph to care for, Beryl attempted to concoct some passable meals, but in the making of bread she failed miserably. Her efforts produced two batches. One was too hard for a regular knife to slice, and the other came from the stove raw in the center. After the latter, Joseph volunteered his help.

"Mother, I mean no disrespect, but Douglas and I baked bread every week. Would you allow me to try?"

Beryl happily gave Joseph the use of the kitchen in the partially completed convent house. As it happened, her doing so created a storm of protest from Mrs. Maloney who caught the boy at work kneading dough when she came to deliver some fresh vegetables. The rectory housekeeper immediately looked for Beryl, whom she discovered in the barn mucking out Sir Prize's stall.

"I declare! The Indian does woman's work in the kitchen while the good nun shovels manure?" She stood, arms akimbo, scowling at Beryl, whose habit was tucked up above oversized barn boots and her forehead beaded with sweat under the line of her coiffure.

Beryl straightened. She stood tall and met the eyes of the irate Mrs. Maloney. She had lately discovered that the lady's name was Violet. *Surely not one "hidden by a mossy stone" as the poet said,* Beryl thought. "Mrs. Maloney, I'm certain it does not surprise you that I cannot cook. Joseph needs more nourishment than soggy dough or loaves he could not cut with a hacksaw."

"But to let the heathen in your kitchen!"

"I don't think of Joseph as a heathen, Mrs. Maloney."

"Obviously. But he isn't baptized! If he dies tomorrow, he'll go straight to Hell. Haven't you told him that?"

Beryl checked her temper and replied firmly. "How fortunate for Joseph that in such a tragic circumstance he will stand before an ever merciful God rather than you."

Mrs. Maloney gasped, but was briefly tongue-tied as she stood before the woman who towered over her, head proudly erect, the wrath of judgment shining from eyes that could have shattered stone. She capitulated. "Far be it for me to condemn the lad. All of us own that he is a good worker and respectful of his betters. But there is talk about him not being baptized."

Respectful of his "betters," Beryl thought as the lady left the barn. *Joseph is respectful of all life, both animal and human. I myself would never claim to be his better.* She would not force Joseph to betray his conscience. Father Donnelly was of the opinion that her example and that of their community of Christians should be more than sufficient to attract Joseph to the Church. It would not have been wise for her to point out that Joseph saw her as the exception to the general run of Christians. Joseph had endured a long history of abuse from "the faithful." Preaching by good example was not a lesson he had learned from his acquaintance with Christians.

The result of Beryl's weeks on the trails with Lizzie had confirmed several pupils for the Vancouver school to start when the new sisters arrived. She had promised the settlers at Yakima Bend that when her sisters were settled, they would establish a school there if the settlers would guarantee a building suitable for instruction, plus a dwelling place for three sisters. The families, Catholic and non Catholic alike, responded with promises, and by spring the promised accommodations were ready.

The sisters from the East were not due until August. The convent building was on schedule, and Beryl would have enough time to supervise finishing touches on the first floor, the school wing, and the sisters' chapel. The refectory, future community rooms, and the second floor, would be completed later. For now, the space that these facilities would occupy in the future would be used for school rooms. There was room enough for twelve small private quarters for the sisters. Beryl would claim no more space than any other sister for her personal quarters. Community business would share the office, also reserved for the principal of the school.

Joseph and Beryl set about painting the sisters' rooms and the hallways. *It was better*, Beryl thought, *to let the workmen continue construction for the second floor*. Joseph painted halfway up the wall and Beryl followed with the part he could not reach.

"Mother?" Joseph, who had never called either Fiona or Douglas "Father" or "Mother," was perfectly comfortable with Beryl's religious title. He thought of her both as Earth Mother and his mother.

"Yes, Joseph?"

"Would you like to have the sisters' names carved on their doors?"

"Carved? That would be difficult with the doors already hung, wouldn't it?"

"I mean on wood plaques. That way if a sister were to go to another place, she could take her name with her."

Beryl wiped her brush so that it wouldn't drip on Joseph's finished portion. "That is a wonderful idea, but who would do the work on such short notice?"

"I will carve the names if you write down the exact spelling for me,"

Beryl had noticed the boy whittling bits of wood Father Brouillet gave him. She hadn't seen any of the finished pieces, if there were any. There was surely no harm in letting Joseph contribute to the sisters' welcome in this way, even if the end result were less than professional.

"You'll have to begin soon. Will you have enough spare time, or should we give you a vacation from your lessons?"

"Aren't you going to Seattle to see the furniture Miss Ordway wrote you about?"

"Yes, next week. I'll be gone from Sunday through the next Saturday."

"I'll do the work then. But I would need proper tools. There's a set I've seen in Mr. Peabody's store. Will you give me enough of my savings so I may buy it? There are four good carving wedges of different sizes in the set. It's $1.50."

"That will be on the school's budget, not from your savings. I was going to order nameplates when I was in Seattle, but I like your idea much better. Do you need wood?"

"At the lumberyard there are nice pieces left for people to use as kindling. That's where I get wood for things I am trying to carve."

"When am I going to see these pieces, Joseph?"

Joseph smiled at her. "When they're ready. Most of them have already gone in the schoolhouse stove. Now that it's summer, I chop up experiments for the kindling pile."

"So you won't let me see the efforts?"

Joseph smiled again. "Not yet." He had great dreams, but he didn't know how to put the images in his mind onto the wood. Simple letters with a border design he knew he could carve easily from birch or cedar scraps.

The day before she left for Seattle, Beryl stopped at Mr. Peabody's store to purchase a store of dried meat, potatoes, and beans that Joseph could fix for himself while she was away. The boy was completely reliable, and Beryl didn't worry about her horse or the schoolhouse. Joseph would be a good caretaker. Mr. Peabody was not behind the counter; his wife was taking his place.

"Mrs. Peabody, I am also looking for a set of carving tools—four of them in a leather pouch?"

"Oh, yes. Charlie took them from the counter and put them aside for our son's birthday."

"I see."

"But I know where he put them, and there's plenty of time to order another set from up Seattle way. You're welcome to this one." She reached under the counter and brought out the leather container that Joseph had described. "They're quite dear, Mother Charbonneau."

"I understood they were a dollar fifty."

"Oh my, no!" She opened the leather case. "Here are four larger chisels, but inside there are five more, and a little mallet of hardwood to complete the set. They are all mounted in ebony with pure silver trim. It's $15.00. But it's well worth the price. Our son will be an apprentice to a cabinet maker next year, and he says that this is the finest set money can buy."

"Then, if you're certain that you can replace it for your son, I will buy it."

"Are you meaning it for yourself, then?" she asked.

"No. For a woodcarver of my acquaintance." Beryl was wise enough not to tell the woman who the carver was, especially at that cost. There was no need for Joseph to know that he had mistaken the amount, and she was delighted to bestow the gift.

* * * * *

The trip to Seattle was successful. Lizzie had found a warehouse of used furniture. Some had been abandoned by settlers who had moved away, but the majority of pieces had belonged to passengers who died on the sea voyage to the west. In the latter case, relatives, if there were any, did not want to pay the freight back; they were content to have what the auctioneer would realize. Beryl needed to furnish a visitors' parlor. For their own convent, the sisters needed only the simplest wood benches for their refectory, and locally built bookcases and wardrobes for their rooms. Beryl found everything she needed, including a piano and drapery. The greatest treasure was an ebony table which could be modified and installed as an altar in the chapel. She found silver candleholders for the chapel, and also for the parlor. Her final purchase was a discarded Oriental rug, which she realized was of far greater value than was marked. The dealer saw that it had faded in one place, by the sun Beryl judged, and was selling it cheap. She could place the piano over this flaw and no one would be the wiser. Her collection would be shipped within the week.

IV

More than satisfied with the results of the trip to Seattle, Beryl looked forward to returning home. She was eager to view the signs Joseph would have begun. Mrs. Maloney met the boat, for which Beryl was grateful, as it was pouring rain. The woman seemed unusually formal.

"It's a shame you had to come alone, Mrs. Maloney."

"My husband is waiting for us with the other men," she said cryptically.

As they approached the convent property, Beryl noticed that Sir Prize was in a paddock seeking shelter against the barn wall only partially out of the downpour.

Mrs. Maloney noted her reaction. "Well, we told you there would be trouble. You wouldn't listen."

"What do you mean by trouble? Why isn't my horse in the barn?"

The woman shook her head. "Without the boy to feed him and clean his stall, we thought it best to turn him out so he could at least have grass. My husband tossed him a flake of hay once or twice."

Beryl felt numb. "Where is Joseph?"

"In jail. We knew no good would come of your taking in a heathen!" Her face had turned purple as she spoke to Beryl, but she was clearly enjoying this moment of revelation.

"In jail!"

"He was caught stealing the very day you left. A thief! A sneak thief!"

A group of townspeople had gathered in the shelter of the unfinished wing of new construction. They were waiting for Beryl. Mr. Peabody stepped forward. He was obviously the leader of the men who stood scowling at her. She faced him, and tried not to feel fear when she looked at the crowd behind him.

"Is Joseph safe? You haven't harmed him?"

"He got a beating from my son when we found him thieving," Peabody said, "but no more than he deserved. I dragged him to the sheriff and he's been in jail since. We're civilized people, Mother Charbonneau. Another place— well, he might have been run out of town, even tarred and feathered. But we kept him at the jailhouse until you got back. After all, you did take responsibility for the Injin."

"What are you accusing him of stealing."

"I ain't accusing, ma'am. I'm telling you. I caught him red-handed."

"Yeah! Indian red-handed," one of the men behind him said.

"I repeat. What do you accuse him of stealing?"

"This!" From his back pocket Mr. Peabody pulled out the leather pouch of carving tools. "I had this put away for my son. The damned little sneak thief had to have gone behind the counter to find it. My boy Eddy and I were out behind the lumberyard and we saw it sticking out of his pocket. He's lucky Eddy didn't beat the hide right off him he was so mad. He knew that set was going to be his."

"Did Joseph give any explanation?" Beryl asked in a deadly calm voice.

"Nope. The kid's mouth has been shut tight as a fresh clam—won't talk to nobody, the sheriff included."

"Mr. Peabody, where is your wife?"

The grocer looked confused. "My wife? What's my wife got to do with what we're about here…"

"Where is your wife?" Beryl repeated.

"Minding the store, where else?"

"Let's meet at the store, gentlemen, please?" *Gentlemen*, she thought. *In a pig's eye.*

"Get in the carriage, Mother Charbonneau," Mrs. Maloney called. "It's pouring!"

"Thank you, I prefer to walk," she said. At least the walk would cool her temper. Words she hadn't realized she knew were close to the tip of her tongue, and it would never do to pronounce them. The aftermath would become a legend more infamous than the first time she rode Sir Prize.

Inside the store, all of them drenched to the skin, Beryl asked Mr. Peabody for the leather pouch. He fished it out of his coat pocket.

"Mrs. Peabody, do you recognize this set of carving tools?"

"Indeed I do. It's the set you bought before you left for Seattle—the day you was in to buy groceries. I forgot to tell you, Charlie. I knew there was plenty of time to order again for our Eddy."

Peabody's eyes widened. "You bought this?"

"I did. For Joseph, so that he could carve signs with the names of each sister who will be coming from the East. May I have the set, please?"

He sputtered. "Well, why didn't the boy say? Why..."

"Would you have believed him?" Beryl looked at the other men, meeting their eyes. "You have done the boy a dreadful injustice. I want him brought to me at once, and I insist that each and every one of you, especially you, Mr. Peabody, apologize to him. And I will also expect an apology from Eddy. If he has harmed Joseph..."

"No! He's done him no harm, Mother Charbonneau. It was just what boys do to each other in a friendly scuffle."

"What you described was not a scuffle, nor was it friendly. Eddy is fifty pounds heavier than Joseph, and in your own words, Eddy was giving him a beating." There was an awkward silence, followed by murmuring from the group that had stood up against Joseph. Beryl continued, "I believe there must be some compensation made here."

"You mean money?"

"No," she paused for emphasis, "Joseph intended to use wood from the scrap pile for our sisters' names. I was quite content with this frugality, but I am not disposed to settle for second best under the circumstances. I want you to find the finest oak wood at the yard and have it cut to Joseph's specifications. I expect these pieces to be delivered to my barn no later than tomorrow afternoon."

There was no argument. The incident was over. Joseph was brought to her at the schoolhouse, and rather than embarrass the boy with her relief, she put her hands on his shoulders and said, "Sir Prize would be most grateful if you would rub him down and bed him in a dry stall."

Joseph looked up at her. "I could leave."

She drew him to her and stroked his head as his arms encircled her. "My dearest boy, you have nothing to be sorry for. None of this was your fault." She looked into his eyes. "And where could you find a better teacher?" She pressed the boy to her again before letting him go. "We live in a harsh world, Joseph. And don't forget your tools." She handed him the pouch.

As Beryl held Joseph to her once more before he went to his room in the barn, she felt him trembling. "Shhh, hush! There is nothing to fear now."

"I'm not afraid, Mother."

"But I feel you trembling."

"I feel a great anger. I kept it from rising—like when you take a cooking pot further away from the fire. But now these feeling are boiling up inside of me. This must be a great sin, Mother."

"No, Joseph. It is no sin. If you were to let this anger rage uncontrolled and then do harm to those who harmed you, perhaps even hurting innocent people, that would be wrong."

"Shylock's pound of flesh."

"Of course!" Comments like this never ceased to amaze Beryl. "You studied Shakespeare with Douglas. I've neglected to build upon this. Sister Sarah Dufrayne will be here soon, and when she is settled, I'll ask her to continue. Now that you are older, you'll find even deeper meaning in the Bard's plays. Meanwhile, try to put this incident behind you, as I must also try," Beryl confessed, looking into Joseph's eyes. "I, too, let anger rise within me."

Part Five

I
On the High Seas
1868

Father Louis Bertrand and his band of nuns embarked for the voyage through the Panama Canal on the Pegasus. The boat was fully booked. The majority of the passengers en route to the New Frontier were optimistic; others were not. The bloody conflict was over, but putting the union back together was like repairing a broken pot. The assassination of President Lincoln had thinned the glue. Most could not agree whether the new administration would help or hinder the process of healing.

"The South will recover," one of Father Louis Bertrand's companions at ship's table affirmed. "Meanwhile, I intend to strengthen my interests in the West where the future of the union lies."

"This will come through education," the priest said.

The gentleman seated next to Father Louis was Cornelius Adamson, an officer of the Union Pacific Railroad. In the midst of the Civil War, President Lincoln had ended the three decade controversy over the building of the railroad and its route. It had been a bitter debate. Daniel Webster originally supported a route to the Pacific, but later claimed that the west was a "worthless void." His soured attitude toward what he saw as savage land, impractical to settle, did not prevent others from wanting to develop it. Men like Cornelius Adamson knew that the only way that the far reaches of the continent could be made a vital part of the union was by the railroad.

"Ah, good Father. For education in the West to bear fruit, we must also have the link between East and West. The railroad is the key to the future. It is not enough that the sea route we are now taking through the Isthmus has reduced the journey to some thirty days. It is too expensive and, as for the journey around the Cape—well, it is obvious that the rail connection will enhance the union."

"Will the project be completed, do you think, by the end of the decade?" Father asked.

"I believe it will. Perhaps the next time you journey back to the east you will ride on the Union Pacific!"

The talk of the great railroad was interesting, and Louis Bertrand was well aware of how it would affect his own dreams for the Northwest. But for now, and for the time of this voyage, his focus was on the sisters and the future of Beryl's congregation. In his close contact with the sisters during the first two weeks they were at sea, he was able to observe them on a day to day basis. It took him little time to judge that Sisters Lavinia, Sarah, Grace, and Gertrude were natural leaders. Marietta, the youngest, was by far the brightest. She would be a future mainstay of the community, even, perhaps, Beryl's successor. The others were affable and committed to their new life. They would be a solid foundation of dedicated teachers.

After Beryl left for the Frontier, Father Louis Bertrand and the Archbishop agreed that there would be no further recruitment in the East beyond those now committed to their novitiate training. Once the Sisters of Martha and Mary left the Visitation Convent, the Archbishop was not in favor of Mother Eulalie's group draining their own resources by devoting time to new applicants. But they had not suffered from their involvement. Prudence Taite had joined the ranks of the Visitation just as their Sister Gertrude had transferred to Beryl's group. Several others who came while Beryl was still with them had decided to remain as Visitation Nuns. All told, Mother Eulalie had gained a half dozen new candidates as a direct result of assisting Beryl and Father Louis Bertrand.

In the West, Beryl had gained two applicants, although the purpose of her travels had not been to attract candidates. She had committed the community to staff a school at Yakima Bend on the Columbia River in September, and she would be able to accept boarders in Vancouver once the second story and adjacent structures of her convent school were completed. Henri Charbonneau's generous endowment to the Congregation had made this possible, and put development of the community years ahead of what Father Louis Bertrand and Beryl might have expected.

Beryl had become a legend in the New Frontier. Louis Bertrand was both proud and alarmed when he heard the stories of her breaking wild horses, surviving mountain mud slides and adopting an Indian boy. The latter disturbed him more than the possibility of Beryl's being thrown by an unbroken horse. When the story of Joseph reached him, followed by Beryl's letters, he was not pleased. Beryl was besotted with the boy, as her lengthy descriptions of his mind and talents indicated. Fortunately, for her reputation, Joseph was still a child. But children grow into young men, and Father Louis was determined to take the boy to Spokane and remove him from possible controversy. The Jesuit University would accept pupils soon, and Beryl should be pleased to send Joseph. If Louis Bertrand's plans materialized, there would be a high school academy and boarding facilities for whites. He hoped that the Motherhouse of the Congregation of Martha and Mary would be located in the same complex, and Spokane would be the hub from which Beryl's community would expand to Montana and Wyoming. And he would be near Beryl in this holy enterprise. Marietta McGinnis, an orphan girl and youngest of the first Sisters of Martha and Mary to take her temporary vows, celebrated her sixteenth birthday on board the steamer bound for the Pacific coast. The high spirits with which she had begun the journey hadn't diminished, even though she had shared a bout of seasickness with almost every passenger before they entered the Isthmus of Panama. In comparison with the other sisters, she was a child, but they treated her as one of them, not as the baby in their midst. This was due in part to the directives Mother Charbonneau had sent during their canonical year.

Marietta was endowed with remarkable intellectual ability. Since her tenth year she had wanted to enter the order whose sisters staffed the orphanage. But the sisters would not encourage her. They judged her background too vague. This was not their sole reason. Marietta's efforts to prove her scholastic value seemed inappropriate for her youth and place in life. Her ease in learning and her supplementary reading in the boarders' library put some of the school nuns at a disadvantage. They accused the girl of pride and self will.

During her fourteenth year, Marietta met Father Louis Bertrand. The Jesuit was quick to get to the heart of Marietta's confessed "sins of pride," and he suggested a meeting outside of the confessional. When he told her of the new Congregation of Martha and Mary, Marietta was eager to meet Mother Charbonneau. Soon after, Marietta left the orphan asylum to join the band of sisters who were in training at the Visitation convent.

"You need not fear that Mother Charbonneau will accuse you of self aggrandizement for your desire to learn, my child," Father Louis told her. Marietta soon found this to be true. Beryl Charbonneau was nothing like the sisters at the asylum. However, Beryl's admiration of Marietta's intellectual gifts did not blind her and Father Louis to an impatience they sensed in the girl. Perhaps, they agreed while discussing the candidate, intolerance would be a better term. Marietta was quick to judge the intellectual limitations of others, even her older companions.

"Humility is truth, Marietta," Beryl counseled the girl. "You never need apologize for your own gifts. But you must learn that gifts of intellect are not the only ones God bestows upon those He loves. Do not judge a person's worth, or a child's for that matter, by quickness of mind alone." Marietta seemed to take this admonition to heart, but Beryl knew that this sister would have a lifelong struggle in curbing her natural intolerance to the slowness of others.

As the Pegasus approached the Golden Gate passageway into the Port of San Francisco, Sister Lavinia joined Marietta at the railing. A hefty wind would have blown their habits like flags had they not wrapped themselves in shawls held close to their bodies.

"Perhaps someday our Congregation may expand to be a presence in this part of the frontier," Lavinia said.

"Oh, I do hope so!" Marietta responded passionately. "There are great centers of learning here!"

Lavinia looked at the younger sister intently. "I hope you will not be disappointed in the frontier, Sister Marietta. Fort Vancouver is hardly a center of intellectual activity!"

"Oh, no, Sister. And, besides, most of the universities are not yet ready for women scholars, even if I were prepared. No, I won't be disappointed. I have faith in the future of our congregation and in Mother Charbonneau."

"And in God?"

"Of course!"

Lavinia left the windy deck and Marietta continued to gaze at the approaching port. Her first glimpse of the western frontier! Her eyes were bright. She could be more patient than Sister Lavinia knew. She acknowledged she was a plain girl, not remarkable for any of her features or her thick set figure. She was aware that her hair beneath the wimple was more the color of mouse, than blonde or brunette. Still, a fire burned within her that she wouldn't trade for all the good looks of silly girls her age—some of whom were companions on this journey. Yes, she could wait. Beryl Charbonneau's vision of a vital community involved in education wouldn't be forever limited to one room schoolhouses. And who better than herself would be chosen to receive the training that would enable the Congregation to grow?

II

The new convent kitchen was spacious and well appointed. It had two woodstoves, sinks, and barrels for fresh water which Joseph brought daily from the well. Mary Louise Doheny peeled the last potato and set the lot aside in a cauldron of cool water. Her curly red hair was moist under the black postulant veil. This was the very first time she had worn the simple brown postulant dress of the Sisters of Martha and Mary. On this great day, nine sisters would arrive from the East. One other local woman would begin her formal religious life in the Vancouver convent. The celebration day meal would be shared with Father Brouillet, Jesuit Provincial; Father Joseph Cataldo; Father Donnelly; Mother Joseph; Father Louis Bertrand, and Mother Charbonneau's friend, Lizzie Ordway.

The superior of the Society of Jesus in the Northern Rockies Province had called for priests, and Father Cataldo was returning from Santa Clara, California, where he had been sent from Boston to regain his health after a long illness. He was looking forward to reestablishing his friendship with Father Louis Bertrand.

Mary Louise had been scandalized earlier in the day when Mother Charbonneau told her she had not counted the places for the table correctly. "You are one place short, Sister." The girl had been delighted to hear herself called "sister." She was beaming when she recounted and told Mother that she thought she had the number right. Mother had recited the list ending with Joseph.

"An Injin at our table?" Mary Louise gasped.

Mother Charbonneau remained mild and unruffled. "Yes, Sister Mary Louise. An Indian. Our friend Joseph, whose ancestors walked these hills before your Gaelic ancestors shook hands with Saint Patrick!" Beryl spoke without anger or harshness, but Mary Louise took her meaning to heart. Accept those whom Mother Charbonneau calls to her table, or else. She was not a stupid girl, nor was she vicious. It had simply never occurred to her that Indians should be thought the white man's equal on any terms. But she wouldn't risk finding out what the unspoken "or else" meant; she'd set another place at the table.

The time of docking approached. Beryl went through the convent checking its readiness. Joseph had completed the carved Christian names of the sisters on wood plaques. He had chiseled each name so that the letters stood out in bas relief. He had added borders to each in appropriate liturgical designs. On the slightly larger plaque for Mother Charbonneau he had sculpted the suggestion of an eagle's feather in the top right corner. It blended into a wheat and flowing water design that completed the piece. Joseph's face flushed as he watched her reaction.

"I'm so grateful, Joseph. Thank you." There was more she could have said, but she gave him a smile and a brief hug instead. She had led the boy into the hall where she placed the name plaques beside the door to the rooms she'd assigned each sister so he could hang them on the doors. It would be the last time Joseph or any other outsider would be allowed in the cloistered section of the convent unless, of course, there was a formal visitation from an ecclesiastical superior, or the need for medical help.

The sisters' accommodations were monastic in their simplicity. A rough wood wardrobe stood in each room. There was a small window, a bookcase, writing table, and a plank bed with a thin straw mattress covered by a flannel sheet. A crucifix hung on one wall. In a cabinet there were warm blankets and a chamber pot. There would be room for each sister's trunk at the end of the bed. It was in the bylaws of Beryl's community that no sister would ever accumulate more personal belongings than could fit into a single steamer size trunk, and, like a pilgrim on a journey, each sister could be ready to travel where God and her superior decreed on a moment's notice. There was an exception, and that was books which could be considered a sister's own. When she had no further use for them, they would become the possession of the community.

The bell at the front entrance rang, and Beryl hurried from the chapel where she was arranging flowers to answer. It was Mrs. Maloney, dressed in her best fur collar coat and a navy blue straw hat with a duck feather as decoration. "It's time to go!" she said. "My! It smells a fair treat in here!"

"Our neighbors gave us a quarter of beef. It's almost embarrassing to offer such fine food!"

"I don't think your people will think about it that way! Father Brouillet has a crate of oranges coming on the boat. Now there's luxury, and that's a fact!"

How this lady has mellowed since that first day she showed me the school, Beryl thought.

III

The sloop's journey from San Francisco had been through calm waters, and Father Louis Bertrand's party of sisters had seen the westernmost mountain range before entering the Straights of Juan de Fuca between the Washington Territory and Vancouver Island. The ten thousand foot peak to the northeast was clear as were the foothills of the great mountain range to the south. Father and his group disembarked at Seattle and immediately re-boarded a steamer that would take them back the way they came to Fort Vancouver. It was a roundabout way, but the Seattle to San Francisco sloop made no detour up the Columbia River inland.

Father Louis Bertrand stood on the deck from the time the steamer entered the Columbia between Fort Canby on the north and Fort Columbia on the southern shore. The waters had remained placid. Father regretted that Beryl had not seen fit to travel to meet her group in San Francisco as he had suggested some months before he departed the East. In spite of the fact that she had promised that she would meet him and her sisters in Fort Vancouver, he had searched the dock at Seattle hoping that she would have changed her mind. It would have been fitting that she stand with him and the Sisters of Martha and Mary at the last of their long journey. Her presence would have blessed this holy alliance, the beginning of their mission in the West.

As the steamer approached Fort Vancouver, Father Louis Bertrand shielded his eyes from the eastern sun. The sisters surrounded him. He was the first to catch a glimpse of Beryl on the dock. She stood tall and slender beside a woman he supposed to be Father Brouillet's housekeeper. Seeing Beryl, the sisters began to wave.

Beryl had accomplished wonders. That could not be disputed. Father had been alarmed to read of some of her exploits, but that a young woman barely out of her girlhood could have managed to prepare the way for her Congregation with such boldness was altogether remarkable. The building in Vancouver meant that Beryl and the sisters would not work closely with him in Spokane, and he regretted this. He had not expected Beryl to accumulate the numbers of pupils she had attracted to her first small school. And then to fill not only the new building, but to plan another convent closer to Walla Walla east of Vancouver, was unprecedented in so short a time. Although he had not written her any words of caution, he thought that she was proceeding too swiftly.

Beryl's building and recruitment program were not the only reasons for his distress. She had told him she had established a close friendship with a Seattle woman, Elizabeth Ordway, a Protestant with links to the womens suffrage nonsense. Then there was the Indian child. These emotional ties disturbed Louis Bertrand. They were outside the scope of his advice and his control. While he had praised Beryl for the wisdom to include holy friendships in her spiritual life, he had not meant her to go so far.

"Isn't this glorious, Father?" It was the voice of Sister Sarah Dufrayne as she waved again to Beryl, who they could see clearly now. As the sister spoke, he realized that he had been scowling.

"The sun is rather bright, is it not, Father?" Sister Lavinia said, noting her spiritual guide's frown.

"Unusually so," he said, shielding his eyes. He would put his concerns aside. Nothing must mar this day.

* * * * *

The celebration dinner was memorable, and afterward there was singing and an exchange of stories. The travelers, tired after their voyage, had been glad to see the guests leave so they might retire to their rooms for the night.

When the guests were gone, Father Louis Bertrand remained talking to Beryl in the parlor. He admired its furnishings, the upright piano, a sideboard and several chairs and the fine Oriental rug. Beryl described how she had come by them at an estate auction in Seattle. She did not follow her story with the incident of her return to find that Joseph had been jailed.

She sensed a coolness on the part of Father Louis toward Joseph, It was probably not more than the result of exhaustion after the long journey. Tired as he was, he did not seem inclined to end their conversation, so Beryl suggested that she show him the seedling fruit trees Mr. Peabody had planted in the convent garden. She led him back to the Rectory instead of returning to the convent. They said their good nights, and Beryl left her friend, still wondering why she felt uneasy.

* * * * *

The day after the sisters' arrival dinner, Lizzie prepared to leave for Seattle before Father Louis Bertrand came to the convent to meet with Beryl. She had not appeared in church for the morning's services. She didn't care for Roman Catholic ritual, and she cared less for the priest who was so high in Beryl's estimation. There was something ill disguised by the courtesy and the polite conversation that made Lizzie suspicious. She had caught him studying the boy Joseph, and there was an expression on has face that told her the man was not pleased with the child's place in Beryl Charbonneau's affection. She caught a glimmer of something else, and this niggled at her thoughts until she named it. That priest is in love with his Mother Foundress. Perhaps he has fooled himself into thinking that this plan for the new Roman Catholic community was God's plan, but clearly it was a way that Louis Bertrand could be a vital part of Beryl's life. Lizzie was absolutely certain that, notwithstanding all Beryl's intelligence and intuition, this fact had never occurred to her friend. The idea made perfect sense to Lizzie. She remembered a conversation with Beryl on their trail trip. She had asked her about her life in the cloister.

"What would you have done if Father Louis Bertrand had not rescued you from the Carmelite Monastery?"

Beryl laughed. "I wouldn't put it quite that way!" Then she became serious. "I would have taken my vows, as I had determined to do."

"But would you not have been desperately unhappy? Surely your frustration with some elements of the life would not have changed. Certainly there was no intellectual challenge."

"Yes, there was, Lizzie. Oh, not in books, but I was reaching. I was taking all the secular wisdom I had learned to a higher level."

"So if a Knight Templar had not come to carry you away—and you don't fool me, Beryl Charbonneau; you would have been fascinated, not by the knight but by his horse—you could have been happy?"

"Yes. I know that the concept of the cloistered life is difficult to understand, especially for one as devoted to social reform as you are. My own family, steeped in the Roman Catholic traditions, found my choice incomprehensible. And to answer you specifically, if Father Louis Bertrand had not come when he did, I would have been there yet."

Lizzie remembered Beryl's words and once again marveled at her friend's innocence. Not that she would have wanted Beryl to stay locked behind those monastery walls, but it was obvious to Lizzie that Father Louis Bertrand was the Tempter, not the Messenger of God. She shook her head as she entertained another side of this complex situation. If there were a benevolent God watching over human affairs, He could have used the priest's motives to fulfill His plans for Beryl Charbonneau. What a very complicated story. I wonder how it will all end?

"Hello in there!" Beryl knocked at the door of the schoolhouse where her friend had spent the night. She entered the room and saw that Lizzie was ready to leave. "I must apologize to you for these stark accommodations."

"I've endured worse in your company," Lizzie replied.

"I think some of the sisters were shocked at your version of our pack trip!"

"They would have been more shocked had I included the possibility of our having shared Harriet Lathrop's bed and chamber pot! Nevertheless, Beryl, I regret that you will have other companions on the trail from now on."

"Never more preferred than you, dear friend. I hear your carriage. Mother Joseph said that she would send one. Please tell her again when you're en route how much I appreciated her making the trip south to welcome our sisters."

* * * * *

Father Louis Bertram thanked Mrs. Maloney for the breakfast she had heaped on a plate. There was a helping sufficient for a family of five. When she returned to the dining room with a plate of flapjacks, he once again smiled his appreciation, but when this was followed by sausage and buttered toast, he protested. "Good Heavens! I am grateful for your generous preparation, but this is enough to feed an army!"

Father Donnelly nodded his agreement, but was eating his portion with gusto. "We eat hearty out West, Father, particularly on Saturdays. It's a long ride up to Yakima Bend for confessions and Mass."

"Just take what you wish, Father, and leave the rest," Father Brouillet said. "Thank you, Violet."

She understood that she had been dismissed. She had hoped to linger to hear more of their breakfast conversation. After Father Brouillet's Mass, the Jesuit had asked her why there was no one to serve the Mass, and she had enjoyed imparting the information that there should be—especially if that Indian boy of Mother Charbonneau's was as bright as she seemed to think he was. "But, of course, he isn't baptized," she added. Father Louis Bertram had not replied, but from the expression on his face it was quite obvious he did not like what he heard.

"I was surprised," the Jesuit said addressing the pastor, "that you had no server at Mass."

"Violet's husband reads the responses on most mornings. I expect that the sisters will train some young boys who are capable of learning the Latin."

Father Louis Bertram ate a piece of toast before pursuing the subject further. "As I understand it, the boy Joseph is capable, but Mrs, Maloney tells me he is not baptized."

"Violet should have left that information for Mother Charbonneau to tell you. She has been diligent in instructing Joseph. He knows the catechism, and I would baptize him immediately upon his asking for the sacrament."

"But why does he delay? Isn't he aware of the serious consequences to his soul?"

"I have discussed the matter with Mother Charbonneau at length, Father. The boy spent his formative childhood years with a man who was not well disposed to Church doctrine. He was then shamefully treated by many who professed to be Christians. I believe that the good example of Mother Charbonneau with the sisters will bring him the grace. Meanwhile, I pray for the lad."

Father Louis Bertrand finished his breakfast without any other comment about Joseph. He was already planning his conversation with Beryl. He was annoyed with her and he would let her know his feelings.

* * * * *

Beryl could not recall her spiritual father having been as distressed as he appeared to be this morning. She characterized the monologue directed at her as "ranting," perhaps even "ranting and raving,"

"The boy must be baptized at once," he ordered in conclusion.

Beryl remained calm. She understood Father Louis Bertram's serious concern, and she also understood that her response must be framed with tact and delicacy. She was under obedience to Father Louis Bertrand, and if his vexation escalated, it was not inconceivable that he could order her to disassociate herself from Joseph. Could she accept such an obedience? She most certainly did not want to try.

"Father, Joseph is not an infant. Baptism without his full consent of will, without the gift of faith, would surely be invalid."

"Your charity toward him has given him abundant proof of God's love for him. Are you certain that his rejection of this gift does not come from some flaw—some deeper arrogance or pride inspired by the devil?"

"I did not rescue Joseph from the unbearable circumstances that trapped him for the purpose of converting him."

"You profess fondness for the boy and yet you neglect his soul? Has he studied the catechism?"

"Indeed. Would you like to test him?"

"To what end? Beryl, I am deeply disturbed by this situation. You must let me take him to Spokane where he will associate with others of his kind who have accepted the way of salvation."

"Of his kind? You mean with Indian orphans who will have little in common with Joseph at his present stage of development?" Beryl realized that she should have controlled her tongue. This was a crisis for Joseph and for herself. She would not send Joseph off to be indoctrinated by men—yes, even the Jesuits—who would not value his potential. She did not know what was in the future for him, but his continuing education was at present his only hope. She continued more carefully. "I have written to you about Joseph's life before Miss Ordway and I discovered him. The boy has suffered greatly. He does not deserve to be uprooted again so soon from a life where he is giving every evidence of hard work and dependability. I intend to enlist Sister Sarah Dufrayne to help with his continuing education. She will be objective and appropriately strict."

"I don't understand you, Beryl," Father Louis said simply. "I urge you to make a sincere effort to bring him to the faith and to prepare him for his future by steering him in the way of a skilled trade—perhaps that of a farrier. I've heard he is exceptionally skilled with horses. The classical education you are so determined to give him is a waste of time. It will also do him the disservice of allowing him false hopes."

They spent further conversation discussing plans for the development of the Congregation, and when Sister Sarah Dufrayne joined them, all talk of Joseph was abandoned. For his part, the priest realized that in this matter

Beryl was not going to accede to his advice, and he did not want to risk an ultimatum which might bring Beryl to the brink of defiance.

When he heard her confession before the following Sunday services, Beryl mentioned nothing regarding her Indian protege. Perhaps what he perceived as something sinister was rooted in his own desire to be foremost in Beryl's affections. Assuredly, she had not neglected her mission, and if truth be faced, the Ordway woman was a far more dangerous alliance than Beryl's sympathy for a half-breed orphan.

Beryl made eye contact with every sister as they were seated around the long refectory table. She had posted appointments on the chapel door for the sisters to see before Father Louis said the first Mass in the new convent chapel. Sister Sarah Dufrayne was to be in charge of schools; Sister Grace Ford would supervise the postulants and future novices; and Sister Lavinia would have the responsibility of all procurements for the house, an appointment the older communities called "bursar." Sister Gertrude was to be First Counselor, and in charge of the community in the absence of Mother Charbonneau. Other counselors were Sisters Sarah, Lavinia, and Grace. There were no surprises in these vital appointments. Every sister would take her turn in the kitchen and share in housekeeping. The community would begin its schedule of work and prayer immediately. Beryl inexplicably gave in to peals of laughter when Sister Grace asked to make their bread. She promised to explain her mirth at their evening recreation.

Beryl looked from one to the other with love and respect. "Welcome, Sisters! And so we begin."

IV

1872

Beryl was caught daydreaming, so absorbed in her thoughts she hadn't heard the tap on the office window. She had been listening to Sister Grace's gentle voice as she instructed the dozen new novices who sat clustered around her on the garden lawn. In just a little more than six years from its inception, the Congregation of Martha and Mary had grown to thirty sisters. The community was looking forward to Sister Sarah Dufrayne's return from Portland where she had visited the mansion deeded to the Congregation by Jonas Hopkins, who owned the Vancouver Flour Mill. It had been inherited by his wife, and having no use for it, he offered it to Mother Charbonneau for a girls academy.

All this, and now the Seattle convent that was established two years ago needed to be expanded. She would go north to supervise this herself. She would leave Fort Vancouver in Sister Lavinia's capable hands; the Portland project, Sarah's responsibility, would be in the planning stage for more than a year. In Seattle she would have the company of Lizzie Ordway occasionally. Joseph would come to Seattle with her, but he would be leaving for Spokane within a few weeks. Father Louis would finally have his way. He had been urging Beryl to send Joseph for the past four years, but she had balked. She no longer had a good reason.

The Gonzaga school was ready to accept students, and Father Louis Bertrand promised that Joseph's entrance examinations had placed him in the highest group. Beryl could no longer put forward the excuse that Joseph's continuing education was best left in her hands. Three years ago she had resisted Father Louis Bertrand's compromise that he would find tutors for the boy if she sent him to Spokane. "He's just twelve years old, Father! I plan to continue his studies, and what I cannot teach him, Sister Sarah Dufrayne can."

Louis Bertrand wished he could impress upon Beryl that the townspeople would feel better about her Indian's being off the premises. His argument, which insinuated that Joseph might be attracted to the young candidates, fell flat as Joseph had barely grown by the time Father Louis Bertrand left for Spokane. She was glad that he had been occupied in the eastern part of Washington Territory and had not seen Joseph for close to two years. He had gained height, and now at fifteen stood inches taller than Beryl. Beryl had a distaste for any accusation that novices were unsafe in Joseph's proximity. Father Louis was her trusted spiritual advisor, but he did not know Joseph as she did. Beryl was not ignorant of the facts of life or of the temptations male adolescents experienced. But she was unreservedly trusting in Joseph's honor.

"Mother Charbonneau?" Joseph tapped again on the window of her office. He seldom came to the front door. Beryl had explained that it was a convent now, and there were rules about outsiders entering, especially males. When he brought wood for the kitchen stove, he'd stack it neatly against the back porch and swiftly retreat. He came to the school for his lessons only after the students had left, and was mindful to have all the chores Mrs. Maloney expected him to do for the rectory before he did his school work. Mrs. Maloney never tired of repeating to him that he was only a servant in God's community.

"No matter how Mother Charbonneau indulges you in book learning and such, or what foreign tongues you speak with her, you must remember your place and not set your heart on rising above your station," she'd tell Joseph.

He used to wonder what was in Mrs. Maloney's mind when she referred to his "station." Did she think it was a place? Where did she believe it was? He knew that the lady thought it had something to do with "putting on airs." He'd overheard Mrs. Maloney scolding Mother Charbonneau when she'd discovered that she was teaching him French. He'd heard the conversation.

"Begging your pardon, Mother Charbonneau, but you're hurting the boy!"

"Mrs. Maloney, in the North there are settlements of French Canadian immigrants. Surely it cannot harm Joseph to be prepared to work as a translator."

Mother Charbonneau's calm voice and logical explanation pacified the housekeeper. Joseph marveled how Mother could speak the truth and yet circumvent it. It wasn't that she spoke with forked tongue as the saying went, but in a way that protected his dignity and privacy. He loved her for it.

Joseph kept his resentment of Mrs. Maloney's attitude to himself. For as long as he could remember he had felt confusion about his place in the white man's world. On the one hand, Mother Charbonneau believed that Jesus loved all children as His own, and that all were precious in His sight. But Indians and people of darker skin were not precious in the sight of God's people.

At the sound of the tapping and Joseph's voice, Beryl left her paperwork and raised the window. "It's Saturday, Joseph. Did you think I was late for lessons?"

"No, Mother. I wanted to ask you if I might have this to take to Spokane." He showed her a large flat piece of cedar. "It was on the wood pile."

"Of course! You didn't need to ask. Wait for me; I was about to walk to the rectory to see Father." She straightened her desk and took a shawl from the clothes hook. She had been at her correspondence for hours and was glad for a break. Joseph held the piece of wood under his arm as they walked.

"Do you need more wood, Joseph? You don't need to use scraps. We can ask Mr. Hopkins for finer pieces from the mill."

"I really want this piece in particular. When I started to chop it for kindling," the boy flushed, "I thought I saw something." Beryl was looking at him questioningly, but she let him continue on his own. "There's a shape inside. I'd like to carve it out."

Joseph left his piece of wood by his stable quarters and went to the blacksmith. Before he left for the new Jesuit school in Spokane, he wanted to take advantage of Caleb's willingness to make him new carving tools. After he had been cleared of theft years before, Caleb, the smithy's son, had been friendly to him when he hung around the livery. Joseph had a soothing effect on animals and had often held the head of a nervous horse, even when he was with Douglas and barely tall enough to reach a horse without the help of a footstool. Under Caleb's tutelage, Joseph had learned how to treat many equine ailments such as hoof thrush, splints, and worms.

"A handful of pipe tobacco will keep a horse free of worms," Caleb told him.

He also taught him how to recognize bot fly eggs that clung to a horse's legs and body in late summer, and how to scrape them off delicately with a knife. "Then burn the scrapings, boy. Don't leave them to hatch more flies." From Caleb's tutelage, combined with that of Mother Charbonneau, Joseph had developed an excellent eye for a horse and was experienced in handling and grooming. Beryl instructed him in riding, and he was now possessed of what she called "an excellent seat." Joseph was the only one aside from herself who was allowed to ride Sir Prize. She also praised his light hands. The smithy hired him to exercise his horses both on the longe line and astride. Joseph gave all the pennies and nickels he earned to Beryl for safekeeping. "Whatcha going to do with your fortune, boy?" one of the smithy's regular customers asked him.

"I don't know." Joseph answered. But he did know. He wanted to buy books, and he wanted to have some money of his own to do so when he went to Spokane to enroll at Gonzaga College, which the Jesuits were building for Indians. He was wise enough to keep such plans to himself. At sixteen, he was young to be admitted at the university level, but he had passed the entrance exams, and he was eager for the challenge.

Caleb listened to Joseph's need for a wider carving tool than any he had. It didn't take him long to fashion it. Ever since the incident when Joseph had been put in jail, the townspeople had treated him more kindly. Caleb went so far as to think of him as a friend, but he kept this to himself. Tolerance was something his father would accept. Calling Joseph a friend was not.

Joseph practiced his carving without showing any of his efforts to anyone except Mother Charbonneau. He had inured himself to disparaging remarks about his book learning, but his artwork was too profoundly a part of who he was to risk the judgment of those who would not understand his work. He didn't count the signs he made. Before he traveled north, he was ready to show his latest creation to Mother Charbonneau, but decided to wait until they were in Seattle, for he wished to make it a departing gift. It was a large bas relief about a yard across and eighteen inches high. His theme was Princess Angeline, Chief Sealth's daughter, whom he had seen when he accompanied Father Brouillet to Seattle's waterfront. He had carved her in the long dress and shawl she typically wore, and she was carrying a pail of clams to sell. In the background was the shape of ships against the representation of Elliot Bay and the Olympic mountains, The piece he kept was his third try. The first one he chipped badly when he slipped and cut into the grain. The second one was well made, but his main figure was as stiff as the statues in church. It needed the illusion of movement to make it come alive. Imagining the brisk breezes that come from the south across Elliot Bay, he carved his figure bent to the wind, her garments rippling as the wind pressed against her body. Then he added gulls above her, braced to ride and turn against the currents of air. The swirl of birds above and the flow of Princess Angeline's clothing pleased him. He was learning his craft, and his skill came less from practice, than from the instinct of a born artist.

V

When Beryl arrived at the Seattle convent it was in a sea of mud. Joseph's sculpture had to be forgotten as he had spent this first week in Seattle building a wood walkway around the convent. The school, on higher ground, was an older house, which was now being painted and furnished for several additional classrooms. Torrential rain had cut rivulets in the dirt as it poured from the hill down to the road.

Once the hard rain had changed to occasional showers, Elizabeth Ordway came to town and stopped on the street outside the convent. Joseph, noticing that her carriage was not balanced, took the horse and wagon to the barn. He discovered that a wheel fitting was dangerously loose. He unhitched the horse and put it in a stall while he fixed the wheel.

"I'm in town to find a sign painter," Lizzie told Beryl as they sat drinking tea. Lizzie was passionately involved with the women's suffrage movement and there was to be a meeting with important guests from San Francisco and the East.

"Joseph is very good with signs," Beryl said. "You might give him the opportunity to earn money."

"If he's really good, we're prepared to pay a silver dollar."

They found the boy grooming Lizzie's horse. "Your wheel needed fixing, so while I did that, I unhitched Charlie. I thought he could do with a good brushing. Of course, the road mud will spatter him as soon as you leave!" he said, smiling. Joseph didn't need to be careful of his speech in front of Miss Ordway. She was always kind to him, and more than that, she treated him as Mother Charbonneau did, as an equal.

139

"Joseph, Miss Ordway needs a sign painted. Would you do it for her?" Beryl asked.

"Sure—on that piece of wood in the back of your wagon?"

"Yes. I have the information here. Can you read, boy?" she teased.

"Some," Joseph replied in the same vein, and Beryl laughed.

Joseph put the grooming brush down and wiped his hands before taking the paper from Lizzie. "This may take me a few days." He looked at Beryl. "The sign for the convent is finished, Mother. It's in the barn."

"I'd like to see your work," Lizzie said.

They found Joseph's stable room tidy. His books were on a shelf above his cot, and there was a heavy workbench against the far wall loaded with wood and tools. But it was the oak sculpture mounted above Joseph's study table that attracted the attention of the two women. Both Beryl and Lizzie stared at it.

"How did you come by this magnificent piece?" Lizzie asked, approaching it to examine the sculpture more closely.

Joseph's face reddened, and instead of answering Lizzie, he turned to Beryl. "I was going to show it to you as soon as it was finished. It's barely dry from the stains I used to bring out the design. It took a few attempts before I got the carving right."

"You did this?" Lizzie was incredulous. "My God, this is one of the most beautiful things I've ever seen! Look at the movement! The detail! It's obviously Princess Angeline!" Lizzie had been amazed since she first met Joseph by the young Indian's manner of speaking, but not so shocked with his gentility, as with this evidence of genius.

Joseph was pleased by Miss Ordway's reaction, but he looked to Mother Charbonneau for the approval that would be its own reward. "It's more than beautiful, Joseph," Beryl said. "Through the work of your hands you bare your soul!"

Lizzie and Beryl spoke of little else than Joseph's talent that afternoon. "The boy is a genius, Beryl. We must see to his development."

"He'll be going to Spokane with Father Cataldo and Father Louis Bertrand. He passed the university entrance exams."

"Did anyone tell you his score?"

"No. Father Brouillet monitored him and he said the score was surprising and congratulated me and Sister Sarah Dufrayne."

Lizzie shook her head. "I don't think that is the place for Joseph, even if it were to be possible."

"What do you mean 'were possible?' The building has been completed, and he qualified for entrance."

"There's more than buildings and test scores at stake, Beryl. There's politics. The supporters will not give substantial funds to an Indian school, even if it begins that way. Rumors are already suggesting that whites will have to be accepted before benefactors will promise funds. And once that happens, mark my words as an educator in this territory, it is only a matter of time before it is an all white school and Indians are forbidden."

"Gonzaga was my hope for Joseph's future," Beryl said sadly.

"But that was before we saw the work of his hands! I've something else up my sleeve. Will Joseph trust me with his sculpture for a few days?"

* * * * *

Joseph had never thought he'd be climbing the front steps of the Henry Yesler mansion, but here he was, flanked by Mother Charbonneau and Lizzie Ordway. Benefactors and regents of the Territorial University were assembled in the parlor, curious to meet the Indian boy so highly praised by Captain Lilly, one of Lizzie's good friends. Joseph's carving was mounted on an easel, covered by a silk scarf, which added to the mystery. The men Yesler and his wife had invited to the meeting had been skeptical about the genius boy Captain Lilly and Yesler were sponsoring, but they agreed to support Yesler's proposal that he be admitted to the university under certain conditions.

"He may be registered in spite of his race and youth," Yesler told Beryl and Lizzie Ordway, "but he will be required to pass the university's entrance examinations."

"We understand that he has had some schooling," Percival Browne, the registrar, addressed Beryl.

"Yes. I began his instruction in Vancouver, and Father Brouillet was kind enough to oversee his Latin studies. For the last two years he has had the attention of our Sister Sarah Dufrayne, who is a graduate of Catholic University in Georgetown. He is also fluent in French. I am confident that Joseph would pass his exams today with no further preparations,"

"That is very interesting, and I might say impressive, Mother Charbonneau. But in fairness to the university, we should be certain that there are no serious gaps in his preparation," Browne said.

Joseph flushed with resentment that he was being spoken of as if he were not in the room, but no one of Yesler's group saw as no one acknowledged his presence.

"Then our offer to receive him—Joseph Wolf is his full name—provided he acquits himself well, shall remain open for the year," Browne said.

"Gentlemen," Sarah Yesler said, "it is time for you to see evidence of this young man's exceptional talent." She removed the silk cover from the Princess Angeline carving.

All three women in the room looked at each other with satisfaction as eight pairs of bespectacled eyes viewed Joseph's work.

* * * * *

Beryl and Lizzie lingered at the bottom of the mansion steps after Joseph had hurried off, his sculpture under his arm. "He looks relieved to have this meeting over," Lizzie said.

"I'm sure he is. I sensed that the gentlemen were impressed, and it was clear that not one of the crowd would dispute Yesler's patronage and deny Joseph a chance, but..."

"But not one of those bearded dignitaries honestly expects him to pass the entrance exams," Lizzie finished.

"Exactly."

Lizzie looked back at the gathering on the wide Yesler porch. There had been handshakes, smiles, and patronizing compliments when Joseph had left them with his sculpture. They gave the boy solemn nods and wished him well. But Lizzie had sensed their feelings. In spite of his talent, Joseph had little in his favor. "The only thing worse for him would have been if he were female," she said to Beryl with an edge of bitterness in her voice.

Beryl returned to the convent and to the garden where she had left heather cuttings to plant against the back wall. They would fill the space between the fast growing pines Joseph had planted. Her thoughts were filled with the boy and the latest manifestation of his special abilities. Many times during the last six years she had examined the feelings she had for Joseph. She felt respect, admiration, and friendship, but these were inadequate words. She loved him. Certainly not a romantic attraction; theirs was a union of soul. In another sense he was her son, as closely linked to her as any child she might have borne in her womb.

VI

Adam, the hostler, stood well back from the house staff who were gathered at the foot of the staircase. He had never been inside the Charbonneau residence. He kept his eyes down and clutched his cap with both hands. Farewells would be said, as most of the servants were to be dismissed now that the house was sold. Gossip had it that the master had bequeathed a modest sum to each of his faithful servants. Adam would welcome a few coins. He'd take himself down to the Olde Oak Barrel and stand a round in honor of Henri Charbonneau's blessed memory. His master had been a fair and honorable man. Adam looked up as Madame Constantia's upstairs maid hushed the cook who had broken the silence to mumble a few words to the footman.

Constantia appeared in the hallway above them. She was attired in solemn black, attended by Phillipe and Pierre. Her sons wore black bands on the sleeves of their grey cut away jackets. The three descended the staircase that was bare of the cloisonne vases of flowers that had always decorated the landings. Pierre still needed the support of a cane since his injury in the war.

Constantia faced the line of servants, her grief showing in the tight lines of her mouth. She nodded her acknowledgment of their thanks as she gave each of them a small black velvet bag tied with a drawstring. The women curtsied. The butler, the footman and the gardener bowed gravely. When she came to the hostler, she turned to Pierre, who handed Adam a leather pouch.

"'I thank ye kindly," Adam said with simple dignity.

"If you have nowhere to go, Adam, please stay in the stable quarters until the Fontaine family arrives. They have already indicated that they would appreciate your continued service," Phillipe said to him.

Adam was taken aback at being singled out. He felt the stares of the group. He glanced up at Phillipe, making brief eye contact. "Mindin' yer pardon, sir, I'd best be on me way. But I'd be thankin' ye most kindly. Most kindly."

The housekeeper dismissed the servants and Adam followed the others, grateful to return to more familiar surroundings. In the privacy of his stable room, he sat on his cot and filled a pipe. He sucked its stem, but he didn't light it. By his own rules there was never an exposed flame in the barn. The kerosene lamps were all well trimmed and hanging over dirt, well away from bales of straw or alfalfa. Here in the stables, the tack he himself had crafted, gleamed with cleanliness on sturdy wood pegs; saddles with well brushed pads were stacked and buffed. The grain was stored in barrels tightly covered against the intrusion of rats and mice. If rodents left droppings, they would not be noted because Adam swept daily. If the surroundings were well tended, the horses were pampered. They were turned into pastures daily, their stalls mucked out and laid with a bedding of fresh straw. The master's stallion, fractious to strangers, would nuzzle Adam with the gentleness of a kitten. Only with the master's daughter Beryl had the great chestnut been so docile.

Adam's rough hands held the pouch Pierre had given him. He tossed it in his hand. This legacy was heavy. The equivalent of a few shillings should be no more than a light jingle. He untied the knot in the leather thong that secured the top and shook the contents out onto the blanket. For a moment he stared down shocked out of speech. "God's Blood!" he gasped. "Gold!" He counted. There were forty-two coins, one for each year he had served Charbonneau as Hostler, harness maker and master of the Horses. Adam scooped the coins in his hand and dropped them back into the pouch. He felt dizzy and his eyes had filled with tears. This was a fortune. It exceeded the sum total of his father's life work and that of his grandfather before him. His Dad had scraped together passage from Liverpool to New York for himself, Adam, and his wife, but he had not survived the voyage. His mother toiled in their Hester Street fourth floor walkup taking in laundry and ironing. Her death left Adam alone in the world at ten. From that time he apprenticed at the local hostelry, learning the trades of farrier, tack and saddle making, and care of horses. His employer came to value the lad's soothing effect on horses. Young Adam could put the flightiest animal at rest so that it gave its feet to be shod so long as the youth stood at its head.

Adam was sixteen years of age when Henri Charbonneau brought his team to be stabled. One of the horses had thrown a shoe and its hoof was badly cracked. Charbonneau watched as Adam fashioned cushioning between the shoe and the hoof wall to prevent further damage. The young man's manner with the team so impressed Charbonneau he asked Adam if he were indentured.

"No, sir. I'm me own person," he said in the Yorkshire brogue, which was the result of his years with his mother.

"Would you consider returning with me to Maryland? I've recently added a second barn for our guests and have need for a man of your skills."

Adam accepted. He had been called a man! He worked for Henri Charbonneau until his employer's death, faithfully caring for the stables and for the mounts and carriage horses of their guests. Charbonneau's guests spread the hostler's fame. Horses always left his stables in better condition than when they came, their tack and harnesses polished and mended.

Adam had been particularly fond of Beryl Charbonneau. From the time she could toddle, her favorite place was in the stable. Adam patiently taught her the ways of horses, how to read their moods and predict their behavior. His instruction was kind, but strict, all under his protective eye. The hostler selected mounts for all the Charbonneau children, but he chose with special care for Beryl. The girl was given a ten-year-old mare with a kind eye and excellent training. The horse required consistent discipline, and her successful handling of this mount gave Beryl confidence. The ability to control a spirited horse, added to her naturally balanced seat, made Beryl an accomplished horsewoman before she was ten years old.

As Adam sat on his cot clutching the leather pouch, a thought entered his mind. Why not take passage west? He could now go to California by rail, and then take a boat north. Or he could procure a team and experience the challenge of the Oregon Trail, but he judged himself ignorant of the skills needed for such a grueling journey. He could take a ship. In the wink of an eye possibilities had opened for him. The sound of a sliding barn door roused him from his reverie. He looked up and stood when he saw Pierre.

"Adam, I should have told you that you are welcome to take harnesses of your choice, a saddle and your favorite tools."

"Oh, sir...I couldn't...yer father's gift..." Adam was a man of few words, and stammering was not his habit, but he stammered now.

"Father wanted you to know how you were valued. Please accept these gifts with our appreciation. What will you do, Adam?"

"I was thinkin' I might go west. Perhaps your sister could use my help in one of her convents."

"Can you read?" Pierre asked kindly.

"Tolerably well, sir."

Pierre took a card from his pocket. On it was written, *Seattle, Fort Vancouver, Yakima, Olympia and Tacoma.* "My sister's Congregation is established in these towns. If you go west, perhaps you'll be kind enough to take messages from home."

"I'd be honored. I am of that mind, sir."

"Then I'll bring letters by this evening. We'd be in your debt."

VII

Beryl waited with Sister Lavinia outside Bishop Blanchet's office. The appointments of this room, from the Oriental rug to the beautifully upholstered chairs of deep red brocade were grand. A priest secretary attended to his paperwork. Beryl's polite attempt to make conversation had not seemed welcome. He was an underweight and uneasy young man; far better suited to the secretarial job he was now doing than tramping out into the frontier as a parish priest. The paneled oak door to the Bishop's inner sanctum opened, and Beryl was surprised to see Henry Yesler in a dapper grey suit, his top hat in his hand. When he saw Beryl, his response was instantaneous and gracious.

"I have a young hunter that needs basic education," he said quietly with a wink. The legend of Mother Charbonneau and her horse breaking ability wouldn't fade away.

Beryl wondered what brought Yesler, who was a Protestant, to the Bishop's office, or maybe he had been asked to call. There was talk about property for a future cathedral overlooking the waterfront in Seattle. Yesler probably owned the land.

Yesler, having taken his leave, the Bishop ushered Beryl into his office and left the door ajar as he indicated that she take a chair next to his desk.

Propriety, Beryl thought. Their conversation would not be heard, but they were in full view of the priest secretary.

It was not a surprise for her to hear that his Excellency wanted to speak about the invitation from the Bishop of the Montana territory for the Sisters of Martha and Mary to found a secondary school and college for Catholic women.

147

"This will not stretch your resources too thin now that you have added Seattle and Portland to your convent locations?" the Bishop asked.

"At first, perhaps. But it is no more of a challenge than our first years in the Northwest."

"Likely not." There was a pause, which indicated that His Excellency was reluctant to speak his mind.

Beryl sat in the straight back chair and gazed unflinchingly at her superior, her eyebrows slightly raised in expectation. If the rumors to which Lizzie Ordway had alerted her had reached the Bishop, she knew what the man intended to say. She was not going to make it easy for him.

Bishop Blanchet cleared his throat and riffled through some papers, selecting one in particular. "A matter has come to my attention, Mother Charbonneau," he began. "One of a delicate nature."

"Is that so?" Beryl realized that her tone was similar to an echo of her father's voice; certainly not that of the humble nun. She softened the effect with a guileless expression of innocence. Not meekness; innocence.

"Ah, it seems that…there are certain accusations…"

Beryl's expression lost the benign look. "Accusations? From whom directed at whom?" she asked with a quiet intensity calculated to rattle her superior.

"I'm not at liberty to be specific."

"Then why, Bishop Blanchet, are we having this conversation?" When the man in his red trimmed robe looked pained, Beryl continued, "The accusation. Is it directed to my Congregation?"

"No, not to your Congregation, I assure you."

"Then to me personally? Once again, Your Excellency, I ask you from whom do these accusations come and to whom do they pertain?"

Blanchet stood fingering his pectoral cross. "It is insinuated that there may be a danger to you and your young Seattle sisters, specifically because of the Indian who lives with you. He is, I am told, not a child, but old enough to be considered a man."

Beryl did not hesitate to respond, nor did she show any discomfort. She decided instead to laugh. "In the first place, Joseph does not live with me and the sisters! While he is attending the Territorial University, he has a room in our barn where he also tends to our carriage and horses. It is well away from the convent. Secondly, your grammatical use of the passive voice is unfair. I do not accept 'it is insinuated.' Who is the accuser?"

The Bishop felt a flush of anger. He dealt with nuns frequently—the Holy

Names Sisters, the Sisters of Providence, and recently the Dominicans. The superiors of these communities were well educated women, but not one unnerved him as did Mother Charbonneau. He was annoyed at the lack of deference coming from a woman, especially a nun, and in his estimation she was very close to being disrespectful. He'd call it aristocratic insolence, but he had to admit that her challenges to vague accusations were justified. He had hoped to shock her; to inspire regret and contrition that one under her care had caused talk. He knew, however, that it was not a problem put forth by the faithful, but concern expressed in a letter from the Congregation's spiritual advisor, Father Louis Bertrand.

"Mother Charbonneau, I do not believe there is a foundation for attributing any unseemly behavior to you."

"Then to Joseph?" Beryl interrupted.

"No. It is the appearance of impropriety that concerns me."

"The appearance of impropriety." Beryl repeated dryly. "My Congregation has provided for Joseph since he was twelve years old. He was to attend Gonzaga College, and I need not remind you what political pressures came to bear in converting the original intent of that facility to a white man's school. Joseph remained in Seattle when it was apparent that he had no future there."

"This I know."

"Did you also know that Mr. Yesler, the gentleman from Seattle who was in your office before you admitted me, is Joseph's sponsor for matriculation at the Territorial University and his patron for his remarkable artistic talent?"

"Truly?" He had not known. "I am pleased to hear this." He spoke the words, but he was not pleased that Father Louis Bertrand had put him in a potentially awkward position with Henry Yesler, of all people. He wanted nothing to interfere with the land purchase he was negotiating with the gentleman.

Beryl decided she should, for "appearances," as the Bishop would say, modify her defensive attitude. "Your Excellency, Joseph has quarters in the convent barn. It is, as I said, well away from our enclosed cloister area. If you deem this unacceptable, taking into consideration the wagging tongues of a few narrow minded individuals, then we shall seek other accommodations for him. But I do so with a heavy heart. I deny any misconduct on Joseph's part. Is the charge leveled at me?"

Bishop Blanchet sighed. "No, of course not."

"In a way I am relieved. I would have been appalled to think that any poisoned words would implicate the young man and myself."

"Oh, no, Mother Charbonneau, categorically not!"

"I should hope not," she said crisply.

Bishop Blanchet and the Mother General parted in a spirit of forced cordiality. On the way to the convent Beryl remained silent, occupied with her thoughts. Lavinia, sensing Beryl's distress, asked no questions.

Beryl had never taken her feelings for the boy to any local priest in the confessional. She had avoided any mention of Joseph when she confessed to Father Louis Bertrand. She knew that the unusual relationship would surely be held suspect by many priest confessors and perhaps, regardless of his protestations, by the Bishop himself. She was confident there was no sin and, therefore, she had never broached the subject to a priest either in private conversation or spiritual counseling. One could never be certain what predispositions of mind and deeply rooted prejudices resided in the clergy.

Father Louis Bertrand had cautioned her about external appearances often enough. It was his hope that the boy would be removed to Gonzaga before there was "talk." There was no real evidence to fuel rumors' fires; only fear. She must find a way to protect the reputation of the community and Joseph's as well. The solution was to come from an unexpected source.

Lavinia interrupted Beryl's thought when from the hill where the convent was located she noticed a large sloop at the Elliot pier. "*The Kidder* is in port," she remarked. "Doesn't that bring back memories for you?"

"It certainly does," Beryl responded, recalling her first view of the Seattle. "Much water over the dam, as is said." After hesitating she said, "Lavinia, have you heard any talk—any gossip—about our Joseph?" Beryl had not planned to mention the Bishop's concerns to anyone with the exception, perhaps, of Lizzie, but Lavinia was dependably discreet.

Lavinia raised her head, peering through her spectacles at Beryl, a frown creasing her brow. Beryl continued, "You've heard nothing about Joseph and improper behavior toward our young sisters?"

Lavinia was genuinely shocked. "Jesus, Mary and Joseph! Nothing of that nature whatsoever! Who would have such an idea?"

"I don't know." Beryl confided the gist of the Bishop's concerns to Lavinia.

"It shouldn't come as a total surprise. There are non Catholics in Fort Vancouver who are convinced that there are secret tunnels between the convent and the rectory."

"So you and I and the other sisters in Vancouver could have clandestine meetings with Father Donnelly under the watchful eye of Mrs. Maloney? Or with Father Brouillet who can barely totter to Mass?" Beryl became serious. "I wish I could dismiss all such rumors, but I must listen to the Bishop when he tells me there is talk, no matter how outlandish. We have to be careful about any appearance of impropriety."

"I see. I am outraged that we should have to listen to such rumors."

"I've been trying to view the matter objectively, Lavinia. When Joseph first came to us, he was small for his age. His size made me wonder if perhaps he had been younger than we believed when Lizzie and I found him. He could have been an extraordinarily precocious seven or eight."

"I doubt it. He was more likely a late developer physically."

Beryl continued, "So our little Indian suddenly emerges like a butterfly out of a cocoon, more than six feet tall and as handsome as a prince from the Arabian Nights. Given that you and I might have had different backgrounds and were heir to the prevalent prejudice against other races, would we have been concerned?"

"Possibly," Lavinia conceded.

"I must put distance between Joseph and the convent. Immediately."

"You will miss him."

Beryl reached for Lavinia's hand and pressed it.

As they approached the convent, Beryl noticed that another carriage was blocking the front entrance. "If that's someone for me, I'd rather wipe off the dust from my face and habit before going to the parlor," Beryl said. They turned the carriage to the back of the convent.

"Mother!" Sister Sarah Dufrayne came out to meet her sisters. "There's a gentleman at the door who says he has letters from your family! I asked him to wait in the parlor, but he won't come in."

Beryl wiped her face and washed her hands in haste while Sarah and Lavinia brushed the habit that had collected dust even though both sisters had worn cloaks. At the door Beryl had to restrain herself from not rushing to her visitor with a spontaneous hug.

"Oh, Adam," she cried, and reached for his hands. "Adam!" Henri Yesler had told Beryl about a piece of land at the foot of Madison hill that could be procured for a good price. This area of Seattle was growing and town residents with the means to maintain a lakefront home away from the dust and construction being done on the Denny regrade, had built cottages close to the shore of the lake which was known as Washington. The land and structure had been intended as a general store, but the owner had abandoned it to join the Klondike gold rush.

Adam saw that the main building and sheds could be converted to livery stables, tack and saddlery, with blacksmith facilities. Cured leather was cheap in the west, and Adam knew his craft. Hunters the caliber of Sir Prize and the Yesler horses were increasing in numbers, and few farriers on the frontier were accustomed to horses of this quality. Beryl had no doubt that Adam's reputation would be established swiftly.

"I'll need a good man," Adam told Beryl, which was exactly the opening she had prayed for.

Joseph warmed to the Charbonneau's former hostler immediately. Beryl had told him stories about Adam's teaching her to judge horseflesh. Although she had had excellent equestrians for coaches, it had been Adam who taught her the little tricks of disciplining her mount and anticipating its movements.

Joseph helped the older man with remodeling and gratefully accepted lodging in exchange for work. Lower Madison was closer to the proposed site for the Territorial University, a location opposed by many who felt that it was too far from central Seattle. By the time the newest group of sisters arrived from Vancouver where they had spent their postulancy, Beryl was able to take their parents and visiting relatives on a tour of the Seattle convent and its outbuildings as a part of investiture ceremonies. Although there was no explanation given to him, Bishop Blanchet, who presided over the rites observed that there was no evidence of the young Indian's presence anywhere on the grounds.

The Vancouver blacksmith had sent his father, who had been a storekeeper, to the Seattle convent as a general handyman. His seventy year old parent had recently become a widower, and he was pleased to serve the sisters. The old man was bent with arthritis. *No one could fret over his proximity to young novices*, Beryl thought grimly. He was not skilled in the smithy trade, having worked in the lumber mill since settling in Vancouver. Beryl assured him that Adam would take care of that task.

Beryl had been spared the burden of telling Joseph the reasons for her hastening his move away from convent property. Joseph himself brought the subject out in the open. "This is the best possible move, Mother. It's wise to avoid trouble before it is trouble."

Part Six

I

Lizzie Ordway carried the last of her boxes to the convent porch. Beryl, her habit tucked up to keep it from the mud on the road, was securing the trunks and crates Adam had already taken to the wagon with strong rope. The horse waited patiently. Adam checked the wheel brakes. Only last week still another man had been killed when his wagon, brake faulty, went out of control and plunged down the hill, finally careening over one of the deep ravines created by the construction on the Denny Hill, a project that literally flattened a natural cliff to permit access to what would be known as "First Hill." Accidents were tragic and all too frequent occurrences.

Beryl delayed Lizzie's departure by insisting she have a cup of tea. "My prayers will be answered if you are happy in San Francisco," Beryl said. "I wish there was an academy like Marcia Rankin's closer."

"It is certainly not a copy of the traditional finishing school. I was impressed by Marcia Rankin when she was in Seattle. Do you remember the meeting for which Joseph made the sign?"

"How could I forget? It was our first glimpse of his talent."

"Miss Rankin was our speaker. She put the question of suffrage into a perspective my impatience did not consider. No general would take ten men to fight a hundred on the battlefield. Those of us in the movement are too few to make a difference. She believes that we must begin by educating young women, convincing them that they are equal to men and should claim not only the right to vote, but the right to be honored as equal in value. It is an effort that may take many decades." Lizzie, whose conversation on this subject was habitually passionate and intense, softened her voice. "Our friendship defies logic, Beryl. You have, with negligible support from your church, created a remarkable entity. It has drawn intelligent women to it like lemmings to the sea..."

Beryl interrupted. "What a dreadful image, Lizzie!"

"Yes, 'dreadful.' These women who follow my dear friend Beryl Charbonneau have sacrificed their freedom of choice and their right to self determination to the paternal stronghold of the Church. They are afloat in waters controlled by men—exclusively controlled."

"And that church, through my congregation, has educated many young women above the level society would have recommended!" Beryl countered defensively. "And who knows what the ultimate result will be? I have not envisioned an institution where the members learn just enough to teach catechism!"

"Paradoxes. Contradictions. Forgive me, Beryl, I was unnecessarily harsh. Are we still friends?"

"Always," Beryl said as they moved to the door. Adam had put the last boxes in the wagon.

"That's the last of it, my dear," Lizzie said, holding out a key. "Now the house is yours. I see that Sister Imelda is already scrubbing the kitchen floor."

"She doesn't mean to offend, Lizzie. She has an incurable passion for wax and polish." Beryl rechecked the hitch. "I wish you had let Adam drive you," she said.

"Piffle! I despise helpless women. You of all people should know that!" she said decisively. She gave her friend a hug before climbing onto the driver's seat. "Adam may come to retrieve the wagon this afternoon."

"You'll find a lunch tucked in your valise," Beryl told her. Lizzie's inability to cook was well known. They didn't linger in their farewells, but Beryl embraced her friend once more. "How I'm going to miss you, Lizzie! Our loss is San Francisco's gain."

Lizzie felt awkward. She was not a demonstrative woman. "Yes, well, let's say I tried." She shook the reins abruptly and clucked to her mare. Beryl watched her drive down the road toward the docks. Lizzie sat, her back straight. She wore a dark russet traveling suit wearing her ever-present sailor hat with its red ribbons trailing down behind her. Life in the Northwest hadn't been easy for Lizzie. She was devoted to the cause of women's suffrage, as well as being an excellent teacher. She had come west with a rare education and a generous heart. Lizzie spoke, read and wrote five modern languages, and had knowledge of Greek and Latin. She never seemed to look down upon the West's lack of culture; she had been determined to have an effect upon its future. When her suffrage cause was ridiculed and suppressed, she decided to accept a position in San Francisco as headmistress of a prestigious academy for young ladies.

Lizzie deeded her Seattle home to Beryl's Congregation. "I have plenty of money, Beryl dear," she told her friend. She had built a structure adjacent to the house for a future schoolroom and knew that the Sisters of Martha and Mary would put it to good use. Two other communities had offered her a generous price, a fact that she did not reveal to Beryl. "There are more candidates than there is room for them at your present Seattle convent. You can sell that smaller place and add to this one. Your group will help the cause of education, and therefore I am proud to assist them."

"But what if you return?"

"Oh, I've already thought of that, although the prospect is unlikely. I have the property on Bainbridge Island, which I have kept."

Sister Sarah Dufrayne came out on the porch. "So, Miss Ordway has gone."

"Yes," Beryl replied, coming back into the house that was now to be the Seattle novitiate. "But I have a feeling she'll be back." *Dear God, I hope so. I will miss her,* Beryl thought. "How is Imelda's floor coming?"

"Finished. Please come in and admire it!"

The two women went toward the house arm in arm. Sarah had suggested that some of the second year novices live in this convent to be a part of the school as a training period. They would assist the experienced sisters and learn while in the classroom without the pressure of being completely on their own. Sarah had proven to be all that Beryl hoped. She was also an excellent judge of the novices' academic abilities, and placed each according to her gifts.

Adam came from the school building before the two entered the house. "We'll have the seats and desks fastened by the end of the week, Sisters."

"You're a treasure, Adam!" Beryl said, smiling at her old friend. Adam was still respectful and unfailingly courteous, but he had lost the habitual hang-head attitude. Here in the frontier he had discovered that he was well respected for his skills, and his confidence grew. He was now a businessman in his own right and relishing every minute of it. When he had built his livery at the end of Madison Avenue, he had no doubt that he could attract the patronage of customers with fine horses if given the chance. His opportunity came when a lady from the town nearly collided with a runaway horse and carriage within view of his establishment. Her horse had slipped and was down. It righted itself, but came up lame. Miss Matilda Perkins was stranded with a carriage of young ladies out for a picnic on Lake Washington. Adam took over.

Matilda Perkins was tending to plumpness, but she was faultlessly groomed and never ostentatious. The girls who accompanied her on frequent outings were her young lady boarders, but the rooms above the saloon and eatery she owned in town had another purpose. The facade of a boarding house was a thin disguise. Matilda saw to it that her girls were scrupulously clean, well mannered, never flamboyant in their dress, and without paint on their faces. Matilda herself never entertained privately, and she was most particular about the gentlemen admirers who sought her girls' company.

When Adam first met Matilda Perkins, he was struck with what he saw as a homespun, almost Yorkshire style beauty. She had reddish hair that was inclined to friz around the edges, although it was neatly pulled back. In spite of her age, her round face was still youthfully sweet, with a spattering of freckles. Her one mark of adornment was her jade earrings, which Adam later learned had been a wedding gift from her late husband.

After the accident, Adam concluded that Miss Perkins' horse suffered a pulled stifle. "It'll heal sur'n' nuff. But this animal shall be needin' stall rest."

"However will we get home?" Matilda asked. It was a long wagon trip up Madison Street from the lake back to town.

"Ye'll be takin' a steed I have right here, ma'am. And I'll not be chargin' board for your other horse. Ye'll be feeding this here one proper I 'spect."

Matilda spread the word, and from the chance encounter Adam's livery was launched.

II

Matilda Katherine Perkins, or Mattie Kate as she was known to customers who frequented the Rainbow Trout Saloon and Eatery, took off the steel rimmed spectacles she used only in private. The letter on the table blurred. Sunlight through the lace curtains speckled the oak table, and through the window Elliot Bay gleamed under a clear sky. The fine June day gave her no pleasure.

She put on her glasses again and reread the words from her daughter. Polly's handwriting had matured. There was nothing left of the childish scrawl Mattie loved. Her Polly, now Sister Paulina of the Congregation of Martha and Mary, was becoming, no, had become a young lady. Polly! Her beautiful Polly, slender, with smooth olive skin and the Mediterranean look of her father's people. Her daughter's dark eyes and ready smile could turn the darkest day into Heavenly light. Her father, Luis Soldano, had been a handsome man. *Oh, yes*, Mattie Kate thought, *he was a beautiful sight to behold.*

Matilda Katherine Perkins, daughter to a widower mill hand, had gone with her fellow hotel waitresses to a party on Italian hill. They had laughed, danced and eaten food with tomato sauce and tangy spices. Luis was instantly attracted to Matilda, and she responded. Motherless, she was overwhelmed when Luis' mother, father, and sisters surrounded her with love. Mattie's dour father had ranted and raved about the damned Italians who reeked of garlic and worshipped the Pope. When it came to a choice between him and the fun loving and accepting Soldano family, the decision was easy. The only reservation that the family expressed was her religion, or lack of it. Matilda went to Father Mercelli twice a week after her shift at the hotel for instructions. Within two months she was baptized a Catholic and married Luis Soldano.

Their first months together sharing the family house gave them very little privacy, but it helped the newly married couple build their dream. They began to cook the family recipes and brought pots of sauce and pasta to the hotel in town daily. They delivered the same hot food to the taverns, and catered dinners for the wealthy families, some of whom had tasted Italian food in Europe. Henry and Sarah Yesler were enthusiastic customers, and whatever the Yeslers liked, others imitated. The couple earned enough to put a down payment on a two story house at the edge of what Seattle residents called Italian town.

Matilda and Luis turned the first floor into Soldano's, a restaurant with paintings of Sorrento, Naples, Venice, and Florence decorating the walls. They covered the tables with red checkered cloth and lit the premises with an abundance of candles dripping from Chianti bottle holders. They hired waitresses and Matilda was the hostess. Luis cooked, assisted by his sisters, whom he paid generously. Matilda and Luis saved money by establishing their living quarters on the restaurant building's second floor.

Matilda withdrew from her public role when her first pregnancy began to be evident. Their firstborn lived only a few hours, being born prematurely. They lived through their sorrow only to lose Luis' father and mother within months of each other. Luis' business continued to prosper and he supplied the dowries for his two sisters, who married within the Italian community.

Matilda's second pregnancy was confirmed after two more years of marriage. This time Luis insisted that she not keep the long hours the business demanded. Felice and Rosa, Luis' sisters, had persuaded their brother that since Soldano's was a family restaurant, and could more than support all of them. He must allow them and their husbands a greater share in the restaurant work and profits. Rosa's husband handled all the books.

Matilda gave birth to a healthy baby girl. Luis named her Paulina, in honor of his mother. Bright and pretty, Paulina thrived and Luis pampered both his daughter and his wife. His trusting nature and ignorance of financial matters paved the way for his sisters' greed. Legal contracts were drawn that made the restaurant the exclusive property of the Soldano family, specifically Luis and his sisters. As long as Luis lived, Matilda was secure, and it never occurred to her to question money matters. She assumed that Luis was making bank deposits mindful of their future. She was not envious by temperament, and was happy for the sisters when they built large homes at the bottom of Italian hill while she and Luis remained above the restaurant. During the next five years, Felice had two children and Rosa three. No more children were born to Luis and Matilda.

The darkest day of Matilda's life came suddenly. Luis' carriage plunged from the muddy road on the Denny regrade. He was killed, and she was alone. Soon she realized that the business was totally controlled by the sisters and brothers-in-law. She had no voice in its management, nor claim to its profits. The family allowed her to live upstairs, but told her that she would have to help if she were to receive any benefits from the business. The girls who had embraced her just eight years ago felt no remorse in reducing their brother's wife to the role of servant.

Matilda was no fool; she conceived a plan. Refusing the position of hostess, she declared that she would wait tables. Her in-laws told her it would pay less, and she demurely responded that, after all, they were allowing her to live upstairs rent free. She was experienced in the ways of waitressing. A hostess wouldn't earn the tips a waitress who knew her job could. For two years Matilda pocketed tips, and when the silly girl who showed customers to their tables took long breaks, she would see to it that payment on several tables never reached the cash register. Each month she would bank only what she was paid in wages. The rest she hid. She had given Luis all her own savings, and she had worked for this "family" business without taking a cent for herself. She determined it was just for her to be repaid, and concealing the tips she kept for herself was to that end. She also had a plan. She had her eye on a space near the opera house where she could build her own saloon and eatery. She had memorized the family recipes and she knew as much about the making of ravioli, pastas, and sauces as anyone in Luis' family.

It broke her heart, but she sent her Polly to boarding school with the Sisters of Martha and Mary in Tacoma. It wasn't so far that she couldn't take the boat for a visit once every week. It was best that Polly not be in Seattle if Matilda were to complete her plans for her family business. She paid the sisters in cash for a year's board and tuition, and used bank funds for a down payment on the building for her restaurant. She had never deposited a cent over what she was paid in wages. The family reacted with anger and accused her of cheating them. They hired a solicitor who audited Matilda's bank accounts and announced to the family that Matilda had not deposited any more than her fair earnings. She had been able to save almost all of her wages and tips since she was fed and housed in the home she and Luis had created. There was nothing the family could use against her.

Matilda didn't try to compete with Soldano's restaurant on the hill; instead she introduced the new culinary delights to the working man. At her place, the Rainbow Trout Saloon and Eatery, men and women could have a cheap meal and the men could drink spirits. Matilda had her name legally changed to her maiden "Perkins." Her daughter, Paulina Soldano, would never have to be embarrassed that her surname was connected to a tavern. The Speckled Trout thrived under Matilda's ownership. Within a few years, Matilda, now Mattie Kate, had added another attraction: her girls. Ostensibly, she took in young lady boarders, but no one was fooled. Her girls entertained only customers who enjoyed Mattie Kate's approval. Mattie Kate never accepted favors, nor did she give any. She might not have retained Luis' name; but she was faithful to his memory.

Polly loved her mother, and she knew that Matilda gave her everything she could ever wish for, but the Sisters of Martha and Mary became her family. It was no surprise to Mattie Kate when her daughter told her she wanted to enter the Congregation. Part of her wished a more normal life for her beloved child, but the frontier was still a rough place, and if a suitor of breeding and family connections were to discover that Polly's mother owned a business which included a "house of ill repute," Polly's life could be destroyed. The girl was only fourteen, and Mattie Kate asked her to wait one more year before entering the Congregation. She obeyed. Mattie Kate took her on a boat trip to San Francisco where she treated Paulina like a princess. Mattie enjoyed being the perfect lady and the two had a month together that both would remember always.

But Mattie Kate was uneasy about her daughter's desire to become a nun in the Sisters of Martha and Mary community. She knew that her friend Adam, owner of the Madison livery stable, had connections to Mother Charbonneau. She confided her dilemma to him. Adam listened with respect and sympathy.

"T'would ease yer mind to speak to Mother Charbonneau. She'll be hearin' ye out, and she'll nae be lookin' down her nose."

Mattie Kate sought an audience with Mother Charbonneau. She told her how she had been betrayed by her husband's people, and how she had had to compete in the harsh world of Seattle's waterfront. She confessed that her girls sometimes entertained gentlemen, but the euphemism didn't deceive Beryl. Mattie assured the Mother Superior with tears in her eyes that Paulina was completely ignorant of her mother's business beyond the obvious eatery and, in fact, Paulina had her father's name, which further disconnected her from Mattie's business.

"Mrs. Perkins, I will not judge you. Nor will I refuse your daughter entrance into this community because of your, ah, business connections. Paulina is a good and gentle girl, and you have done everything in your power to protect her."

Mattie Kate had wept tears of relief, and Beryl told her to forget that this conversation had ever taken place. Paulina entered the convent, received the habit, and had been teaching in the community for several years.

But now, sitting at her table on this fine day, Mattie Kate held a letter that told her Paulina was coming to Seattle to be a teacher in the Italian community's new Catholic school. This could be a disaster for Paulina if Luis' sisters connected her with Mattie Kate—and how could they not? The Sisters of Martha and Mary, unlike other orders of nuns in the Pacific Northwest, kept their surnames as well as their Christian names.

Adam sat in the well padded wing back chair Mattie Kate reserved for him. On an end table beside it there was always good tobacco in a thermidor, and several of his pipes. He always removed his boots at the door, and his stocking feet rested on an ottoman that matched the chair. Mattie kept a quilt over both chair and ottoman not to protect the upholstery, but to insure that Adam would never hesitate to stop by even if he were in working clothes.

Adam never availed himself of Mattie's girls, nor did he ever seek or receive favors of a carnal nature from Mattie Kate. It was well known that Matilda Perkins was faithful to the memory of Luis Soldano. Yet the two were intimate in the manner of old and comfortable friends. There was no one else with whom she could have shared her concerns about Paulina.

Mattie Kate's first desperate thought was to seek another audience with Mother Charbonneau, but Adam told her that she was on a tour of community convents and would not be back until just before the beginning of the school year. Then she would be preparing to journey to Rome where the Pope would give his blessing to her Congregation. The date had not been confirmed, but it was to be in the near future.

Mattie Kate remembered that Mother Charbonneau had been compassionate and understanding when she had spoken to her some years before, and she judged that she would be unlikely to place Paulina anywhere that would bring disgrace upon the Congregation or Paulina. She wondered if she should consider selling her business so that connections would not be made.

Adam convinced her to forget her concerns, and emphatically advised against any extreme action such as selling her business. No one in Seattle would associate Sister Paulina Soldano with Mattie Kate Perkins. Or so Adam thought.

III

Seattle
1876

Joseph put a few drops of ammonia into the bucket of sudsy water in the precise amount Adam had specified. Dipping and wringing out the cloth until it was almost dry, he began to rub the leather harness strips. They had looked clean, but the telltale dirt that appeared on the cloth told otherwise. Joseph repeated the cleaning process four times before he was satisfied that the tack was free of dirt. Then he took some of the oil that Adam himself mixed and worked it into the leather until it gleamed.

Joseph liked this work. He liked the smell of leather and linseed oil, and the way it blended with the scent of alfalfa and horse droppings. Not that these droppings remained. Adam's horses and those boarded at his livery stable were turned out into spacious paddocks daily, and these were rotated so that the grass did not go to mud. All horses were groomed daily and Adam saw to their proper shoeing, floating their back teeth with his heavy rasp to ensure proper chewing, and keeping their fetlocks and manes trimmed neatly. It was well known in town and the surrounding settlements that Adam Piggoty could have pleased royalty with the way his stables were managed.

Adam and Joseph suited each other. Adam was in awe of the sculptures produced in his work room, now newly refurbished and expanded. He confessed to being embarrassed by having a Territorial University graduate working for him as a common lackey. He confided this feeling to Beryl.

"Joseph is aiming higher academically, Adam. He still has years to complete his graduate studies, and he is content. After all, you did insist upon building a real house for him so that the shed would be his working studio."

The house was at the back end of Adam's property with a view of Lake Washington. It was modest, but roomy. If Joseph should consider marrying, this would be a beautiful spot to share with his bride. Beryl knew that there was someone, a Chinese girl. Joseph had told her that the chances of an Oriental girl marrying outside of her race and culture was as unlikely if not more so than a white man marrying an Indian.

Joseph was tall and fine featured. At twenty he looked less like the white man's image of an Indian as he grew to manhood. He could have passed for one of the boys on Italian hill except for the name of Joseph Wolf, the surname he and Beryl decided was the most meaningful and appropriate to the circumstances of his childhood. He could have worked in one of the mercantile shops, or as a waiter in a hotel. Mattie Kate would have taken him on in an instant if Beryl had asked her. But she was very satisfied with the arrangement with Adam.

Joseph had worked for Adam for two years before he met Mai Ling. Adam was partial to Mattie Kate's cooking at the saloon, but Joseph, who frequently went to town with his employer, didn't like the tomato sauces that were permeated with garlic. He found Wong Chen's restaurant and discovered its foreign cooking style was wonderfully pleasing to his palate. Wong Chen's daughter, Mai Ling, pleased his eye. Not only his eye; his very heart and soul. In her there was meaning and purpose, and its form was a delicate girl with shining black eyes and hair glimmering like raven's wings. Her white silk dress made her complexion seem as smooth as rich cream, and the same warm color.

Joseph fancied himself the hunter and Mai Ling was his prize. This image did not mean that the girl was his prey. Rather it focused his mind on a quiet approach that would neither alarm nor frighten her. He wanted Mai Ling for his own, but in this hunt she must want to be captured, and there would have to be a miraculous change of heart within her family if he were ever to have her.

He brought his books when he came for meals and identified himself as a student. The elder Wong Chen respected learning. Soon Joseph was exchanging lessons in English for his meals. After closing, the family, comprised of mother, father, Mai Ling, and her brother, gathered for their lessons. Mother Charbonneau gave Joseph primers and slates for his willing pupils. Before long Wong Chen's friends came and within a few months Joseph found himself teaching thirty Chinese.

In the months of lessons, Mai Ling came to understand that Joseph thought her very special. She had learned enough English to tell him that for two such as they, there were many stones on their path. Joseph loved the way she could speak in poetic images.

"But are they such stones as you wish to be in our way?" Joseph asked.

"Oh, no!" she said shyly, but firmly, not meeting his eyes.

One night there were few students and the Chens were greatly agitated. Refugee Chinese had come from Tacoma where an anti Chinese mob, unchecked by the police, drove men, women and children out of their homes, burning the dwellings as the victims fled. Some of them had made their way to Seattle seeking shelter.

There was anti Chinese sentiment in Seattle, but not with such viciousness. *Surely his friends would be safe*, Joseph thought. The Tacoma incident went unpunished. This was in November. Winter was mild this year, not like that month in 1881 when Seattle was completely snowbound. There had been thirty-eight inches in a single night and the snow and cold had continued unabated for twenty-eight days. The Tacoma refugees found shelter during a mild winter.

One afternoon in early February Joseph had brought the last of Adam's boarding horses to their stalls. The days were still short and there was a chill in the air. Joseph had not heard the commotion in the front of Adam's stables and was surprised to see Mai Ling's brother, Chang, wild-eyed and out of breath. Adam had brought him to Joseph as he couldn't understand the youth's words.

"Oh, Mister Joseph, sir! Terrible news! Terrible!"

In a garbled combination of Chinese and English, Chang told Joseph how his family had been downtown at the market while he stayed in the restaurant preparing the steamed rice and other parts of the evening meals. A mob, well organized, had rounded up over three hundred Chinese from all parts of the city and herded them to the docks forcing more than half of them to board *The Queen of the Pacific*, a sloop docked at Elliot Bay. Oriental men, women and children were to be deported to San Francisco. The rest were locked in a warehouse to wait for the next boat. Chang was sure that his father and Mai Ling had been forced on board.

The Chinese were huddled in the belly of the ship. There was no heat and no sanitary facility. The captain and crew seemed to be cooperating with the vigilantes who had herded them onto the docks and on board threatening them with rifles. Most of the group were afraid to speak, but the elder Chen

167

approached the crewman who had followed the last of the mob downstairs.

"Why do you do this?" he asked.

"Keep yer peace, old man!" the fellow replied, raising his arm as if to strike.

"Please!" Mai Ling intervened.

The man regarded her. "Yer on yer way back where you belong!"

"Yeah!" said another man who was peering through the opening at the top of the ladder. "Like all you foreigner blokes." He pronounced it 'fur-in-ners.'

"All foreigner sent away?" Mai Ling asked the man in the hold. "Surely the Indians will be glad."

The shipmate might have struck her for her insolence, but he was unarmed down in the crowded hold. People who were trapped could be dangerous as wild animals. Also, he'd singled out this little chink for some fun once they were underway. She was pretty and virginal. Yes, sir, he'd have a bit of his own back for her remark.

The captives huddled in family groups, painfully aware of the futility of resistance. A few had already experienced expulsion from Tacoma. This vessel was bound for San Francisco. If they could disembark there, they would become part of an established Chinese community. They would have to bear the present humiliation with the hope of a better future in the south. It was, after all, free passage in spite of the degrading circumstances.

Mai Ling thought only of Joseph and her younger brother, both powerless to help. She hoped that Chang was safe in the restaurant, which was frequented by many whites who might offer some protection if only for their own convenience. But Joseph, her dear, gentle Joseph. When would she see him again?

Upon hearing Chang's story, Joseph made his way to the home of Captain and Mrs. Lilly. The captain was friend to Elizabeth Ordway and he knew men of power. Lilly also boarded some of his fine mounts at Adam's stable and Joseph had been known to him from the time his first major sculpture of Princess Angeline was viewed at the Yesler home. Joseph reasoned that Captain Lilly would recall this and it might gain him an audience with the gentleman. Then there was also his connection to Mother Charbonneau through Miss Ordway. In his panic he made the mistake of going directly to the front door. When a maid peeked through the entry window and beheld a disheveled dark faced man in coarse working clothes, she would not open the door and told him to go away. Joseph pounded on the glass of the double doors, then afraid he might break it, began to beat his fists on the wood rim.

The noise attracted the attention of Lilly. When he saw who was causing the disturbance, he received the distraught Joseph. After he heard what the mob in the town had done, he bade Joseph wait in the foyer while he put on riding boots.

He returned ready to ride. "This way, Joseph," he said, leading the way to the back of the residence. "You may use one of my horses."

"I have one of Mr. Piggoty's, sir. He's tied at your gate post."

"Very well. Wait for me there. Arthur, please see my friend out."

Arthur, Lilly's butler, opened the door for Joseph, and wished him well. It was a courtesy that touched the young man. He was satisfied he had come to the right place for help.

Captain Lilly led the way over First Hill, past the Yesler house, and to another large dwelling.

"Come with me, Joseph," Lilly ordered, dismounting. Territorial Chief Justice Roger Green listened to the two men." This was no spontaneous occurrence," he said. "There must have been planning and organization." The Justice went to a bell pull on the wall of his study. He stepped out of the room as his secretary answered, and returned with a look of grim resolve. "I have dispatched the Home Militia, but we must deal directly with the captain of the *Queen*. He went to the ebony desk that spanned the bay windows that overlooked his back garden. He took parchment and quill, and when he had finished, he put his seal on the document and gave it to Lilly.

"Captain, this is a writ of habeas corpus addressed to the steamer's captain demanding that he put all Chinese ashore to attend a hearing in my court tomorrow in person. The Home Guards will be at the docks to protect the Chinese and to escort them. I authorize you to make whatever other threats seem necessary. I do not imagine that the man would like to hear that his ship could be forbidden a berth at any Washington port. I will also initiate an investigation to determine who paid him to take the Chinese. I doubt he did it in charity."

The *Queen of the Pacific* had not left the docks. The prisoners in the hold endured the chill of the February afternoon in the darkness of the hold. Suddenly the light streamed in as the hatch at the top was pulled back and fully opened. Mai Ling looked up to see Joseph descending the ladder. He told the prisoners that they would be leaving the boat in the morning, and he chose to remain with Mai Ling and her father until that time.

The Chen family was safe, as were hundreds of others, but the treatment of them in Tacoma and Seattle made a majority accept deportation to San

Francisco. The effort to keep the peace afterward was bloody. The next day a fight broke out at the corner of First and Mill Street, and forty anti-Chinese were wounded and the Canadian who led them was killed. The rebellious anti-Chinese secured warrants for the arrest of Captain Lilly and the Justice, as well as three other judges, but Governor Watson declared martial law and nullified the complaints.

Weeks later, life in Seattle had returned to normal. Both sides had learned a lesson. Joseph realized all too clearly that it was not love of the Chinese that had inspired Justice Green and Governor Watson, nor the merchants and other men of power who had supported their cause. The city would use the incident to its economic advantage, even though comparatively few Chinese now remained in Seattle.

"Seattle is already claiming that it is the friend of the immigrant and the downtrodden," Joseph explained to his students once his tutelage after hours at the restaurant resumed. "Our town is proclaiming Tacoma's unfairness compared to our defense of the Chinese."

"But why?" one of his pupils asked.

"So that future trade with the Orient will come here, not to Tacoma."

The elder Chen was philosophical. "So the greed that brought about the troubles takes another form. It now protects us!"

The now small Chinese community was aware that it was Joseph who was their true benefactor. The elders decided that it was right and just that they break with established tradition and allow Mai Ling and Joseph to be married.

IV

Mattie Kate was surprised to see Beryl Charbonneau in Adam's office.

"I'm so sorry—I didn't mean to barge in, I apologize, and I'll wait outside."

"Mrs. Perkins, I was the one who sent for you, not Adam. Considering that many of our citizens are obsessed with the appearances of propriety," she smiled knowingly, "this was the most prudent place to meet. Too bad, really. I should have loved to taste that soup you are so famous for—what is it called?"

"Minestrone. It will be my pleasure to send a tureen to the convent! How may I help you—assuming you are not here to order soup." Mattie would not bring up the subject herself, but she wondered if this meeting had anything to do with Paulina's assignment to the Italian school. It did not, as she realized when Beryl explained her purpose.

"You are in a position to hear—what shall we call it—'scuttlebutt' from your customers. I'm interested in whatever you may have heard about the murder of Douglas McFee, a homesteader up on the Cascade Trail. It happened about fifteen years ago."

"McFee. Yes, I knew of him, and once or twice I encountered him at the hardware store. He came down to sell horses and to purchase them. As a matter of fact, I bought my team from him. He said they were too good for trail use. I got them for a very good price."

"I've seen your team. The man must have had a good eye. What was the talk when he was killed?"

"At first the sheriff put together a posse to look for the Indian who lived up there with McFee, but they couldn't find a trace of the boy. Then one of the fellows down here spotted McFee's gelding on a sloop bound for Vancouver. One thing led to another and his bridle was seen on a horse outside the tavern. McFee had a special head stall with inlaid silver trim—quite unusual. One of the poker tables was doing business with a lout who sported a big roll. When the sheriff questioned him, he admitted that his buddies overtook McFee on the road, but all he was supposed to do was meet them in town. He could neither name nor produce the buddies. Considering the money he carried and the bridle, the sheriff didn't buy the story and he was jailed. I can't tell you more than that."

"So from that time on there was no question of Douglas' Indian boy having committed the crime?"

"You're asking about Joseph Wolf, aren't you?"

"In the strictest of confidence, yes."

"How was Joseph connected with McFee?"

"He was left on his doorstep when just an infant. This was when his wife was alive. Douglas and Fiona raised the child and made every effort to keep his existence a secret. Ultimately, they made up a story about an Indian family coming to work for them, and then in time told another story about the adults abandoning the boy. Douglas and Fiona taught him arithmetic and to read, and when Fiona passed away, Douglas continued Joseph's education. Even as a child, Joseph was exceptional."

"He ran away thinking he would be blamed for the murder?"

"Yes. He survived in unbelievably primitive conditions, pretending to be an idiot. He hung around the Yakima Bend settlement, which is where I found him. Elizabeth Ordway and I had a serious accident on the trail and I almost lost my horse. Joseph saved him. And then I discovered that the boy was not in any way retarded, but, as it were, in disguise. The rest you know."

"Douglas McFee had a lawyer here who handled his affairs. Would he be a help to you?"

"It is what I had hoped for!" Beryl said smiling broadly and pressing Mattie's hands in hers.

* * * * *

"Mother Charbonneau, this is an amazing story. I was aware of a half-breed Indian boy, and for years made an effort to locate him. Douglas McFee made this child the sole beneficiary of his land and goods. Actually, there was nothing of value left in the cabin except an impressive collection of books. The horses were moved to Seattle and sold, and I have set aside the proceeds. I took the liberty of removing the books. They're stored at the Territorial University with the agreement that they be given to the institution if not claimed in twenty-five years. Regarding the land, the government dissolved ownership rights to the homesteads in the valley for the proposed transcontinental railroad. This was done legally, if not generously, and the beneficiary is entitled to that money.

"Mr. Gridley, are you familiar with the sculptor, Joseph Wolf?"

There was a brief silence as the lawyer removed his reading glasses and peered at Beryl. "Are you telling me that Joseph Wolf and McFee's Indian boy are one and the same? This is remarkable!"

"Joseph would not have cared about the land or whatever disposition was made of it, but I know he will wish to claim the books."

"Would he do me the honor of coming to our home? I would have the volumes there for him."

"If it is agreeable to you, will you bring them to our Seattle convent?"Beryl knew that the return of Douglas' books must be a private moment for Joseph. He would not want it shared in any public display. Only she would be present in the convent parlor to tell Joseph of his inheritance.

When Joseph opened the trunk that contained the books that were beloved and familiar, he lifted each volume in turn, remembering his last sight of them on Douglas' shelf. Then he knelt by his Mother Charbonneau and let himself be cradled in her arms. When the tears that flowed freely had stopped, Beryl stroked them from his face and held him close once more. Joseph would share his joy with Mai Ling and other friends, but this moment was for them alone.

The wedding was celebrated in Chinese fashion. Beryl ignored Father Mercelli's outrage at the "pagan union" and attended the ceremony. Captain and Mrs. Lilly, and Adam also attended. Afterward there was feasting, firecrackers, and a great paper dragon brilliant in red, yellow and green. It was placed over the heads of three children who snaked up and down the street. Its great mouth gaped at the guests, and the children's high pitched laughter rose from underneath their disguise. The street was lit by paper lanterns that glowed red and yellow from the candles within. Joseph's friends from the university kept a watchful eye from the dark outskirts of the celebration, prepared for a disturbance, but there was none. Without leadership, the anti-Chinese movement was ineffective. Citizens, however, claimed it had stemmed the tide of what propagandists termed "The Yellow Menace."

V
Seattle
1880

Beryl could look back on twenty years since the idea of the Sisters of Martha and Mary was born. At the Mass celebrating the final profession of twelve sisters, the first profession of ten more, and the reception of the habit for the class of fifteen postulants, Father Louis Bertrand praised the years of growth and grace. There were now schools in Tacoma, Seattle, Fort Vancouver, Portland, Olympia, Yakima, and Spokane, and the invitation from the Bishop of Montana for a secondary school and college in Missoula had been accepted and its first semester would begin in the fall.

Beryl received notification from the Holy See that her application to establish a Congregation would be blessed by Rome and approved by the Holy Father. While this was only a first step, Father Louis Bertram insisted that the Mother Foundress be present to receive the Pope's blessing. He would accompany her to Rome. Beryl chose Sister Mary Louise as companion, since she was not yet qualified to teach. The Congregation's resources were stretched so thin Beryl had made the decision to take Mary Louise, who would delay her normal school training for the time Beryl was in Europe—as long as eight months counting travel. They would sail to San Francisco, take the boat through the channel at Panama to New York where they would be joined by Beryl's elderly mother.

Before embarking on the historical journey, there were details of the coming year's assignments to consider. The day before the departure for

Rome, Mother Charbonneau, Lavinia, and Sarah Dufrayne made last minute adjustments of appointments.

"Sister Paulina seems exceptionally bright. It's a shame we can't let her continue schooling beyond her two years of normal school," Sarah said.

"She will continue," Beryl answered, "but she's young and her knowledge of Italian makes her an ideal person for Father Mercelli's new Italian parish school."

Sister Mary Louise interrupted them, "Excuse me, Mother. This letter was delivered by special messenger."

Beryl opened the envelope and smiled. "I'm so glad this came before I left! Saint Mary's College in Indiana has accepted Philomena, our student from the Tacoma boarding school," she announced, "and any qualified sister the Mother General of the Congregation of Martha and Mary chooses to send to them. The sister we select will have a four year scholarship funded by Philomena's father, Mr. Duffy!" Beryl read the news to Sarah and Lavinia.

"Marietta?" Sarah asked.

"She is brilliant and she has worked hard. Yes, I believe she deserves this opportunity," Beryl affirmed.

Marietta knelt in the convent chapel. She shivered with the excitement after the news she heard. Within a month she would be traveling east to Indiana to one of the most prestigious colleges for women in the United States. She was thirty-two, but young enough and still burning with a desire to excel in the academic community. After normal school she had been allowed to take some summer classes at the Territorial University, and she had established herself as a bold and brilliant scholar. She was aware that behind her back, sisters from other orders who were attending thought she was offensively and inappropriately "singular." Now she would come into her own. All her thoughts were of the college in the Midwest, and she was determined to prove her worth.

* * * * *

Beryl was finally on her way to Europe and Lavinia settled in the Mother General's Seattle office. "I do not feel comfortable in this chair," Lavinia whispered to herself. In her imagination was the picture of a tiny child amongst a crowd of adults, so small she could barely sit at a table without cushions or books boosting her height. She smiled to herself at the image since her feet were clearly on the floor, and as for stature, she was inches taller than the average sister, almost as tall as Beryl Charbonneau herself.

She was pleased that all the assignments were completed and in front of her on the desk. There would be no important matters for her to consider on her own! Had she been aware of the outcome of her first major decision, she would not have been so sanguine.

VI

Old Father Mercelli climbed the stairs of his pulpit with effort. Overlooking his parishioners, he gave his customary audible sigh and, making the sign of the cross, intoned "In nomine Patris et Filii, and Spiritui Sancti, Amen." He surveyed his Sunday Mass attendance and calculated that they were about twenty-five heads short. He also saw that the absentees were men. He'd hear about it in the confessional, and he wouldn't be too hard on those who depended upon Yesler's mill for their livelihood. Sunday or no, if the mill let off all the Catholics for Mass, there would be precious few working. And now the men had to be careful. The completion of the railroad had brought an influx of Chinese and Irish to Seattle and these men would work for almost nothing. *Oh, well,* he thought, as he concentrated on his notes, *Holy Mother Church had given him the power of absolution and he'd be generous with it for the sake of these hard-working laborers on Italian hill, even if it might compromise his reputation for enforcing Church law with no leniency.* He cleared his throat.

"I have news for our parish. The good Sisters of Martha and Mary will open our new school next month. Any child not yet enrolled should be registered no later than Friday next. There is a fee per family, but if it cannot be paid, no child will be turned away. The sisters who will staff our parish school are with us today. Sisters, will you please stand?"

The sisters had occupied the front pew, and all the parishioners had seen of them was their backs with the navy-blue tunic, brown scapular and black veils. Now they stood and faced the Congregation.

"I would like to welcome Sister Joanna Zimmerman, Sister Mary

Catherine Fernandez, and Sister Paulina Soldano." Father Mercelli did not note the gasp from twelve rows back as Felice Contino heard the last name and looked at the nuns. Her eyes narrowed, scrutinizing the sister with the fine features and dark eyes. This was surely her brother's child. But she was also the daughter of a known whore and her presence would bring down disgrace upon the family. Rosa sat across the aisle. Her eyes met Felice's, and the two knew they were of one mind. They would not permit this person, nun or no nun, to teach in their parish school.

* * * * *

Sister Lavinia Boucher, acting Mother General of the Sisters of Martha and Mary, sat in the parlor of the Seattle convent listening to Mrs. Felice Contino and Mrs. Rosa Bersanto. With affectedly apologetic tones and expressions of regret, they told her that were it up to them, there would be no problem whatsoever. But since the Italian community had been scandalized by the immoral and reckless behavior of Sister Paulina Soldano's mother, the prospect of the young nun's teaching in the parish school was unacceptable.

And who would know if mean spirited gossips didn't point it out? Lavinia thought. She suggested that perhaps she could send for Sister so they might see for themselves what a devoted nun their niece was, lady-like in every way with nothing of scandalous behavior about her. But no, they did not wish to speak to Sister Paulina. The memory of their brother's death and his widow's unthinkable betrayal of the good family name required them to maintain their distance, painful as this choice was to them.

When they departed, Lavinia retired to the small convent chapel. She hadn't been taken in by the pious protestations of the two women. Neither could she ignore their cause. It would be best for all concerned, the Congregation of Martha and Mary as well, if Sister Paulina were sent away from Seattle with all due speed.

She thought back over the years. There had been a mystery about this girl. Paulina was a painting with no detail. Now she understood. Mother Charbonneau must have known, and how typical of her superior to ignore the mother's circumstances and think only of the girl's value. Some of the established orders would not have accepted Paulina Soldano if the story of her mother had been known. They received "girls of good character," and the unwritten rule was that the parents had to be of the same unblemished reputation. It took a dispensation from Rome to admit an orphan with unknown parentage, and then only if the community petitioned, which was rare.

Lavinia organized her thoughts. Paulina was blameless. She was obedient, intelligent, and her cheerful willingness to accept any task made her an asset to any of the Congregation's convents. Yet, in this situation, she would have to be removed from her appointed post, and in such a way to prevent these vindictive aunts from proclaiming their hatred of her mother to Paulina's face.

Saint Mary's College in South Bend, Indiana, was run by the Sisters of the Holy Cross, and had been a pioneer institution for the education of young women. Marietta, packed and clearly deserving of the honor was looking forward to the train trip and the academic challenges at Saint Mary's. She would have to wait. Marietta would stay in Seattle and Paulina would take her place at Saint Mary's. It would be a blow to the older sister, but delay wouldn't hurt her. In fact, in the interim she might continue at the Territorial University, which had already accepted women, and where Marietta had established a reputation for academic excellence. She dreaded the ordeal of informing Marietta of the change, especially since she was not at liberty to give her the reason.

Mother Lavinia had extracted a promise from the aunts that if Paulina were to be removed, no whisper of gossip would surface. The promise had been given. After all, it was best for them. And speaking of promises, Lavinia told herself, she would move Heaven and earth to avoid a nomination to be Mother General. She found, and this incident reaffirmed it, that she had no taste for being responsible for the community at large. Mother Charbonneau had told the sisters before she left for Rome that it would be in the best interests of the Congregation if they picked new leadership for the future. Mother's efforts had borne fruit, and her role as pioneer foundress was finished. Beryl was certain that the community would look to Lavinia, the woman who had nurtured them through their novitiate years, and if she herself remained firm in her decision not to put herself forward as the first Mother General, Lavinia was certain to be elected. "Well, not if I can help it," Lavinia muttered half aloud as she genuflected and left the chapel.

Sister Marietta McGinnis accepted her superior's change of assignment with unconcealed resentment. She seethed outwardly and inwardly. What right did this slip of a girl, only six years in the community have to go St. Mary's? Marietta had taught Paulina in Tacoma. She had seen the mother and had taken stock of the fine clothes and expensive gifts to the community.

Paulina's favor had been bought. Now the girl was on her way east, and Marietta who had served the community for fifteen years would remain in Seattle teaching dirty little immigrant brats. She had been tossed a bone by way of placating her: she had been registered to attend classes at the Territorial University.

Marietta confided her disappointment to Sister Gertrude, and only to her. Gertrude had to agree that the switch of Marietta and Paulina was very hard to understand.

"Don't tell me it's God's will," Marietta said. "I've already heard that from Mother Lavinia."

"I can't very well tell you anything else, but I promise you I'll try to get to the bottom of this."

"Isn't it obvious?" Marietta cried. "Paulina comes from money, and I'm a dispensable orphan that Mother Charbonneau allowed to come west because she needed volunteers." She made no effort to disguise the bitterness in her voice. "If I had a rich mother, I'd leave."

"Surely you don't mean that!" Gertrude replied, but she feared she did.

Sister Gertrude approached Mother Lavinia in Marietta's behalf, but without success. "I wish I could explain, Sister, but there are confidences involved and a situation that makes the change necessary."

Although Lavinia wouldn't speak, Gertrude saw that the older sister was deeply distressed. She concluded, as Marietta had, that money was involved somehow. There was no point in begging further for a reversal. She would pursue the matter when Mother Charbonneau returned and, meanwhile, she'd counsel Marietta to accept the change with no external show of opposition.

Lavinia tried to soften the disappointment for Marietta. "We look to you, Sister Marietta, as Sister Sarah Dufrayne's successor as Director of Schools, not Paulina Soldano. Maintain your dignity, and believe me, Mother Charbonneau and all the sisters will credit you highly."

Sarah urged Marietta to be realistic about the education she would receive. It was equal to, if not superior to St. Mary's. Objectively, Marietta knew this to be true, but the disappointment never left her. The resentment remained and grew like a slow, deadly poison. No honor, and there were many, healed this infection of her spirit. Yet her surface demeanor was placid. She was not given to revealing her feelings. She wrote a brilliant Master's thesis on William Blake's "Songs of Innocence and Experience" and never once reflected that she had intimate knowledge of the invisible worm that gnawed the heart of the rose.

Part Seven

I

The ceremony in Rome was a colorful kaleidoscope of ritual and pageantry. Nowhere but inside the Vatican could the sounds and images of the Roman Catholic Church convey such a sense of history and authority. The dramatic red and white attire of the attending cardinals was reflected on polished marble floors. Beryl's simple habit was a contrast to Pope Leo XIII's velvet and ermine robes. The audience with the Holy Father was brief. He presented Beryl with documents that proclaimed her Congregation to be protected by the Holy See. The Sisters of Martha and Mary had come a long way from their temporary foundation in the Visitation Nuns' guest quarters. The audience of a few minutes confirmed and blessed the Congregation of Martha and Mary. After a few days of sightseeing under the guidance of the Jesuit college in Rome, the group from Seattle began the long journey home.

Constantia and Sister Mary Louise were enjoying a tour of Notre Dame Cathedral under the tutelage of Father Louis Bertram. Beryl asked to be excused until later in the afternoon, giving as her reason the quantity of correspondence from America that had been saved for them at the Jesuit novitiate in Paris.

Since Beryl had left Seattle, there had been very few hours that she could call her own. She had felt obligated to be companionable and particularly attentive to her mother on the voyage from New York. After they had docked at LeHavre, the accommodations Father Louis Bertram had arranged in religious communities and monasteries on their way to Rome invariably demanded stories of life in the "Wild West." When Beryl demurred, Sister

Mary Louise would urge still another story. "Mother, what about the time when…"

Now that she was on the way home, Beryl was impatient for the familiar and simple surroundings of the Congregation's convents. Alone in the room provided for her, she began to open her letters. She selected Lavinia's first, passing over two envelopes in Joseph's hand. She would save her dear boy's words like the wine at the wedding feast of Cana—the best for last.

Lavinia's letter appeared to be a long one, and she spread the pages out on the desk in front of her.

Dear Mother,

> *I am pleased to report that the Seattle elementary school was at full capacity just a week after your departure. Sister Sarah, who was with us for the first week in Lent, reports that the student body of twenty girls at the Portland High School will be increased to thirty-five in the coming year.*
>
> *As you remember, we had yet to name the school and the convent and you charged Sarah with the responsibility. She decided to sponsor an essay contest in which a name would be submitted, and in paragraph form the writer should clarify the reason for the name suggested. Mt. Hood School of Martha and Mary won. At first, neither the bishop nor the sisters approved. The bishop wanted the school to be named Our Lady of Perpetual Help. When Emily Peabody read her excellent essay, Mt. Hood School was accepted. She described the ascent to the peak of Catholic holiness through Catholic education and pointed out that the year round view of snow covered Mount Hood would be a reminder of this ideal. "A life devoted to God always points up to the summit," she wrote.*
>
> *Even the bishop was impressed. So much for the good news. Reluctantly, I was made aware of a situation which compelled to exercise the authority you granted me for the time you were overseas. Briefly, I made the decision to send Sister Paulina Soldano to St. Mary's and retain Sister Marietta at the Italian School…*

Beryl read Lavinia's account of the circumstances surrounding Mattie

Kate's vindictive sisters in law. She pondered the details with regret. No one should fault Lavinia; it was an unfortunate situation. *Would I have made the same decision?* she asked herself. *Probably not.* Whether or not there may have been another way, she would support Lavinia's judgment and give no indication of disapproval. Still, she wished Paulina could have been sent to the Territorial University and Marietta to St Mary's as planned. But where was there a sister to fill the post at Father Mercelli's parish? The Congregation was stretched to its limits. Her first priority upon reaching Seattle would be to reward Marietta for her obedience, notwithstanding the fact she had given it grudgingly, as Lavinia described in her letter.

The placement of sisters and other essential reorganization must be addressed before the next school year began. If, when their boat reached New York, Father Louis would escort Constantia to her new home in Georgetown, Beryl could leave New York and be in Seattle by August if she traveled by the railroad to San Francisco and then by sloop to Seattle. She wanted to see firsthand the progress of the three sisters who were establishing a charity health care station on Market Street in San Francisco. Beryl was apprehensive about this departure from the mandate of the Congregation to establish schools. However, she took seriously Sister Gertrude's concerns about the value of sisters trained to assume the care of the elderly of the community in the future.

Urged to rest by the Paris Jesuits after his months of travel, Father Louis Bertrand had advised that Beryl also plan to spend time with Constantia in her townhouse on the outskirts of Georgetown. This was also close enough to the Visitation Sisters' convent for extended conversations with Mother Eulalia. Before reading of the conflicts at home, Beryl had agreed. She also looked forward to a visit with Mother Aimee at the Baltimore Carmel. After reading Lavinia's letter, she determined that her concern for her Congregation must take precedence. She would write her regrets to the Visitation nuns and to Carmel.

There was another problem. Sister Mary Louise was unwell. She had lost weight, and coughed with alarming regularity. It was Beryl's intention to let her stay with the Sisters of Saint Joseph, whose Motherhouse was near New York until she was strong enough to return west. The St. Joseph order rotated their sisters from east to west, so there would be no question about an unescorted trip home. Who would be her own companion? She had already decided upon a perfect solution to that matter.

Father Louis Bertrand was neither pleased by nor supportive of Beryl's intention to forego visits in the east in lieu of returning home early. Beryl was at a loss to understand his refusal to accept her serious obligations to the order the Pope had so recently blessed. Constantia was both distressed and angry at Beryl's change of plans. Her complaints were tearful and persistent.

"Maman," Beryl cried after a particularly bitter tirade from her mother, "How can you be lonely when you are surrounded by such a loving family?"

Constantia lived within a short carriage ride of Yvonne and Evangeline, and almost as close to Pierre and Phillipe. A dozen grandchildren took turns visiting their grandmere.

Constantia made use of her scented handkerchief, delicately blowing her nose. "Father Louis promised that you would remain with me as you begin the restoration of the school the Madams of the Sacred Heart abandoned during the war!"

Beryl was speechless. She knew that her spiritual father had been considering a post at Catholic University, which puzzled Beryl, since his heart was so devoted to the schools in the west. Catholic University was close to what had been the Madams' exclusive finishing school. The nuns' proximity to the University, plus their reputation for academic excellence had caused some Catholics to call them "female Jesuits." The term was, in most cases, a compliment. Closing the school had left the region without its most honored facility. It would be a challenge and an honor to rebuild their school, and to continue the institution which placed an emphasis on classical education rather than the manners of the socially elite. But for the Sisters of Martha and Mary, such a task would be ten, even twenty years in the future. Father was being manipulative. Beryl would not be pressured into a premature venture. Thank Heaven for Constantia! She had opened an otherwise tightly closed bag so the cat could creep out. Beryl would deal with this situation with tact and compassion. And firmly.

If Father Louis Bertrand was distressed that his secret plan was exposed, he concealed his displeasure. Instead, he told Beryl that he had renewed his commitment to developing Gonzaga College in Spokane as a major Jesuit institution. Relieved, Beryl prepared for departure from Paris and for the voyage home. Her lips would be sealed regarding the failed plan for the Madams' school. What hay Lizzie would make if Beryl let the sun shine on that scheme!

Although Joseph had nothing to do with her unwillingness to strain the resources of her Congregation, Joseph was at the heart of all her decisions. Did Father Louis Bertrand guess how profoundly she missed Joseph in this long journey abroad? Beryl tried to suppress the suspicion that Father Louis Bertrand had been contemplating a means of separating her from "her Indian." Before leaving Paris she had written to Joseph suggesting that he read John Donne's *A Valediction Forbidding Mourning.*

> *I know that Douglas introduced you to Seventeenth Century poets. Do you remember an essay you wrote as you began your University classes? I believe your title was "No Man Is an Island," a reference to John Donne. Read the stanzas that refer to the compass image in Valediction.*
>
> *You and I are like the twin compasses. "Thy soul the fixed foot, makes no show/ to move, but*
> *doth, if the other do." I hold one compass and you the other. They will always bring us home.*

II

Beryl's boat from Northampton docked in New York. The usual crowds huddled on the pier to welcome friends and relatives home. Immigrants had been separated and ferried to Ellis Island. Beryl scanned the crowd until she spotted Elizabeth Ordway, who was waving frantically. It was, of course, easier for Lizzie to spot the nun than for Beryl to locate her. The friends were reunited on the pier where Beryl saw that Lizzie was supervising several stewards who were hauling five oversized steamer trunks on board a boat bound for Panama and the west coast of America. The trunks would go to Seattle by boat while Beryl and Lizzie braved the rail route.

"Lizzie, dear friend! Does this mean what I think it does?" Beryl asked inclining her head toward the trunks.

"Good guess. Yes, I'm western bound and may God have mercy on fools and suffragettes."

When Lizzie had received the letter Beryl sent from Paris asking if she would accompany her to Seattle on the newly completed railroad, she decided to return to Seattle permanently. Two years in San Francisco's foggy climate had depressed her usually indomitable spirit. She had returned to the family home in Lowell, Massachusetts, but once there she found it impossible to forget the West. The mountains, the beautiful Puget Sound, and the friends she had made haunted her. She seized the opportunity to be Beryl's companion on her early return from Europe and packed her trunks.

Father Louis Bertrand had agreed to deliver Constantia safely home to Georgetown. Beryl sensed that he was unusually quiet and commented to

Lizzie when she described their parting that she hoped he was not unwell. Lizzie gave an innocuous smile and brushed off Beryl's concerns. Privately, she judged that the man was annoyed with Beryl's independent decision. The Jesuit's moods were crystal clear to Lizzie. Anything or anyone who interfered with his exclusive time with Beryl Charbonneau suffered his displeasure.

III

Beryl and Lizzie stood on the deck of the *Windjammer* as the boat docked at its Elliot Bay berth. They could see the group of welcomers waiting to greet them. Sisters Lavinia and Sarah stood with a group from the Seattle convents. Asa Mercer, Captain Lilly, Henry Yesler and Justice Green were on hand to meet both Lizzie and Beryl. Then Beryl saw Joseph. He was standing a little aside from the men, a nosegay of daisies in his hand. She felt a wave of relief. The few days of delay during the crossing might have meant that Joseph and Mai Ling could have departed for the exhibition of Joseph's sculptures in San Francisco.

The sisters surrounded their Mother Charbonneau as she descended the gangplank. Joseph stood back, patient for his turn, knowing that his "mother" should not greet him first. When his turn came, he extended his arms, still holding the daisies. Beryl put down her valise and returned the embrace spontaneously.

"You're home and safe," Joseph whispered.

As they embraced, Beryl was shocked by her reaction to their closeness. She experienced a physical sensation that throbbed through her body. She drew back, stunned speechless. Stepping away seemed to have no other significance than an expression of friendship and gratitude for the nosegay. To any of the welcoming party the moment was perceived as innocent and appropriate. Even Lizzie, well known for her cool reticence regarding any outward display of emotion, accepted the hugs of the sisters and handshakes of the men. But the intensity of Beryl's brief encounter with Joseph, and its evidence of physical desire shocked Beryl, she who presented herself to the world as a virgin clothed with the vows of chastity.

Before they made their way to the convent carriage, Lavinia, her voice barely audible, asked Gertrude if Beryl seemed depressed. "She's unusually quiet."

"Heavens no! Think of the long journey, not to mention the stress of honors and the challenges for the future!"

Lizzie was welcomed by Captain and Mrs. Lilly, who had invited her to be their guest until she found accommodations of her own. She said a quick goodbye to her friend before Beryl's sisters escorted her to their waiting carriage. At the convent, Beryl smiled mechanically and answered the many questions from her community. As soon as she could, she excused herself for the night promising to tell the full story of the momentous trip when she had had a good sleep, and the community was gathered for her welcome home celebration.

Alone in her office/bedroom at last, Beryl stood by the window and pulled the curtain aside so she could see the convent garden two stories below, From this location she could also see the great Mount Rainier. As if keeping vigil, Beryl watched the magnificent peak that dominated the southern sky as it faded into the night.

"Oh, Father in Heaven," she whispered to the stars that had begun to appear, "If you had made me a saint, I would confess my weakness and separate myself from the occasion of sin." Slowly, as there was no other way to fall to her knees without experiencing pain in her back, Beryl knelt. She covered her face with her hands, the face the world saw with veil and wimple: the symbols of consecrated virginity. Slowly she removed the hands and raised her head. "Have I sinned?" she asked aloud. There had been no sufficient reflection; no evil intent. She must not rush to self-accusation, seeking the confessional and God knew who to hear her! She wouldn't risk confessing this incident even to Father Louis. Understanding of her failings as he had always been, in this matter he would recommend a penance which would mean sacrificing all association with Joseph. Not to see her Joseph? Not to know the warmth of his affection and share in the images of his art? No. She could not bear such cruel deprivation.

Beryl rose from her knees and paced the room. She must confront her feelings and mete out such punishment as they deserved herself. She was a woman. Hidden under the folds of her religious habit, she was a woman. Not one of beauty, but tall, awkward, aging and plain. Hardly the image of a seductress. She had, for one shocking instant, lost control. The sheer force of her response to Joseph's innocent embrace had shaken her. Was it a temptation sent by the Father of Lies? If so, what she had experienced came with the swiftness of a totally unexpected attack. From her first days in the monastery so many years ago, she had been lectured about purity. She had tired of the preoccupation religious superiors and many priests entertained regarding chastity. "Beware of 'special friendships,'" they had repeated ad nauseam to the novices. Well, she didn't accept most of that. But then she had never been confronted with her own frailty. *Why now?* she thought. She conjured the image of her first mare whose sudden reaction to a bee sting in its ear would have sent her flying from its back if she hadn't had her heels well down in the stirrups. She had been taught to be ready and alert, prepared for the slightest signal of a "spook." She smiled. "Wait, Joseph, my dear love, don't hug me until my heels are well down!"

IV

Beryl's return from Rome was an occasion to celebrate in every convent of their Congregation. She brought certificates from Pope Leo XIII for each sister, and gifts of medals blessed by the Holy Father. On their way to his San Francisco exhibit, Joseph and Mai Ling came to the Seattle convent to say goodbye. Mai Ling was overwhelmed by the celebration in progress. "Perhaps we shouldn't have intruded on this occasion," she had said to Beryl.

"Joseph knows us better than that, my dear."

"What may we bring you from San Francisco, Mother?" Joseph asked.

"Do bolts of silk come to the Chinese settlement from the Orient?"

"I believe so."

"Then bring us back a length of fine silk that we may use to make a vestment. One of our sisters in the infirmary is confined to a wheel chair, but she does beautiful embroidery. It would give her great pleasure to work on a lovely piece of silk." She accompanied them to the door where their carriage waited and was prepared to accept his brief hug. *Heels are well down,* she thought to herself.

* * * * *

All the Congregation's sisters from the Seattle and Tacoma area had gathered for the homecoming. Mattie Kate, insisting upon anonymity, had sent cooks and servers to the church hall on Denny Hill providing food and caterers for the event. Adam had been her delivery man. The local sisters had decorated tables. There was a head table with place markers for Father Cataldo, Father Brouillet, Father Mercelli, the local pastor, and Mother Charbonneau herself. Other guests included Lizzie Ordway, Captain and Mrs. Lilly, and Henry Yesler and Asa Mercer.

Lizzie had brought a profusion of dahlias from her gardens on Bainbridge Island. In her absence, the tubers had gone wild and multiplied. Blooms graced banquet tables with splashes of yellow, pink, red, and white set off by deep green wild blueberry leaves.

Sisters Sarah Dufrayne and Lavinia came into the hall looking for the redoubtable Miss Ordway. They took her aside purposefully.

"We'd appreciate some advice," Sister Sarah said, her eyes on the door.

"It's a private matter. Somewhat, shall we say, 'political' in nature," Lavinia added. "You are experienced in matters of voting and elections."

"Not as much as I'd like to be. But I have submitted my name for superintendent of the Kitsap School District. The Seattle *Post Intelligencer* has already said it must be a joke!"

The day after Lizzie and Beryl returned to Seattle, Lizzie had placed her name on the ballot for superintendent of schools in Kitsap County. She immediately faced the ridicule that had driven her away five years before. "It's simply the misinformed opinion of a male dominated newspaper!" she had said when she read a reporter's words in the new Seattle *Post Intelligencer*:

> *It may be a good joke to put a woman in nomination, but I do not regard the office of school superintendent of so little importance as to vote for a woman at the polls.*

"We would vote for you if we could," Sarah said. "We will at least pray!"

"We do have the power to vote for our Mother General—the first official superior since our Congregation was blessed by the Holy Father."

"Beryl," I would assume, Lizzie interrupted Lavinia, thinking at the same time how she disliked terms such as 'Holy Father.' If she thought the Northwest was male dominated, it was nothing in comparison with the Roman Catholic Church.

"That's the problem," Sarah said. "Mother has told the community that someone else should take over now that her pioneer work is done."

"Typical of her," Lizzie remarked. "And extraordinarily silly at this time. She's not ill, is she?" Lizzie asked, concerned. The two sisters denied the possibility in unison. "Then your community has the power, vote for her!"

"She doesn't even want her name placed on the ballot!" Sarah said.

"We were thinking of circulating a petition and presenting Mother with our overwhelming support," Lavinia added.

Lizzie frowned and rearranged a flower bowl as she pondered the situation. "No matter how well Beryl is appreciated, the community has grown, and it's just possible that not every one of your sisters may want to sign such a petition. Some may sign with reluctance because they don't want their names to be conspicuously absent. No, you must be more subtle."

"But how?" Lavinia asked.

"Who is likely to be elected if Beryl is not?"

Lavinia," Sarah said firmly.

"Unfortunately," Lavinia agreed. "And I have no desire for the honor."

"Then it is up to you to encourage the sisters to retain Beryl. Are there nominees?"

"Yes," Sarah said. "We circulated ballots for nominations and picked the top two. The sisters were asked to leave Mother Charbonneau's name off. They have placed myself and Sister Marietta on the ballot."

"Sister Marietta. The sister at the Territorial University?" As they nodded, Lizzie resisted the impulse to roll her eyes. She'd met that one at school planning committees. She thought of the Indian maxim, 'speaking with forked tongue.' "Is this a secret ballot?" she asked, and when they affirmed that it was, she concluded, "Then have a blank line after the two names for a write in vote. It will be an opportunity for sisters to speak their mind with privacy and voluntarily. If there is an overwhelming majority of votes for Beryl, she won't refuse. Now it is up to you, Sister Lavinia, to spread the word that this is your choice."

Other sisters were entering the hall and the group concluded its conspiratorial conversation. Both sisters whispered their thanks to Lizzie.

The banquet was memorable. Roasted lamb and fresh raised rolls, together with an assortment of vegetables in succulent sauces. Mattie Kate had seen to it that there was nothing "Italian" in the cuisine which might have revealed the identity of the caterer.

After dinner, Beryl told the sisters that when the new Gonzaga College was built, the sisters were to occupy the building that had been its temporary school in Spokane. "And there is more for us to consider," Beryl said to the group. "The Bishop of Montana has requested that we open the high school academy this year, even if we are not ready to staff the college. I have assured the Bishop that if our current novices and the twenty who are entering in the autumn persevere, we will be happy to accept." There was applause. "As we grow, we must consider our need for a permanent Motherhouse. I commend this intention to your prayers. God will guide us and show us where and when."

Lizzie listened to her friend and wondered how in Heaven's name this Beryl Charbonneau could be so naively unaware of her vital importance to the community at this time. She had been chugging along on an uphill track, and had reached the first summit. But the way ahead was not all level. Beryl's leadership was crucial during these developing years. She found herself praying that God would inspire the sisters to write in her name. *What a Tom fool thing to ask*, she chided herself. Lizzie believed in an omnipotent Creator, but she didn't believe in bothering the Master of the Universe with piddling details.

Whatever power, human or divine, inspired the Congregation of Martha and Mary in the election, there was unanimity in the community, and Mother Beryl Charbonneau accepted the office of the Congregation's first official Mother General. She had suffered Lizzie's lecture in regard to the important years of development. Sometime later, when they were alone, Beryl had looked at her friend with a penetrating scrutiny. "I must be losing my good memory," she said to Lizzie.

"In what way?" Lizzie demanded, falling into Beryl's trap.

"I didn't recall that you had been appointed Mother General over the Mother General. Whatever inspired the Holy Father to give such power to a Protestant—perhaps the fact that you won the office of Superintendent of Kitsap Schools by a significant margin?" Lizzie had won, 244 votes to 165.

"You know very well that I cheated," Lizzie said wryly. "I listed my name as 'E. Ordway' so as not to draw attention to my being a woman! Enough men were stupid enough not to question the initials, and it served them right! But you know that there was no such subterfuge in your election. You are needed by your Congregation, and they had the sense to realize it."

Beryl wrote a long letter to Father Louis Bertram before the elections. Father Louis had responded:

> *You shall take up your cross and follow what your Lord asks*
> *of you.*

Beryl hadn't needed her spiritual Father's words, nor Lizzie Ordway's admonitions to tell her the obvious. She had known Lavinia's mind. This good sister had no desire for the burden of leadership. The incident with Paulina's relatives brought that clearly home to her, and Sister was still agonizing over the consequences of her decision to exchange Paulina and Marietta.

Gertrude Oldfield, one of the original five, had been of invaluable service to the community as both teacher and nurse. Beryl had taken her from full time classroom duties and appointed her a traveling health care supervisor. Gertrude instructed the sisters regarding the teaching of hygiene and made them aware of the early symptoms of contagious diseases. She tested students' eyesight, hearing and physical fitness, and visited parents when there were serious health concerns. Gertrude was an asset to the community and well loved by its sisters.

It was Gertrude who had approached Beryl to put before her a problem that might arise in the future. Where would the community care for its aging or infirm sisters? Individual houses could care for occasional illnesses, but as the community grew, inevitably there would be aging sisters and those who with various complaints could not care for themselves.

"We do need a Motherhouse," Beryl told Gertrude. "Had you approached me before we had accepted the Bishop of Montana, we might have been able to redirect our efforts to this important cause. Now it will be foremost in our prayers and plans."

Beryl had acted on Gertrude's advice by establishing the experimental group in San Francisco. The three sisters there were working for a degree in nursing, as well as providing health car and education for the underprivileged near their convent.

Unlike her sisters in other pioneer communities, Beryl did not want to continue to approach the people in the little towns begging for funds to finance any Congregation project. Mother Joseph had done this with success, and the Dominican Sisters from Newburgh, New York, were now following the same pattern in towns south of Olympia. She supported their efforts, which in the case of the Dominicans, were for funds to build hospitals. But Beryl could not bring herself to beg money for a Motherhouse, in spite of the need.

Beryl asked a Jesuit colleague to be retreat master for their ten days of spiritual renewal, and for the theme she chose St. Teresa of Avila's words:

To give Our Lord a perfect hospitality, Mary and Martha must combine.

The Jesuit had delighted the sisters with an anecdote about the great saint and her wonderfully balanced view of the spiritual life. He told them of the time that Teresa was served a fine dinner of roast partridge which she began to eat with unbridled enjoyment. Someone admonished her saying that such gusto in eating was not in keeping with her life as a nun. Saint Teresa had responded, "When it's prayer time, pray; when it's partridge time, partridge!"

Mother Charbonneau's nuns had laughed, some so heartily that tears rolled down their cheeks. Beryl noted that Marietta was not moved to mirth. *Perhaps*, Beryl thought, *she is distracted by concerns for the newly formed school for young ladies in Montana.*

After consultation with the local bishop, the Congregation had decided to add two years of college, making the secondary school a six year program. They would progress from there. *And*, Beryl thought with some regret, *Marietta is still unhappy that she was forced to accept Sister Paulina as a faculty member*. Her opposition was illogical, as Beryl had told her firmly. Whatever personal complaints she had because of Paulina's degree from Saint Mary's must be put aside for the good of the school and the community. Marietta had complied, but not graciously. It puzzled Beryl that this sister, so well honored by the University and so respected in the ranks of her sisters, could bear a grudge for so long.

V

The Congregation welcomed a visit from Father Louis Bertrand. As he said Mass for the sisters, Beryl noted that he looked tired. He was not aging well. After Mass she walked with him in the convent garden.

She scrutinized her friend's expression, and it came to her that it was not any physical infirmity that brought this strained look to Louis Bertrand. If there were something troubling his mind, perhaps he would confide in her.

Beryl was correct. Father Louis Bertrand suffered, but it was not a matter of mind. It was one of heart. Beryl Charbonneau was never out of his thoughts. She invaded his heart and soul like a cancer in his body and with an equally deadly effect. He wanted to be near her desperately, but in her presence, the resentment of her joy in comparison to his torment compelled him to withdraw. When he was miles away, he longed for her letters, but when they came, he was more despondent over her ignorance of his love. In spiritual terms he was lost in the dark night of the soul.

It required all his strength of will to maintain the appearance of spiritual strength and tranquility as the Congregation's confessor. It was as much for Beryl's sake as for her community. When he received the invitation to say a Mass in honor of her most recent election, he doubted that he could accomplish the task, especially with Beryl in such close proximity. And there was no one to whom he could go for help. He tried confessing to one of the older Jesuits in Spokane, but he was berated in an appalling manner with no gram of pity. Instead of hearing the words of absolution, the priest had slammed the confessional screen in the penitent's face.

Louis Bertrand walked with Beryl, his head down, and his senses overwhelmed by his interior agony. She had touched his arm, and he drew back from her as if he had been burned.

"Father!" It was an exclamation of concern. "Are you unwell?"

He did not dare to look at her. "Yes, but not in any way that could be helped by a physician."

"May I help?"

He laughed bitterly. "No, I think not." His eyes were still averted.

"Would you rather be alone?"

He took a deep breath. "No. Continue to walk with me, Beryl, and pray with me, but let us keep silence."

Obediently Beryl walked beside him.

Somehow her presence within the embrace of silent prayer eased his pain. This was how it must be. What if he spoke? The years between them were no longer significant. Suppose she shared his feelings? Yes, she understood such feelings of devotion, but her heart's love was for an Indian who was as much her own as if she had conceived him. If he spoke, if he told Beryl how deeply he was suffering, no good would come of it. He might blurt out that he hated Joseph for the claim he had in her heart. It would be an unbearable burden upon her, and it was not his right to place such a heavy cross on her shoulders.

"I have decided to take a leave of absence from the Order," he heard himself say. "There is a community of Benedictines, Trappists, in France, and I intend to live with them for at least a year." *Or however long it takes to purge this cancer from my soul.*

"I had no idea, Father. But I can understand your need. Many times during these last years I have felt my spiritual strength slipping away, and I've longed for just a month in Carmel."

Louis Bertrand just nodded. The idea had been germinating in his mind, but it took form when he spoke the words to Beryl. And she had blessed his intention. He would go as soon as he could obtain permission from his superiors.

Before new appointments, Sarah Dufrayne, director of the Congregation's schools. asked Beryl to let her step down. "We need women like Marietta in administrative positions," she said.

Beryl questioned the wisdom of placing Marietta in a position of power. Before Father Louis returned to Spokane, Beryl confided in him.

"It's Marietta, Father." She told him the story of her having to give up St. Mary's.

"So now your two most highly educated sisters, Marietta and Paulina, have completed their degrees and the position of Director of Schools is the prize. You don't have to let Sarah resign."

"That would not change my problem; it would only delay facing it."

"Paulina is of your mind. Marietta is not."

"I know. But if I give Marietta just recognition of her achievements, she may be a happier member of the Congregation."

"So, in essence, you'll reward her for being a voice of opposition and hope she will have a change of heart? That has another name: bribery. It will lead to a community war."

"And what kind of a war will I have if she isn't rewarded?" Beryl argued.

Father Louis sighed deeply. "She doesn't value her position as chairman of the new school in Montana? She will ultimately be dean of the future college. Perhaps she would be happier in one of the older orders she admires so much."

"She knows full well that our spirit of singularity gave her the academic honors she enjoys today."

"Yes. Ironic, isn't it? Pray about this, Beryl, then make a decision. However, prepare yourself for disappointment. I don't believe any honors will silence Marietta's personal bitterness."

Marietta had not expected to be given any administrative position in the community. She accepted the Directorship of Education with a return to the feeling of awe and respect that had first inspired her to be a part of Beryl Charbonneau's congregation. This honor would mean more work for her since she would have to continue in her appointment at the Montana school. Hard work did not concern her. This was an opportunity to make herself known to the entire teaching community, and through this directorship she might eventually be a candidate for Mother General. She understood at last that it was not Lavinia, nor Mother Charbonneau who had deprived her of St. Mary's. Paulina herself should have deferred to Marietta's seniority. She focused blame entirely on her.

Part Eight

I
A Tragedy for Seattle
1889

Joseph had made his mark on the fine arts community of San Francisco. He and Mai Ling had not planned a prolonged stay in the City by the Golden Gate, but it was five years before they returned to Seattle. On her inspections of California convents, Beryl visited Joseph, and she was well content to see him honored and, more important, happy. Since their marriage, Mai Ling had given birth to three children in succession: Su Ping, a girl, and Lee, her brother, fraternal twins. They were followed by Sung Chow, now four years old. Mai Ling loved San Francisco, but her parents remained in Seattle, unwilling to leave the restaurant that was the symbol of their success in America. Joseph was planning to complete a body of work intended for exhibition in France. He judged it would be at least six years before he was ready to accept the invitation. The French were patient, especially with artistic genius. They had not imposed a deadline.

Since Mai Ling's family was in Seattle, Joseph had hoped his wife would consider remaining in the north. He judged that in Seattle he would have the solitude necessary for his sculpting, and he would be closer to Beryl. It was a surprise that Mai Ling's parents informed them that they had resolved to let Chang have the restaurant. They would move south. It would be cruel, he knew, to separate Mai Ling from her parents now, and the Congregation's business let his Mother travel to the Bay Area.

Joseph and Beryl sat in the Seattle convent garden. "Somewhere, deep within me, there were dreams to be carved, and many are yet to be created. The Paris showing is in the future, but already the images are crowding to my consciousness demanding expression!"

Joseph's hands were on a burlap covered package he had placed on the garden picnic table. They sat under the shade of the maple trees Joseph had planted in the back of the property many years before when Lizzie deeded her property to the Congregation. It was a warm June day, and birds sang from their perches on the ivy covered stone wall that separated the convent yard from the street outside. The road had become a thoroughfare for wagons and carriages from the hill to town. Seattle's population had grown to eighty six thousand since Beryl had arrived in the west. There were twenty five blocks to the main downtown area, and the city showed every promise of continuing to thrive.

Joseph pushed his gift to Beryl across the cedar table. She untied the string that secured the covering and unwrapped a carving that had been worked on a long piece of ebony.

"Mai Ling's father had this wood sent to me from China," Joseph told her. "I have wanted to bring it to you for some time, but this was my first opportunity to travel north."

Beryl found a representation in bas relief of the beginning of her Congregation. Carved figures flowed with harmony of form and detail. There was the great mountain, the ship that had brought the first sisters of Martha and Mary in the foreground. In front of them, wonderfully chiseled and detailed, was a perfect portrait of herself, and back from the group, smaller in perspective, was Father Louis Bertram. The design of figures gave way to the Seattle waterfront and then to the hills beyond. In Joseph's vision, the denuded landscape surrounding the city was transformed into a wilderness setting. Among great trees was a wolf and, in the sky, seeming to come right out of the work itself, was an eagle, wings spread. A waterfall flowed through the forest into Puget Sound itself.

"This is earth, and your time on it," Joseph explained pointing to the group of sisters. He moved his finger to the wilderness. "And this is the Great Spirit Land beyond. From here the waters of life flow to nourish the earth. I am the wolf, and you are the Eagle. You live in the earth and at the same time your spirit flies in the sky of the Eternal Lands."

Never in her life had Beryl been so moved by a gift. It was not just the emotion inspired by the deep sentiment of her love and friendship, she experienced awe in the face of genius. She met Joseph's eyes, unable to speak.

"I knew it would please you," Joseph said, reaching for her hand.

"Please me!" she whispered. "I have no words." She pressed Joseph's hand in hers without fear of the love that flooded her heart.

II

Joseph and Mai Ling were present when one of Joseph's most celebrated works was presented to Justice Green. It was a representation of the attempted deportation of the Chinese. The bas relief sculpture in the form of a mural would hang in the new federal government building.

Beryl attended the presentation dinner, which was hosted by Captain and Mrs. Lilly. It was an eclectic gathering. Joseph Wolf's lovely wife sat next to Justice Green; Justice Green's wife was positioned next to Joseph; Beryl sat to Captain Lilly's left, while Lizzie was at Mrs. Lilly's left. Other guests included the editor of the Seattle *Post Intelligencer*, Harvey Cox, who had long since acknowledged that a woman could fulfill the position of a school director. Henry Yesler was present with Minnie Gogle, a young cousin fifty six years his junior, to whom Yesler was rumored to be engaged to marry.

Lizzie, unfailingly courteous, looked across at what she thought to be a mere child with an aged grandfather, and she grieved anew for Sarah Yesler, who had died two years before. Lizzie and Sarah had been deeply involved in the women's suffrage cause, and Lizzie had been a frequent guest at the forty room Yesler mansion which took up an entire city block on James and Jefferson Streets.

The Lilly dining room was a long room with wood panels decorated with patterned wallpaper within each framed oblong panel. Candles in each panel supplied soft light, and there was a chandelier of a hundred more candles above the long table. The table and chairs stood on a thick Persian carpet. The sideboard held a silver service, bottles of wine, and more candles. The chairs were of mahogany wood and well upholstered. The table was likely of the same fine wood, but it was covered with a superbly ironed linen cloth with lace inlays. The silverware gleamed, heavy with a rose pattern. Beryl appreciated the beauty of the atmosphere; she had been born to such luxury, although the Charbonneau home decor was understated. This room's sumptuous decor stopped just short of ostentation.

One of Joseph's early creations, a larger than life free standing piece, "Air to Sea" was on display in the entry hall by the dining area. It was a rendition of whale, deer, and hawk, and had not been greatly appreciated until Captain Lilly saw it. "Joseph is far ahead of his time," he had said when he purchased the piece.

They were served several courses, beginning with soup and a light wine. There was roast beef with the Yorkshire pudding favored by Captain Lilly and the other men at the table. Several kinds of potatoes, buttered asparagus fresh from the Lilly's own garden, and condiments accompanied the meat. The conversation was relaxed and Beryl found the captain well informed and sincerely curious about her several communities, especially the college for young ladies in Montana. Yesler's young companion who sat on her other side was equally interested. Beryl found her intelligent conversation a pleasant surprise.

No one around the table sensed that the sound of distant commotion in town signaled Seattle's greatest disaster. In the Lilly home, following dinner conversation, there were the compliments called for by good etiquette. "You have outdone yourself, Melissa," Lizzie said to her hostess. "I've heard that this pie is your own creation."

"Yes. It's made of dates and pecans. The Captain has a friend who brings us fresh dates and nut meat from California." She herself had mixed the dates and nuts in a caramelized sauce. The pie was topped with rich whipped cream.

The Lilly butler approached his employer quietly.

The captain rose and tapped his wine glass with a spoon. "Everyone, we will delay our coffee. Arthur tells me there is a fire downtown."

Joseph and his wife were immediately concerned about their children who had been in Chang's care. It was possible that one or more of them may have accompanied Chang to downtown Seattle when he went for supplies. Everyone moved to Captain Lilly's wide front terrace. From their vantage point they saw smoke gathering at the corner of First and Madison.

"It could be any of several buildings," Lilly said, peering down the hill.

"All that sawdust on Ziba's Hardware Store floor," muttered Henry Yesler, who was more correct than he knew.

"They should bring it under control easily," Mrs. Lilly said. "Shall we return to our coffee?"

"If you would excuse us, Mrs. Lilly," Joseph said, "Mai Ling and I are concerned about our children."

"Oh, must you leave?" Mrs. Lilly asked.

Mai Ling nodded, but Joseph spoke for them. "I do apologize to you and your guests, but it would relieve our minds to know that Chang has returned safely from town."

The remainder of the guests decided to take their coffee out onto the terrace where they could watch the smoke, which had not abated.

"I can see flames now," Lizzie said to Beryl and those within hearing.

"It's definitely spreading," Yesler said.

"If you'll excuse me, dear lady," Harvey Cox said. "I think this is a story I should not leave to some junior on staff."

"We understand. By all means do discover the extent of the blaze," the captain said.

No one in the group lived where their homes were threatened, although Beryl worried about Mattie Kate's establishment. Surely the fire would be put out before it reached that far down the street. But within another half hour it was clear that the conflagration was not going to be stopped. There was silence on the terrace. The smell of smoke had reached the top of this hill, and the horses waiting with the guests' carriages were agitated. The captain's gelding was saddled by his gate when he had ridden to the docks with a mount for Justice Green when he met the boat from Kitsap County. Lilly gave orders to have the grooms take the carriages to the back of the house.

"My God!" Justice Green squinted through what was now unpleasantly acrid air, obscuring the view. "I believe the flames are eating up the town!"

The Lilly's guests did not have time to react, as a wagon pulled by a frightened and sweat covered horse reeled up the hill. "It's Chang!" Beryl cried. "With his children!"

The captain bolted down the steps and grabbed the horse's lead. Chang sat forward, exhausted. His girl, Su Lee, stood in the back of the wagon howling. Beryl rushed to her and lifted her out, holding her close. Through her tears she sobbed, "Fall out! Sung Chow fall out! He out!"

Chang straightened immediately. "Where, girlee? Where?" he demanded.

The child could only sob "He fall out!"

Beryl took a look at Chang's horse. That one would never go back down the hill. It was suicide to try. The other carriages had been taken to the back. Only Captain Lilly's hunter stood, nervous, but calmer than the other horses had been. Beryl wasted no time. She untied the reins, and with a deft movement put her foot in the stirrup and mounted the horse. She gathered the reins, made a quick circle, and impelled it down the hill toward the town while the dinner guests stood too astonished to speak. Even after Beryl had galloped away, all Yesler could say was "My God!"

Beryl pressed her knees into the horse's sides and kept the feel of its mouth on the reins. The horse recognized the mastery of its rider, and did as it was bade. Beryl didn't allow herself to think how long it had been since she had been on a horse. She willed herself to ride. At the bottom of the hill, a crowd was gathered, but they separated at the sound of hooves. They were awe struck at the vision that came toward them. Beryl, astride, reined in to question them.

"The boy—a child four or five, Chinese! He was in a wagon! Does anyone have him?" No one in the crowd had seen a child, certainly not a Chinese child.

"I saw a wagon driven by a China man, Sister!" someone cried. "There were two children in the wagon."

"It came from over there!" someone else offered. "Just before that building collapsed and blocked the way!"

Beryl surveyed the obstacle. Without further word she headed toward it. Taking the reins with one hand and ripping the belt from her tunic with the other, she headed the horse, which was a well built hunter type, toward the wreckage. *Dear God, I hope Lilly has jumped this animal!* Just before she reached the barricade, which was black and smoking, she used the belt against her mount's rear. He jumped without hesitation. There was burning wreckage on either side of the street and heavy smoke. Two blocks ahead Beryl spotted a crumpled figure in the middle of the road huddled against the streetcar tracks that went the length of First Avenue. He was moving, but dazed. Beryl pulled the horse to a halt, and shouted to the boy. "Sung Chow!"

He sat up. Beryl leaned over. "Take my hand!" She had to repeat the words before he complied. Grabbing his wrist, she hauled him up in front of her so that he faced her, his little legs astride over the English saddle. "Hang on to me, tight," she ordered. He clung to her, but he was disoriented. She would have to ride back the way she came, but now more beams had fallen onto the path. She could avoid the first by riding near one building, but it was dangerously close to flames. She prayed the horse would continue to obey her. She skirted the first obstacle, but there were two more barriers in front of her before she would reach safety. She judged it to be a double jump similar to those she had ridden in her youth at horse fairs. But did this horse know about clearing two obstacles? No time to ponder its skills. The child was clinging more tightly now which was good for she would need one firm hand controlling the horse's head and another to use the belt if need be. She headed toward the barricade, but she sensed her mount's back stiffening. She would not risk a balk. She rode back and turned him in a few tight circles then aimed straight for the debris. She pressed her legs against his belly and gave him a whack with the belt just before the first wreckage. He cleared it and bounded for the street over the second barrier on his own impulse. The crowd scattered and cheered.

"As God is my witness, Sister, I've never seen a finer piece of riding!" one man shouted.

Other expressions of praise followed, but Beryl headed directly back up the hill to the Yesler mansion at a steady trot. Captain Lilly's horse was in good shape, but he was covered with foamy sweat. Lilly and the others had come halfway down the hill to meet them, followed by Joseph and Mai Ling. At the restaurant they had discovered that only one of the children, Sung Chow, had ridden to town with Chang and Chang's daughter Su Lee. They rushed to meet Beryl, who clutched Sung Chow tightly to her breast.

Joseph took his son from her and looked up at Beryl with infinite gratitude. Beryl dismounted and tied her belt around her habit's tunic. She was certain she looked a fright, but she was more concerned with the horse. She gave him a swift once over and said to Lilly. "Please forgive me. I had to act swiftly."

"You are an amazing woman," was all he could say.

Lizzie appeared at her side with a damp cloth. Soot had darkened Beryl's face. "You'll have one hell of a time stopping this escapade from appearing in the history books!" Lizzie whispered, and hugged her friend, kissing her cheek in a spontaneous gesture of relief uncharacteristic of the dignified Elizabeth Ordway.

The flames were still sweeping through the town. At least twenty five blocks had been destroyed, including the Rainbow Trout Saloon. When the facts began to unfold and the complete catalog of the day revealed, there were stories of heroism and loss. Matilda Katherine Perkins had gone back into the flames attempting to rescue one of her girls, and horrified spectators had seen the building collapse before she could have reached the stairs. Mercifully there were comparatively few casualties, but the town was a smoldering ruin.

Beryl sent a telegram to the Bishop of Montana and asked him to notify Sister Paulina of her mother's death and to request that she return to Seattle immediately. Beryl had a frustrating conversation with Father Mercelli, who refused to say a funeral Mass or give Catholic burial to "the fallen woman" who was also a "fallen away Catholic."

"How do we know, Father, that Mattie Kate had not confessed that very afternoon? Can you not give her the benefit of the doubt?"

"It would have been unlikely," he said coldly.

She appealed to a Methodist minister and also to the minister of the new Baptist Church. If anything, they were more adamant than Father Mercelli had been. Lizzie Ordway was incensed at the narrow-mindedness. "Mattie Kate shall have my plot on Bainbridge," she said emphatically.

Lizzie arranged for a service in Kitsap where the clergy was not privy to Mattie Kate's reputation. Hundreds of mourners came by boat to pay their respects, Sisters from the Congregation, Beryl and Paulina among them.

* * * * *

Beryl watched as Joseph set the panel he had given Beryl into the entryway of the convent chapel. He was to return to California the next day, but he would not allow the sculpture to be installed by anyone but himself. Also, it was a good excuse to see Beryl. He was eager to tell his Mother about the island property he had seen as he hunted for suitable old growth to carve.

The doorbell sounded. It was Mattie Kate's solicitor, Foster Gridley. Beryl showed him into the convent parlor.

"Miss Perkins had her will drawn some time ago," he explained. "The building, of course, is beyond repair, but the property is still worth something. It is her bonds and other investments which have the greater value, and they are all willed to the Congregation of Martha and Mary, with one condition."

"What is that?" Beryl inquired automatically, not yet grasping the import of what the solicitor was saying to her.

"It is simply this: if at any time in the future, her daughter, known as Sister Paulina Soldano and a member of this Congregation, should leave the convent, she is to be given a legacy equal to one third of the value of the monetary bequest. You do not need to be concerned with sharing the future value of the town property, which, if I may be so bold, I advise you to keep. It may someday have extraordinary worth." The solicitor took off his reading glasses and looked at Beryl. "You have been willed two hundred thousand dollars," he told her, "in immediately available assets. There is triple that in various investments." When Beryl did not respond, he asked her if she understood what he was saying.

"I understand the words, of course. But I am shocked. I had no idea we were the beneficiary of such a fortune."

"It is that, without doubt. I trust you will find a use for the money?"

"Yes. I regret that the answer to our prayers came in this way, but yes. We have a use for the money." The Congregation would have its Motherhouse.

III

"For the life o' me, I dunno what we'd be goin' over there fer!" Adam grumbled as he led two horses onto the barge, securing them safely away from the stern. Captain Lilly led two more and tethered them in the rear. Sister Bernadine Malloy, a newly professed sister with a cheerful disposition smiled broadly, waiting for her legendary superior to respond. Beryl accepted Adam's growling and was happy for it. It was a bit of his own crotchety self which she hadn't seen for many months. He was still mourning Mattie Kate. Adam had contemplated closing down the livery stable and leaving the Territory.

"Where would you go, Adam?" Beryl had asked.

"Dunno. Away." His head was bent and she couldn't see his face under the ragged felt hat which he'd worn since Beryl knew him as a child.

Beryl begged him not to leave until she had found a location for her Motherhouse, and he had agreed to help her. She embarked on a search for a site that took her to Montana, Spokane, Bellingham, and Bainbridge Island. A promising piece of land was available north of Seattle, but Beryl was put off by the denuded hills. The lumber mills had wreaked havoc with the town's surroundings. The Seattle site was close to the University of Washington's acreage, and the value of the land would surely increase as time went on. "It's a good investment," Lizzie had told her, but Lizzie was urging her to consider another woodland site on Bainbridge Island as well. "My reasons are purely selfish. I'd like to have you close by," she had told Beryl.

"As for investment, I think the saloon property in downtown Seattle will be of great value in the future," Beryl told her. "I want more acreage, and I want solitude," Beryl explained. We don't need the Motherhouse to be 'convenient.'"

She had considered property near Bellingham, which had a view of ten thousand foot Mount Baker, but she felt that the site should be centrally located. Sisters from most every location in Washington State should be able to travel the distance to a Motherhouse within a single day. The last location she investigated was the site Joseph had seen before he returned to San Francisco after the fire.

The island east of Seattle on Lake Washington was heavily wooded. The clear cutting around Seattle hadn't extended to this island the natives called Mercer's Island, not after Asa, but to honor Asa's brother Thomas, who had come to Seattle before Asa. Before he left for San Francisco, Joseph had discovered the property when he was searching for naturally fallen old growth cedar for his work. Before he left Seattle he told Mother Charbonneau what he had discovered.

"There is access only by barge, but that won't hamper builders. Building materials are already transported around the Seattle Tacoma area by water. To the east, the island is closer to the mainland, and it is possible to reach Seattle by public ferry."

Beryl was interested in the island from the first description Joseph had given her, but until the legacy had come to the Congregation, it had not been appropriate to consider the location. When none of the properties she visited seemed right to her, Adam and Captain Lilly helped her organize the trip to Mercer's Island.

When Lizzie heard Beryl was going to look at Mercer's Island, she complained, "You'll be virtually isolated!"

"Elizabeth Ordway," Beryl scolded. "It's not like you to be so shortsighted! You've lived on an island for years. There's going to be growth, perhaps even a bridge someday."

"Over Lake Washington? You're an incurable dreamer."

"Yes, I am! And I think you should remember that when you and I stood on the deck of *The Kidder* thirty five years ago. Seattle was a sad little settlement of mud and sticks. Look at us now. Why, the week after the fire, merchants were back with their wares under tents! The town is unstoppable, and I think Mercer's Island has a future."

"Not in our lifetime,"

"My dreams are for the lifetime of the Congregation."

Adam had already made a trail from a location on the west beach through the woods. The beach would be part of the purchase. Letting down the back door of the barge to make a ramp, Adam and Captain Lilly led the horses, one at a time, down the ramp, into the water and up to the beach. When the horses were tethered, they placed planks for the sisters over the water.

The five of them mounted, both sisters astride, and set off along the rough trail. Beryl and her mount followed from the rear. The trees were thick and they had to break through underbrush of Oregon grape and wild blueberry. The horses bit off tender greenery to eat along the way. The well trained animals had only a light snaffle bit and their browsing in the greenery wouldn't hurt them. They entered a cedar grove in which the needles had made a forest carpet free from brush. There were several fallen trees around the edge, green with soft moss covering the wood. From this grove the trail led up the hill, and at the summit they found a natural meadow. To the east, the Cascade Range rose from the forests, high and purple in the summer haze. The great Mount Rainier, snow covered with the grey blue of its perpetual glacial snow pack, dominated the view to the south. The lake below glittered below them, fragments of sun fire reflected in its depths. "Eureka," Beryl breathed. "This is the place." No argument from that moment forward could dissuade her.

IV
1900

Beryl had written to Father Louis faithfully while he was in France with the Trappists. After his return to America, he had taken up residence at the Jesuit University in Santa Clara, California where Beryl continued to send letters.

Beryl's correspondence described the progress of the Mercer Island construction at each stage. Barges brought wood and foundation materials by water. The Congregation's council decided to leave as much of the original forest as possible with clearings for garden, a road, and trails. The Jesuits at Gonzaga sent an architect from inland to help the community plan their home. He was intrigued with Beryl's idea to have a two story building in a square shape, but with one section on the entry level enclosing an inner courtyard.

"Our infirm sisters will be able to walk in protected gardens within sight of their sisters, and guests who visit and tour the grounds will not have access to our private convent garden."

The architect had a more ornate house in mind, similar to Gonzaga and that of the Providence Sisters. Beryl resisted and ultimately had her way in her unusual, but practical design. One wing joined the chapel in such a manner that sisters on the second floor could pray in a consecrated place without having to go the length of the convent and downstairs. The one story section contained a large community room and an infirmary. There were plans for smaller meeting rooms, a library, and private rooms for sisters, who as they aged might not be able to reach the second floor. Even with their increasing number of candidates in the novitiate there would be no common dormitories.

The interior design was simple, but not cold. Wood flooring graced the entryways, which would be polished to luster. Beryl, with the approval of the community, had commissioned Joseph to carve panels of the Congregation's history combined with the growth of the territory. For the foyer there was to be a panel depicting the story of Martha and Mary in the scriptures. She accepted the gift of a long Oriental rug for the front hall from Captain and Mrs. Lilly, but aside from that there was little ornamentation. All was in harmony with Beryl's desire for simplicity. However, the effect was not harsh. Even on the single floor wings, the ceilings were higher than normal, and great stained beams broke the otherwise stark lines.

When construction on the interior was finished and the school terms over, sisters began to come to the island to help with the library, kitchen facilities, and the boarders' schoolrooms scheduled for opening some months ahead. It was almost time for the dedication.

Beryl wrote to Father Louis:

> *I know that the way here is difficult, but I will hold you to your promise to stay with us for a few days after the dedication. I am happy you have chosen to go to Santa Clara where the climate will be easier on "your old bones," to use your own words. Yes, I would think we'd be receptive to the idea of schools in California should we be asked to come. I thank you for your offer to greet the three sisters who will be arriving to attend Santa Clara. I am sending Sister Danielle, Sister Agnes and Sister Leona. Our dear friend Lizzie pointed out how humorous this trio is: a Lamb, a Lion, and a Daniel! The three are eager to study. You asked about the name of our Motherhouse. The sisters are sending suggestions. So far my choice is Highland Home of the Congregation of Martha and Mary. I realize it is wordy, but it can be shortened to "Highland Home." I confess I like the sound of it. And speaking of confession, you must prepare to hear mine.*
>
> *I fear it may take some time! The sins of omission and commission have accumulated, and though I have received the sacrament from the cathedral priest weekly, I've saved my deeper concerns for your ears.*

She continued with more details of their plans for the dedication, then signed it with her usual "Your daughter in Christ," conclusion. Father Louis had written only infrequently during his stay in France. One very brief message had said, *I am at peace, and that state is the greatest gift God has given me in my lifetime.* Beryl wondered about this comment. There was a deep mystery in her friend's heart. Father Louis Bertrand wrote a single sentence on the holy card he had saved for Beryl. He would have written more, but he could not prevent his hand from shaking. He sealed the envelope that had been addressed by the courtesy of a house brother. He looked at the name. *Reverend Mother Beryl Charbonneau, SMM.* He possessed no portrait of Beryl, and he didn't need one. The years had changed her, but her blue eyes and generous smile burned in his memory and he needed no other representation.

He knew what the doctor would say to his superior, but the advice was not necessary; Louis Bertrand knew that neither his heart nor his lungs would withstand traveling from Santa Clara to Seattle. He did not choose to be a corpse thrust over the side of a sloop in alien waters. Neither did he wish to be interred somewhere along the coastal rail route. From where he sat in the partial shade of a great oak, he could see the cemetery garden behind a stone wall, under the shade of trees that had been growing for fifty years. This was the resting place for many of his brothers. Yes, among them would he lie, under a simple stone with his name, the dates of his birth and his death chiseled deeply enough to withstand the weather and the years.

He pulled the wool blanket Brother Albert had left for him around his shoulders. It was cold today in spite of the California sun. He felt bone tired. It would not be unseemly to rest his head against the pillow that braced his back and sleep a while.

He thought of Beryl, and smiled. It had not been the prayer and the fasting at the monastery that had brought him peace. He had fled to France troubled in heart and soul, and he had pondered his state quite alone. In the silence of monastic life he had confronted the demons of jealousy, the unfaithfulness to the spirit of his calling. But it was not the days and nights of prayer and fasting that exorcized his demons. To his great wonder it was the brilliant light of his love for Beryl Charbonneau, the power of her shining goodness that won the day. The monsters of envy and discontent against which he grappled were brought out to be confronted with her purity of dedication. They would never again tempt him to diminish Beryl's bright place in his heart.

Father Sean Fitzgerald, the superior of the Jesuit House of Studies and

Priory in Santa Clara, California, showed the doctor to his carriage. As he walked up the steps to the oak paneled front door, he knew that he would have to tell Father Louis Bertrand that his physical condition would not permit him to attend the dedication of Mother Charbonneu's Motherhouse. It would be a sad task. Father Sean had hoped that the rail journey north, now a mere three days from Oakland, might be a possibility.

"I have taken that rail route, Father," the doctor said, "and it took some five days with unavoidable delays to reach Seattle. The trip by sloop, though much longer, is preferable for anyone whose health is impaired. I do not believe Father Louis Bertrand could survive either. The priest is not so old in years, but he is worn out physically. In fact, he will in all likelihood leave us before the month is out."

Father Fitzgerald was tempted to keep the physician's judgment to himself. The dedication was still several months away. He could at least promise Father Louis that he could travel north once his health returned. But as soon as he entertained the deception, the Jesuit rejected it. It was a lie unworthy of this exceptional priest.

Father Fitzgerald did not have to accomplish the sad task. Brother Albert met him in the hall with the news that Father Louis Bertrand had slipped quietly away in his sleep.

V

"God blessed us with a perfect day," Mother Lavinia said as she walked with Beryl and Sister Gertrude, their health care supervisor, in the twilight after the long day of the dedication. Bishop O'Dea had come from Vancouver where the seat of diocesan government was located. The setting sun was red in the west, and the mountain in the south held a soft pink color against a deepening blue sky. Just the tips of the trees in the foothills caught the last of the sun and stood out golden against their darker green. Swallows fed on the wing and a few birds still called their farewell to the sun. In the building, lamps had been lit in the large hall, and the glow would be a beacon across the waters of the lake.

"Sung Yee planned these paths well, Mother," Gertrude remarked. "As we grow infirm, our postulants can wheel us about quite comfortably!" The other two agreed. Care of their elderly sisters in the future had been as important a consideration as their plans to house the postulants and novices. In her personal journal Beryl had made special note of their community "family" responsibilities.

> Let no Sister of Martha or Mary lack the loving care of her community in any sickness of body or mind, or in any circumstance of age or infirmity. Let no concern for the Congregation's work keep our sisters from this solemn obligation.

Sister Sarah Dufrayne had agreed that some of the entering sisters be given an opportunity to train in nursing and health care rather than for teaching. Lavinia had supported the proposal, as did a majority of the community. "Don't misunderstand me, Sisters," Lavinia had spoken in open meeting. "I intend to teach until I am one hundred and two, but facing the possibility of infirmity is realistic. I, for one, would more willingly accept being cared for if I knew it was one of my own sisters changing the bedpan!"

More squeamish sisters were shocked until Beryl laughed heartily. "Sister may be blunt, but she has a point!" To herself she thought that however indelicate Lavinia's image was, it was well expressed and pertinent. She appointed Sister Gertrude as Infirmarian, using the term borrowed from her Carmelite monastic experience. Before she left office, she promised that she would make certain to install this office in perpetuity.

The Congregation gathering at Highland Home convened with the traditional ten day retreat. A priest from Gonzaga College gave the meditations each day and a monastic silence fell over the house. Beryl welcomed it and maintained her solitude as well as she could, considering the demands of her office. The activity of the past several years had sapped her strength. Ever since her wild ride on Captain Lilly's hunter the day of Seattle's great fire, she had suffered chronic back pain. She accepted the discomfort, and no one knew the cost to her, as she maintained her calm and patient demeanor. She chuckled to herself that her walk had become stately. Some of her community assumed that she was making a supreme effort to take Marietta's counsels regarding proper religious deportment to heart. The truth was that she had to move more slowly and deliberately if she weren't to cry out before she could repress her response to the pain in her lower back and legs.

Lizzie was not fooled and scolded her. "Beryl! See a doctor!"

"And be told my back hurts me? I know that. At my age I expect to have some aches and pains."

"Piffle! You're not that far on the other side of the half century mark! If I had a tenth of your vigor I'd be happy," Lizzie remarked.

Beryl had concluded she experienced an increase in pain when she was worried about one thing and another. Relaxation and prayer had the effect of a dose of laudanum.

Just before the dedication, Beryl received word from Father Cataldo, now the provincial for the Rocky Mountain area, that her dear Father Louis had died peacefully in his sleep. Beryl had heard that he was not well. She hoped that the California climate would help, and it did somewhat, but his body had finally given out. After the news, Beryl knelt in the chapel where Joseph's sculpture was inlaid on the side wall. The carved portrait of the Jesuit would be a perpetual reminder of his great role in the Congregation. It had been his dream, and as the community grew, he had been supporter, advisor, and spiritual father. Beryl had gazed at the carving. In spite of Joseph's intent, she saw the eagle with its spread wings as Father Louis Bertrand, not herself. Please God he would spread the wings of prayer over them protectively from Heaven.

There were family losses for Beryl as well. Constantia had died, also peacefully, and her sister Evangeline and her brother Phillipe had contracted diphtheria in an epidemic that raged in the swampy environs of the nation's capital. Their deaths followed Constantia's. Beryl accepted death as a part of life, but still she grieved.

Here in the solitude of her retreat, Beryl pondered the mystery of love, human and divine. What was this force that inspired her friendships and vocation? It had many facets. She had loved her home and family, but her emotional attachment to Father Louis Bertrand had been greater. Here in the West she loved her work and her sisters, but her feelings for Joseph were deeper. He was friend and son; he was the voice of her soul. Her friendship with Lizzie eluded definition.

None of these passions, and she admitted that the word was appropriate, took her away from her basic love of God and her dedication to His work. In fact, as her love of others deepened, so did her capacity to pray and be one with her Creator. How strange that much of the Church's spirituality emphasized "detachment." It was the way that Marietta proclaimed was ideal, and certainly the way Marietta chose. It was the theme song of other communities, including active modern congregations such as Holy Names and the Dominicans. It was a concept basic to Carmelite spirituality.

In her room she opened the sealed envelope that Father Cataldo forwarded from her friend. It was a scrawled sentence written on the back of a holy card. It was a single phrase: *I shall love you better after death.* Tears of pity and compassion filled her eyes.

Deep into the night, Beryl left her room to sit in the sisters' chapel. There in silence, the darkness lit only by the vigil candle beside the altar, she summoned the image of Father Louis Bertram. In her memory, he was not bent and frail as she had seen him last, but straight and vital, the vestments of Mass draped over his tall body in graceful folds. She could see his hands outstretched and hear the voice she had known in her youth, strong, full and true.

She pondered his last words to her. Louis Bertrand was a holy man, dedicated to his priesthood. She had never known him in any other way, and it had not occurred to her that he suffered from human temptations. She reached for one of the shawls left on the pews for the sisters' use. It didn't relieve the chill she felt; this came from a coldness within. How could she not have understood her friend's bitter trial of soul?

The fragments of memories scattered over half a century of her life began to fit into a clear picture. Louis Bertram hadn't wanted her to live in the solitude of the cloister, and even as she left the world through the enclosure door that shut so solidly behind her, she took his words of other possibilities with her. The improbability of an unqualified, inexperienced young woman founding a new order was not a prudent choice, but how else would she have come to the Frontier? His reluctance to share her devotion to Joseph had disturbed her, irritated her. Now that, too, was clear.

It had been for the best that her spiritual father had kept his dark secret from her. Enlightenment would have dislodged the foundation stones of the Congregation more threateningly than any challenge Marietta might make. In the chapel, Beryl realized that the great endeavor had been inspired by a motive less than perfect. And yet God had transformed its beginnings into one of His shining creations. Ignorance might not be bliss, as the proverb said it was, but it had preserved Beryl's calling and her confidence in a divinely inspired mission. *Inspiration*, she thought, *the breath of the Deity within.* God had permitted Father Louis' trial, and in the black night of his suffering, the Sisters of Martha and Mary had shone all the more brightly.

When Beryl looked toward the eastern sky where the rising sun began to emerge from behind Mount Rainier, she went to her room to find a warm cloak. As she walked toward Highland Home's Cedar grove, the sun burned through the leaves above her. The birds were singing their welcome to the morning in a cacophony of calls. She walked on the soft carpet of needles that covered the ground, hardly noticing the soreness in her back. In the silence of this mighty stand of trees, she reflected that in Carmel she could have spent her life ripping away loving attachments from the womb of her soul. And like a woman's miscarriage, her lifeblood would have been drained from her. She had chosen to nourish the embryos of love and friendship with an absolute certitude that she had chosen rightly. Perhaps her way was not the path of heroic virtue that the saints had followed, but, as she used to say to Father Louis Bertram, she was neither heroic nor a saint.

"My dear, dear friend," she said softly, "Now you may be by my side all the days of my life. Without sin, without fear. Take my hand, and we'll go forward together."

VI

Shortly after the dedication of Highland Home, Beryl made a journey to Bambridge Island. Lizzie was still settling into her new home. She had hoped to build on her property before she moved to San Francisco, but those hopes never materialized. Upon her return to the West, unsure of her future, but in high spirits after her successful election as Kitsap Peninsula Superintendent of Schools, she began to made plans for a permanent residence. She served Beryl tea on a steamer trunk using apple boxes as chairs. "We're not fancy, but this will do! You can't fault me for rushing to construction—how long has it been? Too many years!"

"I remember tea on the trails made over campfires! With far less comfort than this!" Beryl exclaimed with what seemed to Lizzie to be forced jocularity. Lizzie, always sensitive to her friend's feelings, put down her tea cup and frowned at Beryl.

"My dear, dear friend. You are always as welcome as a warm day in spring, but you should tell me why you're here—especially now."

"I'd rather talk about you and your hopes for the emancipation of women! Your campaign awakened women to the fact that 'love, honor, and obey,' when strictly observed, keeps them shackled."

"That is an exceedingly ironic opinion coming from a woman married to Jesus within a Church that is dominated by men."

"Ironic. Yes, I admit it is. But historically, strong and independent women have brought about spectacular changes in the Church's male society."

"Name some."

"Catherine of Siena, Teresa of Avila, Hildegard of Bingen, and Joan of Arc—even though I think she had more than a few bats in her belfry."

"But, Beryl, don't you see the fundamental difference between my thinking and yours? I am constantly knocking my head against the wall of male power, and even if I come away bloodied and bruised, I won't ever stop the challenge. You accept your walls and vow obedience to those who built them!"

"Walls are metaphors, Lizzie. They have no solid reality that can imprison thought. As a matter of actual fact, if the extent of my private philosophy were known, I would not be allowed to preach, teach or retain any position of authority within my Congregation or the Church. Not so long ago I would have been publicly burned at the stake. Not even Father Louis Bertrand knew what a heretical turn my thinking had taken! It is what troubles me now. Do I have a right to think for myself, while externally accepting what I no longer accept."

Lizzie was stunned. "In all the years I've known you, you have never once hinted that your faith was unsteady. What has happened?"

"I am probably guilty of thinking too much!" Beryl said lightly, pouring herself another cup of tea. "And I am mourning Father Louis Bertrand's death."

"Understandably," Lizzie said sympathetically, "but I'm not letting you off with your first facile reply. As I see it, I am the one person on this earth, aside from your Joseph, with whom you can speak honestly without fear of damaging your reputation or of giving scandal. If I may ask," said Lizzie, pleased that there was an opening for a question she had long wished Beryl to answer. "whatever inspired you to become a nun in the first place?"

"The idealism of youth, I suppose. And…" She hesitated.

"And?"

"I had an adolescent crush on Father Louis Bertrand. He was my spiritual and academic knight in shining armor. I wanted to please him and to be a part of the religious life he represented. He was my radiant ideal! There was no young man who came close to him in manners, intellect, and spirituality. I chose the Carmelites because I believed they were the most perfect expression of a woman's' religious vocation. But it wasn't dishonest; I was sincerely attracted to their contemplative life."

"As I remember, Father Louis wanted you to be a Holy Names Sister, or to join that other order with the embarrassing name."

Beryl laughed. "You mean 'The Madams.' I agree that is an unfortunate appellation! It has caused many a snigger, which the ladies do not deserve. They are a uniquely well educated group."

"So why didn't you choose the community that would have pleased Father Louis?"

"I don't know. While I absolutely adored him, I was also independent. As things worked out, it was providential—if we accept the premise of God's personal involvement in every detail of our lives."

The two women talked far into the night. "I call myself a Christian," Beryl said, "and there is no one other than Jesus Christ who claims my first loyalty and passion. He is my path to the truth and I walk with Him gladly and freely. Yet, I see beyond what He Who is at one with the Father and the Holy Ghost is to the Church. I see the Father as the Indian's Great Spirit, as Buddha and Mohammed. I see in Him the force that moves all creation. And I do not," Beryl paused for emphasis, "do not regard Him as the exclusive possession of Rome. Jesus Christ has been greatly wronged by those who have conquered, killed and plundered in His name. Since the earliest days of Christianity, supposedly religious men have taken a lease on Hell itself and in a self-serving concordant with the Father of Lies condemned their fellow humans to the land of everlasting fire." Beryl reddened slightly. She had not meant to give such an impassioned speech.

Before she could comment, Lizzie spoke. "You are not a hypocrite, Beryl. You are an honest woman who has answered her faith's extraordinary calling. Do you believe all those strong women you mentioned never questioned their place in the grand scheme of things? Perhaps the Church just hasn't caught up with your thinking!"

"Tell that to the authors of the Baltimore Catechism!"

"They say 'the devil's in the details,' Beryl. I know it's out of context, but you're putting doubts where they don't belong. Can you imagine what irreparable harm you'd do if you stood in front of your Congregation and told them that you're out of step with strict Roman Catholic theology?' Don't even think about it. March to your own rhythm and know in your heart that there's as much room for your beliefs as there is for those of that weasel Mercelli!"

When Beryl made her farewells to Lizzie, she departed far lighter in spirit than when she had come to her.

"Be at peace, my friend," Lizzie said.

VII
1904

Joseph stood alone on the deck of the *I'il de France*. Mai Ling was asleep in their cabin suite—a blessed change from the storm tossed crossing three months ago. He wondered if his wife's passionate pleading that she and Joseph remain in Paris permanently wasn't in part due to the dread of seasickness and fear that the ship would sink before reaching home port.

"You could be content to live an ocean apart from our children, and forego the possibility of seeing your parents and brother Chang?"

"The children are almost grown." She did not mention Su Ping, who was a deep disappointment to her mother. Her daughter had chosen to convert to Christianity and planned to enter Beryl Chabonneau's Congregation. Mai Ling begged and cajoled her daughter not to abandon the traditions of her family.

"They are the traditions of half our family, Mother. Father approves."

"Why did Mother Chabonneau have to take our daughter?" Mai Ling had complained to Joseph. "She left you alone!"

This was true, and in his youth this had puzzled Joseph. As a child, he had wondered if he were undeserving of joining Mother Charbonneau in her faith. The priests never ceased trying, in their terminology, to wash him in the Blood of the Lamb. The image of the sacrificial lamb and the theology it represented was powerful. Jesus had laid down His life willingly. His fetters, even on the cross, bound him by His own choice. Those which Joseph was urged to accept would deprive him of his freedom. He would have to put on the chains of his old nemesis, Torquemada. Nevertheless, had his beloved

231

Mother Charbonneau offered these shackles to him, he would have kissed the hands that locked the chains around him.

Once he had challenged her. "But Mother, since I'm not baptized, the priests say that I cannot enter Heaven. Even Father Brouillet says that I will be separated from you for all eternity."

"Joseph, my child, I would not pass through the gates of a Heaven that would lock behind me to keep you out. And believe this: God the Father and His Son do not live in such a place. Popes, inquisitors, bishops, priests and even ministers such as the one you knew as a child in your settlement will be roaming in the Elysian Fields searching for the God in whose name they condemned their fellow man. They'll still be walking on the endless path of exile with no joy while we are happy and free in our Creator's presence."

"Mother, they would call you a heretic," Joseph said softly.

"Yes, I expect they would. But it's our secret, Joseph. It wouldn't do my Congregation any good to have me burned at the stake."

"It wouldn't do you much good either," Joseph said.

Up to the time Mai Ling and Joseph boarded the ship to take them home, Mai Ling had continued to express her fervent wish that they live in Europe. She was attracted to the culture, the gracious permanence and stability. Her eyes were not closed to class divisions and poverty, but she and Joseph had been accepted by the French. What was the word—assimilated. Joseph's lectures and exhibits were well attended.

Rodin himself had been moved by Joseph's vision of form and content. The great sculptor had understood that the raw life of the New World's western seaboard with its juxtaposition of natural beauty and man's brutality in an unlikely symbiosis was the soul of Joseph's art. "I have never seen such harmony of form in works that depict violence and disorder," he said to the museum's board of directors. "Some works are at war from within: the persecutor and the passive victim."

The curators of the Louvre had waited patiently for Joseph to complete the body of work they would display at Paris' world famous center of art. There were delays beyond Joseph's control—the rebuilding of Seattle after the fire, the responsibility for his three young children, and the problem of obtaining properly aged wood. The museum directors had seen Joseph's work and, being men who were familiar with collections that spanned many decades, they waited. The excitement generated by the display had proven well worth their patience.

In the collection, Joseph had shipped one of his most graphic sculptures, a vast bas relief carved on a laminated oak board. Shortly before the exhibition he had judged it too graphic and instructed that it remain crated. "The Hanging" was eventually shown in Paris; Joseph had been convinced by Rodin himself.

"Do you think that your work would shock the city that invented the guillotine?" Rodin asked. "No. In this work there are layers that show the faces of death, vengeance, and compassion."

The emotions in "The Hanging" began at the top, with grotesque figures of men in the throes of death. In his subsequent representation of spectators, Joseph had carved hatred, shock and, finally, at the bottom, a woman set apart, her arms flung wide open as if to receive the souls of the dead in forgiveness. The figure was a perfect portrait of Beryl Charbonneau.

Joseph promised Mai Ling that they would return to Paris one day, and he made a compromise that seemed to comfort his wife. The University of California at Berkeley across the bay from San Francisco had offered him a renewal of the honorarium which would allow him to pursue his art with only a portion of his time devoted to teaching. Mai Ling was secretly pleased that there would remain distance between her husband and Mother Charbonneau. She had feared that with the Paris showing over, and with the security of abundant funds from the sale of some pieces, Joseph would want to return to Seattle. Her parents had relocated to San Francisco, and for this reason alone she looked forward to living near the growing community where her Chinese dialect would be spoken. She couldn't put her feelings into words, but she knew in her heart that although her husband loved her deeply, he was not "her Joseph." She could not claim his whole heart.

Part Nine

I

Beryl had a year left in office, a year to exercise the authority of Mother General. She determined to make certain that the bequests in Matilda Perkin's last will and testament would be carried out as Mattie had specified. In particular she was concerned about the provision made for Paulina should she ever leave the Sisters of Martha and Mary. Beryl made the trip from Highland Home to the Seattle convent and asked Lavinia to accompany her downtown. Traveling from the hills to town was a dangerous drive in the early days of Seattle. As Seattle rebuilt after the great fire, work on the Denny regrade continued. The coming of the motor car demanded roads of better quality than those a horse and carriage could negotiate. Beryl did not like the "horseless carriage," but she had seen enough change in her time to understand that it was a matter of time before the motor car would replace the horse. She was happy that Adam had come in an automobile to drive them downtown.

"'I detest this trip off the hill," Lavinia said, averting her eyes from the steep drop on her side of the conveyance.

"No harm will come to us when we are in Adam's care. Relax, Sister!"

"I have confidence in Adam, but I lack your nerve. I am still in awe of your taking the railroad across the country when you returned from Europe."

"It was more uncomfortable than unnerving. Yet, I cannot imagine any other experience which would have given me a sense of the vast distance between the Atlantic and Pacific."

"Oh? I can conjure the vision of the Beryl Charbonneau of thirty years ago

237

on the Oregon Trail driving a covered wagon pulled by longhorn steers and followed by spare horses and pack mules!"

Beryl could not help but laugh. She said, "If I had been a male, well…"

"If you had been a male you'd be a mighty queer looking Mother General!"

Their laughter distracted Lavinia, and before the sister could give in to her fear of Denny Hill, Adam had guided the vehicle to the level stretch of First Avenue. He stopped at the new office building where Foster Gridley had installed his practice.

Gridley welcomed the sisters. He was cordial and reserved at the same time. Gridley had not had business dealings with nuns, although he was the lawyer who had saved Douglas McFee's legacy for Joseph, executed Matilda Perkin's will, and who had informed Beryl of her legacy to the Congregation. As a member of a Masonic lodge, he had regarded Catholics in general with suspicion, but he found it impossible to feel anything but profound respect and a measure of awe for Mother Charbonneau. Ignoring the warnings of his lodge fellows, he had enrolled his daughter in the Congregation's Tacoma boarding school after the Seattle fire. At first his excuse was that rebuilding demanded that he make temporary quarters for the firm in his home. It was more convenient for his girl to be away at school. However, she had remained there until graduation. To his knowledge, no nun attempted to convert her, and to the surprise of the legal community and his Masonic brothers, Henrietta still sat with her family in the front row of Seattle's First Presbyterian Church every Sunday.

As the sisters entered his office, Gridley indicated chairs and took his seat behind the desk. "Mother Charbonneau, I have asked you to see me for the purpose of confirming and signing legal documents related to your legacy. I am happy that you have brought a nun from your Congregation to witness these documents. We have members of the staff that could act as witness, but confirmation from your community is preferable."

Beryl and Lavinia signed the papers Foster Gridley had prepared. Afterward, Beryl asked Lavinia to wait for her with Adam. Gridley shifted the papers on his desk until he came to a particular document. "As to Matilda Perkin's concern for Sister Paulina Soldano's future, according to your request, I have drawn a separate agreement for the stipulated amount which will be adjusted as economic circumstances dictate. I have created a trust fund giving the disposition of Miss Perkin's bequest to you, Mother Charbonneau. Therefore, should a need arise to execute this specific term of the will, your signature will be all that is necessary to remit the amount due to Miss Perkin's daughter."

"I understand, Mr. Gridley. But what if I should be the victim of a fatal accident, or die from disease?"

"This is addressed in a codicil. In this event, your Congregation, or whoever is its elected superior—is that the correct term?" When Beryl nodded, Gridley continued, "Paulina Soldano's legacy would be signed over by whoever has the authority."

"Yes." There was a lengthy silence before Beryl decided to speak. "I would prefer that your firm hold the power of attorney for Sister Paulina and that no one other than you and I know of the bequest unless circumstances are such that money is to be paid. I will see to it that if Sister Paulina should leave, I or one of our sisters will notify you."

"What exactly are you saying, Mother Charbonneau?"

"I do not wish to imply that any future Mother General of the Sisters of Martha and Mary would try to circumvent this contract, but dispensation from vows which would make a nun's departure legal and approved by the Church could be delayed by years. You may draw your own conclusions regarding withholding permissions and refusal to submit applications for release from vows. I do not believe Matilda Perkins would have wanted any possibility, no matter how remote, to deny her daughter the benefit of her bequest."

"Mother Charbonneau, I am honored by the trust you place in me."

"I realize we are speaking of trust, Mr. Gridley. There has always been trust between us. May I remind you that you gave your daughter into the Congregation's care? We respected her Protestant heritage. Stealing her would be a far greater sin than anyone's stealing a patrimony."

When Beryl and Lavinia left the lawyer's premises, he stood at the window that faced First Avenue. He puffed the cigar he had foregone in the presence of ladies. A cloud of blue smoke rose to the ceiling. Through the haze he stared at Beryl as she entered the motor car. "Jesus Christ," he said aloud, "that is one hell of a woman."

II

Sister Paulina cupped little Josie's chin in one hand and used her own handkerchief to wipe the child's tear streaked face with the other. "Now let me see the hurt."

The six year old pulled up the hem of her blue uniform and let Sister unfasten the garter that held up her grey cotton stocking. Paulina pulled it down gently over the skinned knee. The fall had scraped a hole in the hosiery, and the knee was beginning to ooze blood.

"It's not so bad," Paulina said giving the child a hug. "But you'll have to go inside and let Sister Marcella put Mercurochrome on it. It won't sting," she promised. "Off you go!"

Josie scampered toward the boarders' door holding her stocking up with one hand. Paulina straightened from the crouch that had put her on a level with Josie. She walked among the children at play, stopping to talk to every one. Nancy, the eleven year old girl who had arrived last week, was sitting on a bench by herself. That wouldn't do. The child was tall for her age, with a habit of scowling with her mouth turned down. Her hair, dark brown and pulled straight back, was unattractive. She was inclined to be taciturn, and Paulina had the impression that this was not from shyness or lack of the ability to express herself, but from wariness of her new situation. She had never been away to school. The girl swung her feet as she sat in an I-don't-care-that-I'm-alone attitude. Paulina decided that Nancy did care. Loneliness and homesickness had to be remedied as speedily as skinned knees and bruises. She joined Nancy on the bench.

"I need an older girl as a volunteer," she said.

"For what?"

" 'For what, Sister?' " Paulina corrected.

"For what, Sister?" Nancy repeated. Paulina's corrections were so sweetly made, no girl reacted petulantly.

"Come along with me. It's a secret." She took Nancy's hand and signaled to Sister Dorothea that she was leaving the play area. The two entered the house and went down the hallway to Sister's office. Paulina opened a drawer in her desk and took out a wide band of blue ribbon. Betty Ann's mother had brought several rolls last weekend. The concerned mother thought that it would add a bit of prettiness if the girls wore hair bows to offset the plain convent uniform.

"Isn't that frivolous? We shouldn't be teaching the girls to be vain!" Sister Irma complained.

"They're little girls, Sister, not postulants. There's no reason that they have to be kept as plain as Jane Eyre!" Paulina answered.

"Who?" Irma asked.

"Just a literary character," Paulina responded matter of factly. She often forgot that many of her sisters didn't have the advantage of her liberal arts education. The works of Charlotte Bronte were not found in the Motherhouse library, but they were on her shelves.

Sister Dorothea, who had been busy darning boarder's stockings, said, "I see no reason why the girls can't wear ribbons. But we'll let Sister Paulina wash and press them!"

"Then I suggest we appoint Sister Paulina Soldano as Mistress of Ribbons and Bows!" Sister Millicent, teacher of the first two grades said.

"I accept the obedience, Mother Millicent," Paulina teased. "I promise with God's help to do my best!" She parodied the reply customary for all tasks given by the Mother General.

She had made the same response three years ago, when at her final election Mother Charbonneau had given her an assignment to teach at the Highland Home boarders' school. There were whispers in the community that it was a demotion. Paulina, after all, had taught at the young ladies' college in Montana, and had been successful as far as anyone knew. There were rumors that she and Sister Marietta were far from amiable.

Paulina heard her new assignment from Mother and a wave of relief swept over her. She would not have cared if Mother Charbonneau had assigned her to full time scullery chores, which every sister, Mother General included, shared. To be free of Marietta's constant criticism and hostility was a gift from Heaven. Marietta was now full time dean of the college, now a four year school.

Paulina taught the older girls in the Mercer Island Boarding school. Sister Dorothea was principal; Marcella, and Millicent were also on the staff, assisted by second year novices whose training Sister Paulina would supervise. Later, after their first profession, the novices would be sent to a one or two year normal school program, but they would have had some practical experience to add to their formal training.

The professed teaching sisters were capable, and they were friendly. There were others at the Motherhouse engaged in the training of postulant and novices. They, too, contributed to the general spirit of the community. Paulina had never been so happy. Every day she awoke to the sound of birds singing their premonition of dawn before the sun appeared over the Cascade foothills. Her own heart sang a prayer of thanksgiving.

Paulina showed the ribbon to Nancy and asked her if she could experiment with different bows on her hair before they showed the other boarders. Nancy was pleased to be asked. Paulina had her sit on a straight backed chair and she undid the child's braids. Nancy's hair fell in waves. Paulina smoothed it with a brush and then pulled back a bit of each side, but not tightly. She tied a large bow that sat on top of Nancy's head, slightly back. Her hair fell loose and soft. It had the effect of lifting the girl's features. Paulina found a mirror in another drawer and showed Nancy what she had done.

"What do you think?" Paulina asked.

"I like it!" Nancy replied.

Recess was almost over, and Paulina told Nancy to stay in the office until she knocked on the classroom wall next to it. She would have the girls assembled, and at her signal Nancy would be the one to show the new addition to their uniforms.

The boarders were delighted and their squeals attracted the attention of Mother Charbonneau. The Mother General peeked in to discover the source of the mirth. She joined in their pleasure by putting down her cane and assisting the sisters. She now moved with an effort, and had to accept the cane to steady her. The back pain had spread to her lower back, which a doctor told her was the result of damaged nerves in the spine. There was little he could do except prescribe laudanum, which Beryl refused. "It clouds my mind, doctor. There are many who suffer; why should I try to be free of pain that reminds me I am only human?"

Paulina's decision to include Nancy had made the girl a part of something that was special to the boarders. The girl had made friends that day, and as the other sisters remarked later, there was no comparison between the face that had been on the playground earlier. They thought it was the way Paulina had loosened the girl's hair. Beryl, listening to the sisters at their recreation hour, had thought to herself that it was nothing at all to do with a hairdo, and everything to do with Paulina's sensitivity to a child in need of kindness.

Beryl was well pleased with this sister, whom she knew had suffered from Sister Marietta's coldness. In so many ways Marietta was a good sister, faithful to her commitment and remarkably intelligent. Marietta was accepting of every other sister, including those who could be maddeningly obtuse. She was patient with her students, and never seemed unduly proud of her academic achievements. But she seemed to have no good will toward Paulina.

Beryl knew that Lizzie didn't care for Marietta, who she thought was unnecessarily rigid. Lizzie was accustomed to a certain amount of stiffness from members of the older orders, but in Beryl Charbonneau's community, it struck a sour note in her mind. It seemed inappropriate.

At one time Beryl had considered bringing Paulina and Marietta together in her presence, but she concluded that the confrontation would increase Marietta's bitterness and add to Paulina's pain. She had left the situation to God, and it was in her prayers every day. Now she had done what she could do for the good of Paulina, as well as the community.

III

Once again at retreat, Beryl had begged the sisters to release her, but a majority felt it significant that the next term would be the beginning of the new century's first decade. She had allowed her name to be proposed, and she was elected, as there was no name in opposition. However, she insisted that the community by-laws be amended for this election and this election only. She would serve for two years and not a day after. The Council agreed to honor her request and reluctantly accepted Beryl's terms.

Against the advice of her doctor, Beryl prepared to make the annual visitation to the convents in California. "I'm happy you're going with her," Lavinia told Paulina as they loaded the portmanteaus into the wagon. "For her sake I wish the trip weren't so long." She looked back to the house to see Mother Charbonneau emerging from the front door with the entire community, including postulants and novices, following to wish her "God speed."

"She seems in fine fettle!" Paulina said. The young sister had not been with the Congregation long enough to know what drew Mother Charbonneau to San Francisco like a moth to light: Joseph lived close to the city. Beryl had assured him that her duties as Mother General of the Congregation would mean frequent visits to California. The promise made their parting easier, but this trip had been the first one she was able to schedule in two years, and she had seen him only briefly after his return from Europe.

"Her back bothers her, but she's still strong," Paulina assured Lavinia.

"And it is futile to hope she'd ever spare herself," Lavinia added.

"The greatest favor we can do for her is to find a successor. But if there's no clear choice, will she…"

"No. She won't accept. Definitely not."

The group escorting Beryl came close and they cut off their conversation. Paulina followed her Mother General into the carriage and waved to her boarders, who shouted farewells. The children ran for a time beside the wagon as Adam shook the reins and began the trip to the waiting boat. He had advised Beryl to procure a motorcar, but she was not enthusiastic. "What would we do with the horses?" Beryl teased. Adam would make certain that Mother Charbonneau's and Paulina's luggage would be transferred to the ferry going to Seattle.

Beryl's journey would begin with a steamer trip south, so they would begin visitation at the point of greatest distance from the Bay Area and then work back north. There were three schools and a clinic in places within reach of San Francisco. The clinic was set up in San Francisco's Market Street and gave care to the poor and to migrant workers. The depression of the decade had affected the big city, although the wealthy seemed untouched, as the many buildings on the surrounding hills proclaimed. The Sisters of Martha and Mary ministered to those at the very bottom of the social scale. Occasionally, a patient would pay or bring some offering of food, but part of Mattie Kate's legacy was set aside to fund the good work. Already contributions from wealthy parishes were making the sisters' services possible without the reserve money.

The clinic community numbered eight sisters, four of them in nurse's training. It was the first group to depart from the community's teaching mission. They all realized that in the future care of their own sisters would be their work. Already three sisters were cared for at Highland Home. At present, Sister Gertrude needed no other help than what the postulants and the other sisters gave her. One of the infirm sisters was afflicted with a loss of memory, although she would participate in prayers that were familiar to her. Beryl saw the safekeeping of sisters who had worked for the good of the Congregation as one of the most important obligations of the Sisters of Martha and Mary.

"Only three more convents to visit and you may go home!" Beryl told Paulina. The young sister would travel with two of the nursing sisters from San Francisco who were in need of a rest.

"And I'll miss all the cake and rich food!" Paulina said in mock disappointment.

Her evaluations completed, Beryl was now free to make a side trip on her own. Joseph's home in the Berkeley hills was a harmonious blend of oriental simplicity and Joseph's selection of art. Beryl could not help but compare his formal dining area to the homes of Henry Yesler's and Captain Lilly with their opulent decor. Mai Ling had found a long ebony sideboard which was placed along one wall. Above it was a portrait of the three children, Sung Chow, Su Ping and Lee.

"A portrait of Mai Ling is being painted now by an artist friend of ours," Joseph explained. Two Tiffany dragonfly gas lamps were placed on either side of the portrait echoing its shades of red, lavender and blue. A length of silk that repeated the same hues covered the sideboard. The opposite wall was a wide glass door paneled in the French tradition, which framed the gardens outside. The dining table, also of ebony, was set on an unadorned crimson carpet.

Before her trip, Beryl had tried to conjure the image of Joseph's new home in the Berkeley hills, but her imagination had not come close to the gracious reality.

Mai Ling's cook prepared a special menu in the style of northern China's cuisine. The taste pleased Beryl, even though the spice called "kung pao" made her eyes water. "Many of our sisters suffer indigestion," she told her hosts, "and for the first time I am grateful that only my bones give me trouble! I would not have wanted to deny myself this pleasure!"

Joseph and Beryl walked in the garden after the meal. Arm in arm, Joseph noticed that his Mother Charbonneau seemed to have lost inches in height. She permitted him to steady her as they strolled on a path of fine gravel.

"Are you in pain, Mother?" Joseph was the only living being who could ask Beryl such a direct, personal question. And he was the only one who would receive an honest answer.

"It's chronic and often distracting, but I'm a tough old bird, Joseph. I've learned to box up the pain and hammer it shut like a crate of rosy apples from the Yakima Valley. Don't worry about me. I suffer the expected consequences of old age."

Joseph squeezed her arm. He hated the thought of Beryl's aging. "There are Chinese physicians who do wonderful things western doctors know nothing of…"

"If pain comes to be an unbearable burden, I'll trust you to find such a treatment. Meanwhile, tell me about your work and let me see what is in progress."

If Joseph were the only one permitted to ask personal questions of Beryl, she was the only soul on earth given the privilege of viewing a work of his in progress.

IV

Paulina returned to Mercer's Island to find Highland Home in the grip of an influenza croup epidemic. Gertrude was near collapse, and Lavinia alarmingly ill. Many of the boarders were confined to bed. They needed help. She was happy that Beryl remained in California and that the sisters who accompanied her home to Washington were trained nurses. The sickness at Highland Home was out of control.

"Please, Sister," Nancy Collins said weakly. "I need my daddy."

"I know, dear. But it's not wise that we have visitors while there's illness here. Will you take more juice?"

Nancy took a sip. "But Sister, Daddy's a doctor," Nancy told her.

Paulina sent for him immediately.

With Gertrude exhausted and Lavinia too ill to make decisions, Paulina took over. She sent their caretaker's son, Sung Woo to Seattle to fetch Nancy's father. They were back on the grounds before mid afternoon. Paulina took Doctor Collins to the children first, then made the rounds of the community with him. She was distressed to find the situation worse than she had known. "We should have called you sooner," Paulina said.

"Nancy tells me you just returned this morning?"

"Yes. At first I thought there were mostly sick children, but our older sisters were trying to continue in spite of feeling ill."

"Influenza can get out of hand very quickly. How many sisters can you spare to help?"

"As many as you need. But how much danger are we asking them to face?"

"Good question. Send only those sisters who have had the croup as a child, or those who have already been exposed to influenza."

"I can send the novices. But I'll need their Mistress' permission. She's ill in the infirmary, but I'll see her immediately."

"Is there a place for me to stay over?"

"Yes. The chaplain's quarters. Sister Gertrude sent him off island. He's elderly, and with weak lungs and a bad heart."

"She's to be commended for her sensible decision. Now, Sister, see that I have ice. Lots of it. I assume you have an ice cellar."

"Yes."

"Also get me sacks—anything to put chips in. It's for the high fevers." He went into his bag. "This is ipecac. Have you used it?" When she nodded, he instructed her to have it administered to two of the youngest sick children who were beginning to have trouble breathing.

Sister Gertrude staggered into the parlor. "Doctor! We're losing Sister Lavinia."

The words stuck Paulina like a blow.

"We'll lose you if you don't get some rest," he snapped, but followed her down the hall.

Paulina was astonished at how Sister Lavinia had failed, even during the course of a few hours. She was pale against the infirmary bed pillow that Gertrude had propped up to help her breathe. Paulina took her thin hand. It was unexpectedly cold.

"Sister..." she whispered. "Tell Mother...I will pray..." Her eyes were fixed and there was a faint gurgling sound in her throat. The barely perceptible pressure on Paulina's hand loosened.

"Oh, no!" Paulina groaned.

The doctor's efficient hand checked the carotid artery and her eyes. "She's gone, Sister."

Gertrude came to the bed and knelt beside it. "May God and His angels meet you!" she said softly. Looking up at the doctor, she said, "It's true that I'm exhausted, but I'm not sick and I am strong. I'll take care of the body."

"Very well, Sister."

Paulina found a sister to show Doctor Collins back to the children's wing, and went to the novitiate. Sister Dolores Mary, Lavinia's assistant, was with the group trying to keep their schedule of study and prayer. She looked at Paulina, surprised to see her in this area forbidden to all except the Mistress and her assistant.

"Excuse me, Sisters," Paulina said, "I have sad news. Sister Lavinia has just left us—peacefully and promising her prayers." Many of the novices' eyes filled with tears. "I need your help. You're dispensed from your normal schedule. From this moment until further notice, you will have charge of the kitchen and all housekeeping duties. Those of you who have had the croup as a child will come with me to help with the sick. Sister Dolores Mary will show you what we need. Perhaps you would like to stop at the chapel first to pray for our dear Sister?"

Paulina sent their gardener to the mainland for Adam Piggoty's help. They would need a grave dug—pray God only one—and a casket. But he would need to be prepared for more. She instructed the caretaker to send a telegram to Mother Charbonneau, which she wrote hastily. She warned her not to return until the danger was over. Paulina had taken charge decisively and efficiently. She didn't hesitate to make decisions, knowing that if she made a mistake, Mother Charbonneau would understand.

In the next three days they lost another one of the older sisters in the infirmary, and two of the younger professed teachers in the boarders' school. Doctor Collins told Paulina that the younger sister was already ill with undetected consumption.

"But she had such a healthy glow about her!" Paulina protested.

"An unfortunate phenomenon of her condition."

The bishop sent a young priest to the island to counsel and provide the sacraments. The sadness of the house's loss was accentuated by a series of stormy, heavily clouded days typical of early June in the Pacific Northwest. On the seventh day, the clouds were gone, the day shone brilliant, and Doctor Collins was certain that the worst was over.

"I need some fresh air, Sister. Will you come for a walk?" he asked Paulina.

They took the trail to the cedar grove, the ground steaming with the warm sun that now flooded the woods and brightened the grounds. The Cascade range glowed white to the east as they reached a clearing. There had been a late snowfall on the higher elevations.

"Beautiful country," the doctor said.

"The sisters will have the blessing of God's sunshine," Paulina said, referring to the burial which was to be later that day.

"Did you come from this area, Sister?" Dr. Collins said changing the subject.

"I was born in Seattle. I went to school in Tacoma, and to college in

Indiana, but Seattle has always been home. Were you born here?" she asked in return, realizing that this walk and this conversation was not customary for a young nun.

"No. I'm a Boston boy, raised and educated back East. I came west during one vacation from medical school to see my Uncle Barney. He was a tough old codger, who used to run cattle over the Snoqualmie trail mid century. I took one look at these mountains and knew I was home. I had to return. I climbed Mount Rainier that summer."

"To the top?"

"To the very top. I don't have the words to tell you what it was like. I met my wife on that climb."

"Do you still climb?"

"I do when I can."

"Does your wife still climb with you?"

"Adele died giving birth to Nancy."

"I'm so sorry," Paulina said. "How did you manage with an infant?"

"The Providence Sisters had a charity ward whose baby had been stillborn. Mauve came to take care of Nancy. She was an Irish girl who had been literally owned by her employer. He discarded her when he got her pregnant. It was a mess. He reclaimed her, and I ended up buying her freedom. I enrolled Nancy here when I sent Mauve back to Ireland to care for her aged parents."

Doctor Geoffrey Collins was devoted to his work. He was a senior doctor on the staff of Seattle's Providence Hospital, as well as having an associate private practice. He was known as brilliant, dedicated, and efficient. He was not noted for warmth or friendliness, as any nursing sister at Providence could confirm. He met their formality in kind with a curt, brusque manner modified with courtesy. The truth of it was that he didn't like nuns. His early education in Boston had been in a parochial school. As a little lad, he had suffered the tutelage of a sister with a sadistic streak. He was continually on the wrong side of her tongue and her switch. As he progressed in school, he had nothing but contempt for sisters, who, if he had been old enough and wise enough to understand, were woefully untrained. His pre-adolescent arrogance saw these nuns as stupid and he didn't consider that there was any excuse for it.

When he moved from the sisters' school to a Jesuit preparatory institution, his life changed. The staff recognized an exceptionally bright boy. Most of the Jesuits shared Geoffrey's contempt for the teaching sisters' lack of training. Geoffrey studied hard, and by the time he graduated from prep school and entered Harvard University, he was committed to a career in medicine. Even if he had been more inclined to a course of studies in the liberal arts, he would not have been attracted to a life in the Church, even though the Jesuits made every effort to attract the young man to their ranks.

When he married Adele, he had been happy and had planned for a long life with her, and they hoped for several children to enrich their marriage. At her death, he withdrew into his work. After a suitable interval, his friends and associates introduced him to "eligible" young ladies, but Geoffrey wasn't attracted to them. Examining his disinterest, he wondered if it were because he didn't want to be hurt again, or if he were too particular. The Irish au pair, Mauve, had taken care of Nancy and the house, so he wasn't in any hurry to find a helpmate. His conclusion was that there was a right person for everyone, and perhaps he had found his and there wouldn't be another.

Geoffrey did not have to remain on Mercer's Island for the entire week. After the first few days he could have left his powders and instructions in Sister Gertrude's able care. But he stayed. He stayed for the stolen moments with Sister Paulina Soldano. He stayed to watch her slender, delicate figure walk down the hall. He stayed to hear her voice, soft as satin, as she sang to the sick boarders with tones as true and clear as a flute's. And he stayed to catch the smile that made bright those thickly lashed dark eyes. He imagined her hair, black and shining. He knew from the strands that frequently escaped from under her wimple that her head was not shorn. He imagined the firm body not entirely disguised under the tunic with the belt that revealed a minuscule waist.

Nancy had told him about her beloved teacher, whose kindness and guidance toward his awkward daughter had already effected a dramatic change. Nancy was growing into a lovely girl. But he had never had more than passing curiosity about "Sister Paulina." By the time he left the island he admitted to himself that he was in love with this young woman, and he also recognized that nothing would come of his infatuation. She had given him absolutely no opening to speak, although there had been many occasions when confidences could have been shared. He felt like the stable boy who sneaked looks at the young princess while painfully aware that his love was an impossible dream. He had asked Paulina to walk with him hoping against hope that she would speak in some way that indicated a mutual attraction. She did not.

He had been offered a position in San Francisco, which he had not considered seriously, partly out of unwillingness to uproot and start again. He thought now that he should accept. Nancy could stay in school on the island if she wished until she completed her elementary education, and come to him for vacations. For himself, he needed new challenges, new faces, and new surroundings. Perhaps then he could forget Sister Paulina Soldano.

V

The time to elect a new Mother General would come in a few months. Beryl was anxious to give up the Mother Generalship, but first she would embark on her last visitation of convents. She would make a particular effort to express her concerns about maintaining the unity of the expanding Congregation. Their membership had grown, and their convents were established in five western states, with invitations to establish schools in Nevada and Arizona.

Beryl spent many prayerful hours analyzing her personal feelings regarding a successor and trying to balance them with objectivity. The thought of Marietta as Mother General gave her no peace. Was her unwillingness to accept Marietta's succession a retaliation for the opposition Marietta made publicly whenever circumstances gave her the opportunity? Marietta had modified her views over the years, and the majority of professed sisters were unaware of any disagreements. If the matter had been discussed, it had long since lost the glamour of controversy between two women of power. Marietta had a reputation for scholarship, and for fairness. Not even sisters who were unsuccessful teachers resented her criticisms. If those in Montana who noted her coolness to Sister Paulina Soldano wondered why, their conclusions would be to question Paulina, not Marietta.

Beryl tried to put herself in younger sisters' minds. Why not choose Sister Marietta? She was an appropriately mature age, and she was one of the first pioneer sisters. She had a fine education, was experienced as a supervisor of schools, and a natural leader. But as Mother General, what would Marietta do to Paulina? Paulina would be an ideal administrator of the community's schools, but it was not likely that Marietta would give her nemesis a position that would set her up as the Mother General after her own terms.

Beryl sat in the darkness of the cedar grove. She was up and dressed before Mass on this day when she would be leaving for visitations. This time she had asked a young sister from the Lake Forest Park convent north of Seattle to be her companion. They would meet in Seattle. "Oh God, give me a humble heart!" Beryl prayed. "You have begun our work, and I must let You bring it to perfection!"

While Beryl didn't want to stop the growth that seemed to be based upon the need in many cities and towns, she was concerned that the Sisters of Martha and Mary were losing the intimate family spirit that had made the Congregation special. Beryl was accustomed to planning ahead, but she realized that soon these matters would be in the hands of another, most likely Marietta. Beryl had completed her last series of visitations and was visiting Joseph when word came that her dear friend Lizzie Ordway was dying. A steamer direct to Seattle was the quickest way north.

Adam's horses snorted their impatience as he waited by the berth where the steamer from San Francisco would dock. Gusts of wind shook his carriage. His heavy wagon would have been safer on this blustery day, but he wanted Beryl Charbonneau to have protection from the weather as they drove up the hill. Not that she would mind. If there had been no other way north, she would have leapt astride a strong horse and ridden all the way from California to be with her friend. Lizzie Ordway had been ill for several months and the time left to her was now a matter of days. She rested at Captain and Mrs. Lilly's residence with the comfort of good friends and also relatives who had come to settle in Seattle.

The wind found a loose flap in the carriage top and it could have ripped without Adam's swift attention. He secured it just as the steamer appeared northwest of Magnolia Bluff. As the boat docked, he approached it, holding his hat as he waited by the off loading ramp which shook perilously as the craft moved in the choppy water. He spotted Beryl clutching her cloak tightly, her cane tucked under one arm as she balanced herself by clutching the rope on the gangplank. Adam rushed to her assistance, wondering how the ship's crew could permit her to proceed unescorted. There was a uniformed man pursuing her, he noted, and realized in the same instant that Beryl had started down as soon as the gangplank was lowered ignoring efforts of the crew to restrain her. Adam met her half way.

"I've arranged for my baggage to be taken to the convent," she told Adam. "There's no need to wait for it." As he helped steady Beryl, his old hat blew from his head and settled in the bay, bobbing up and down like one of the seagulls who populated the docks no matter what the weather. "Oh, Adam, your hat!"

"No matter," he said to Beryl. He turned the horses slowly from the dock, mindful that the wood planking was slippery even for beasts who could balance on four legs. The rain assaulted them and the wind became stronger as they went up the hill. It was a short ride, and Captain Lilly was waiting for her on his porch terrace. He led Beryl into the parlor where Lizzie, fully dressed, was sitting in a lounge chair in front of bay windows. Her eyes were sunken in dark circles, and her skin was taut against the bones of her face.

"I love a good storm," she said to Beryl as she entered the room. Beryl noticed immediately that Lizzie's voice had lost the full bodied tones typical of her friend. 'My school teacher voice,' Lizzie had called it. She was propped up on pillows. "Were you seasick?"

"My stomach considered rebelling, but I wouldn't permit it," Beryl said, pulling a chair close to Lizzie and taking her hand, which was limp and cold.

"Well, how do I look?" Lizzie asked testing her friend's truthfulness.

"Terrible," Beryl replied. "You should never wear green; I've told you it makes you look like a frog."

Lizzie drew in a breath and smiled. For a long time neither spoke until Lizzie asked, "Beryl, do you really believe in the myth of an afterlife?"

"Probably not the way it's pictured in holy books or in Father Mercelli's sermons. But, yes, I don't believe we end here."

"Can you picture me with wings sitting on a cloud," Lizzie rasped with a cough.

"Yes," Beryl said, looking out the window at the wildly swaying trees and muddy streams pouring down the road. "On a day like this, frankly, yes!" She squeezed Lizzie's hand. "But the stories I heard all my life about the greatest bliss being to sing and pray all day with the angels…well, I personally would have little taste for it."

"Possibly because you can't sing," Lizzie said weakly. "So what would it be like, if we did go on?"

"I think we go on becoming," Beryl answered trying to find the right words. "We spend our lives trying to get the better of all the nastiness flesh is heir to. And when we succeed, it brings us closer to what we should be."

"And hellfire?"

"Oh, you know I don't really believe in that either. That would mean God gave up on us, and I don't think He would. Somehow we're meant to get it right, sooner or later. What we didn't finish on Earth, maybe we'll learn after. And don't ever quote me, my dear. As you well know, Mother Foundresses aren't supposed to be heretics."

"But you surely are, as I well know, and you have admitted! You may convert me yet, Beryl."

"I don't want to convert you. How would I answer to God if I tried to change what He meant you to be?" They sat in silence again, and Beryl noticed that Lizzie was beginning to doze. Pressing her hand she rose and kissed her forehead. "I'll be back later," she whispered.

Lizzie slipped away peacefully a few days later.

"Will she be taken to Bainbridge?" Beryl asked Captain Lilly.

"She gave her place in the cemetery to Mattie Kate. We're going to have her in our plot at Lakeview."

"There will not be another like her in my time," Beryl said. "She was a great woman, a great human being. "You're still with us, dear, and always will be," Beryl told Lizzie in an unspoken farewell at the cemetery. Many sisters from the Congregation attended the funeral in the company of men and women prominent in the community of both Kitsap and King counties. In the eulogy, her vision and determination was proclaimed and also her accomplishments, including her exhibit of Washington's education system for the Chicago World's Fair. Not the least of her legacy was the establishment of many schools in Kitsap county. The Seattle *Post Intelligencer* gave her high praise and admitted it had been mistaken in its opposition to her bid for superintendent of schools years before.

Lavinia's death during the influenza epidemic had been a grave loss for Beryl, but Lizzie's left her indescribably lonely. Through the years, Lizzie Ordway had been the voice of reason and inspiration, of truth and friendship. Her love of Lavinia was deep, but Lizzie was there for her in another way: she was alter ego, a part of her being, in much the same way as Father Louis Bertrand had been. In her grief she wondered if she would ever see these dear friends again. Astonished at her doubts, she realized that two of those to whom she could have expressed them were gone. And this is where the truth of all I believe must be faced. *Dear Lord, I believe, help Thou my unbelief!*

Part Ten

I

The community was gathered for the historic election, and there was nowhere for Beryl to have a private conversation with Joseph, who had arrived from San Francisco. His delicate Mai Ling had died. Beryl grieved for Joseph. She would have sent Su Ping to California, even though rules established by the Church for the "Canonical Novitiate," forbid a candidate's being absent. Beryl suggested that she circumvent this rule by leaving the convent and then returning to enter again as a postulant the next year. Su Ping had told Beryl that if she could have seen her mother while she was still living, and if there had been the slightest hope of reconciliation with her, she would have followed this advice.

So that she and Joseph might speak in private, Beryl asked Adam to drive her to Lakeview where they sat near the ferry dock. Joseph was thin and looked ill. He told Beryl of Mai Ling's valiant fight to overcome lung fever, but she was not strong enough. Sung Chow and Lee had come to be with her at the end.

"Joseph! Why didn't you ask to have me send Su Ping? There are no customs or vows that should keep a daughter from her mother at such a time!"

"The bitterness between them was never resolved, Mother. I know you would have sent Su Ping, but how would she have taken a refusal by her mother to see her?"

"What will you do with your beautiful house? Surely you won't sell it. And what of Sung Chow?"

"I would as soon burn the house as sell it. I gave it to Lee, and over time he must give Sung Chow a third of its value. Lee loves the place, and he's welcome to make any changes. I will never go there again. Sung Chow wants to attend school in San Francisco. He should have the choice. Mai Ling had several relatives in the city."

"What are you going to do?"

"I gave my resignation to the University. I don't need the money. I think I will imitate your Carmelite days, my Mother, and become a hermit. Solitude might give me the clarity of vision I need. Right now I don't have the heart for work."

"That will return."

"I don't know. Has my soul become a sieve that cannot contain creative wholeness? I feel my essence is slipping away."

"If you were a Christian mystic, I would tell you that you are wandering in the dark night of the soul. Stay here on the island, Joseph. The gardener's house is empty. I will see to it that no one—not even myself will disturb your solitude. We won't even feed you. Bring your own supplies. Be alone; accept the darkness of your spirit; let it cover you like a night without moon or stars. One day there will be a dawn."

Beryl put her arms around her beloved Joseph, now a man whose years had finally betrayed him. She pressed the heavy garden house key into his hand. "If you decide to use it," she whispered. Beryl walked with Joseph back to the carriage where Adam waited without giving in to a limp. If the march of years had overtaken Joseph, they had stomped upon her with crushingly cleated boots. But never mind. Joseph had come back to her.

II

1903

The sisters were crowded in the Motherhouse. Every member of the Congregation of Martha and Mary was present for the election that would end the era of Mother Beryl Charbonneau. It was the beginning of a new century; it was a turning point for the Congregation. The community had voted to elect first, then enter their retreat. The new Mother General, and few doubted that it would be anyone other than Marietta McGinnis, would be able to decide upon new appointments and announce them while the sisters were in silent retreat.

The election took three ballots before Marietta was declared Mother General. In a development that shocked Marietta, the first ballot had an overwhelming majority of write-in votes for Beryl Charbonneau. It was merely a tribute, for the sisters knew her mind. Still, it was an indication to Marietta that the community was still very much Mother Charbonneau's, and that Beryl was beloved. This support came as a shock to Marietta. It put her in the uneasy position of "second best." When the second vote was counted, there was an alarming thirty-five percent for Paulina Soldano. This necessitated a third ballot, and by a very small majority, Marietta was elected. With so many sisters declaring support for Paulina, it would be logical for the new Mother General to appoint her to a high office in the Congregation. Director of Schools would be an expected appointment, but Marietta couldn't bear the thought of working with Paulina so closely. How could she get around this?

Sister Philomena Duffy was popular with the community, and equally qualified to be in charge of the Congregation's schools. No one would question her appointment as Director of Schools, which was the first assignment Marietta posted.

Philomena had entered the Academy for Girls in Tacoma when she was in the ninth grade. Michael Duffy's family of three girls and two boys moved to Seattle when Michael was appointed regional director of a San Francisco shipping line in 1873. The family had been happy in San Francisco, but Duffy was ambitious and there was less opportunity for advancement in California. By accepting the Seattle directorship, he would rise in the company faster and more surely. Seattle was a growing town, and social advancement was also promising. He envisioned himself as a political candidate if his reputation as businessman and civic leader were properly established.

Philomena was the middle child. She possessed a quiet intelligence that singled her out in spite of her unassuming ways. She did not think of herself as pretty, although when she sat in front of her dressing table mirror, she judged that her features were tolerably regular, classic even, but then there was the fact of her freckles and the red hair that frizzled around her face defying all efforts to keep it under control. These two aspects of her appearance loomed large in Philomena's mind and saved her from vanity. However, she was satisfied with her taller than average, slender frame, and she also knew that her quickness of mind was not a common gift.

The older Duffy girls were left to finish school in California in the care of their maternal grandparents. Philomena had graduated from grammar school and was eager to join in the adventure of moving north. While her parents searched for a suitable home, Philomena enrolled at the boarding school operated by the new Congregation of Martha and Mary. A young sister, Paulina Soldano with dark eyes and a Mediterranean look was just out of normal school and she was Philomena's advisor and English teacher. Sister Paulina had gone to school at the academy before she entered the order and was a capable and enthusiastic teacher. Philomena and Sister Paulina became friends during the three years of Philomena's studies. The girl confided to the young sister that she might want to enter the Congregation, but she pledged Paulina to silence. Her parents had no objections to their daughter's entering, but Philomena told them she would like to finish her education first.

Ever since the sixth grade her goal had been to attend St. Mary's in Indiana, and her teachers had encouraged her. The Duffy family had no financial problems, and they promised Philomena that if she wished to go east to school, she could do so. Philomena loved the Sisters of Martha and Mary and appreciated the fact that the community was less restrictive than others. But she was realistic. If she began the three year novitiate after high school, she wouldn't have any advanced schooling until her first profession, and then she'd be sent to Normal school for one or two years. If she waited and entered with a prestigious degree, her life in the community would be different.

Philomena's pastor and confessor was not pleased with what he judged to be the girl's calculating appraisal of her future, but he had to admit that she had a point. The girl was modest, generous, and sufficiently pious, so he agreed with her decision. Philomena said nothing to the sisters, made no application, and kept her future plans to herself. Her pastor warned her that she might lose her vocation, but Philomena insisted that if it were real, it would stand the test of time.

When Philomena's family discovered that through their generous financing of a scholarship Sister Marietta McGinnis would be traveling to Indiana to school, they were pleased that their daughter would have a companion at school. Sister Marietta and Philomena would travel together on the rail trip east. But when the Duffys brought Philomena to the station, it was Sister Paulina Soldano who was being sent off by Mother Lavinia and several Sisters of Martha and Mary. Philomena fairly squealed her delight, and Paulina told her that it was the greatest surprise of her life. "I never dreamed of St. Mary's, but I'm thrilled to be going. One day I was enrolling my pupils at the new Italian school in Seattle, and the very next I was packing my trunk to go east!"

Philomena came home for two of the four summers, but Sister Paulina remained at school taking extra classes so she could complete a Master's Degree by the end of her four years. Philomena met Mother Charbonneau and Paulina's mother when the two came east. Mattie Kate took an instant liking to Philomena and teased her about the undisciplined kind of red hair they shared. "Fortunately for her, Paulina inherited her father's Mediterranean looks," Mattie Kate told Philomena.

When Beryl visited St. Mary's, Philomena was just a year from graduation. She decided to speak to Mother Charbonneau about admission to the community. Beryl was pleased. Not only would the Congregation benefit from her ready-made education, Philomena seemed to possess good sense. The sisters of Holy Cross told Beryl that the girl was popular and uncommonly mature. At school Philomena earned the nickname "Old Iron Trap" because of her ability to keep any secret and also not to divulge her own deeper thoughts.

Paulina went home to receive an appointment to the new girl's high school in Bellingham, Washington, and Philomena entered the postulancy in Fort Vancouver. The day Philomena received the habit, she laughed with the others that the wimple which would cover her wild hair was very welcome. It was unusual that Philomena would make any personal remark, and her contemporaries remembered it. Many of them had confided their ups and downs to this sister, who was older than the majority and who had become their natural leader. Philomena always listened, but gently deferred advice to Mother Lavinia, their Mistress of Novices. Philomena never broke a confidence, and any concern could be trusted to her.

After her profession, Beryl assigned Philomena and Paulina to the new college for young ladies in Montana, where Sister Marietta was appointed dean. Within two years Philomena had been promoted to be history department chairman. It was obvious to the staff that Paulina did not enjoy Marietta's approval. Her superior took any opportunity to criticize and publicly reprimand her. The college complex included the grades, high school and the two year college. In one incident, Father Catrell, the chaplain, questioned Sister Paulina's curriculum content. Not wanting to embarrass a capable teacher, he approached Paulina directly.

"Emile Zola does not seem an appropriate author for Catholic young ladies," he commented.

"Possibly not, Father, but we're studying the Dreyfus affair and comparing it to other such parodies of justice in works such as Ibsen, and bringing our discussions directly to the study of Our Lord's wrongful persecution by the Pharisees. I have not used this author's antipathy toward the faith."

Father Catrell was satisfied and mentioned the matter to Marietta, intending to praise the young teacher. Marietta used the information to give Paulina a reprimand and announced the chaplain's concern in a general meeting without presenting his conclusions. Such incidents troubled Philomena. In her own history classes, the content and discussions were sometimes off the mainstream of Catholic doctrine. At St. Mary's, the students had been encouraged to face criticism of the church and respond to it intelligently, aware of the fact that some of it was legitimate.

Philomena was aware of questions and whispers on the part of others who were more puzzled with Marietta's obvious antipathy toward Paulina as time went on. Philomena distanced herself from gossip, but wrote frequent private notes of support to Paulina. Without having to say so in words, both knew that it was best for the community that sides not be taken. If Philomena had made an issue of supporting Paulina, others would follow. Some sisters, seeing loyalty to Marietta as their duty, would take her part. Such division always compromised the peace of the house and ultimately that of the Congregation. Both Philomena and Paulina were relieved when the Highland Home was completed and Mother Charbonneau appointed Paulina to teach in the boarders' school.

After Marietta's election as Mother General, Philomena received a summons from her. Their meeting was cordial, and at that time Marietta made no mention of an approaching appointment. She had always treated Philomena with respect, but now there was a subtle change. It seemed to Philomena that she was being enlisted as an ally. Subsequently, she was surprised to discover that she was named supervisor of the Congregation's schools. It would have been pointless to dispute the appointment by protesting that Paulina was better qualified. Marietta was not one to listen to advice. And if she had been persuaded, how would Paulina and Marietta work together? They would not. Philomena accepted and wondered what role Paulina would be given. After all, the sisters had given her a sizable percentage of their vote.

Philomena was heartsick as one appointment after another was posted, and Paulina's name was absent. The prestigious positions went to others, often to those far less qualified. Mother Charbonneau was named Mistress of Novices, which no one in the community would dispute. Sub Mistress would be young Sister Joan Sinclair. It could have been Paulina. Mistress of Postulants was Dorothea, who had experience as Mother Lavinia's Sub-Mistress, but there too, Paulina would have been the better choice. Sister Gertrude continued as Infirmarian with an assistant; principals were named to every school, and in one posting after another Paulina's name was left out as those less qualified were appointed.

Philomena was distressed at the degree of unfairness. More than distressed, she was angry. Many times in her life she had been told that it was fortunate she didn't have a flaming temper to match her Irish ancestry. *It may have come late,* Philomena thought to herself, *but it is most definitely present now.* Marietta had scheduled conferences with four sisters before the retreat master's afternoon homily. It was a perfect time for Philomena to speak to her former superior. She slipped a note under Mother Charbonneau's door which requested a meeting. Philomena suggested a classroom in the boarders' wing which was empty for the summer.

Beryl was waiting when Philomena came to the rendezvous. The younger sister came to the point without wasting words. She had not brought the Mother Foundress of this Congregation out of retreat to inquire about her health or make small talk.

"Mother, I am concerned, gravely concerned that Sister Paulina Soldano has not been appointed to any position she deserves by experience and ability."

Beryl, seated at a study table, indicated a chair to Philomena. "God has blessed our Congregation with vocations and material goods. He has asked us for sacrifices along the way…"

Philomena interrupted. She was in no mood for platitudes, whether they came from the celebrated foundress or not. "Respectfully, Mother, it is not God who asks a sacrifice from Philomena, it is Sister Marietta."

"Mother Marietta," Beryl corrected mildly. "No, Sister, it is God. And it is for us to give Paulina to His care for His purposes."

"Mother, I don't understand. How can you not be offended by the obvious affront to a sister as faithful and valuable to our Congregation?"

"Sister Paulina left us several hours before Mother Marietta's election. Our retreat master and I witnessed her signature on the papers of exclaustration and dispensation from her vows."

Philomena sat in stunned silence. She hadn't seen Paulina for several days, but retreats of the Congregation of Martha and Mary were designed to give maximum privacy to the sisters. Meal tables were set up, but sisters could take their repast out of doors, or in their rooms. There were no seats reserved in order of their rank in the community, and in chapel sisters might sit in the balcony area unobserved from the lower floor. Freedom and solitude characterized the ten days of retreat. There was no conversation or socialization except for the necessary business the Mother General might have to conduct. Philomena had not thought to look for Paulina.

"So that's why Mother Marietta didn't appoint her," Philomena said, feeling embarrassment.

"I didn't say that. Marietta doesn't know yet."

To Philomena, this news was more startling a revelation than that of Paulina's leaving.

Beryl continued. "If Marietta had appointed Paulina to a high office, I would have told her immediately. I was quite certain that she would not." Beryl had taken the measure of Sister Philomena's character years ago, and she had not been disappointed in her. She could be trusted with a confidence.

"God gives us trials in different ways, Sister. I pray that Marietta will one day realize that her antipathy toward Paulina is the single most important challenge to her spiritual life. You know that in all other ways she is fair. Her ability and accomplishments are unquestioned."

"But why does she hate Paulina?"

"I would like to be able to modify your terminology, Sister, but I cannot. I will answer your question, but you must never repeat what I tell you."

"You can rely on that, Mother."

Philomena listened as Mother Charbonneau recounted the events that led to substituting Paulina for Marietta's place at St. Mary's.

"Paulina never suspected the reason?"

"She believed, as did the community, that Marietta was given an opportunity for greater honors at a secular institution where she would compete on an equal basis with men and women. The results of her success bear witness to that conclusion. Neither you nor Paulina received such accolades, nor were your degrees valued more highly by the community or those we serve."

"It is still difficult for me to grasp that Paulina is gone. She must have decided this some time ago. She was my idea of a perfect sister. Was she really so unhappy?"

"No. Not unhappy with her life as a sister. On our last trip together we talked at length. It was Paulina's belief that she stood in the way of Marietta's peace."

"But that is Mother Marietta's failing! Paulina shouldn't have to answer for someone else's sins against charity!"

"True. Paulina also knew that Marietta would not want to work with her, and for the next six or twelve years there would be constant tension. She was aware that Marietta's feelings could lead to a serious split in the community if sisters, quite understandably, took sides. Paulina is a woman of deep spirituality. She doesn't need to wear a habit to be a light of faith."

Philomena nodded her agreement. "Where did she go?"

"She accepted a post as headmistress of a private school in San Francisco where Elizabeth Ordway went to teach many years ago. I'll give you the address and I hope you will see her each time your position calls you south. Your friendship may be easier to maintain now that it doesn't have to depend on clandestine notes pushed under doors!"

"You knew about that, Mother?"

"Paulina told me you gave her courage when she felt most alone and unwanted."

"I tried. Now I think I should have spoken out openly in Paulina's defense."

"You would have forced Marietta to compound her sin. I'm glad you didn't," Beryl said, rising to her feet. "And one day I look to you to lead our community." She didn't wait for a response, but smiled at Philomena and left the room.

Beryl concluded that the best way to inform Marietta of Paulina's departure would be in written words. Beryl did not want any confrontation, and she believed that a direct statement that could be read in private and reread was the best means of communication. She sat in her new room that was located at the end of the novitiate. Her desk was by the window and overlooked a stand of trees beyond which was the lake and Mount Rainier. She had pen and ink and a page of foolscap in front of her, but she had put no words to paper.

The room was undecorated, except for the cedar crucifix on the long wall. It was a gift from Lizzie, who had commissioned Joseph to sculpt it for Beryl's twenty-fifth anniversary of vows. Lizzie had written a note with the gift which Beryl had folded and attached to the back.

My dear friend,

As I look at this work of art that so profoundly represents your faith, I am reminded of the words in the Gospel: "Greater love hath no man than that he lay down his life for his friends."

Lovingly,
Lizzie O.

Remembering the words in Lizzie's note, Beryl knew what her words to Marietta would be. She dipped her pen in the well and began to write.

* * * * *

The Congregation's second Mother General had worked all afternoon on the last day of retreat. She scarcely noticed the magnificent sunset that turned low clouds blood red. Marietta turned up her oil lamp as it grew dark, and labored over charts that represented community assignments for the next year. She didn't notice the envelope on the floor by the door until she resigned herself to the fatigue that demanded rest for her body and mind. She pushed uncompleted work back on her desk and reserved the list that was to be posted. She thought that she would take it to the bulletin board by the chapel entrance tonight so early risers could read it. She picked up the envelope and noted her name in Mother Charbonneau's writing. She experienced a flash of annoyance. It had seemed up to now that Mother would leave her alone without imposing recommendations or advice. This was a new beginning and Mother should be content with her appointment as Novice Mistress. She had endured conferences with many sisters who took special pains to extol Beryl Charbonneau and encourage Marietta to preserve the spirit of the Congregation she had established.

The very mention of Beryl Charbonneau seemed like slaps in her face. Objectively, she knew that the sisters did not wish her ill. Yet, she wondered if she were destined to be an extension of the legendary Beryl Charbonneau rather than a leader in her own right. Whatever the former Mother General did seemed to be tolerated. One example was that Indian who was now installed in the gardener's cottage. What kind of religious rule permitted a Mother General's friends to invade premises that should be exclusive to members of the community?

She took a letter opener and slit the seal. The contents informed her simply and directly that Paulina Soldano was no longer a member of the Congregation of Martha and Mary. At the end of the note there was a cryptic message. *Sister Paulina made this decision unselfishly for the unity of the community she loved. Remember, "greater love hath no man than he lay down his life for his friends."* What did Mother Charbonneau mean? Was she praising Paulina for defection? Was she telling her, Marietta, to continue in the spirit of sacrifice for her community of which she was now the leader? Was she saying that in spite of Paulina's breaking her commitment, Christ, with His sacrifice on the Cross would redeem her? Whatever the message, she would not have to face the problem of placing Paulina. Thank God, she was free of her.

There was one more thing she could accomplish before the end of retreat, and she needed to get it off her mind. She sent for Beryl Charbonneau.

Marietta wasted no time in pleasantries. Beryl hoped that her note had inspired the new superior to speak to her openly about Sister Paulina. She had underestimated Marietta's sense of fairness. Demons of the past could be expelled and a new beginning, unmarked as a fresh new slate would bless her office. What did come from Mother Marietta was unexpected and vicious.

"Mother Charbonneau, I am told that your Indian friend is residing in what was meant as the gardener's cottage. Please inform him that the community will be hiring permanent help and the premises must be vacated immediately."

Beryl stared at Marietta, the words wounding her like physical blows. She willed her voice to be calm. "Joseph Wolf, whom you have known as a friend of our community, professional colleague, and a world renown artist has recently lost his wife. He was in profound spiritual distress. He occupies the gardener's cottage at my invitation."

"He has my invitation to go elsewhere."

"The Council has made no plans to employ a gardener. Adam Piggoty is still capable of supervising our modest landscaping."

"Will you inform your friend that he is to leave, or must I ask the law enforcement from Lakeview to convey the message?"

Beryl regarded Marietta without a reply, then turned away from her to fix her gaze on the view of Highland Home's southern acres. The length of her silence was beginning to unnerve the younger woman. Beryl spoke quietly and with an intensity that left no doubt that what she said she meant literally. "When I go out your door, it will mean that I reject any obligation of obedience to you and, therefore, it follows that in acknowledging such a great sin I must accept expulsion from the Congregation and such punishment as ecclesiastical superiors give me. You must convey your decision to Joseph face to face. Joseph Wolf must find another place of rest and solitude which he will need if he is to complete an important work of art commissioned by His Excellency for the new cathedral. As to my…"

"Oh, stop it!" Marietta spat the words. "You can have your way. No one has ever dared oppose you, but the time will come that the great Beryl Charbonneau will be a feeble legend hardly remembered in a vital new community meant for its future, not its irrelevant past!"

The two women regarded each other without further words. Beryl left and shut herself behind the locked door of her room. She would repeat this conversation to no one. Did the Congregation have any idea of Marietta's character? First thing tomorrow she would contrive to have Joseph invited to another location. Oh, how she wished she could have had Lizzie's counsel.

The sun had set hours ago, and even the great mountain had faded into the night. It seemed to Beryl as she stared at the darkness that Lizzie's voice spoke to her. "Look up, my friend, and you'll see the stars."

III
San Francisco
1906

The young applicant looked familiar to Paulina, but then this was not the first group of fifteen year olds she had seen, and there had been many faces. The girl had stepped in the room, then retreated as if she were afraid to come any closer. Paulina wondered if she had become grim in the space of two years as headmistress. The door opened again and the girl returned, dragging a tall man.

"Doctor Collins!" Paulina exclaimed, "And, yes! It's Nancy! What a pleasant surprise!"

"See, Daddy, I told you it was Sister Paulina!"

Paulina came forward to shake the doctor's hand and to give Nancy a hug. "It's not 'Sister' anymore, it's just Paulina," she told the doctor. "And 'Miss Soldano' to all our students," she told Nancy.

"Had I known you were in San Francisco," the doctor said, "I would have contacted you."

"Oh, it's just as well. I'm only beginning to feel comfortable out of the habit and in the wide world," Paulina said lightly. "You've come to enroll Nancy?"

"We were out comparing schools, but I think that won't be necessary anymore, do you, Nancy?"

"Most definitely not! This is it!" Nancy said fervently.

"We do have an excellent curriculum, Doctor Collins, but so does the high school operated by the Sisters of the Holy Names. Marcia Rankin's Academy won't give Nancy the same kind of Catholic instruction."

"Now that you've dropped the 'sister,' please drop the 'doctor,' and call me Geoff. Actually, Nancy and I have discussed that aspect. We want a broader base than a school for Catholic young ladies. I understand that there is no restriction here as to race or religion."

"That's correct."

"That is rare. We've been to several schools whose headmistresses assured us that only the right kind of people would be accepted. That is, no Jews, no Chinese, only rich Roman Catholics, and no persons of dark skin. It didn't entice us, it offended us."

"Marcia Rankin, our founder, fought that attitude, as did Elizabeth Ordway after her. But we insist upon very high admission standards, which I'm sorry to say does limit the variety of girls here. In accord with the nature of our school, similar to the boys' preparatory school, we've maintained our academic standards. However, this coming September we plan an experiment whereby we will admit students for a practical certificate without the requirements of the academic program."

"That sounds interesting."

"Interesting, perhaps, but successful? I don't know. We're in uncharted territory." Paulina handed a folder to Geoffrey. "These are admission forms. I already know Nancy's qualifications. If you choose Marcia Rankin Academy, we'll be happy to have Nancy."

"Please, Daddy?"

"No question in my mind," Geoffrey said. "Let's plan a celebration. Are you free for dinner, Paulina?"

"I'm not," Nancy said. "Remember I'm spending the night at Laura's."

"Then we'll celebrate without you! Will you come to dinner with me?" he asked Paulina.

"Yes. I'd like that very much," she replied, feeling her cheeks go warm.

Paulina's Powell Street apartment on the second floor of Miss Wellington's home was luxurious in comparison to the plain room at the Motherhouse. She even had electricity, the miraculous lamps that glowed without the use of gas or kerosene. The Seattle convent had witnessed the first electric lights down the hill in town, but she had not thought she would live in a home with such a modern invention. Certainly it would be many years before Highland Home would have such an improvement. Paulina still preferred simple surroundings, and her rooms were bare of all but necessary furnishings. When Mrs. Wellington entered them after Paulina had settled, she cried out, "My Lord in Heaven! You're living like a nun!" The little lady had no idea how close to the truth she was, and while Paulina had been momentarily speechless, Mrs. Wellington prattled on, obviously unmindful that Paulina had ever been anything but a school marm. But not just an ordinary school marm, Mrs. Wellington would brag to her neighbors, the headmistress of a fine academy for young ladies!

Paulina tried to dress well as her position demanded. It wouldn't have done for a headmistress to be shabby. But she was unaccustomed to style. Sensibly, she chose a fine dressmaker, and confident that the seamstress would produce a wardrobe appropriate for her situation, Paulina left choices to her. She had one frock nicer than her business-like assortment of skirts, blouses and serviceable dresses, and that was a royal blue with a matching cloak. She had spread everything she owned out on the bed, and found herself wishing she had something just a bit frivolous. Everything she owned was so unimaginative! She finally decided that the Sunday best blue dress was the best for the occasion. With a pearl choker around the high lace collar and her hair swept up fashionably, she would feel comfortable as a companion to the handsome doctor.

When Geoffrey Collins had stayed at Highland Home during the crisis of the influenza and croup epidemic, she had felt an unfamiliar warmth in his presence. When he told her he was a widower, she had been tempted to reach for his hand and look a little longer into his kind grey eyes. She resisted, not only because she was mindful of her vows, but because she was aware how inappropriate the doctor would judge such forwardness on her part. Today, he had seemed genuinely pleased to see her. She looked in the mirror. Her face was flushed like a silly girl in a dime romance novel.

Dr. Geoffrey Collins judged his own behavior this night as a return to adolescence. He nicked himself twice with his razor, fumbled with his cufflinks and winced when he saw his thinning hair, graying at the temples in the mirror. He was forty-seven, and what age was Paulina? When he counted the years from her entering the convent at sixteen, then her schooling and assignments to the present day, she couldn't be more than thirty-two. It wasn't too wide a separation. At least he wasn't old enough to have been her father! And he was strong and healthy. There would be time for another family. He thought two boys and another girl would be nice. He could picture them around the dining room table, walking in the park, putting candles on the Christmas tree…suddenly he threw his head back and laughed a long, hearty laugh. He'd given Imogene the night off, and Nancy was at her friend's home. He could make fun of himself as loudly as he wanted. His imagination had spanned years and had him wedded, bedded, and a new family gathered at his knee. But even though he saw the humor in his fantasy, he also knew it would all be true.

Six months later, Geoffrey and Paulina walked out onto the balcony of the Cliff House watching the distant fog roll in toward the shore. Paulina wore her new velvet dress, plum colored and designed to show off her slight figure. The high lace at her throat accentuated her swan like neck, and the wind that blew constantly from the ocean had taken little wisps of her black hair which fell over her shoulders and curled about her face.

"Aren't you cold, my dearest?" Geoffrey asked her, and when she turned to meet his eyes he stroked her cheek. He had rehearsed his proposal speech a hundred times, but the words wouldn't come. He took her hand and slipped the ring with its diamond surrounded by rubies on her third finger. "Will you marry me?" was all he could say.

"Oh, yes!" was the immediate response, and he took her in his arms.

IV

Beryl read Paulina's letter with satisfaction. Although Paulina had taken her post at Marcia Rankin Academy as soon as she arrived in San Francisco two years ago, the words she wrote to Beryl about her work thinly disguised loneliness. Paulina had been happy in community life. Her vocation came with a natural ease, and she had borne the trial of Mother Marietta's antipathy with remarkable good will. Beryl didn't think she herself would have done half as well. Now Paulina was to be married and there was the hope of her own family.

Philomena also had a letter that described the simple wedding ceremony performed in the presence of Geoffrey's closest friends, Paulina's staff, and Nancy as her maid of honor. More friends and associates were invited to the dinner and reception which followed at the Cliff House. Paulina wrote Philomena describing Geoffrey's home on one of San Francisco's hills, and invited her to spend as much time as she could with her at her next visitation.

When the visitation trip to California became a reality, Philomena looked forward to seeing Paulina, but there was a new problem. Mother Marietta had decided to accompany her to California. This was a surprise because Marietta had specifically delegated convent visitations to her Director of Schools. It would be awkward getting away from the Mother General's company, but Philomena would contrive to extend the Marcia Rankin visit. There was nothing to connect Paulina with Marcia Rankin Academy, and some of its experimental curriculum was reason enough for Philomena to plan to spend at least a day there. Philomena had written on her schedule, *Afternoon and evening with Mrs. Collins, head mistress of Marcia Rankin Academy.* She had shown the entry to Beryl.

"I'm calling this 'prudence,' but in my heart I know it's shameful deception, pure and simple."

"Perhaps not pure, and certainly not simple," Beryl had replied. "But you will be evaluating Paulina's new policy of admitting students for a program other than the traditionally academic."

Philomena's visit worked out more perfectly than she had anticipated. There had been structural problems with the old clinic/convent building on the Market Street flats, and when they arrived in San Francisco, Marietta suggested that Philomena ask Mrs. Collins if she could lodge with the boarders at the Academy during the time of visitation.

"I believe Mrs. Collins would prefer I lodge in her home," Philomena said, hoping her tone sounded indifferent.

"Certainly, if that is how it will be arranged."

"How perfect!" Paulina exclaimed when Philomena appeared on the Collins' doorstep carrying her valise. "We'll be able to stay up and talk like a pair of novices hiding from Mother Mistress!"

"Did you do that too?" Philomena challenged.

"No, but I knew a few who did. You must remember that the silence and isolation of our novitiate was harder for some than for others."

"And Mother Lavinia knew, you can bet your life on it. She could have caught me once or twice!"

Philomena admired Paulina's new look. She had taken to her married state with grace and flair, and even filled out a bit. Just as she had been the perfect sister, now she was the perfect wife and stepmother, as well as outstanding headmistress.

"Not headmistress for long," Paulina said. "There will be four of us come August!" she said, patting her stomach and smiling happily.

After their dinner, Geoffrey was called to the hospital, and once Nancy had gone to bed, the two friends sat in the living room warmed by a fire on the hearth. It had burned to embers by the time Geoffrey returned, and he teased them about staying up like Nancy and her friends at an overnight party.

"We had a couple of years of news to tell each other," Philomena said, rising from her comfortable chair, "but now I think I'm ready to..."

She was interrupted by a strange rumbling sound followed by a violent swaying and shaking. Philomena was thrown back in her chair. The chandelier in the dining room came loose from its mount and crashed on the table at the same time that the china cabinet seemed to walk several feet before toppling and shattering its contents. Bricks jarred loose from the fireplace and one narrowly missed Geoffrey's head as he bent to scoop the embers that had jumped from the hearth onto the rug. It hit him on the shoulder, which was well protected as he had not yet removed his coat. Nancy, too frightened to scream, was making her way down the stairs which shook and swayed so that part of the hand railing was coming free of its bolts. The girl edged down along the wall, then ran to the couch where Paulina and Philomena still sat. It was pitching like a boat in choppy water and she clung to Paulina. Finally the shaking subsided, and all was quiet.

"We're all right," Geoffrey said.

The furniture had moved, paintings on the wall were thrown to the floor, and books in the hallway shelves were scattered. "I imagine upstairs is just as bad," Geoffrey said. "I need to check the outside." Paulina, Nancy and Philomena followed as Imogene, the Collins' cook and housekeeper, emerged from her room still in her nightgown, but with a shawl wrapped around her. "I declare!" she said. "I was tossed clear out of my bed and rolled under my table. Good thing, too. The plaster from the ceiling fell all over it." She brushed the white residue from her nightgown.

Their neighbors were out in their yards and on the street, most of them in their robes. Chimneys were down, and brick porches similar to the Collins' home were cracked and out of shape. The homes, as far as could be seen, had withstood the shaking. The house at the end of the street had a stone wall which was now a heap of rubble scattered on the street.

"I'll have to go back to the hospital," Geoffrey said.

"And I need to see if our sisters are safe," Philomena added.

"That could be dangerous." Geoffrey looked up the street. "Wait here. Perhaps Mr. Fletcher would help." He left to seek out the man who had been the first one on the block to own an automobile. If the roads to the north of the hill were open, he could cut back and down one of the through streets to the lowland. The sisters' clinic was in the worst part of town, an area heavily populated with indigent and poverty ridden families in over crowded tenements.

Fletcher was retired, and a Baptist, but he respected the work of the Roman Catholic nuns, and was quick to volunteer to drive Sister Philomena as close as he could get to the convent clinic. He told Geoffrey he would bring the nuns back up the hill if need be. It hardly crossed Philomena's mind that Marietta would thus learn of the "Mrs. Collins" deception.

Paulina convinced her husband that she must go with Philomena so she might stop at the school to check on the welfare of the boarders. Nancy remained at home, picking up and filling available containers with water as her father instructed.

The Marcia Rankin Academy boarders were safe, and the building didn't seem to have serious structural damage. As they had been in the Collins' home, books and furnishings were scattered on the floor, and the electricity was out. Paulina gave instructions for the three teachers who lived at school and left with Philomena. Aftershocks swayed the ground several times, but not with the intensity of the first quake.

Mr. Fletcher drove them within three blocks of the convent and decided it would be prudent to stay up the road and watch the car. Aware of the rash actions of men who were frightened and intent upon saving their families, Fletcher had decided to stash a rifle in the boot of the car. Men, women and children were already coming up the hill, some weeping, others in silent shock. At the bottom of the incline, the clinic building was leaning, and the back seemed to have collapsed. Philomena ran to two sisters who were taking medical supplies out of the building to the street. "Where is Mother Marietta?" she cried.

"The others are trying to get to her. She was back there!" The sister pointed to the rubble where a brick wall had fallen in. Some of the wooden walls inside had splintered and collapsed. Paulina followed Philomena to the back, stepping over pieces of plaster and wood.

"Sister!" A flash of recognition lighted Sister Nelda's face as she saw Paulina. Paulina smiled, but didn't stop. In the back area, three sisters were frantically clearing the mound of bricks that covered the part of the room where Marietta had slept. With two additional pairs of hands, they uncovered her head and shoulders. She lay still, her eyes staring as if in surprise. She was not breathing.

Philomena made the sign of the cross on her Mother General's forehead, then stepped back. "There's nothing we can do for Mother Marietta. Go back and get everything you can carry out of the clinic, but hurry. Come, Paulina. There will be people who will remove the body."

"I'll come. Give me a moment," Paulina said softly.

She knelt on the rough pieces of bricks and pushed back a strand of hair from Marietta's face and closed her eyes. Because of this woman she had left the community, and because of her she had found and married Geoffrey Collins and now carried a child. Marietta had given her a blessing, not a curse. She bent over the body and kissed her forehead. "Be at peace. We all find forgiveness in Heaven," she whispered.

The five sisters and Paulina worked quickly to stuff gauze, antiseptic, and anything else they might use in pillowcases and bags. They were within sight of the waiting car when still another trembler hit. Some people on the road screamed as the sound of falling structures accompanied the shaking. Geysers of water were now spewing from the cracks in the street below. "The water mains!" someone shouted.

Up the hill, the sisters were shocked to see Mr. Fletcher standing beside his automobile, a rifle in hand, ready to challenge anyone with a mind for theft. The sisters loaded the supplies swiftly. "I'll have to make a second trip. The weight of all of you would be too much," he told them as he cranked the motor. "I can take three of you now."

Philomena acted without hesitation. "Paulina, you go with Winifred and Nelda." She added in a whisper, "Do the sensible thing, you have more than one life to consider."

By the time Mr. Fletcher made the second trip, fires were burning in isolated areas of the city. "Without water to fight the blazes, the whole town could go up in smoke," he said grimly.

For the next three days the sisters helped treat injuries in a tent they had set up in Golden Gate Park where refugees had created a community. A hospital for more serious cases had been located downtown in a building near City Hall Park, but had to be abandoned when the fire went out of control. Geoffrey worked with the sisters at the Park.

It was not a surprise to Geoffrey when city officials came to condemn his home and those around them on Nob Hill. "We're awfully sorry, doctor, but unless we blast a barrier there'll be greater loss," the department official told him. Residents were given only hours to gather whatever belongings they could carry away. There was very little they could save. Geoffrey decided that it was time to leave the city. He arranged transportation for his family and the five sisters after making certain Marietta's body would be buried in the Catholic cemetery until the community could make other arrangements to bring her home to Washington.

The ferry landing that had been mobbed for three days after the quake was still crowded, but the group waited only hours before boarding the boat for

Oakland. Once across the bay, there was no time for rest. Geoffrey arranged for a private rail car to take them north. The cost was exorbitant, perhaps because they were leaving the state. The railroad had donated its services by taking refugees anywhere the rail serviced in California free of charge after the catastrophe. Geoffrey, concerned for his family, and solicitous of the five Sisters of Martha and Mary, was satisfied the money to leave safely was well spent.

On the east side of the bay, they were able to send telegrams to the Motherhouse and to Captain and Mrs. Lilly. The captain met the group at the station along with Adam, Joseph, and Beryl.

"God bless you for your generosity to us, Dr. Collins," Beryl said.

"The sisters worked heroically, Mother Charbonneau. You have reason to be proud of them, and they are well deserving of a rest."

The sisters left for Mercer's Island while Captain and Mrs. Lilly welcomed Geoffrey, Paulina and Nancy, together with their housekeeper, Imogene. At last they were able to bathe, rest, and try to put the nightmare of the past days behind them. When they were alone, Geoffrey sat down with Paulina and told her how serious their financial situation was.

"I put all my resources into the house and property," he told her. "I have very little in reserve, certainly not enough to reestablish us. It will take time, but I promise after some hard years, we'll be on our feet again."

"My dearest," Paulina said taking his hand. "Don't you remember that I told you my mother left some money for me should I ever leave the convent? All that is yours, my love—ours. You could buy back into the practice you left and we can find a home.

"Paulina, it would take a fortune to do that!"

"Will two hundred and fifty thousand dollars do?"

V

Beryl looked fondly at Joseph, who was visiting his beautiful daughter, the image of Mai Ling. Su Ping had entered early in her teens and possessed a gracious spirit of reserve which Beryl decided was a natural outcome of her mixed heritage. Joseph's son, Sung Chow, was now in graduate school on the East Coast, and Lee was in charge of an engineering proposal which would ultimately join San Francisco and the Bay Area.

Joseph had recovered from the depression he had endured after Mai Ling's sudden death. Although still thin, with a touch of grey at his temples, he stood straight and tall. The Archbishop's commission had forced him to leave his self-imposed exile from the land of the living, and he had not stopped working since.

The day was warm. Late August weather was almost always fine on the Island. A cloud of dust rose from near the lake to the north. A long promised road would soon connect the Motherhouse with East Seattle, the community on the northern tip of Mercer's Island. It would be convenient in many ways. There was a steamer that toured the island each week, blowing its whistle at each little dock. The sisters would take baskets and walk down the trail from the Motherhouse to go aboard the craft to shop. It was outfitted as a miniature grocery store and was much appreciated for smaller purchases.

"You'll be happy for the road," Joseph said following Beryl's gaze.

"I dare say. Did you know that we've purchased property in Lake Forest Park north of Seattle?"

"Yes, and something else, I understand," he said with a twinkle in his eye.

"You've been talking to Adam."

281

"Yes. He can barely contain himself. He has the Congregation's motorcar at the livery that he's turned into half a garage for all the Madison Park people who have bought automobiles. I can't wait to see you riding in it with hat and scarf, your veil flying as you go twenty miles an hour down the road!"

"Twenty miles an hour! Can an automobile go that fast?"

"Even faster if there were decent roads."

"I'm not afraid of progress, Joseph, but last week when that flying machine passed over, I thought some of the sisters would faint. I was walking with Sister Gertrude at the time, and she was thrilled. She said that on her hundredth birthday she wanted a ride in one."

"What did you tell her?" Joseph asked smiling.

"I promised her I'd see to it. Of course, my memory might fail me as then I'd be one hundred and ten, but I promised to do my best!"

The evening after the services Beryl opened mail that she had neglected for several posts. She saw Paulina's handwriting and opened the envelope immediately. She read the news with delight:

Dear Mother,

> *You will excuse me I'm certain for not being present at the services for our dear Gertrude and also for Mother Marietta. But I have just given birth to a beautiful baby girl, and the little one won't let her mama go off quite so soon! All three of us made suggestions for her name and it is Olivia Katherine Anne Collins. Olivia is Geoffrey's mother's name; Katherine is for my dear Mattie Kate, and Nancy's choice is Anne because she says she's never forgiven her parents for not naming her "Anne with an E" in honor of the Montgomery novels she treasures.*

> *I can hardly wait for you to meet Olivia. Do visit when you come to look at the Lake Forest Park property. By the way, Geoffrey bought an automobile! It's a bewildering, noisy, and terrifying monster.*

> *I also want to thank you and Philomena for being so understanding about Nancy's going to the Holy Names Academy. It is, as you know, only a few blocks from our home. She says the sisters are quite "starchy stiff," and not at all as much fun as the Sisters of Martha and Mary!*

Beryl finished the remainder of the letter and saved it to give to Mother Philomena as Paulina had asked her to share it. "Starchy stiff," She chuckled.

The community had assembled for Marietta's funeral services and burial. Philomena, appointed acting Mother General, had scheduled a convocation as soon as the school term ended for emergency elections and to discuss business.

Marietta had not concluded the purchase of the Lake Forest Park property, although it was generally understood that this was her intention considering the approval the sisters had expressed. When Philomena went through papers in the Mother General's office, she was appalled to see that rather than establish a "business house" north of Seattle, Marietta was going to propose a split in the community.

As she skimmed through the Mother General's notes, Philomena was shocked to read of a long range proposal which would, after her second term as Mother General, have established a separate Congregation of the Sisters of Martha and Mary, independent of Beryl Charbonneau's foundation. Depending upon growth and support, the Montana group and schools would be part of this plan, together with Idaho and Spokane. In this event, there were proposals allowing the community to push east to the Dakotas, Minnesota, and any points beyond. If the separate Congregation began with California, it would include northern and southern California, Nevada, Arizona, New Mexico and perhaps Colorado. Beryl's original group would be in western Washington and Oregon, and those locations that were not the new community—whichever combination was selected. In either event, it seemed to Philomena that Marietta intended to be the Mother Foundress, and she had outlined a new book of by-laws. Her charts of assignments over the next eight years would place Beryl's faithful supporters in Washington and Oregon, while the sisters who favored changes in the community's structure would be shifted to either Montana or California.

It became clear now why Marietta had been delaying the purchase of the Lake Forest Park house and acreage. She didn't want the restructuring most sisters of the community envisioned. Philomena and others supported proposals that the Mother General be the business head of the Congregation. Like a Benedictine abbess, this person would be the contact for the public. Like the same order's custom, the Sisters of Martha and Mary would elect a Mother Prioress who would take care of the spiritual needs of the community. The five major geographic areas would elect sisters to be counselors charged with representing the interests of all their convents. In any conflict or deadlock, the Mother General would have the deciding vote. Philomena had spoken on behalf of the sisters to Mother Marietta and to Beryl concerning a move in this direction. She thought she had Marietta's support. Now she saw that she had not.

Philomena decided she would not make this matter public. She knew Beryl's mind about preserving records for the Archives, so she would not destroy the material. But she could seal it as personal papers and bury it in the multitude of documents kept by the community. In years to come it wouldn't matter who read it or what they concluded. For now it was important that the community function undivided and in peace. She was certain that Marietta had not yet begun to find allies. There was no correspondence from any sister that suggested she had gone further than her personal agenda.

At the mandated Convocation following the death of a Mother General, the new plan for shared duties between the Mother General and the office of Prioress was approved. Philomena was formally elected Mother General, and Beryl Charbonneau Prioress. Sister Philomena appointed Sister Margaret Blanchard Mistress of Novices, Sister Nelda Fenner as Sub Mistress of Novices, and Sister Clara Petersen Mistress of Postulants. Five others from the various localities: Sisters Winifred, Margaret, Joan Marie, Josephine, and Sarah Dufrayne, one of the original five from the Seattle convent, were elected counselors.

"It's a good group," Philomena told Paulina after the meetings. She had considered asking her friend's advice in the matter of handling her knowledge of Marietta's plans, but she decided to remain silent. It wasn't a matter of loyalty; she could never consider Paulina an "outsider." Rather, it was that there was nothing Paulina could have done except to advise her, and she already determined her course of action. No, she would let the knowledge gather dust and hope that it would be many years before it came to light, if at all. She also decided to appoint the Archivist with great care, preferably some sister who was too busy to do much more than keep files in order.

VI
1912

The first of September, the traditional date for receiving the new class of postulants, was a sunny day, a pellucid blue sky without clouds. The sisters set picnic tables out in the front park in the shade of the fir and cedar trees. Because of the island's isolation and the difficulty of getting on and off, the postulants assembled at the Leschi dock so that they might come in a group. There had been Mass at the new St. James Cathedral, a farewell to parents there with promises to write and a few tears. The group of twelve arrived on the Motherhouse dock and were met by a smiling group of first and second year novices.

After a ceremony in the chapel and afternoon Vespers, the twelve, each with a novice as hostess, joined the community for a dinner picnic. They had identification tags pinned on their dresses so that the older sisters could call them by name. Beryl and Philomena made their rounds trying to spend some time with each new entrant. Beryl approached a girl who stood alone looking at the mountain, which was white and clear. "I hope you're not homesick, my dear," she said.

The girl turned quickly. "Oh no! I'm just wondering what words would describe that gorgeous mountain. It would be easier just to paint it with all these surrounding trees and the water!"

Beryl paused to read the name tag which was pinned on lopsided with an oversize safety pin. She stared at the name: Elizabeth Ordway.

"You knew my aunt," the girl said with a smile that would have brightened the bleakest day. "And you're probably thinking that the family wasn't Catholic!"

"You're right," Beryl replied.

"Mom is, Dad isn't," Elizabeth said simply.

Beryl regarded the pert posture, the intelligent eyes, and ready smile that showed the space between her two front teeth, just like Lizzie's. "Is Carl your father?" The girl nodded. "I met him at your Aunt Lizzie's memorial service. You must have been…"

"Just nine years old! But I remember you and the sisters."

"How does your father feel about your entering?"

"Oh, just hunky dory. He says I'll last about a week."

Beryl laughed out loud. "How about lasting two weeks so you'll be with us for my feast day celebration?"

"Sure, Mother, I can manage that!" The laughing eyes were just like Lizzie's.

Beryl left the postulants and said to herself, *Well, Lizzie my dear, what a lovely surprise.* She sought out Philomena to tell her about her conversation with new Sister Elizabeth. They shared Paulina's letter.

"It sounds like a week would have just about done it for Sister Elizabeth if she'd gone to Nancy's starchy stiff sisters!" Philomena laughed.

"I think Sister Clara will find her a treasure, and Elizabeth will recognize Clara as a kindred spirit."

VII

Sister Clara Petersen was experiencing what an older sister called butterflies in the stomach. She had never been a superior, and was nervous about the great responsibility of Mistress of Postulants that she had been given. She was also a convert, having been received into the faith only four years before her entrance. Mother Philomena and Mother Charbonneau assured her that she was their choice and they had confidence in her ability.

"Most importantly," Philomena had told her, "you understand Mother Charbonneau's philosophy of religious discipline tempered by charity."

Sister Clara remembered her own early days as a young professed sister when Beryl would tell her group that holding one's tongue was more often in the interests of charity than simply obeying a sterile rule of silence. Mother Charbonneau had also told them that there was a fine distinction between retaining individuality and being self-centered. "Singularity" was not against Beryl's bylaws. Each sister had an obligation to explore her talents for the good of the Congregation and those it served. But this wasn't to be an excuse for self aggrandizement.

In a private conference with Mother Charbonneau after her first year of teaching, Clara had discussed the problem of using one's talents and, yet, at the same time retaining a spirit of sacrifice.

"What do you mean, Sister?"

"As Christ offered His very life, so we should offer that which is of great importance to us."

"Yes," Beryl said, but she wanted specific examples.

"Well, I love to sing, but I gave it up as a sacrifice to God."

Beryl looked at the young nun thoughtfully. "How did you come to do that?"

"Sister Marietta approved," Clara said, somewhat doubtfully.

"Would you sing for me, Sister? As your superior, I insist, and that must override any personal promise." She indicated the piano in the parlor where they sat together.

Clara went to the piano and lifted the lid that protected the keys. One of her proudest accomplishments in high school had been learning to play the piano. "What would you like? A hymn?"

"Not necessarily. Why not choose something you really love to sing?"

Clara sat on the piano stool. "This is a piece by Edward Grieg. It's called 'Solveig's Song.'" She played the opening chords and began the soulful music, which ended with the lilting melody that concluded with an octave ending on a "high A." Beryl was both enchanted by Clara's singing and angry at the audacity of Marietta for trying to silence her, but she wouldn't show her displeasure to the sensitive young sister.

"That was lovely. Thank you." She waited until Clara had returned to the seat opposite her. "My dear, what if I gave you a beautiful rosary with carved beads and a crucifix in pure gold, would you take care of it?"

"Of course!"

"You wouldn't intentionally throw it away, perhaps never to be found?"

Clara's eyes widened. "No!"

"Consider that the rosary is the symbol of the voice God gave you. And what have you done with it?"

Clara was stunned. "How could I have been so ungrateful?" she whispered.

"You weren't thinking of your voice as a gift from God, but it is. I want to hear that voice in chapel, with your sisters, as you walk in these woods, and as you work with your students. Promise me?"

"Yes, Mother."

Sister Clara Petersen, now newly appointed Mistress of Postulants, had been born near Ellensburg east of the Cascades. She was the youngest child of the Petersen family. She had four older brothers, and all of them loved their pretty little blonde baby sister. As the years of her schooling progressed, her wise teacher suggested that Clara try for a scholarship to high school. The woman had attended the academy in Tacoma run by the Sisters of Martha and Mary, and strongly recommended the nuns. Her parents had no objection, even though the family was not Catholic.

Clara passed the entrance examinations and was sent off to boarding school. She sang in the school choir, was an outstanding student, and for the first time in her life studied religion. There had been some Sunday school groups in their church, but it was mostly where they were told stories like Daniel in the lion's den, Joseph and brothers, and Moses taking the people out of Egypt. Her family didn't even say grace before meals.

Clara's announcement to the sisters that she wanted to be baptized a Catholic was received with mixed feelings. On the one hand they were delighted, but at the same time they knew that there were many non-Catholics attending their schools, and it wouldn't do to start a rumor that the sisters were out to convert rather than educate young ladies. Sister Philomena was principal of the Tacoma school and she had presented the problem to Mother Charbonneau. Beryl herself went with Philomena to present the matter to the Petersens. They had no objection, and Clara was baptized at the end of her freshman year.

Four years later, Philomena made the trip to the Petersens to broach the subject of Clara's entering the community. It took more persuasion to gain their permission this time, and then they compromised by agreeing on a year's time at home. Clara promised to join in social activities proper for her age.

"Clara, don't try to be a nun before you enter the convent," Philomena told her. "Your parents want to be sure you've had an opportunity to meet boys and girls your own age and consider whether or not you want to marry."

"I know what I want," Clara insisted.

"I'm sure you do. But both you and I and your parents need to know what you want is what God wants."

Philomena hated the thought of losing an outstanding candidate like Clara and told Beryl about the situation. "Mother, I'm not certain I should have been so conciliatory."

"She's only fifteen, Sister."

"I know. But you and I both know that there are communities that would have convinced her parents that the wrath of God would be upon them if they refused to give their daughter to God."

"Catholic families, perhaps. But not the Petersens. And we are not, as has been pointed out to us even within our own ranks, like other communities," Beryl reminded her.

Clara stayed at home for a year, did what her parents wished, and happily entered the novitiate in Vancouver the next September. She never wavered in her intention to be a member of the community.

Someone less understanding than Clara would have seen only the contradictions in new postulant Sister Elizabeth Ordway. Elizabeth could devote every free minute, pencil in hand, writing in her journal, nose close to the pages, and never budge from her chair. Yet she fidgeted in chapel prayers and didn't like the long periods of meditation.

Clara sought Mother Charbonneau's advice, and Beryl said, "I think she needs to be directed into a more contemplative kind of prayer."

"Contemplative! Mother, she can't sit still for the Rosary! I talked to her about it and she told me it was hard because it was the same last week, the week before, and would be the same the week after!"

"I think she's trying not to pray," Beryl said, which puzzled Clara. "For Elizabeth to keep her mind quiet and content with mere repetition, she must do violence to her very nature. We need to set her free."

Beryl conducted weekly classes in the postulants' quarters. It was an hour of questions and answers, the history of the community, and instructions on the bylaws of the Congregation. Beryl decided to use the next hour to discuss the many ways of prayer.

"Some of the saints had to push everything else out of their hearts to prepare a place for God. Often it was a harsh discipline. Some attempted to forget everyone and everything they had loved in the world. Personally," Beryl told her postulants, "I don't pretend to understand this way, but if any of my sisters chose it, it would be because they knew in their hearts that no other way would lead to holiness for them."

"Wouldn't that be like the hermits in the desert?" Sister Amy asked.

"It could be," Beryl agreed. "But the desert is a place. It's how one thinks and feels in that place that is important." She smiled. "To some of you the postulancy is a desert, and it can seem arid and bleak compared to home and the world. It's similar to the hermit's life, to be sure."

"But we're not going to be in the desert forever!" Sister Bernice said. "We'll get out of the novitiate someday, won't we?" There were giggles from some of her sisters.

"Yes, of course," Beryl affirmed. "But while you're here, you're learning about yourselves and you're learning to pray."

"And pray and pray and pray…" Sister Elizabeth sighed.

Her companions looked at her, then at Mother Charbonneau, wondering what kind of a reprimand Elizabeth would get.

"Sister Elizabeth," she said amiably, "you could define life as 'we breathe and breathe and breathe,' couldn't you?"

Beryl had the girl's attention. Elizabeth wondered what was coming next. Beryl was pleased that the girl had given her such a fine opportunity. She had been circling the point she wanted to make. She continued, "That repetitious intake of air makes everything else, everything, possible. But you don't give your full attention to the process. Look around you, sisters."

It was a mild April day. They sat outside where the wild cherries were blooming, snow white. The green fir and hemlocks had new growth, gold green on the tips of branches. The sky was blue and the stellar jays were scattering the sparrows who were trying to find nests in the highest branches of the flowering dogwood.

Beryl said, "The world is charged with the grandeur of God...He fathers forth whose beauty is past change..."

"Is that a poem?" Elizabeth asked.

"I'd call it prayer. They were the words of Father Hopkins, an English Jesuit and friend of our first spiritual director, Father Louis Bertrand. Prayer is all around us, it's not confined to the chapel, and real prayer has very little to do with repeated words for their own sake. The words are only like the mechanical act of breathing; only the beginning of prayer."

"So we're in chapel and saying the Rosary, and it's all right to think of being on top of Mount Rainier praising God?" Elizabeth asked, not meaning to be facetious although a few postulants laughed.

"Or we can say the words and be kneeling in the garden of Gethsemane watching and waiting with Jesus, and longing to comfort Him by wiping the bloody sweat from his forehead with a cool cloth."

The postulants looked at Beryl, spellbound. All but two of the group went on to receive the habit of the Sisters of Martha and Mary the following September. Elizabeth Ordway was among them.

VIII

Young Sister Elizabeth Ordway made her first profession in September,1914, along with every sister in her class who had received the habit. They were eager to escape the confines of Highland Home and receive assignments for school and teaching. Three in the group had been at Normal school and they were confident they would be sent to teach. Elizabeth thought that she'd probably be sent to Normal school, but secretly stormed Heaven that Mother Philomena would see her way clear to sending her to the University of Washington where she would earn a degree. There was one disadvantage to that, and it was that sisters attending school there lived at the Lake Forest Park convent, and that was almost as bad as the structured life on the Island. Elizabeth was most definitely not inclined to thrive on a semi-monastic routine.

Just before the profession ceremonies, Sister Margaret Blanchard, the Mistress of Novices was diagnosed with tuberculosis.

"We've caught this in the very early stages, Mother," Dr. Collins told Philomena. "I expect her to make a complete recovery if she is sent to a drier climate."

A sanatorium in Arizona was Dr. Collins' recommendation. Philomena informed Beryl. "She'd be better off going in secular clothes. Dr. Collins felt that the regime of bathing, taking the sun, and socialization would be less awkward for Sister if she were not dressed in the habit."

"I myself made a choice to wear secular clothes when we came west with Asa Mercer. Otherwise I would have been conspicuous."

Beryl had come to Seattle for the monthly council meeting specifically to convince Adam to come to Highland Home to spend his last years. Adam was now eighty-three. He had refused Joseph's invitation to live with him on part of Adam's property which he had deeded to Joseph after Mai Ling's death. He had been persuaded to sell the livery, which was now an automobile repair shop. A wise businessman, Adam had learned about automobiles and could drive, but the management of this business was more than his failing strength could manage. Beryl's winning argument was that the community needed a motor car and driver for the trip to East Seattle for supplies and to meet those coming over from Leschi on the ferry. Now that there was a road around Mercer's Island, the commuting pattern between the Motherhouse and the mainland was easier. There was even electricity and a telephone at Highland Home. Adam was cautious.

"Are ye turning me into a charity case?" he grumbled.

"Adam! We're asking you to help us. If charity enters into this, it is your charity to us, not the other way around!"

"I'll not be put out to pasture!" he said. As he mulled over Beryl's words, in his mind's eye he could see the bold Charbonneau girl riding out on her father's stallion. A flood of memories washed over him. There was Henri Charbonneau's legacy to him, his years of serving Beryl and her Congregation, not as servant, but as trusted friend. In the end, he accepted Beryl's offer.

Beryl had said more to reassured him. "You're more steady on your feet than I am these days! When I retire to a wheelchair, you can push me about!"

It was more than a joke. Walking was increasingly difficult for Beryl who was now seventy-two. The pressure on the spinal cord from her back problems caused not only pain, but numbness in her legs, and she had taken a few falls. When Sister Sarah Dufrayne told Philomena about this, Philomena forbade Beryl to go out on the trails alone. Beryl had smiled and responded meekly. "So, at last I am once again the child promising obedience to the 'Mother.' It's time to live the humility I've preached."

Sister Anne Francis, the Infirmarian, had not been able to convince Beryl to use a wheelchair when she went out. "I'm not that humble," she snapped, but she accepted a companion on her walks, and the novices were given permission to go with her. Beryl never lacked for a willing companion. She tried not to show favoritism, but she was particularly delighted when Sister Elizabeth Ordway joined her.

As she sat in Mother Philomena's office, she sensed that there was something else on the Mother General's mind besides Margaret Blanchard's wearing secular clothing. She brought up the subject of Adam to fill an awkward silence. "He's consented to return with me. This way we can see that he's well nourished and we can send for medical help if he needs it. The man is amazing. He's as bright as ever he was, and just as crotchety! I didn't speak of morbid things, but it will give me comfort to know he will be buried on the island."

"Mother," Sister Philomena began, and Beryl knew she was about to tell her what was on her mind. "I'm considering Sister Clara as Margaret Blanchard's replacement. I know she's young, just thirty-two, but she's been professed for ten years."

Beryl listened without interrupting. Philomena would come to her real concerns without prompting.

"But Sister Nelda Fenner has had a year's experience as Sub Mistress, and it would seem appropriate to appoint her."

"As a reward for her experience? That could be a dangerous precedent."

"I realize that, but I've tried to appoint sisters to sub positions who I believed would also be qualified to move forward. It would be an exception not to move Sister Nelda into the Novice Mistress's position. But..."

"But you've noted a certain inflexibility and inability to understand those young sisters with personalities different from hers." Beryl finished her sentence.

"Exactly, Mother. Your eyes haven't been closed, have they?"

"No, and it's probably a fault." She hesitated, choosing her words. "Novice Mistress is not an administrative post, it's our future. You will recall Sister Irma, who was your Sub Mistress. She was a good sister, she tried to set a good example, but she was fearful and tended to scrupulousness. As our bursar, she is perfect. She gives great attention to details, keeps flawless books, and is efficient in all ways. I don't think she has an equal in the community. But reward her by appointing her as Novice Mistress? Of course not."

"There's more to my concern, Mother. We've experienced the result of hurt feelings. Marietta, may she rest in peace, should have taught us something."

"It taught us that no one of us is immune to the sin of envy. But as you once told me so vehemently, the problem of envy was Marietta's, not Paulina's."

"You appointed Marietta Director of Schools," Philomena said quietly.

"But as a reward for achievements that qualified her for the position, and certainly not to buy her favor. I never had her respect, much less her goodwill. But under no circumstances would I have appointed her Mistress of Novices, and I would have fought against her ever filling that role in our community."

"And so the community elected her the spiritual leader of us all. It is ironic."

"God made His own corrections, and there was no damage done," Beryl said.

If you only knew how much damage would have been done, Philomena thought to herself.

"Nelda is a different person altogether," Beryl continued. "She is introspective, prefers to be alone, and does not relate to others easily. She's academically gifted, and has a passion for history. The Congregation has not given her an opportunity to continue her education that was interrupted by the earthquake in San Francisco. We would benefit greatly by her further education."

"I know that her dream has been to attend the University of California in Berkeley.

"Then send her. And send Sister Elizabeth Ordway with her."

"A newly professed?"

"One of the finest minds it has been our privilege to receive. You can bring her home every summer either to live here or at Highland Home. Normal school would be a waste for Elizabeth."

"Oh, Mother. Stay well, stay healthy. Whatever would I do without your wisdom?"

"Use your own, I expect," Beryl replied.

Part Eleven

I

At the ceremony honoring newly professed and those who had received degrees, Beryl found that Sister Elizabeth had lost the childlike look of her novice years. But the spontaneity was still there in the bright blue eyes. Now, six years after her profession, she was a little thinner, but poignantly like her famous aunt in appearance. There were differences in the two that became more apparent as time went on. Elizabeth was a happier person than Lizzie. Lizzie was the intellectual equal of any man, but she had to prove herself every step of the way. Her niece didn't seem to want to prove herself; she wanted to be herself.

Elizabeth, for all her carefree exterior, had rare depth. She had been home from school last summer when Adam had died, her first summer away from Berkeley since the Congregation had permitted her to study for a Master's degree after her undergraduate work. Beryl, under obedience not to go out alone, had been reluctant to have anyone follow her to Adam's grave; she wanted to keep her grief private. Elizabeth sensed Beryl's need and came to walk with her as frequently as she could. She approached Mother Philomena confidentially with concerns about Mother Charbonneau's unsteadiness and lack of balance. As a result, a wheelchair was provided for Beryl. Only Elizabeth and Mother's friend Joseph Wolf had been able to persuade the Congregation's Prioress to be wheeled. Without any request from Beryl, Elizabeth would push Beryl down the trail to the meadow beside the cedar grove where Adam's stone was mounted at the grave. She would bring a notebook and go off somewhere within sight, leaving Beryl with a sawed off rake to tend the wildflowers she had planted in memory of her friend. No one knew Beryl's capacity for friendship better than Elizabeth. They talked about Lizzie frequently. Beryl told her about Joseph and Father Louis, and Elizabeth treasured all she was told.

Elizabeth had now returned to the Motherhouse with a bachelor's degree and Sister Nelda Fenner with a doctorate in philosophy to be awarded officially when she completed and defended her dissertation. The community retreat this year was somber in tone. Many of the sisters had brothers and even fathers who fought in France. Other sisters' families had different problems. Sister Clara's had been the victims of vandalism and abuse in eastern Washington along with other German immigrants. When the United States became involved in the European front, Beryl herself spoke to her community about love within, much in the same way she would have done in Carmel half a century ago had she had the authority.

> *In our Congregation we cannot hide our heritage behind a saint's name We are Charbonneau, Bordeaux, and Fontaines. We are Mahoneys, O'Briens, McMahans, Flannerys and McKays; we are Fenners, Petersen, Deitlers, and Hechts; we are Vecchios, Molinos, Renos, and Angelinos.*
>
> *We love our Su Ping and our Anna Fernando. I could continue to name our ancestors who span the globe from west to east and north to south. But we are not fragmented: we are Sisters of Martha and Mary, a unity of heart and mind. The battles that rage in Europe have nothing to do with the Sisters with whom we work and pray.*

The sisters agreed that they would contribute to international relief, and not participate in any particular patriotic display. Some thought that this policy could be seen as a form of betrayal of flag and country.

Beryl pleaded for compassion and prayers for peace. "Those who are called enemies also pray for their loved ones," she reminded her sisters. "Of course, your private prayers are said in the sanctity of your own hearts."

Since 1917 there had been fewer entering postulants than in previous years. Only four were expected at Highland Home for reception in September. The community suspended their bylaws and eliminated the office of Mistress of Postulants, combining the new candidates with the novices.

The summer was unusually quiet at Highland Home since many sisters were volunteering to help the International Red Cross in Seattle. Elderly

Sister Sarah Dufrayne used her time to put the Archives in order. The room reserved for community records was a place of boxes, documents, and photographs in a shocking state of disarray. During the summer she separated material to file year by year. She had a separate place for material she judged to be confidential.

After Marietta's election, when Beryl left the office space reserved for the Mother General, she sent all her journals to the Archives. Sarah spent many hours perusing these. Much of Beryl's notes were historically significant, and Sarah began to worry that the many details known only to Beryl might be lost forever if they were not properly transcribed with a view to the future. The Mother Foundress's memoirs would span more than half a century, from the Civil War to this great worldwide conflict. How she would love to help dear Mother Charbonneau in such a task, but it was becoming more difficult daily for her to see clearly. Spectacles didn't seem to help and there was a fogginess that wouldn't go away no matter how frequently she rinsed her eyes with the mild saline solution the doctor recommended. He called the condition "cataracts," and said there was nothing that could be done.

The more Sarah thought about it, the more important such a written document seemed. It should not be delayed. True, Mother Charbonneau was alert, and aside from the restricted mobility stemming from her back problems, she was a vital person whose powers of mind had not diminished. Still, loss of memory could happen in a short time as was demonstrated by several sisters who now lived in the Infirmary wing. Three of these had been actively teaching only a few years before, and now they were like children who couldn't even remember how to dress themselves. Sarah found it impossible to imagine such impairment in Beryl Charbonneau, but then one couldn't be certain what trials God might send for one's purification here on earth.

Philomena listened to fragile Sister Sarah when she brought the proposal of Mother Charbonneau's memoirs to her. "I agree. Mother's story is much more than what any sister could assemble from her notes. Would she wish to write of her personal life?"

"She is a Mother Foundress. Her personal life isn't entirely her own. It is part of her community, and consent is beside the point if you charge her with the task."

"If one of our sisters wrote a biography and used not only Mother's journals, but conversations with Mother herself, we might have a rare book," Philomena said half to herself.

Philomena sat in her office at Highland Home looking out the window at the expanse of lawn and the paths that went toward the cedar grove and the lake. She saw Sister Elizabeth pushing Mother in the wheelchair. However, did Sister get Mother to consent to using it? She looked at the two of them fondly. Their conversation was animated, and Philomena was pleased to see that the young sister had managed to draw Mother out of her grief over Adam's death. Beryl didn't lack faith, but she was human, and the ties with the old man went back through all the years of her life. She waited in the front hall for Sister Elizabeth and asked her to come to the office.

"Sister, I had planned to assign you to the Academy in Bellingham or send you to Montana, but…"

"Either, Mother!" Elizabeth said eagerly.

"However, there's another obedience I would like you to accept." Elizabeth looked at her expectantly. "It would delay your teaching and require that you live here at Highland Home for a year. At least a year, perhaps longer," she added.

Elizabeth's bright smile left her face. Highland Home! Community life here was practically cloistered with its never changing cycle of prayers. There were few sisters outside of the novices, and work was so limited. Obediences included gardening, cooking, sewing, cleaning. Elizabeth never shirked her fair share, but staying here was like being in the novitiate all over again. Had she done something to displease Mother Philomena? She had thrived on the stimulation of school and the independence of study and private prayers. Her community had made every exception possible for her. All these thoughts rushed through her mind, and at the same time she also acknowledged that she was the youngest sister ever to be sent to a secular university. In simple gratitude she would take the assignment she was to be given on faith with as much good will as she could muster. "Tell me what you want, Mother, and I promise I'll try my best."

When Elizabeth left Philomena's office it was with elation and a sense of being a privileged part of the most important work any sister could do for the Congregation of Martha and Mary. Mother Charbonneau's biographer! For such an assignment as she had been given, she would have lived anywhere, made any sacrifice. Mother General had told her to keep the task to herself until Mother Charbonneau was informed. However, she could seek out Sister Sarah Dufrayne and gather as many of the documents in the Archives as she wanted to read. She was also to accompany one of the sisters back to Lake Forest Park this afternoon so that she might select a typing machine in Seattle for her use. There was an empty room next to hers, and this would be reserved as her office so the work wouldn't invade her personal space. There were even greater thrills. Philomena was going to suggest that Mother Charbonneau journey to the East with Elizabeth so that Elizabeth could see first hand the origins of the Congregation in Georgetown, and even the Baltimore Carmel and the Visitation Nuns. She would ask that Joseph accompany them.

Elizabeth went to the chapel and prayed that she would be equal to the momentous task she had been given. As she finished her prayers, she noticed that the shadows were long on the grounds. She stepped outside just as the bell calling the community to Compline began to toll. It was the time of swallows feeding on the wing, of bird song and light winds from the water. Overhead, she saw a great bird circling. She shaded her eyes and looked up. High in the evening sky she saw an eagle, wings spread, lifting on the air in ever greater circles. As she stared at the great bird in flight, she knew what the title of her book would be. She had not put one word to paper, but her biography of Mother Charbonneau would be called *Under Eagle Wings*.

II

It was 1920 before Elizabeth finished her book. The title page might read "by Elizabeth Ordway, SMM," but she had been only the painter who used oils and canvas to complete the portrait. All the details revealed Mother herself. Every nuance was there. The woman that was Beryl Charbonneau fairly leapt from the pages. Beryl gave Elizabeth permission to show a manuscript to one of her professors who now taught at the University of Washington. But only to him.

"Sister," Professor Stoltz told her, "this is perhaps the finest biography I have ever read. And your departure from a neutral third person commentary to telling her story from her point of view was brilliant. I felt like I knew Mother Charbonneau intimately when I finished." He gave Elizabeth the name of a publisher with a letter of recommendation. "I can guarantee that he will publish this," he told her.

Mother Philomena and Elizabeth sat in the garden with Beryl, who held the manuscript in her lap. "Your professor is right, Sister dear, anyone who reads this would know me intimately."

Philomena was pleased. "Sister Sarah would have loved it," she said. "As would your Aunt Elizabeth, Sister."

"I'm sure both were little birds on Elizabeth's shoulder." Beryl chuckled. Sarah Dufrayne had died the day before the new year.

"Professor Stoltz gave us the name of a publisher," Elizabeth began.

"No." It was just one word, but Philomena and Elizabeth looked at Beryl curiously. Beryl put her hand up. "No," she repeated. "I can't allow it to be published, at least not yet."

"But when, Mother?" Philomena asked.

"Sixty years after my death." She looked at Elizabeth with affection. "You could still be here to take the credit, my dear."

"I don't want credit! For all I care, we can say Sister Serendipity Sunbeam wrote it! It's important to publish it for the Congregation, and for anyone else really interested in the beginnings of education in the Northwest."

"Yes, that may be true, but it's too soon. When it is brought out and the dust is blown away from the manuscript, the Congregation will read it as history and perhaps others will learn from it. But now, it's just too soon."

Sister Philomena sat without adding her views for what seemed a long time. "She may be right, Sister," she said to Elizabeth. She was thinking that there were too many private stories told in this book.

"You have the authority to ignore me," Beryl said to Philomena. "Tell me that it is to be published regardless of what I may think, and it shall be. I am not the Mother General; you are."

"We can't do that, Mother!" Elizabeth said. For some weeks she had sensed this outcome, and it was all right. She meant it sincerely when she said it didn't matter whose name was given as author. To Elizabeth, the book itself, completed, was its own reason for being. It was Beryl Charbonneau, and whether it was read now or in sixty or more years was unimportant. Knowing Mother Charbonneau as she did, Elizabeth realized that the publication of *Under Eagle Wings* would put constraints upon the spontaneous growth of the community. It would be forever chained by the powerful image of Beryl herself. *Besides, we still haven't written the last chapter*, Elizabeth thought.

Sister Elizabeth Ordway left the Motherhouse in September,1921 for her assigned post at the Academy of the Holy Trinity in Bellingham. She had dreaded saying goodbye to Mother Charbonneau and the Motherhouse, but it had been easier than she anticipated.

"My dear," Mother Charbonneau said to her, "this is your home and always will be. I hold you forever in my heart."

Elizabeth loved her Congregation, but without sentimentality. After her book she saw it as living and growing. There were weeds mixed with the flowers, and even some of the loveliest blooms had thorns. She had seen the community through Beryl Charbonneau's eyes, and the Mother Foundress didn't wear rose colored glasses.

Saving the book for publication, however, could be dangerous. *Under Eagle Wings* must be protected from short-sighted or self-serving sisters.

There were potential Mariettas, just as there were Claras and Philomenas. Who knew what would be done with an historical biography as truthful as this? Elizabeth examined her motives. Did she fear for the book because it was uniquely hers and she felt protective of it? Did she anticipate that credit might be given to someone else? No, and no. Should she trust that the two extant copies would emerge, one from the community archives, and the other from that of Gonzaga College's Archives in sixty years? Again, no. What should happen and what could happen balanced precariously teeter totter fashion, and Elizabeth couldn't guess which end had the greater weight.

Elizabeth had typed a third copy which she had not confessed to making, even to Mother Charbonneau. In this one she placed a letter from Mother Charbonneau which affirmed the truth and authenticity of what Elizabeth had written. She had assumed her most ingenuous look and asked Mother Charbonneau for a second letter. "Just in case." Mother had complied without question.

What to do with the secret volume was the problem. She could put it at the bottom of her own trunk to protect it. But it was not realistic to think she could guard it until she was close to eighty-five years old. What if her mind and memory failed like little Sister Imelda's? The manuscript needed a safe haven. She needed advice.

The Collins home was a happy one. Olivia, now a young lady of sixteen years old, herded her little brother and baby sister like the collie dog who was their constant companion. Nancy was in the second year of her novitiate at Highland Home, having entered after two years at the university. She hadn't chosen the "starchy stiff" sisters. Geoffrey and Paulina had not opposed her. "You get one and you give one back," Geoff had said, putting his arm around both Paulina and Nancy as they left her at the Motherhouse.

Elizabeth explained her concerns to Paulina and Geoffrey, whom she had come to know during her writing and interviewing. "I'm making a confession here," she told them, "because I've taken it upon myself to make this copy." She held the manuscript that was well wrapped in brown paper and tied with hemp cord. "I can't even let you read it."

"I understand your concern," Paulina said. "I've lived some of those pages."

"My worst fears might never be realized, and I admit I may be overly cautious."

"I can't imagine anyone who would know better the dichotomies within the community than my wife," Geoffrey said.

They decided that the manuscript would be left in the safekeeping of Geoffrey, Paulina, and herself. Dr. Collins would place it in a safety deposit vault where it would be protected from fire and theft. Only the three of them would share access, and as the years claimed any one of them, another would be admitted into the custody pact, selected by the survivors. Should Elizabeth be incapacitated or dead, another of the surviving caretakers would become the chief caretaker. There would always be three. Sixty or more years was a long time. If, during the decades, Elizabeth saw fit to change this custodial arrangement, she had the authority. Elizabeth left them with the weight of her worry gone.

III

"Philomena, dear," Mother Charbonneau said, dropping the formal 'Mother,' "I was in your position many years ago, and I gave in for the good of the Congregation. As I see it, there is no one ready to take your place."

"There are quite a few almost ready, Mother. Couldn't they learn by the experience of the office?"

"Who? Clara? She needs more years, more variety of experience within the community. She's been confined to the novitiate charge for too long a time. Margaret Blanchard? Her illness gave her patience and a look at the world outside. She would be my personal choice, but what would the travel, the responsibility, and the long hours do to her? I don't think Dr. Collins would recommend her accepting election."

"There's Nelda."

"Whom you did not want as novice mistress. She's ready for Director of Schools, and would be good at it. But you need to get Clara out into the community. Director would accomplish that. I suggest you split the school position into primary and secondary. Let Nelda work with the secondary teachers."

"And who's to be Mother Mistress?"

Beryl laughed. "We're beginning to sound like politicians! If it were a few years from now, I'd hope you'd think about Elizabeth. But she's young, and she needs to be out and about. She should also work for a higher degree. Why not consider Rose Ellen or Winifred? They are kind, well respected by the sisters, and love the Congregation."

Philomena accepted a third term, and once again she appointed the recovered Sister Margaret Blanchard as Mistress of Novices, posted Clara and Nelda as Directors of Schools, and Sister Elaine as Sub Mistress. Mother Charbonneau remained Prioress, always willing to give spiritual advice to her sisters. By now a staff of five sisters were needed in the Infirmary, and Sister Winifred, who had survived the San Francisco earthquake, was appointed head Infirmarian.

Sister Elizabeth wasn't the only young nun who was shocked to see that Mother Charbonneau had become much weaker in the year she had been away from the Motherhouse. Returning to Highland home after a year at the Bellingham Academy, Sr. Elizabeth's heart sank when she saw how difficult it was for Mother to move. It was Sister Winifred's responsibility to monitor every sister's health, but, nevertheless, Elizabeth asked Sister Nancy to write a note to her father asking him if he couldn't find some excuse to come to the island for a health check visit. Geoffrey came ostensibly to check on Sister Margaret Blanchard. He was pleased that she was doing well, and congratulated Mother Philomena for letting Sister assume the position of Novice Mistress. "Part of continued recovery is a good attitude, and Sister would not have been happy elsewhere," he told her. "I haven't seen Mother Charbonneau, is she off island?"

"She's in her room, doctor, and I'm glad you're here, for if you hadn't come I would have called you."

They found Mother fully dressed. She was sitting in an easy chair that Winifred and Philomena had placed in her room over Beryl's protestations. She was stubborn about not wanting special care.

"Well, Mother, you'll just have to grin and bear it, as the saying goes," Sister Winifred said. The Infirmarian was a strong woman, round of face with little smile crinkles around her eyes indicating her cheerful disposition. If it weren't for her size, she might have looked like a story book elf. Philomena's features were sterner. Her long face with its Roman nose could take on an intimidating appearance, especially with the wild red hair hidden under the coiffure. It was still unruly, but grey was toning down the carrot hue.

"Don't give me your look, Philomena," Mother Charbonneau grumbled. "I remember you as a saucy little miss in the Tacoma Academy!"

Notwithstanding her objections, the chair had stayed, and Beryl had to admit that with her feet supported on a well padded footstool, it was more comfortable than her straight backed desk chair.

Geoffrey sat down beside the indomitable legend, who was now past eighty years old, and not liking it very much. For someone as stubborn and vital as Mother Beryl Charbonneau, he could imagine the suffering being a semi-invalid cost her. She had to be content to be wheeled to chapel and to the refectory. She could still walk, but the process of getting from one place to another was exceedingly slow and the cost was great pain. She still refused strong medications, but Geoffrey insisted that she take aspirin round the clock. "It won't dull your mind, Mother, it might help any inflammation of your spine."

Geoffrey had consulted with the orthopedic physicians at Providence Hospital, and they had suggested the new treatment of traction to stretch the spine and relieve the pinching of nerves. Geoffrey had rejected this, as he noticed Mother was beginning to have some difficulty breathing. The total inactivity of traction combined with her being in the hospital for a prolonged stay didn't seem to him a wise treatment considering her age and temperament.

Another orthopedic doctor had suggested water therapy. If Mother Philomena agreed, he could see to it that a small heated pool could be built. They had electricity now, so the water could be kept at a comfortable temperature. It would also be good for other older sisters. "Would the old girls object to bathing suits?" he asked Paulina. She supposed that some of them might, but they could arrange their time so there would be privacy. Philomena agreed readily, as long as the cost would not be excessive. Geoffrey solved this problem by making it his and Paulina's gift. Beryl never benefitted from the pool.

It began as a sore throat, developed into a cough and then a low grade fever. Philomena had a bad feeling about this illness, slight as it now appeared. Elizabeth, at the Motherhouse for retreat, agreed that Mother's condition could deteriorate. "Mother, have you sent for Dr. Collins?"

"I'm about to do so."

"Please, Mother, would you have him bring Joseph?"

Elizabeth had not needed to explain. Philomena had read *Under Eagle Wings*.

The retreat continued, but there was a more profound hush at Highland Home than the silence of retreat. The sisters seemed to know that Mother Charbonneau was going to leave them. Her back pain was almost intolerable and Winifred administered doses of morphine, telling Beryl it was augmented strength aspirin. In chapel, Beryl sat in her wheelchair, head bent, unsuccessfully trying to stay awake. With increasing frequency, pain overcame her. She knew that her work was almost finished. Philomena had told her that Joseph was coming along with Dr. Collins. She understood.

They arrived on the first ferry. Mass was over, and Elizabeth asked Philomena if she could take Beryl outside in the sun. Mother's fever had risen, and Philomena couldn't speak for the tears that she tried to push back. She nodded. Joseph found his Mother in the meadow near the cedar grove. She was so still. He looked at Elizabeth. "She's just asleep, wake her, Joseph. She's waiting for you."

Elizabeth, unable to hide her tears, moved away. She saw that Philomena with all the community was coming toward them, and she walked up the trail to meet them and to keep them from intruding on Joseph's visit.

The farewell between Joseph and Beryl was a page that Elizabeth would never write. Beryl Charbonneau died peacefully in the arms of the one human being most precious to her.

IV

The sisters kept a watchful eye on Joseph in the days before Mother Charbonneau's funeral. Philomena was worried that he was keeping his grief in too tight a control, and confided her concerns to Elizabeth.

"I was apprehensive, I'll admit," Elizabeth said, "but I don't think he will experience the same depression as when Mai Ling died. Their friendship transcends death." She would have said "love" rather than "friendship," but she and Philomena were within the hearing of a number of sisters. There had always been dark suggestions about "Mother Charbonneau's Indian," as certain sisters had whispered over the years. Elizabeth was not about to add to the absurdity of these implications.

Alone in the gardener's cottage, Joseph grieved, but in his sorrow he felt his mother's presence. He let the memories of her, the joys and challenges they had shared wash over him like a soothing balm. In a few days her body would be buried in the cold earth, but her soul flew free. Elizabeth's biography had been well titled. When tears came, he let them flow.

The memorial Mass had brought dignitaries, friends, and colleagues from great distances. The chapel was overflowing, and the entry doors as well as the outer doors were left open so those who didn't have seats inside might at least hear the music. Joseph sat at the back of the sanctuary, not wanting to deprive any of the sisters a place. Elizabeth would not leave him in solitude. She, along with Su Ping, Philomena, and the Collins family, joined him in the back pew.

The Archbishop had a eulogy prepared, but he made the mistake of asking for comments from the assembly. It was a full two hours before remarks were ended. No one was inclined to depart early. After the first fifteen minutes, His Excellency decided to sit in the chair usually occupied by the celebrant during Mass. There were as many moments of laughter as anecdotes that inspired tears.

It was a shock to the sisters when Joseph, normally so reticent to put himself forward, rose to speak.

"I called her 'Mother,'" he said, "just as all of you honored her with the title. My Mother Charbonneau gave me life, not biologically, but spiritually. She was the inspiration for every work of art it was my privilege to create. She was my teacher, my mother and my friend. I will walk in her presence all the days of my life."

A week after Mother Charbonneau's funeral, life on the island began to return to normal, Mother Philomena and her friend Paulina Collins walked together on the grounds accompanied by Joseph. It was a misty October afternoon. In the cemetery Beryl's grave was covered with flowers.

"They look fresh," Paulina remarked.

"With the foggy mornings and sunny afternoons they're likely to last a week longer," Philomena said, picking off a wilted dahlia bloom.

"Did you read Sister Elizabeth's biography of Mother?" Paulina asked Joseph.

"Not all of it. I did read some excerpts and Sister Elizabeth and I spent many hours together. Mother wanted me to be free to say as much or as little as I felt was appropriate. Actually, it was easy to confide in Elizabeth. Mother trusted her completely."

"Did you read it?" Pauline asked Philomena.

"Yes. I wish you could have. You were in it, you know. Your story reads like a romance novel."

"Oh, dear! And my mother?"

"A strong, heroic woman. The community has been honored to have her as a benefactress. I have vivid memories of her when she came to visit you at St Mary's."

"Of course. I had forgotten. But you didn't know her as 'Mattie Kate' then, and I suppose that is in the biography?"

"Only in the most sympathetic way, Paulina. Such concern is precisely why Mother did not want the book published now."

"Even so, sixty years is a long time to wait."

"What are your plans, Joseph?" Philomena asked.

"With your permission, I would like to sculpt a standing image of Mother for the Motherhouse entry."

"I give it with all my heart!" Philomena exclaimed. "Will you remain with us to do the work? You are more than welcome."

"I am grateful for your invitation, but I have a commission to complete in France and a place to work there which will give me the solitude I need."

Philomena continued to remove faded flowers from the hundreds that blanketed Beryl's resting place. "I'll be sad when these have to be taken away. Cut flowers have such brief beauty."

"You'll be able to plant the potted azaleas and the hydrangeas," Paulina said.

The three stood at the grave, each with private thoughts. "In God's time there's really no difference between the life of a cut rose and the sixty years a biography lies dormant," Philomena observed.

Joseph nodded. "Yet it might be more fitting to use those cedars as a symbol. Some of them were growing here when Michelangelo carved the Pieta."

"True."

The bells from the tower above the chapel began to toll the time of evening prayers. Paulina voiced her thoughts. "All things have their beginnings and endings, dear friends. Who knows what will be in half a century? The Congregation will be almost over a hundred and fifty years old, and we will be approaching the last decades of the century."

"Or nearing the beginning of a new one," Joseph said.

Alone in the sisters' chapel, Joseph waited to make his farewells to Su Ping, His thoughts naturally turned to Mai Ling's bitter opposition to their daughter's conversion and subsequent entry into Beryl's congregation. He knew that Su Ping often wondered why he had never accepted the beliefs by which his dear friend and Mother lived her life. Truth told, he and Beryl were more in agreement than anyone knew. Through Beryl, Joseph had come to honor Jesus, but he could never align himself with the Christians whose actions contradicted the essential teachings of their man-God. He supposed that if he, like Beryl, had been born to the Church he might have come to terms with the paradox. He knew in his heart that his "beloved heretic," as he often called Beryl in the privacy of his own thoughts, rejected the strange zeal that followers of her God of love used to justify all manner of hatred and

314

violence. He smiled to himself. In Beryl's loving heart she could forgive even such as these.

What he had not confided to the sisters, or even to Su Ping, was that he intended to spend his last years living in a French monastery. They would know soon enough when he gave them his overseas address. He did not want his daughter or the Congregation to assume that this meant "conversion." He was not seeking a place of worship or a particular expression of a religious way of life in France, but an atmosphere of creative silence. He believed this would make further growth in his art possible.

He prayed, *My dear Mother, when it is my time, come to meet me as I seek to slip through the back door of the life beyond. Just be sure the gate stays open? If, by some joke on me you may have arranged with the Master of the Universe, I die in a monk's robes, embrace me. for I am forever your Joseph.*

Epilogue

Under Eagle Wings by Elizabeth Ordway, SMM and PhD, was published at a time when many religious communities were in a downward spiral to ultimate disintegration. The work was praised as a document which brought to life a fascinating woman in an historical setting. Beryl Charbonneau's vision, sadly, was no longer relevant to modern religious congregations. Read by a few who were witnesses to the collapse of many communities, it might have been a caution for those who would abandon the spirit of their origins. This lesson came too late.

Before the biography was printed, bitter controversies raged within Mother Charbonneau's community. One powerful group of sisters led by Sister Esther Harding wanted to sell the Motherhouse on Mercer Island in order to finance a new concept of religious life which would combine what was left of the Sisters of Martha and Mary and three other congregations. Sisters would no longer live in traditional convents, but devote their lives to a variety of causes more agreeable to a majority of members than staffing schools and hospitals. Sister Esther realized that selling the property in downtown Seattle, as well as the Mercer Island Highland Home would launch a newly merged secular community into the Twenty-first Century.

From the hour she was elected to preside over the hundred and forty year old Congregation of Martha and Mary, Mother General Esther Harding's premeditated decisions began a killing chain of events. At her election, a living community, which like others, suffered a chill from the winds of change, was condemned.

Sister Esther's election was not by unanimous acclamation, but a simple majority after a battle of bitterly opposing sides. Sister Esther's contemporaries voted in a unified block. They were impatient to shed the skin of old traditions that kept the sisters from what they saw as meaningful participation in the modern world. Sister Vivian Morrison, a graduate of law school, realized that the Congregation had all but lost the character of the community she had entered. She applied for a dispensation from her vows. "This will not be the community I entered over a decade ago," she told the Council. Her departure from the Congregation created a rift between herself and Esther, and Esther's followers.

Sister Vivian's opposition to Esther's plan for modernization was inspired by the admonitions of Vatican Council II's renewal guidelines for religious orders: "Return to the spirit of your founder." In the case of Beryl Charbonneau's Sisters of Martha and Mary, this should have been clear. However, the fire at the Gonzaga University Archives destroyed one preserved copy of Beryl Charbonneau's biography which was written while the Mother Foundress was still alive. Elderly sisters who could remember Beryl Charbonneau were convinced that Highland Home should not be sold, but used to house and care for retired and infirm members of the community, the very reason, they claimed, for its being. Modern, younger sisters in positions of authority had placed their senior sister/invalids in nursing homes, often secular facilities where the sisters did not have the comfort of Mass and community prayers.

The two groups took their battle to the highest tribunal of the Archdiocese, both factions hoping to have their case supported by the Archbishop. But, without a clear statement of Beryl Charbonneau's intentions for the community, aside from faded journals and disconnected autobiographical notes, the outcome was far from certain. Ultimately, the dispute reached a hearing before the Archbishop. When the highest authority of the Archdiocese sided with Esther Harding, the sisters who wished to keep Highland Home took the matter to court.

Esther Harding, Mother General of the Congregation of Martha and Mary, entered the courtroom. The sisters of her council followed her. From her place at the plaintiff's table, attorney Vivian Morrison watched the procession. After Esther had planted her bulk in the first row behind her archdiocesan lawyers, Sisters Michelle, Colleen, Ruth, and Ann Rose filed in. Sister Michelle feigned indifference, but scrutinized her surroundings with hooded eyed. Little Sister Colleen had not pulled back her hair with accustomed severity, but she still looked like a ferret without the traditional veil. Sister Ruth's matronly figure and sweet smile gave the lie to the fact that this hard as nails Superior was no earth mother. Towering above her companions, posture stiff and erect, came Ann Rose, alias the "cat hater."

Vivian still felt anger whenever she thought of the inflexible Ann Rose. She remembered the weekend when all the community pets were snatched from the convents. "The decision of the council," Ann Rose claimed. This arbitrary act had pushed dear frail Sister Anita over the edge. And what harm had Anita's fifteen pound cat done to Ann Rose? As chairman of the Congregation's council, Ann Rose claimed the presence of cats prevented allergic sisters from living in the convents of their choice. Vivian had rescued Purr Tuffer from the pound, but Anita had slipped past being comforted by the knowledge. She became still another old sister shipped off to a secular nursing home.

Vivian glanced at her watch. Judge Muriel Hopper hadn't yet entered the courtroom, but it was already 10:00 o'clock. The Murray Care Center had promised to have Sister Elizabeth ready for Paulina Miller to bring to court on time. *Dear Heaven, I haven't allowed a margin for delay*, Vivian thought. Eighty-five year old Elizabeth could no longer walk any distance, and transporting her wasn't an easy matter. But as Vivian turned to look toward the double entry doors, they opened and an attractive young woman steered an invalid sister into the courtroom. The young woman was Paulina Miller, one of the last three custodians of *Under Eagle Wings*. Twenty years ago, when Vivian was Sister Vivian Morrison, SMM, Elizabeth had asked her to act as one of the guardians. Yesterday Vivian had used the key to the safety deposit box where the manuscript was kept.

"Thanks, Paulina," Vivian said, and whispered to Elizabeth, "How are you?" Elizabeth smiled. Vivian loved this brave old nun. It was Elizabeth who had asked Vivian to initiate the suit on behalf of all the elderly sisters of the Congregation. While no one could dispute their the first rate level of care, the sisters were still exiled from the community to which they had vowed faithfulness until death.

Vivian opened her briefcase and indicated its contents to the old sister. Elizabeth's eyes glistened, and she nodded. The package, wrapped with faded brown paper and tied with brittle hemp cord, was safe.

Vivian glanced at Sister Esther Harding, who sat expressionless, her head tilted upward, confident that the power of Church and canon law was in her arsenal of legal defense. Seemingly, all Vivian had on her side was one "useless" old nun, terminally incapacitated. The judge might sympathize with the effort to prevent the Congregation's dissolution so the community's elderly might return to their Motherhouse, but she would not be able to find justification to rule favorably for the plaintiff's case. Vivian took a deep breath and exhaled. *Yes, it would have happened that way were it not for the carefully preserved secret copy of Mother Foundress Beryl Charbonneau's biography.*

Vivian removed the manuscript from her case and placed the parcel on the table. As Esther stared at it, the arrogance fell from her face like a snake's discarded skin. Her eyes widened and a flush rose from her neck in uneven red splotches. *So Esther recognizes the wrapping.* Vivian was now certain that it was she who had concealed or destroyed the Congregation's copy. She wondered if Esther had applied sufficient deodorant to take her through the morning. The sweat would flow today. Yes, it would.

The clerk announced Judge Muriel Hopper's entrance. Once the court was declared in session, Vivian rose. "Your Honor, may I approach?" She took the manuscript with her. "Judge, this is an authentic copy of Beryl Charbonneau's biography completed under her supervision more than sixty years ago. It could not be made public until today because of Mother Charbonneau's specific instructions."

Judge Hopper removed her steel rimmed reading glasses and peered at Vivian, whose scant five foot frame demanded that she stand on tiptoe to be seen. "In the statements I have read, the official biography was lost in the Gonzaga University Archives fire ten years ago," Judge Hopper said.

"Yes. That copy was burned. The community had another which cannot be located. It was presumed lost during several moves of community offices back and forth from Seattle to Mercer Island."

The archdiocesan attorneys who towered over Vivian began to dispute evidence being brought in at this late date. Judge Hopper silenced them swiftly. "In my chambers. Bring your proof of authenticity, Miss Morrison."

Sister Esther's two legal advisors took seats in front of the judge's private desk. Vivian wheeled Sister Elizabeth, still alert, but obviously suffering from the lack of pain medication she had refused in order to participate with an unclouded mind. Vivian pulled her chair beside the invalid. Jack Blanchard, the attorney favored by the archbishop himself, challenged the importance of the wrapped package. "What evidence is there that this has any bearing on the matter at hand?" he demanded.

Vivian turned to Elizabeth, who spoke. "Mother Charbonneau's handwritten authentication is inside." Elizabeth's voice was soft, but clear. Judge Hopper leaned forward to catch her words.

"Why the delay, Sister? And what makes this manuscript pertinent to this case?"

"Vatican Council II urged all religious communities to return to the spirit of their founder. The spirit of the Congregation of Martha and Mary was plainly expressed by our foundress. Her intentions are crystal clear in the biography."

Judge Hopper's admiration of this ancient nun was undisguised. The body might be worn out, but the fine mind was there. "I am still at a loss to understand why this was withheld until now." She looked steadily at Sister Elizabeth. She had no wish to prolong the nun's ordeal, but she wanted the facts.

"A week ago, your honor, we acknowledged the sixtieth anniversary of Beryl Charbonneau's death. At her request, her biography was neither to be read nor published until sixty years after her death. I was bound not only by my desire to honor Mother Charbonneau's wishes, but by a binding obedience given to me by Mother Philomena, Mother General at the time."

"And what is your connection with the manuscript?" Judge Hopper asked, still straining to hear Elizabeth's replies.

"I am its author, your honor. Almost fifty-seven years ago, Mother Philomena entrusted to me the task of writing Mother Charbonneau's biography. Mother Charbonneau was in fragile health, and our Mother General wanted her story told while our foundress was able to oversee the telling of it." Sister Elizabeth paused as Judge Hopper untied the string that bound the manuscript. She put on her glasses and read Beryl Charbonneau's testimony of authenticity. She perused the first few pages.

"This seems more like the beginning of a novel than a biography," she said looking at Elizabeth for clarification.

"Yes. At first I used the traditional biographical style—Mother didn't want a ghost written first person account. I spent two years with Mother Charbonneau as her constant companion and confidant. I saw her life through her eyes, all the history, her personal struggles, her hopes and dreams and friendships. I became a storyteller, as well as a biographer—not to change the facts or fictionalize truth by exaggeration, but to bring Beryl Charbonneau to life…"

"And no one knew you had a copy?"

"Over these sixty years only I and two selected others knew. There were always three caretakers. If any of the three were unable to maintain the guardianship, another would be appointed. The copy was sealed, and has remained so until today."

"You went to such lengths to keep this a secret?"

"Not to keep the biography secret; it was widely known that one was written. You might say I conspired to keep one copy safe. Your honor, sisters share faults and failings with the rest of humanity. I realized, young as I was when I wrote this book, that the manuscript could be lost, or even suppressed. Who could have predicted the Gonzaga Archives fire?" She did not press the question of the Congregation's missing copy.

"Sister, I shall read this with great interest. I'm declaring a recess until Monday morning. Ten o'clock." She stood and came from behind her desk to shake Elizabeth's bird-like hand. "Thank you, Sister."

Outside the chambers, Jack Blanchard took Esther aside. "Sister, the legends repeated about Beryl Charbonneau are common knowledge. I doubt that a collection of biographical anecdotes will have any bearing on Judge Hopper's decision."

"We'll see." Esther said shortly. But she recalled the chapters concerning the building of Highland Home and Beryl's very specific intentions for the Motherhouse. She herself had found and read the manuscript in spite of Beryl Charbonneau's decree. Unless Judge Muriel Hopper was incredibly obtuse, and she was very much the opposite, Esther's plans for changing the Congregation and financing a secular institute were evaporating like fog on a hot summer day.

Paulina Miller took charge of Elizabeth, and Vivian bent to kiss her cheek. "Thank you, dear one," she whispered before her old friend was wheeled away. Vivian stopped at the table and retrieved the coat she'd draped over her chair. As she turned to leave, Esther's substantial figure blocked her way.

"Why couldn't you have left well enough alone? What good can this do now?" she demanded harshly.

"Let's leave the decision to the judge, and go from there. Excuse me, Esther, it's inappropriate for us to be talking." It was difficult for Vivian to remember that this woman was the older girl she had followed about like a puppy through grade school, high school, and into the Congregation of Martha and Mary. Few could call Esther friend, but Vivian had come as close as any. Vivian knew Esther more intimately than anyone else in school or in

322

the Congregation. She was aware that under a plain newsprint cover the teenage Esther had *Gone with the Wind* in her bookcase. Only Vivian knew that when a revival of *Lost Horizon* with Ronald Coleman had come to a Bellingham theater, Esther had seen it at least ten times. This imaginative woman could have been a charismatic leader in the tradition of Beryl Charbonneau, but her vision was flawed by impatience and personal ambition. She could have been a foundress in her own right—and still might be, but without the substantial funds of the Congregation of Martha and Mary, this was unlikely.

Ex-Sister Vivian Morrison edged past the four counselors who waited for Esther. They looked at her nervously, but kept a discreet silence. Vivian, at sixty, was their contemporary, but she looked twenty years younger. Her size six maroon power suit accentuated her slight figure, and she moved with the ease of a woman perfectly fit. She had never dyed her hair, which was a salt and pepper mix styled in a short wedge. Her heels clicked on the polished parquet as she pushed her way outside through revolving doors to First Avenue. The rain had stopped and bright blue patches showed between white cloud puffs. One hundred years ago this very Seattle street was in flames, and Beryl Charbonneau, astride Captain Lilly's hunter, had thundered down the dirt road leaping over burning rubble to rescue five year old Sung Chow. Esther had heard those hoofbeats today. Beryl's dream would not be trampled upon. *Hi O Silver!* Vivian thought, as she made her way to the parking lot.

As a result of the judge's reading and the subsequent publication of *Under Eagle Wings*, the Sisters of Martha and Mary were able to remain at Highland Home Motherhouse. There would be no merger, no dramatic departure from Mother Charbonneau's founding Constitutions, especially in the matter of Highland Home's use. The sale of Mattie Kate's downtown property was more than enough to maintain all the members of the community at Highland Home until the very last sister would take her last breath. Sadly, this unhappy day is not far off. The average age of the sisters when the book was published was eighty, and no new member has taken vows for over twenty-five years.

Sister Elizabeth Ordway sat in her wheelchair, concealed by the semi darkness of Highland Home's chapel. Her gaze was focused on the ebony sculpture Joseph had presented to the Congregation years before she was born. Should this glorious dream of Beryl Charbonneau's Congregation have ended? Elizabeth knew that Beryl herself would have told her all human endeavors have a beginning and an end. Like a match lit in the dark, the flame of the Sisters of Martha and Mary lasted but a brief moment of time.

"But, oh," Elizabeth whispered, "how lovely was the light."

Author's Note

The historical references in *Beloved Heretic* are, for the most part, accurate. However, I have taken liberties with the time line of Catholic parishes in Washington State. The date of the attempted Chinese deportation from Seattle is a few years earlier than it actually happened. The references to the Whitman Massacre, Fathers Brouillet and Cataldo, the founding of Gonzaga College and the political pressures which forced the Jesuits to abandon the college's original purpose as a school for Indians, are based on fact. My research into early Washington State history unearthed dramatic events. As well as the expulsion of the Chinese from Tacoma and Seattle, there was the great Seattle fire, the politics of the trade routes from the Orient, and the destination of the Union Pacific Railroad. Bold men built Seattle's economy: Henry Yesler, Asa Mercer, Captain Lilly, and others. They are incorporated in the story of Beryl Charbonneau.

Asa Mercer, more famous for his "Mercer Girls" than for his role as first president of the Washington Territorial University, did, as in the book, sail from the East Coast with eleven young women whom he had chosen to become wives of the settlers, thus bringing culture to the territory. Elizabeth Ordway, a significant character in the book, and a pioneer in education in the Pacific Northwest, was among this group. The incidents relating to her struggle to contribute as a woman to the Olympic Peninsula's educational development are accurate. Of the eleven in Mercer's group, eight married, and one died shortly after arrival. The tenth, Elizabeth Ordway, remained a spinster; and there was an eleventh of whom nothing more is known. Who better than Mother Beryl Charbonneau of this novel to be that eleventh woman?

Church related references, such as the foundation of the Visitation Nuns by Mother Eulalie in Georgetown and the hardships the community endured, are straight from their archives. The first Carmelite Monastery for women was indeed in Baltimore, and the description of its rule and the cloistered life within its walls is accurate.

In creating Beryl Charbonneau's Congregation of Martha and Mary, I have combined the development of three actual pioneering religious communities which came to the Pacific Northwest. They are the Holy Names Sisters, (actually the first in the Northwest); the Providence Sisters, and the Dominicans, who came from Newburgh, New York, to Aberdeen. The first two of these communities still exists, but in greatly reduced numbers. The Dominicans (formerly Edmonds Dominicans), who founded hospitals in Aberdeen and Chehalis, have given up their identity to merge with another Dominican congregation in the East.

The setting of *Beloved Heretic* in the 19th and 20th Centuries does not make the themes any less applicable in 2007. Women today, as in Beryl Charbonneau's time, must overcome the limitations established by a male dominated power structure. Nowhere is this conflict more challenging than in the Roman Catholic Church. Modern women are denied a voice and must conform to uncompromising doctrines espoused by papal authorities and by societies within the church. The unrelenting control of Opus Dei is not just a figment of Dan Brown's imagination. Ironically, women who founded religious communities a hundred years ago were perhaps more effective leaders than they might be today—barring exceptions such as Mother Teresa.